Praise for

Time-Stopper

"James Young's debut is a smart, surprising exploration of our obsession with control. What begins as a clever premise—a man who can stop time at will—becomes a poignant meditation on perfectionism, loss, and learning to embrace life's beautiful messiness. Young brings his insider knowledge of D.C. politics to create an authentic world where the fantastical feels grounded and real. *Time-Stopper* is that rare novel that's both thought-provoking and genuinely moving—a remarkable first book from a writer with a distinctive voice and keen insight into what makes us human."

–**PATRICIA FORS**, CEO OF MUSE LITERARY PUBLISHING

"If you could stop time for everyone but yourself, would you do it? Imagine the power you would have—acting to get things done while everyone else was frozen. You could get what you wanted and improve the world. In *Time-Stopper*, David Preston finds that he can stop time—and does. But things don't work out as he envisioned in this fascinating, allegorical novel."

–**GEORGE LEEF**, NOVELIST AND AUTHOR OF *THE AWAKENING OF JENNIFER VAN ARSDALE*

"*Time-Stopper* is an outstanding premier novel, rich in character development and insights into the legislative sausage-making process. James Young's first foray into fiction leavens a story of personal tragedy and K Street intrigue with a clever and original sci-fi twist—two people who discover their ability to stop time to their advantage. A page-turner that will keep readers engaged throughout to see what happens next. A winner!"

–**DENNIS TOSH**, AUTHOR OF THE JOSEPH MICHAEL BARBER ESPIONAGE THRILLERS (MOST RECENTLY, *SINS OF THE FATHER: A MODERN-DAY TALE OF REDEMPTION*)

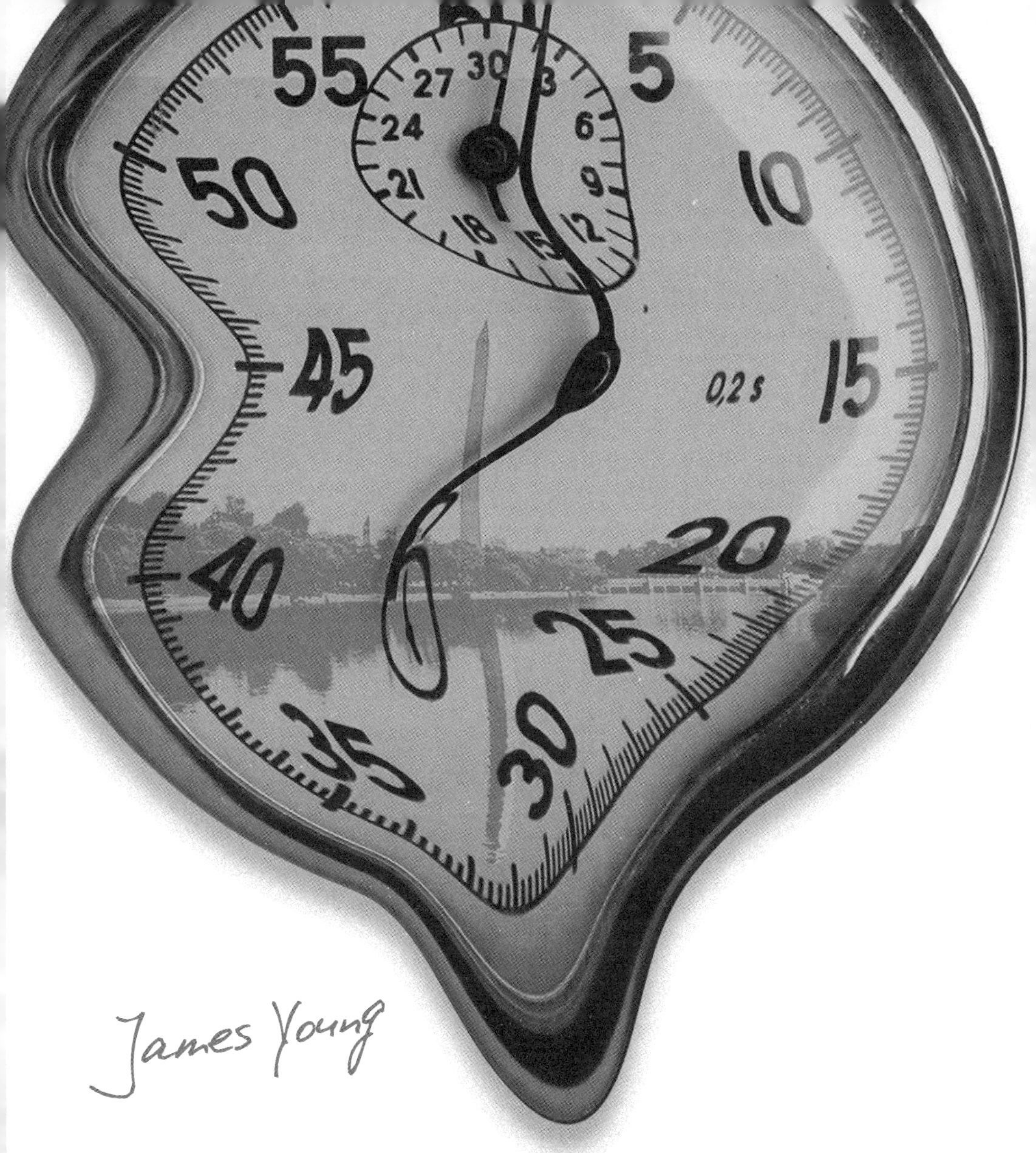

James Young

TIME-STOPPER

Interludes in Time

www.mascotbooks.com

Time-Stopper: Interludes in Time

For more information, please contact:
Subplot Publishing, an imprint of Amplify Publishing Group
620 Herndon Parkway, Suite 220
Herndon, VA 20170
info@mascotbooks.com

Library of Congress Control Number: 2025920609
CPSIA Code: PRV0126A
ISBN-13: 979-8-89138-152-0

Printed in the United States

TO ELIZA, WHO GAVE ME THE IDEA
AND GIVES ME INSPIRATION.

CHAPTER ONE

Time controls people. It defines them. The shortest biography is a tombstone. Often, it tells no more than the person's name with a time ascribed to it: two endpoints—beginning and end—with its quality presumed based on the time between its two points of demarcation.

David knew his day was beginning at 6:49 a.m., even before he looked at his phone. Eleven minutes to go. While he rarely needed it, he always set the alarm for 7:00 a.m. He hated the alarm's jarring sound; switching it off, he resumed thoughtful inertia. A body in motion stays in motion, and one at rest stays at rest. His certainly tended to. At night, he pushed sleep back; in the morning, he pulled it forward. In between, his mind calculated how much time he had before the alarm.

More than sleep, it was morning's solitude he loved. So, he sank back momentarily to feel its stillness and silence. Finished, he quickly reviewed his mental checklist: messages, news, calendar, weather. Then, back to the time.

He had to be out of bed by 7:15 a.m. for everything to fit into place and deliver him to work by 9:00 a.m. A quick prayer, then up. A perfunctory run, shower, dress, and go. He would eat at his desk. By then, he would be hungry because he never was right after a run. Everything in due course.

The Metro ride into downtown D.C. from Alexandria, Virginia, was rarely pleasant, but it was tolerable if he didn't have to stand on the King Street platform too long and if he got a seat on the train. Sometimes he rode the train south, away from work, just to get a seat at the end of the line; then he rode back. Not today, though.

The cars were full of people going to work just so they could return home again. Few smiled. Mondays can do that to people. Few had any expression at all. Unseen and unseeing, each isolated, anonymity despite proximity. He recognized some but hid acknowledgment lest he violate the unspoken rules of anonymous travel.

As he left the train, he began to think about his "episodes." Would he make it through the day? As he had gotten older, these had become easy to induce, more frequent, and longer lasting.

Why did Mondays always seem to be repetitions of the same bad day? At their most insidious, they make you regret the weekend. Work built up behind a two-day break, only to burst forth into chaos heightened by a morass of meetings.

Yet, he had less reason to worry than anyone in the crowded staff meeting. He was extremely good at what he did. No, he was perfect. He always knew his issues inside and out—both the politics and the particulars. Usually, people only knew one or two aspects of an issue. David knew them all. He also had the uncanny ability to anticipate issues before they arose. In the middle of a new discussion, he could produce an outline and argument on something still forming. People had taken to calling him "Radar," partly in jest, partly in awe.

Just thirty-four, and in only three years, he had become the go-to person for lobbying on Whitney Aeronautics' tax issues. A Fortune 50 company and America's oldest aircraft manufacturer, Whitney had a limitless supply of issues, almost all of which eventually morphed into tax issues. It was a hackneyed Washington joke that whenever a big policy debate unfolded, it was dubbed the "Full Employment Act" for its participants. For David, it was no joke. In thirteen years in D.C., he had come to realize that he could always work in this town, no small feat for a place that attracted hordes desiring to do something—anything—in politics, while summarily turning away most.

This Monday's meetings went equally well. The staff meeting passed, despite being too crowded, too long, and too boring. Two calls with Corporate's world headquarters followed.

By late morning, he had a free moment to call Kristin, his girlfriend of six months, to see if she was as excited for tonight as he was. This was the real reason his day had gone so well—and would keep going well, no matter how work went.

They had already exchanged numerous texts and emails, streams of consciousness, minimizing real conversation and trivializing what it did encompass.

It's amazing how few actual words pass between us, David thought. *Usually, only a stream of acronyms, symbols, and emojis. The correspondences of John and Abigail Adams these ain't.*

It was good to occasionally hear a voice, even if it was harried and hurried. Good to know a real person was out there, not just a keyboard. A quick Monday commiseration, a sharing of frustrations, and, finally, a short affirmation of anticipation.

Tonight, David was taking her to see her favorite group. He had shot the moon on the tickets, getting the best seats for a rare, small-venue performance by a band that usually played arenas. He was thrilled at his own unique resourcefulness in getting the tickets. Only he could have done so. What was relevant had been the cataclysmic reaction when he told her. Beyond thrilled, Kristin's response—with squeals, hugs, and kisses—had allowed him to revel in being the cause. Now, just hours away, was what he expected to be the best date of their relationship and likely his life.

It would be perfect.

A knock on his door and a lunch invitation brought his daydreaming up short. Frank and Jeff were his two office favorites; they made the job more than merely work.

It was always "Frank and Jeff," never "Jeff and Frank." They were a set, like shoes or silverware; where there was one, there usually were two.

Saying they made work fun would have been an exaggeration. The Hill had been fun in his twenties, the heady feeling of doing something of national importance in a sprawling college halfway house. The Hill churned with earnest and eager twentysomethings overseen by a small cadre of genuine adults who couldn't possibly oversee everything. Days regularly cycled through late nights and early mornings, fueled with urgency, lubricated by hormones, and populated by other singles doing the same thing and with no other lives than what work provided. People made enough money to get by but not enough to get out. So, they lived their work, and that offered them the things they couldn't afford.

Work off the Hill was entirely different. Here, what he had once done for love and a pittance was a business. A matter of money made it a matter of fact: simple, to the point. There was only one reason you were here, and the people who worked with you did it for the same reason. They rarely went out afterward. For most, instead of being their lives, this work was an interruption of them. Of course, there were an irritating few who desperately tried to relive what they had done in government. The worst were former administration people—the worst of the worst being from the White House. They continued to try to replicate "there" here, "playing White House," David called it, vainly seeking to elevate the now routine to significance.

If Frank and Jeff couldn't make the office fun, they at least made him forget momentarily that it wasn't. Both were married and at opposite ends of the life-with-children and political spectrums.

Frank was a Republican in his early fifties with two children in college. His demeanor was perpetual exasperation, and he could seemingly rumple even a new suit. Jiggling his midsection with one hand and then patting his head with the other, he would grouse, "Why do I have so much here and so little there?" Jeff was a Democrat with a newborn. As Frank was forever on his last nerve, Jeff was always in need of his next nap. Twitchy, and with anxiety as his exercise, he was the Laurel to Frank's Hardy. On the Hill, party affiliation had meant everything; at work, it was just another facet—like where you were from or had gone to college—it was known but not dwelt on. Downtown, it made Frank and Jeff complement each other.

At lunch, quizzing began about his big night. They talked a lot about his activities, his two friends readily admitting they lived vicariously through him. David used to think they were joking, but the longer he had known them, and the more they talked about their lives, the more he realized they weren't.

Frank's children were older, but no less dominated his life. As he regularly said, "The bigger the children, the bigger the problems." This carried over to the time and cost they entailed. Jeff had just had his first child. "Or, rather, my wife did," as he liked to joke. Jeff confessed that getting sleep was now his most anticipated bedroom event.

So, the focus regularly fell on David. Both had once been where he was now, thus his dating life was the three's only shared life experience.

Frank asked, "Are you going to pop the question?"

"Are you kidding? It's just a date!" David exclaimed, launching back in his seat for effect.

"You're the one kidding if you call this 'just a date!' If I'd ever done something this special, I'd have been proposing," Frank said.

Jeff laughed. "You never would've thought of something this special!"

"That's true," Frank confessed.

"Didn't you both just decide to get married without a lot of fanfare?"

"Actually," Jeff said, "my wife decided. And she's never let me forget fanfare's absence."

"Where are you taking m'lady to dine?" Jeff asked in accent when the others' laughter had subsided.

"I figured we'd just grab something quick," David garbled out through a bite.

"Oh," came back in subdued unison.

Their muted response spoke louder than outright disdain.

The last memory I want from tonight is of something falling short of perfection.

"You're right, I've screwed up big-time on this. I've got to fix it. Now."

The pair had plenty of suggestions, but none were easy to execute. Getting into a good place now, just hours ahead of this major event, would be impossible.

"I'll start calling as soon as I get back, maybe someone's canceled."

Frank snorted. "Like that'll happen."

"Oh, come on, think positive. You're the ones who exposed the flaw; the least you can do is send some positive vibes for fixing it," David implored.

"All the vibes in the world aren't going to help you when we get back."

"Yeah," Jeff added, "you aren't doing anything between one and three this afternoon."

"Why not? I'm caught up."

"Didn't you read the email we got just before we left?" Frank leaned forward and widened his eyes for effect. "Mandatory HR training."

"Oh, crap! Tell me you're kidding!"

Both wore the glum resignation that only came from being condemned to one of the inane sessions that Corporate regularly inflicted on their unfortunates. The only difference between the gallows and HR was that on the gallows, they could only kill you once. HR could, and did, over and over again.

"These damn wastes of time are forever crapping on our days like pigeons on a statue," David intoned to no disagreement.

Frank deliberately shook his head. "HR may be a joke, but it's no laughing matter."

CHAPTER TWO

The HR rep, a lanky man with an unctuous voice, began the session with the usual spiel: "The company believes the ESG—environmental, social, and governance—framework is a topic of utmost importance…"

David's mind was already gone, focused only enough to keep him from making eye contact with the presenter. Having done several mental laps around his brain, he thought it safe to check how much time had elapsed.

Twenty frigging minutes? Time's dragging here, but it's flying outside, where I need to fix that missing restaurant reservation.

Either the time wasted in here or the time lost out there would have been enough; together, they were irresistible. *Can't take it any longer, so I'm not going to.*

Time stopped. Abruptly and completely, everything halted instantly. Sound died, motion ceased. Everything, everyone, stood stock-still in place, all objects motionless as though in a snapshot he had taken.

David had done this so often that the extraordinary had become commonplace for him. As a child, his first encounters with this inexplicable phenomenon had simply happened. He hadn't known how or why. They had just occurred, like the electricity shutting down. The events would be unexpected, irregular, often resuming and stopping again in fits and starts. Then time would fully restart as if nothing had happened.

When he first began controlling these episodes, he had needed to squeeze his eyes shut to get the focus to accomplish the task. No more. Just a concerted thought usually sufficed.

Now in the conference room, he was the only movement in a *tableau vivant*. His first action was a primal scream over the now-suspended HR conference. If Thoreau's verdict was that "the mass of men live lives of quiet desperation," his was one of loud separation. A scream into silent stillness did wonders. No longer was he crushed between the pressure of the unending present and his fast-approaching reservation-less future.

He smiled and contemplated the Zen riddle: *Did my scream actually occur since no one else heard it? Easy answer: Yes.* But only briefly; he had a cage to step out of and beckoning infinity to step into.

He threaded his way through the conference room of mannequins. He opened the door, walked out, then flew down the flight of stairs to the building's lobby. There, more statues in various states of halted motion greeted him.

He began walking the five blocks to the restaurants he wanted. Along the way, a pigeon hung in midair, a bus stood suspended in mid-intersection, a bicyclist balanced mid-pedal. David chose as straight a line as he could manage through D.C.'s maze of streets. He weaved leisurely through traffic that had been moving the moment before—and would again in the instant he released time.

He tried several restaurants, searching for the same thing: a paper reservation list. Those who kept reservations on computers were useless to him now. With a lack of movement, electricity and anything that used it were dead; he could punch a keyboard, but nothing would happen. The same applied to phones, an elevator, an electronic door: However they were when time had stopped, there they stayed until he let time resume. David was the only motive force that now existed.

When he finally found a paper reservation sheet, he silently blessed the old-school approach. He gently slid it from beneath the hostess's hand and flipped to the time he wanted. Finding the 5:30 p.m. listings, he scanned for an opening (unlikely) or enough room for him to squeeze his last name, Preston, in among the rest.

There wasn't the former, but there was room enough for a somewhat tortured insertion. *Now, let's add another name in between so mine doesn't stick out.* If not a masterpiece, it looked semi-plausible. That was usually sufficient. Confronted with the obvious—here, a name on a handwritten list—few questioned the fact staring back at them: There it was. An explanation must exist; he never had to provide it. Instead, people simply explained the inexplicable to themselves. He had only to wait patiently while they did. *After all, it's not like I could possibly have done it.*

He hoped Kristin was in the mood for Indian food. Fearing she might not be, he decided to hedge his bet. After all, what is time in pursuit of perfection? He went into four more places before finding an Italian restaurant two blocks away that also had a magic paper reservation list.

He walked slowly back, swinging his arms and kicking his legs out, belting out songs he expected to hear tonight. He had all the time in the world, or, more accurately, he had all the world's time. The serenity that now came from it and the release of pressure with perfection's attainment were sublime. He did not know how long he stayed in this time-stop—or in any of the others, for that matter. But he knew how often he came to them.

His biggest worry—David always had another one—was that he came to these time-stops too often. Being utterly unhurried was intoxicating, if not addictive. Now he often just came to them for no reason other than that time-stops were often more comfortable than being in time.

From a bench at the Navy Memorial on Pennsylvania Avenue, he mused in monologue, "It's good I don't know how long I'm in these. I'll do better. It's easiest if I don't start them at all. Once started, they become progressively easier." He promised himself—again: "Tomorrow, after tonight, none."

CHAPTER THREE

When he returned, the conference room was unchanged, though he was utterly. If not outside, he had changed inside. He was completely at peace. He weaved his way back to his seat to finish what before he felt would finish him. He just had to wait the meeting out and let time carry him through the course he had perfectly set it on: to tonight, to Kristin.

Upon his release, time resumed its headlong rush. Suspended motions restarted—a drink taken, a collar adjusted, a sentence finished—a global pause button released, and everything was exactly as it had been before.

As slowly as the presentation droned to its belated conclusion, the rest of the workday sped by as fast. Work always seemed to. Doing goes faster than being done to. And, of course, the HR presentation had pushed a good bit of work back into the day's remaining few hours. Perversely, this helped to temper, or at least distract, his anticipation.

Frank and Jeff usually beat him out the door. "Fred Flintstone sliding down the dinosaur's back," as Jeff liked to say. Both wished him well on a night that each undoubtedly remembered from their pasts and likely would never have again. Helpfully, Frank gave parting advice: "Do everything I wouldn't do!"

David laughed. "I'll try."

Waiting at the elevator, he texted Kristin. "Leaving now, see you downstairs." He was pleased with himself. Everything was perfect, even down to the final surprise about dinner. He hoped.

To David, their entire relationship was perfect. And he worked relentlessly to be perfect in it. He always thought of the exact right thing to do and spent a lot of time thinking about the next moment and the right thing for it. Once sure, he executed. It was impossible not to notice. Kristin clearly did—a glancing touch, a sighed "Oh, David," a peck on the cheek.

And Kristin was the most perfect thing about the relationship. She was gorgeous, beyond beautiful. Auburn hair made her jade eyes shine out from her porcelain skin. Tall and high-waisted, her slimness exaggerated the angularity of her limbs, so that she looked in flesh like the sketches of models that he saw in her fashion magazines.

Everyone noticed her immediately. She could not be inconspicuous—not anywhere, not anytime, and regardless of what she wore. Men noticed, of course. They could not stop noticing, often to the point of comedy. David watched them over her shoulder; doors would be walked into, things dropped, unfortunate gawkers tripped as their gazes locked on Kristin instead of where they were going.

Women also noticed, but much more subtly. They were more discerning, so it didn't take them long to recognize that whatever they did or said would have no effect on the men in the vicinity. Few, therefore, stayed long in her proximity. They offered noncommittal compliments, like praising how well she dressed.

They have it backward. Kristin makes her clothes look good.

When he had put her picture on his desk, David noticed an increase in his visitors. Some thought the photo had come with the frame. A few had asked if she was his sister—despite David not having one. They assumed it more likely that he had forgotten one than that he had such a girlfriend. The next assumption was that she was only a picture. For the office's summer party, he had downplayed whether they would come. The shock was total when they did; he wondered how much money had changed hands in wagers over her existence.

Their gym offered the same experience. Despite both being members, she had never seen him. Of course, he, along with everyone else, had seen her. Many were the days he had gone just because she might be there. When it became clear they were dating, his stock had gone through the roof. There was a transitive property of coolness that flowed from her to him. His nagging question was whether Kristin knew all this too. But he didn't allow himself to dwell on that tonight.

She was waiting in the lobby when he arrived. That was a good indicator of her excitement. Kristin was always late. Always. He hadn't known her long enough for this to be irritating; he just planned accordingly. Like everything about her, he found this endearing.

Flaws in the otherwise flawless add charm, character; in the already flawed, they simply accelerate opinion's downward spiral. *Life is, after all, unfair,* he thought. Dispelling the fiction that it is fair is one of the first signs of experience; accepting it, one of the first of maturity.

Their greeting was quick, a peck on the lips and the slightest embrace. Then they raced, hand in hand, with the clock and adrenaline.

"You look wonderful as always! You wear Monday well," David said. "Of course, everything looks good on you."

"You're sweet. I'm too excited to think. The whole day has been a distraction to this."

"Seeing me?" he joked as he searched for validation.

She glanced at him. "Uh, yes. Always. But especially tonight because of where we're going! No one I told, and I've told everyone who would listen, could believe where you're taking me."

"What about those who wouldn't listen?"

"I told them twice because they're just envious and deserve it," she said and laughed.

David stopped, and Kristin's momentum brought her up short. "I've got an idea. Let's take this up another notch. Instead of sandwiches, let's go to a restaurant and just relax before heading out. The concert seats are reserved; it's not like they'll be setting up their own equipment. What do you prefer, Indian or Italian?"

"You're kidding, right?" Her eyes widened.

"Do I look like I'm kidding? Which would you like better?"

She rushed into a hug, then pushed him out at arm's length. "I love you, that's what! How'd you do it? When?"

In his mind's eye, David watched them float down the street, she on excitement, he on accomplishment. Just now, her focus beyond him and to the event had put him on edge, but her last comment sent him soaring.

The same streets he had frozen and leisurely strolled to make the reservations just hours before now teemed as they approached the theater. Traffic, always bad during Washington's misnamed "rush hour," crawled. They, along with increasing numbers of other concertgoers, walked past car after car.

He went with Indian, the bolder move, when she insisted that he pick. He rolled the dice a bit; he was playing with house money tonight. Also, his forgery was better there. Even with house money, David didn't like losing.

As they walked, he planned how he would play his entry. Cool, of course. But not too cool. He wanted the appearance of nothing being out of the ordinary. He wanted the hostess to feel that; he especially wanted Kristin to feel it. He had a reservation after all.

Going in, he held the door; then, they squeezed past the other patrons to get to the reservation desk. The hostess looked thoroughly frazzled, like she had already thrown out half of D.C. and had sized him up as next.

"Do you have a reservation?" She appeared to know the answer before she spoke.

"Yes. Preston, party of two for five thirty." Sean Connery as James Bond couldn't have done it better.

"What? Oh, yes. Umm, we had a question about this one."

"No, it's two."

"What?" The hostess's eyes snapped up.

"You said you had a question about this *one*, and I said the reservation's for *two*." He grinned. "A little dinner humor."

"Oh. No, I meant this reservation." The hostess returned to her harried self. "I mean, we have one more reservation in the five-thirty slot than we usually take."

"Sorry, but we have tickets to the seven o'clock show at the Warner; we're a little tight on time. So, you've got our reservation, and we'd like our table. It's not like I wrote it down."

From countless repetitions, David had learned that mentioning what had actually happened was always the clincher. Patently impossible—though exactly what had occurred—it ended any argument over the obvious. Once past the hostess station, they were home free. The table was fine; if a problem arose, someone else would sit in the kitchen. When Kristin's butter knife started to fall, David stopped time to ensure it didn't.

Perfect.

The Warner Theatre was a civilized space for a concert of this magnitude. Instead of a mash, an orderly line slowly transported pricey patrons forward. One thousand dollars a ticket buys more than just a seat. At these prices, he figured no one would be stoned or drunk beyond comprehension. It was one thing to be wasted and have wasted one hundred dollars; it was another to be wasted and have wasted this opportunity.

Inside, the Warner was a great wedding cake of a building. Tier on tier of balconies piled up over and behind the floor seats where they were sitting. It was as far from a rock venue as could be imagined. No plastic molded seats made more to be stood on than sat in or concrete floors intended to be littered, puked on, then hosed down. This was part of the attraction: He hoped that those in front would use their seats as actual seating.

As they had come in, Kristin bought them T-shirts. It was a frivolous expense. David would not have bought one for himself but had planned on buying one for her. Both adjourned to put them on. Hers looked tailored; his looked like someone else was wearing it with him.

Waiting, they people-watched and commented on the surrounding zoo. Even here, some looked to be slumming, like this was as much of a stoop into the masses as they could tolerate. Others, he couldn't imagine how they had afforded these tickets. Then there were many clearly there on their parents' dime—a lot of dimes, really. Perhaps the parents were reliving their love for the band through their love for their children. In any case, these concertgoers wore fan gear older than they were.

The show, the one on the stage, not in the aisles, was everything he had hoped. The band exceeded their reputation, still virtuosos and showing a genuine love of playing.

Of course they did. Why would you still be doing it if you didn't? he thought. It certainly wasn't for the money, and, at this point, nothing could happen backstage that hadn't happened before a thousand times in a thousand ways. *How strange that this is their job. But if you're a drummer, you drum. What else can you do? They're probably better now than in their heyday—honed by more sets than God could count.*

Every song would have been another group's finale, but they kept soaring on and on. David's favorite was an old blues standard—a song they must have loved from way back. Many took it as almost a break in the show. It had never sold a million copies or reached number one—certainly not for the bluesman who wrote it. To David, it was insight. A glimpse into the band if you just looked. For a conversation he knew he'd never have, his question was, "What drew you to Willie Dixon's 'Little Red Rooster'?"

David loved reverse-engineering such things. Taking something—a song, movie, a comedy sketch—back as far as he could. He loved originals, something just emerged from the shadows that no one had heard or seen before. He was forever watching or listening to things way before his time in his constant quest for another link back in the creative chain. It also often made him out of touch with contemporary things—especially with his contemporaries. Sometimes his best insights hung awkwardly, enormous *non sequiturs* lumbering like camels into conversations.

Now transported, he didn't want time to stop. Instead, he wanted it to go on endlessly. He watched with half his attention on the band, the other on Kristin. She danced and sang the songs—back to the band, to herself, and often, turning her head, to him.

The moments encapsulated the very perfection he had sought, that he had created. But there could always be more: When the drummer threw his sticks into their vicinity, David ensured Kristin got one. Because perfect could always be perfected.

Then it was all over. After numerous encores, each surpassing its predecessor, there were no more. His hands were numb, but he kept clapping and shouting, not realizing his voice was as depleted as the feeling in his hands. Only minutes after the lights had come up, and they and the others conceded, did he stop and realize how spent he was. Kristin looked the same. They hugged, like survivors of a near-miss who savored that they were still standing.

She shouted, "The most fantastic thing I've ever witnessed!" Then, in what sounded like a whisper after the din, "Let's go home." David strove to reply but could only come up with squeezing her tighter.

The walk back to Kristin's place was more of a forced march. Kristin lived in downtown D.C., just blocks from the Warner. Such a high-rent district was her guilty indulgence. Kristin's hedonistic reasoning was that she was only this age and this single once; she would be old later, and then she wouldn't live here. David envied her cavalier approach, a lack of control he would never, could never, allow himself. Tonight, he was glad she lived nearby.

They had started with a group of concertgoers, many wearing the same new T-shirts they wore. As the blocks progressed, numbers thinned until only a scattered few stretched into the dark. David was taken by the quiet. Perhaps it was a quickly ebbing Monday's lateness; perhaps it was the contrast to the thundering wall of sound that had engulfed them for hours. It felt as though they were walking through a time-stop.

At her building, they were instantly through the lobby. The elevator took forever. Once in, any questions about the rest of the night vanished. Kristin barely let the door close before wrapping herself around him in a prolonged kiss. By the time they reached her floor, David could barely walk out.

Leading him into her apartment, she pressed him into the door, closing it. For an instant, he thought they might not get to her bedroom, but she pulled him there with urgency. Her cat, Philpot, who had mistakenly chosen her bed for his, was abruptly ushered out, and David, even less ceremoniously, rushed in. Kristin had always been willing, but he had never found her wanting. Now she was.

Usually, there was a theater to their lovemaking, beginning with a candle.

This time, there was no light, save through gaps in the blinds. As she pulled off his T-shirt and then hers, David was momentarily amused. *How will we distinguish them later?* The thought was quickly swept away. Then there was no time or will for thought, only the barest carnal instinct.

As they lay there in the sensuousness of exquisite release, his thoughts slowly returned. He felt himself looking down on them and up at the ceiling simultaneously—as though in two places at once. Grasping for reality, he stopped time.

David wanted to completely take in the moment and the evening. He wanted neither to end. Personally, it also allowed for recovery; already surprised, he had no idea how much more Kristin expected.

On any other night, this would have been a concern. But this was not such a night, and this was not why he had stopped time. It was not that he wasn't into this; it was that he was so much so.

Kristin had just rolled off his chest when he froze everything. She lay just to his left, her right arm draped languorously over him. He now had time to look at her in stillness and low light, a black-and-white photograph. Her head was turned slightly toward him, hair swept across her face's left side, partially covering her left eye. She looked blissfully detached, making her even more beautiful—something he had thought impossible. Her left arm fell across her stomach, and her right ankle just crossed her left. She was completely naked, a figure study of sublime art. He both stared and studied. He wanted to memorize this pose; he would never see a more beautiful woman at a more serene and sensuous moment. After a long, long while, her nakedness made him feel cold for her, even though he knew she was not. He gently covered her.

When he resumed time, they made love again as if they had not just finished. Though just as primal, it was gentler, slower, a complement to the first's complete abandonment. When they were done, she sighed and said, "Oh, baby, let's go to sleep now." David answered with a soft kiss. It was all the perfection he had sought and all he could imagine.

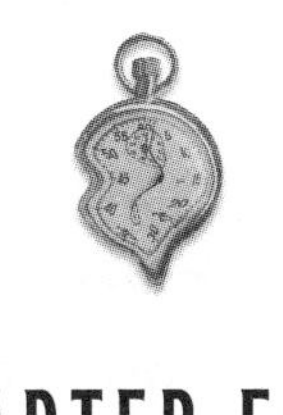

CHAPTER FOUR

When David awoke, he saw that Kristin had gotten up in the night and put on one of their T-shirts. Her back faced him; he almost touched her shoulder, stopping only from fear of waking her. The sun was coming up, and the room was now easy to see. Finding his bearings, he noticed the time—6:21 a.m. He could sleep longer but didn't want to chance Kristin waking up ahead of him, leaving him with a rushed goodbye when he needed to leave for work. Kristin didn't mind being late; David never was.

He wanted his exit to match last night's perfection. He stopped time to guarantee it. He found the other T-shirt in the jumble of clothes jettisoned from the bed. In the kitchen, he found Philpot frozen in examination of his empty bowl. David didn't dare feed him; Kristin was very particular about measuring out his food. David also knew a hungry Philpot would eventually wake Kristin when nothing else would—an alarm clock she didn't have to set. But David had to leave something for Kristin. He sliced strawberries, poured juice, and put a cup of yogurt on a big plate with the strawberries. He left them in the fridge, giving Philpot a stroke as he left.

Returning to the bedroom, he found pen and paper by the phone. It took him a while to mentally compose what he sought. He stuffed several errant attempts into his pocket, unwilling to leave evidence of his inarticulateness. The hardest part was signing it. He had never told her he loved her; it seemed like something he should say first in person. After all, she had told him she loved him last night, hadn't she? For him, that had capped the evening. But had she really meant it? Or was it just an offhand remark uttered in excitement? David agonized, the pen hanging at the signature.

He finally succumbed. *If this isn't what comes with love, then what's so special about it?* So, he added "love" just before his name. He also added a "PS" that he would rather have told her in person, but hadn't wanted to wake her. He put the note on the pillow where his head had been. Compelled, he kissed her as he left.

He closed the bedroom door, then the apartment door. Turning, he was startled by Kristin's neighbor frozen in the corridor. Kristin despised him and would have been mortified if he'd seen David leaving, thereby getting a much-sought glimpse into Kristin's private life. David pivoted by him to the stairwell. Now cautious, he didn't restart time until he was well onto the sidewalk. Immediately, he texted, "I miss you already." He wondered when she would read it.

Despite the hour, the street was busy compared to last night. Others' days were well underway. He stopped only once on his deliberate walk to work. There was a lingerie store on D Street that he regularly saw, and he always wondered how it stayed in business. Even through COVID, it had remained open, its lithe mannequins donning new wardrobes for no one to see. He had never felt self-assured enough in a relationship to shop there. Today he did. He would be back.

Fortunately, his office building had a gym with a shower. Cleaning up, which he desperately needed, was not a problem. Nor was getting dressed for work. He always left a full wardrobe, from dress shirts to suits, in his office.

As usual, he was the first one in; no one the wiser of his return as he was wearing what he had left in the previous day. Kristin texted him with an emoji of a winking cat; he didn't understand, but his heart still soared.

Frank and Jeff eventually passed by his office; they paused to mime inquiries about last night. Busy with a call, David flashed a thumbs-up. Grinning, both returned the gesture.

Then Phil swung by. Unloved by most, he was loathed by David. So distant a number two in the office, his position seemed a title in name only. Having risen by seniority, Phil now nominally supervised people whose work he didn't understand but took credit for. He was generally viewed as Corporate's spy and not entirely trusted—especially by David. David had not told Phil about last night, but Phil must have learned as he always seemed to, by overhearing others and quizzing to fill in the details. Playing an air guitar, he sauntered past David's glass wall. For Phil, this was clever, though, as always, he took it too far. David fake-smiled, pretending to talk on a call he was muted on.

Despite the lingering air of Phil's cringeworthy performance, David always thought Tuesday a great day: It was not Monday and fully six days removed from being so again. The morning went by quickly; despite Frank and Jeff's entreaties, even to the point of paying, he begged off lunch for an errand.

Back outside the lingerie store, it was far more intimidating open than it had been closed. There were now more than mannequins inside, there were people—women people. Even as he entered, he felt he should have stopped time.

"May I help you?"

Too late now.

If it weren't intimidating enough to buy this stuff, why do they have to compound it by having attractive women selling it?

"I'm interested in getting something for my girlfriend," he forced out, trying to speak to, without staring at, a tall brunette who could have worn anything in the store.

"Is there a specific occasion?" she asked.

"No, I wanted something she could wear anytime she felt like it."

"I meant, are you celebrating anything?"

Damn. Fifteen seconds in, and I've already blown it.

Steadying himself on a counter, he vainly sought nonchalance. "N-n-o, I just love her."

I still haven't told Kristin this face-to-face, yet I'm telling a saleswoman in a lingerie store!

"That's sweet. What's her size and taste in lingerie?"

Damn and double-damn; I only vaguely know.

"Well, she's about five-foot-nine and in great shape. Here's her picture." Of course, he dropped the phone trying to show it.

The woman smiled. "She's beautiful. I'm sure we have something that will flatter her. And please you."

Embarrassment's crimson surged up his neck and down his forehead; he felt its red train wreck across his face. In so far over his head, David was looking down on himself—and not liking what he saw.

"Maybe I should just look around." Starting his turn, he stopped and turned back. "Um, in case I mess this up, what's your return policy?"

"As long as it's not worn, we'll happily give you a store credit. Look around, and, if you have any questions, just let me know."

David looked around and tried to disappear. How could so little material cost so much? He rather hastily bought something green to match Kristin's eyes and got it gift-wrapped. It came back over the counter in a gift bag emblazoned with the store's name, something in French that no one in his office could pronounce but everyone would recognize.

He faced a new problem: getting this upstairs and later back outside without being seen. *Surely, I can work this out. Heck, other men buy this stuff and do so without making the world stand still.*

David's solution was to take it downstairs to a gym locker, then pick it up on his way out that night. He checked the lobby before hustling across it and down the stairs to the gym. He placed the bag on his right hip as he walked past the gym attendant. Neatly turning into the hall toward the locker rooms, where the men's and women's doors faced each other, he cut sharply to the left—and right into Stacey from his office. Their nearly knocking heads was enough to make him drop the bag, which of course landed name-side up.

Stacey smirked, and David again felt himself blush, surpassing his chameleon performance just minutes earlier.

"Going for a workout? Or was your run in here enough?" She laughed.

Stacey was the best staff assistant in the office, probably the best they had ever had. She deserved more opportunity but needed an opening in the hierarchy to get it. She was one of only a handful of others from their office who used the gym.

"No, I was just practicing my juggling. I guess I need more work," David said as he force-laughed back.

"I guess so, if you're having trouble with just one!" Still laughing, she left him to try and salvage some sense of dignity.

Back upstairs, he took the long way to avoid Stacey's desk, questioning whether he would ever walk by it again.

The rest of his day was easy compared to lunch. He worked out downstairs to avoid running into Kristin at their gym and spoiling his surprise. When he left, he had the lingerie bag under his coat to avoid getting another surprise himself.

Improbably, he felt more excited than he had last night. Then, he had been completely prepared; tonight, he was thoroughly and uncharacteristically spontaneous. Yesterday, he had been unclear on how he stood. Now, he knew.

His finger trembled slightly as he reached to ring her apartment from the lobby. Her excitement couldn't match his, but, hopefully, it would come close. David never rang the buzzer from downstairs; he always texted—again, another twist.

"H-h-hello?" She answered.

"It's me, David. Last night was so great, and I didn't get to talk to you this morning, so I thought I'd just stop by and surprise you. Surprise!"

"Well, you certainly did. Thanks again for last night and everything."

"Did you get my note? I left it on the pillow. And did you find breakfast?"

"Yes, I found both, thanks. They were sweet."

She doesn't sound like last night at all. She doesn't even sound like herself!

"Well, it's silly for us to be talking over a speaker when we could do it in person. Are you going to buzz me up?"

A pause. It seemed like an eternity.

"David, this isn't a good time. I don't feel well. I didn't go to work today."

This wasn't true; Kristin had mentioned the office in one of today's texts. He started grasping for answers to rescue his visit.

"I know..."

What advantage was there in debating details? The facts were wrong, but the message was clear: Kristin didn't want him upstairs. Reasoning wasn't going to change that.

Even if I get up there, the whole purpose—to build on last night—is already lost.

David tried to think of something to keep even this disappointing encounter going. Nothing came.

"David, thanks for understanding. I'll call you later."

"Look, is there anything I can get you?" Knowing he could, and would, get it instantaneously.

"No, thanks. I'll call you."

"Feel better."

"Thanks. Good night."

The arm he had been leaning on dropped as though lopped from his body. He considered buzzing again. Only the greatest willpower prevented him. He wanted to—wanted to, more than anything. It was not about seeing her, but about not letting this end as it just had, replacing last night as her most recent memory of him—a bad next bite after an otherwise perfect meal.

It would have been infinitely better to have not come at all. Now, he just wanted to climb out and back to where he had been.

Stop time and go upstairs to see what's wrong. You can, no one'll know; then just come back if there's nothing. No. It's been a good day; haven't stopped time since leaving here twelve hours ago. Anyway, what's to gain that would offset what I've already lost? Just have to wait. And worry.

His final impulse was to stop time to, escape and regroup. But here, stopping time would not make him feel better.

Time really needs to go faster. Speed me to the next place. The one where Kristin texts me and says she wants to see me.

The whole way back to his condo, he had stared at his phone for Kristin's text. None came. Countless explanations came to mind, but none ever came from her. So, he filled in the blank with every conceivable one, from concern to condemnation. Some he sought to swat away immediately—she was seriously ill, or another man was there—but the explanations circled back around like horses on a carousel, rising and falling in believability.

CHAPTER FIVE

Always spartan, tonight his place felt barren. Kristin had been here once; that had been enough for them both. He liked it this way, but it was clearly not put together with her, or anyone else, in mind. His home was strictly utilitarian, a place of necessity, for doing what had to be done and then left behind. They had implicitly agreed to meet at her place.

He slept poorly when he could sleep at all. Coming out of the fog of his last of several semi-sleeps, he immediately checked his phone. Again. Nothing.

It took everything David had not to contact her. That was today's debate. Should he, or shouldn't he?

You have the perfect excuse: You're worried she might be in a truly bad way.

This was his emotional side.

She sure as shit hasn't forgotten you'd been there. And she hasn't texted or called. Contacting her now only compounds last night's misstep.

This was his rational side.

Between them, he still clung to the hope that everything would right itself. In desperation and frustration, he stopped time. Even though it made no sense, he needed it.

This was another reason he came to this place outside of time, one that had been growing and increasingly drove him here. In addition to using time-stops to pursue, David also used them to escape. The retreats were not *from* things as much as *to* something: aloneness. He liked it there. The rarest of moments: The sound of pure silence was his on command to be experienced between the still of his breathing and the beat of his heart. It was perfect stillness, perfect silence, perfect solitude.

Others had their "happy places," where they sought mental escape—usually places they had rarely, perhaps never really, been. David had one place he could go to instantly and stay as long as he wished. And more and more, he did. He would come into a time-stop for no particular reason, other than that he wanted to be there more than he wanted to be anywhere else. He couldn't know how long he stayed, but he couldn't help knowing how often he came. And the more he came, the more they seemed to beckon. His biggest worry, and his real guilt about his time-stops, was that he came to them too often. Even more, he worried that he enjoyed them too much—that his trips outside his real life were becoming the best parts of his life.

Kristin's text came in the middle of a meeting. It was one of the rare times David felt flustered at work. His first reaction was to stop time. But this would have been useless—except for allowing him to curb his emotions—because he could not have responded. He bolted from the room as soon as the meeting ended.

"Can you see me tonight?" That was all.

Hell, I'll see you right now if that would help!

He fought to compose himself before composing a response.

His first sentence matched his first concern: "Are you okay?" Then: "Of course I can. I can meet you right now, if you need me."

"Tonight's fine. Seven?"

"Yes. I look forward to it. Hope you're feeling better."

Now, to kill eight hours.

He threw himself into work but was never able to push seven o'clock from his mind. The only thing that really helped was the gym. Regardless of what happened in the office, a workout cleared his head. He did not want to risk seeing Kristin, so he went to the downstairs gym. Escape didn't quite come, but it was as good as he could do in the grip of obsession.

Having finally arrived downstairs in her building, David was hesitant. He had waited twenty-four hours for this, but now he wasn't ready, though not from lack of preparation. He had played through every conceivable scenario and situation. She would say this; then he would say that—all rehearsed. But now, just offstage, he doubted.

One thing's certain: Having not stopped time since this morning, I will instantly if I have to now.

After last night, there was no earthly way he was going to buzz her. Bad karma. While he really didn't believe in it, he also didn't need more of that memory either. He texted, she buzzed, and he was an elevator ride away.

He had left the lingerie behind tonight. That impulse seemed a lifetime ago. He just wanted to get back to pre-lingerie now, or even pre-concert. Tonight, he had flowers. This was his boyfriend cure-all. It showed that he had thought, that he cared, that he had made an effort. Plunging into the unknown, it was all he could think to do.

She opened the door immediately but barely moved back from it. Following her retreat, he scanned to take everything in. She looked anxious but otherwise well. Her smile wasn't real; it went only to her mouth, not her eyes.

He started when she didn't. Once he did, he couldn't stop.

"Are you okay? I was really worried. I'm sorry I surprised you. Sorry I left without saying goodbye, if that hurt your feelings. I'm just sorry and worried and should just shut up." Remembering, he jerked the flowers toward her. "Oh, here, I forgot, these are for you."

"Thanks, you're always so thoughtful," she said, talking more to the flowers than to him. "No, I'm sorry. I wasn't feeling myself. Doing a lot of thinking. I left work early and came home to think some more. I just didn't feel right."

"Have you seen someone? Gone to the doctor?"

"It's not that. I…I…shouldn't have gone to the concert."

"But we had a great time. I mean, I had a great time. I thought you did too."

"No, I did. I loved it. It was great. It was just too much. David…"

"Yes? Kristin, this isn't making sense—"

Kristin blurted out, "This just isn't working, and it's not going to work. You're an old man in a young man's body."

Shifting from foot to foot, David looked for something to lean on to escape his awkwardness. "If that's the problem, I assure you it'll solve itself. My body'll catch up."

He watched Kristin suppress a smile that seemed more pained than amused. "See! You're always coming up with these clever quips to change the subject."

"I'm sorry. I thought you were insulting me, and I was defending myself."

"No!" she said sharply. Then, immediately softening, she continued, "I'm not trying to insult you…I'm trying to break up with you."

Feeling like he had been shot, David sought escape in dark humor—despite knowing it was pointless.

He heard his voice match the imploring tone Kristin had used. "Well, that's worse. Couldn't you just insult me instead?"

She looked in different directions to avoid looking back into his stare. "No, it's not working. You've been perfect…"

"I can be less perfect. I could be downright flawed if that's what you want."

"Look, I'm serious. You've been perfect, and it's been amazing but…"

"But?"

"But I just don't *feel* it with you. I want to. I've tried to…Monday night. I know I should. But I just don't. I'm sorry."

"I'm sorry too. But what about Monday night?"

"I tried so hard to make it right. To make it work."

"What if we tried harder?"

Kristin's voice lowered to a whisper. "Don't think I haven't. Don't think I don't want it to work. Please, please don't think that. I want it more than you do."

"That's not possible," David replied, conscious for the first time of breaking his gaze from her.

"Yes, yes, it is. I know I won't find you again or anyone close to you. That's why I tried so hard. That's why I wanted it so bad. I wanted you to be 'him' and for us to be 'us.' But you're not, not for me, and we aren't 'us.' All the trying won't change it for me. If it could've, it would've. And trying harder will only make it harder when it comes back to this point. And we would—most likely, you would. But regardless, we would."

"I'm sorry." It's all he could think to say because he was, on every level. "I wanted to be 'us' with you too. To be 'him' for you." Her face was in her hands. He watched her shoulders shake slightly. "Why are you crying? I'm the one getting dumped. You'll have someone new in no time. I'm eminently replaceable; you could have your pick."

Not looking up, she replied in staccato, aligning with her shoulders' rhythm, "I don't…want…my pick…of anyone. I just want the right one, and I wanted that to be you. And now it never can be. Not now, not after this."

Despair drove him half a step forward. "Sure, it could—tomorrow, next week, right now."

"No, you'd always remember this—the unfiltered honesty. And so would I. We'd both look back at it and know this wasn't right."

There they hung, separated by a chasm of two feet. There was some talk of still being friends, hanging out, seeing each other at the gym. But he knew, and knew she knew, these were just words to be said. Not to be meant or believed, but to just hurry the transition to there being nothing but the past. Then they stood. Silent. A long time.

When he could stand it no longer, he spoke. "I should just go then."

A failed attempt at a smile. "Yes. Yes, you should. I'm a mess."

"I meant what I wrote. I do love you." He said it because he had to; it was the only way he could let himself leave.

"Please, don't say that."

Reaching for the door, he offered, "Is 'goodbye' okay?"

"Yeah, that works."

"Then, goodbye."

"Goodbye."

He couldn't watch the door close and didn't hear it when it did. Just like that, it was over. Nothing he could say or do to bring it back. All they were now was the past. Forever.

It all had happened so fast that David had forgotten to stop time. Instead, he had been the one frozen. She had stopped time for him, and all he could do was stand there and try to leave with as much grace as a man with no dignity left could muster.

Now alone, he thought to himself, *There's nothing as dead as a relationship when it's over. Even life itself ends with a pleasant memory or two. People do laugh at funerals, remembering good times. But an ended relationship, that's real death. There's no afterlife here. Just cold, empty, over.*

What hurt the most was that David knew deep down that Kristin was right. He had to respect her decision and, therefore, her all the more, which made the hurt all the worse.

Feeling like hell, he finally stopped time now that it was too late. He walked the nine miles back to Alexandria. He didn't restart it until he was back in his condo with the door shut and his phone off. He wanted to be sure no one could reach him because the only person he wanted to wouldn't be trying.

CHAPTER SIX

He didn't know how long he had slept; he had made a point of not looking at the clock last night. He knew it was late; the sun was streaming in.

"Crap."

David never overslept. When he was running late, he just strategically stopped time and let himself catch up to where he needed to be. But for that to work, he still had to have time to stop. Now he didn't. It was already too late.

Of course, he had turned his phone off, so that hadn't helped. There were a hundred messages, half telling him he was late. And not one of them from Kristin. He hadn't expected any. Rather, his hope was one signifying last night had been a bad dream instead of a nightmare. Life wasn't going to let him off that easily, though. He was still short a girlfriend. And now, late.

Instead of trying to salvage the day, David tanked it completely. He emailed that he was sick. This was not totally a lie. He was sick of everything right now. Saying he was sick was more believable than that he was late. Because he never was either, sick was more plausible.

He read each message's first sentence, if he read anything at all.

It's amazing how trivial these are when you don't care about any of them.

Normally, he would have dutifully responded to each and gotten caught up in the ping-pong volley of group messages, each breathlessly sending marginal increases of information as though they were the Ten Commandments straight from God's finger. Today, he wore out his delete key.

He was only responsive to Frank and Jeff. He emailed Janice, who ran the office, and Stacey to tell her he would be missing everything. Then he shut everything back off.

Pity is truly a job that conforms to the old saying about wanting a job done right. David did it right. To do it, he played time like a piano. He started it just long enough to do what he had to do—cooking, showering—then shut it back down. As good as he had tried to be at not stopping it, today he was that bad. He didn't really know if it helped or hurt; he just knew he needed to do it, and that he didn't want to feel at all right now. As much as he hated feeling dependent on anything, he knew he was on stopping time—*this* time—today.

David didn't know how long he had extended his sick day. Only the lengthening stubble on his face gave him a hint. When he was "in time," he played every heartbreak song he could think of. He chose "Broadway" because of the line about a young man in an old man's bar, reminding him of Kristin's first words. Then there was "Breakfast at Tiffany's"; it captured his loss. He settled on an obscure number, "You Ain't Thinking 'Bout Me" by an old band called Sonia Dada. That one worked best in its resignation to hurt's one-sidedness. Kristin wasn't thinking about him, and he was using every trick he could to not think about her—even as she affected his every moment.

Each time he checked his phone, he grew more despondent that there was not only nothing from Kristin, but that there was never going to be. That was the hardest to accept. When he stopped time, he stopped the messages.

Late in however many hours he had crammed into just a few actual ones, he decided to take his motorcycle out. He had a Harley-Davidson Sportster 1200. It was his one decadent personal pleasure. He wasn't a polisher, like the bikers down in Old Town who parked their shining chrome and sat around them. He loved riding, not rubbing, his bike. It wasn't a showpiece, but it was his best in-time escape.

Early on a fall afternoon, he rode the GW Parkway. On the Virginia side of the Potomac, it was a beautiful ride right in the city. Taking it, with some side roads added, he could get a "century"—100 miles in a ride—in almost any weather. He headed south toward Mount Vernon, took a right until he hit Jefferson Davis Highway, then kept going south to Mason Neck. Its fields and horses made it feel like the country solitude he craved. He stopped and watched the horses for a long time before realizing it was nearly dusk. Time to go back.

David didn't like riding in the dark, not from apprehension but from being unable to see the landscape—a big reason he rode. He pulled into the south end of Alexandria as the sun set. Lost in his thoughts and the rumble and vibe of his ride, he was jarred back by the blare of bad music. A car screeched to a stop on his right. It took some music to catch his attention above the Harley's rumble, but everything about the car was designed to catch attention. And then offend it. He instinctively looked over. That was enough for the driver to look up and unleash.

"You gotta fucking problem with my music, motherfucker?" came from a young, grizzled face, tattooed, pierced, and set as though spoiling for confrontation.

David pretended not to hear, gesturing with his right hand that his helmet blocked the sound. He only wore full-face helmets, so it was believable he had not heard what he definitely had. He thought this gave them both an "out."

The driver didn't care and signaled back to lift his visor. David unthinkingly and obligingly did. The driver leaned out, then repeated his obscenity louder and slower.

David had learned early from riding motorcycles: Let everything go. Bikes lose against cars. Period.

Every idiot can drive a car and usually does. You just have to extricate mentally, and sometimes physically, but always extricate.

Not this time. The previous night, the miserable day, and this piece of excrement were too much. He stopped time. Putting his kickstand down, he climbed off and walked over to the car. The window was down, and his antagonist was frozen in pursed-lip insult. David surveyed everything until he found something he could use. He reached across the driver and turned the man's key to the left so that he could remove it. Then he sent it as far as he could throw it down Washington Street. Mission accomplished, he got on his bike, rocked it to the right, put up the kickstand, and resumed time.

The driver's car was immediately, and, to him, inexplicably dead. He flailed around the car trying to figure out the problem.

"Yes, I do. It sucks. It's the soundtrack to stupidity." David revved his engine for emphasis and then brought it back down. "Have a nice day." David left the man in a blare of horns from irate drivers weighing in.

CHAPTER SEVEN

Once back on his street and off his bike, he turned not toward his condo but to the small hill facing it. At the top was a small bench swing that he had never seen anyone use. Trying to decompress, he focused on gently rocking and the chains' rhythmical grinding. With his eyes closed in concentration, he tried to use these sounds and the motion to summon calm. It did not come. Instead, as he walked into his condo, the opposite of calm boiled over in him. Beside himself and by himself, he unleashed at everyone and everything.

"How could this fucking happen? How? I did everything right; more than right, I did it perfectly!"

He was jolted out of himself by a quick pounding from his floor. *Forgot to stop time, damn it!* This was one of the embarrassing side effects of his gift. Sometimes he lost track of whether he was in or out of time. At work, and to his humiliation, he had been caught in extended monologues with himself.

Barely restraining himself from pounding back, his realization only added to spiraling frustration. He struggled to bring himself under enough emotional calm to succeed in stopping time now. It took two tries to summon the concentration. However, David's motivation was not self-restraint; it was to allow himself to fully erupt in complete privacy. When he assured himself that he had, he raced past where he had just left off.

In an extended and exhausting rant, "What did she want that I didn't give? What more could I've done? Why did I have to leave that fucking, stupid note when I should've just stayed and talked to her instead of trying to take the easy way?

"This was perfect! It was just as I planned! Just like it was! I took the perfect job! I picked the perfect fucking girl! She even said she loved me! Then I blew it! Totally fucking blew it! Again!"

"Again" was the trigger. As soon as David said it, if only to himself in a silenced world, he heard it. It resonated deeply, hitting like the unexpected self-inflicted wound it was. Its unintended honesty hurt worse than Kristin's rejection or his self-recrimination.

David knew that it was not the absence or the near-miss of perfection that had ended it with Kristin; it was his single-minded, myopic pursuit of it. This was not the first time.

He had come downtown to K Street to find "perfect" here. He had intended to make a new perfect life: perfect job, perfect salary, perfect girlfriend. He had come downtown to pursue perfection because he had been unable to find it on the Hill.

In the Senate, he had worked for one of the old bulls. Senator Hyde, from his home state of Georgia, had been chairman of the powerful Appropriations Committee. David had risen rapidly up the ranks in the Hyde universe by being perfect as he had always been. He simply could not be held back—whether by youth or inexperience—because he was rapidly seen as the best at whatever he was tasked with. Before long, he was another binder-carrying expert always at the chairman's side. He could, as Hyde said fondly, "Produce anything out of his bag of tricks, like Felix the Cat!"

The critical juncture of David's Senate career had come during a disagreement over legislative language between Hyde and Senator Thomas, an equally senior and powerful committee chairman. David had detected a discrepancy between two of Thomas's versions—one he showed to Hyde and the other he had actually submitted as an amendment. When David discovered it, Thomas had conceded and attributed it to carelessness.

Ordinarily, in the decorous Senate, that would have ended it. But David felt the discrepancy had been deliberate. So sure, he had stopped time on the floor of the Senate. As the floor stood still, he had walked into its well—where only senators were allowed—and searched Senator Thomas's papers. It confirmed David's suspicion; the discrepancy had been deliberate.

Then David went beyond being right. He kept Thomas's paper and, seeking a bow on his discovery, he showed Thomas's paper to Senator Hyde. It was pure hubris. David had already won the issue for Hyde; he could have just basked in yet another coup. But he didn't. He couldn't. Then even stopping time could not undo what he had overdone.

Furious at the revelation, Hyde confronted Thomas, who returned his ire, claiming there was no legitimate way the paper could have been obtained. Because he was the one who had initially discovered the discrepancy, David was blamed without proof by Thomas and his office; he became *persona non grata* in their world.

Hyde and Thomas had both retired since David had left the Senate, but their relationship had never recovered. Nor did David feel that his Hill relationships had—even with his former boss.

Failing in perfection there, David had left the Hill to continue his pursuit of it. To him, the fault lay not in the quest but in the failure to attain. Now it had just eluded him again—losing the perfect girl he loved and loved being in love with.

As he rolled through the two episodes now, he zeroed in on the people—Senator Thomas, Senator Hyde, Kristin. *People are too variable; they leave too much to chance. Things—work, career, goals—these fit what I can do with time. Things, I can control. People? No.*

David knew he was obsessive. But so were others. The difference? His ability amplified his obsession. Stopping time made his nature a strength and a weakness. Others found it hard to stop—to leave well enough alone; David didn't have to. He was infallible to others because his ability allowed him to be truly infallible. Yet David could never appear so to the one person who could see into his inner sanctum: himself. Regardless of his perfection to others, he was not for David. Stopping time meant there were almost infinite ways to improve even seeming perfection.

Now, having been dashed down into the hurt of rejection from the heights of elation, he lashed out.

He did not know how long this time-stop lasted. With time stopped, there was nothing to measure or by which to measure. He could only tell by what transpired with him. Tonight, it was exhaustion, at the onset of which came his decision on what he was determined to do.

CHAPTER EIGHT

David awoke the next day knowing that while it would be tough to get through, it had to be done. He didn't recall the last time he had just discarded a day like he had yesterday. Even when he was truly sick, he kept his oar in the water to some extent. Yesterday—yesterdays—he had consciously sought out the separation from everything except his own thoughts. It had worked, but now he had to face the reality he had so deliberately avoided. Even with new resolve, it would hurt.

He started immediately by stopping time, getting himself ready, out the door, and to the train in essentially no time at all. So early, the train was quiet. He read emails as he rode, pausing only long enough to look out at the gray sky over the Potomac and the crew teams rowing below.

He stopped time again as he exited the Metro and walked past the man who sold newspapers, and he always ignored, across the Navy Memorial, and finally paused at the sailor's statue that he particularly loved. He had never felt closer to the statue than he did today: alone and gazing into forever. He started time only long enough to get into the building.

As soon as David went into his office, he saw Kristin there. She was smiling at him as only she could. There was nothing he would not have done for that look. It was the one he had constantly worked to coax from her; when he got it, he felt he had reached the summit. Though it was just her picture, everything he had resolved to put away last night came back instantly. He was not going back there again, to the feeling that had swallowed yesterday. If he could not break the spell, he could at least break the frame. He swept it off his desk in a single motion before he could think more about it or regret it. He made sure to pick it up face down before putting it into his bag.

He relentlessly used his time-stops to catch up, then released time and waited for the world to catch up to him. By the time people began arriving, he was, as usual, ahead—as if he had never been gone.

Frank came by first, sounding genuinely concerned. "How're you doing? Janice told me you were sick. I corrected her, though; I said David never misses work. He must be dead."

David pulled a slight smile. "I was really flattened, but I'm better now. Fine, actually. Did I miss anything?"

Frank grinned back. "Just a day mining salt. There's no shortage, so you didn't miss anything."

"Thanks. Hey, want to grab lunch today?"

Frank rocked back in mock shock. "You must still be sick if you're asking me!"

"I forgot to bring anything today. I was so focused on getting caught up, it must have slipped my mind. Why don't you ask Jeff when you see him?"

"Sure. Welcome back."

It's better to rip the Band-Aid off and tell Frank and Jeff up front. It'll stink, but it'll be over. At least, I'll control it and won't have to constantly dread it coming up later—especially with some others.

He started to settle back in when Stacey appeared.

"Feeling better?" she asked lightly.

"Yes, thanks." With embarrassment still lingering from their last encounter, he sounded unnaturally stiff and formal to his own ears.

"That's good. Janice wants you to read these and see her at eleven about them."

Stacey extended a large binder that looked to contain his next two hours.

As David reached for it, Stacey exclaimed, "What happened to your hand?"

He hadn't noticed, but now looking, he saw the blood.

"Oh, I don't know. I must've cut it between here and the Metro. I'll go wash it off."

She smirked back. "You better. Janice wants those read, not bled." Snapping back from her joke, she said, "You sure you're okay?"

Embarrassed again, he cupped his hands to obscure them. "Sure, I didn't even know I had it."

That settled it. David stopped time to clean up his cut from Kristin's picture. He had battled to refrain from stopping time for months while with Kristin—trying to save it primarily for her. With her gone, he was going to stop time as often as he needed or wanted to.

David stopped time to read the binder Janice had sent. Then when walking to return the lingerie. Finally, to cancel his gym membership during mid-morning when he knew Kristin wouldn't be there—still, he stopped time to walk through to be sure.

His next excising chore was to tell Frank and Jeff at lunch. David led the way as they jaywalked directly across the street to the place they always went. It wasn't a dangerous act; the light made the traffic pattern perfectly predictable—to the point that David routinely counted it out by watching the pedestrian signal tick down half a block away. Frank and Jeff regularly kidded the routinely reserved David about being a hardened criminal. He had once convulsed them by laconically explaining, "It's my way of sticking it to the Man." He had no such joke today.

Seated at their usual table, Jeff, who David hadn't seen all morning, started. "You sure you're fully back to normal?"

"Yeah, I'm fine. Why? Don't I look okay?"

"You *look* fine, but you don't *seem* fine."

Frank seconded, "Yeah, you seem…not all here, distracted. Somewhere else."

Damn. I hoped I only felt that way. He gave up, rushing it out instead of trying to work it in casually.

"Kristin and I broke up last night…two nights ago. I mean…" He breathed deeply. "She broke up with me."

His friends sat in stony silence. Having lived the relationship with him from the beginning, they knew what she had meant to him. David sensed they also immediately connected its timing.

Frank broke their stunned silence. "Just like that? Out of the blue?"

"Just like that. Lightning from a cloudless sky."

Jeff, never one to beat around the bush, went straight to the economics. "That sucks. Did she at least offer to pay for the show?"

Frank winced and sighed. "Oh, Jeff."

David didn't bother answering. Now, it was out there. "Look, this is new to me…"

Jeff leaned back and squinted. "First time you've been dumped?"

"First time I've cared," David said, leaning over the table.

"That's tough. It takes it from a gut punch to a nut punch," Frank replied.

"A miss is as good as a mile, I'm afraid. And 'close' only counts in horseshoes and hand grenades," Jeff added.

"And love," Frank offered.

"I haven't heard that last one," Jeff said.

"You're the rare person if you haven't *lived* that one." Frank stretched himself far across the table and reached for his tie's knot.

"Uh-oh, there goes the tie," Jeff said, rolling his eyes at Frank's sure "tell" of his coming "frankness," as he'd dubbed it.

Frank turned from grimacing at Jeff. "Look, close is as good as love gets—it's the only thing that counts in it. It's as good as it *can* get. David, once you get through holding your groin and can stand upright again, know this: If you go looking for perfect in love, you *ain't gonna find it,*" Frank said, punching every word with his finger on the table. "And if by some miracle you did find it, you ain't gonna keep it. It would change because you're both gonna change. You're not perfect, and she won't be, so the two of you can't be either. Anyone who's living in day-to-day love—not the momentary stars-in-your-eyes kind, but real honest-to-God, forever, day-in-and-day-out love—knows even if they won't admit it. They know it. They live it. And they do because they're committed to it—not just in it but committed to it."

The two let Frank's diatribe sink in.

"This is supposed to make me feel better? That I have *less* to look forward to? You should be telling this to Kristin; maybe she'd take me back!"

Frank, mellowing, said, "It's supposed to make you feel *normal.* That 'not settling' stuff is all BS. You either settle or you're single. There ain't no perfect, David."

"Look, thank you both for coming out and listening—well, not so much you, Jeff. I wanted to tell y'all up-front. I know it's going to come out, and I don't want a big production about it. I just won't bring her up anymore. Now you know why."

Jeff jumped in first. "You can count on us…or at least on Frank. You need to warn me so I can prep for something like this. All I know about love is that it's something that happens before you have kids."

"No, Jeff, that's sex," Frank responded.

They laughed, even David, who understood no more than the attempt at consolation.

For David, the worst that could still come would be having to relive the breakup through repeated retelling—to all those who didn't really care but would pretend to and then relish the gossiping and speculation.

Unspoken among his band of confidants was the knowledge that the people most to be avoided about this were Phil and Denise, the Washington office's homegrown version of Phil. Of course, there was no way that it wouldn't get to them. They made side careers out of knowing everything that went on in the office—all under the pretense that it somehow had bearing on the office's functioning, rather than just feeding their predilection to pry. They would certainly find out eventually. David hoped that they would find out so late that the news would have aged beyond their ability to pretend to be sharing something fresh. Really good gossip came with an expiration date.

David hoped the worst was over; still not easy, but perhaps easier. He mulled over Frank's comments. It fit his resolve to a *T*.

CHAPTER NINE

Throughout his time downtown, David had not taken great satisfaction from his work. He had come three years ago partly because the money was so astoundingly good that he couldn't turn it down, not because the work was profoundly stimulating. More importantly, he had gotten the offer when all Hill paths to advancement appeared closed. He had accepted it when people had told him that time downtown "would be good seasoning."

For the most part, it had been a good experience and certainly a lucrative one. It gave him insight into another aspect of the legislative game. Still, he often felt he was playing for matchsticks downtown. The stakes just seemed so small compared to the Hill's politics and policy. Maybe people came to Washington with the dream of being a lobbyist, but that was hard to believe. He hadn't known any childhood friends who dreamed of being sportscasters rather than players. Those who truly loved the game wanted to play it, not describe it, regardless of the audience. That was what he now did, though. He translated the Hill to Corporate and Corporate to the Hill. At his most cynical, he saw his job as buffering the "principals" on both ends of his translating from knowing how unimportant each was to the other.

David kept two signs—"work" and "fun"—taped beside his desk.

"That's why they call it work,

and they pay you to do it."

And:

"That's why they call it fun,

and they don't pay you to do it."

When he came back from lunch, he tore the "fun" one down. He didn't see it applying to him for the foreseeable future.

With Kristin gone, he threw himself into work. Before, by stopping time, he had excelled without effort. Now, he was aiming not just at excelling, but at perfection.

He relished work's escape. Trips back to headquarters? Sure. He knew he wouldn't run into her there. Lobby trips, which he had formerly avoided if possible? Pile them on. He welcomed the change of scenery and, even more, eliminating the chance of seeing her and the disappointment she now embodied.

The first week went smoothly as his life shrank remarkably. It was station to station. He went to work, he ate at his desk, he went to the gym downstairs, he went home. Repeat. He stopped time when necessary, but mostly for work, not release. Without much going on, time wasn't precious.

Then weeks and a forgettable birthday had passed the same way. Not quickly, not painlessly, just passed. That was all he asked. There had been no word from Kristin. Not unexpected; and, once David had accepted reality and resolved on a new one, not unwelcome.

He covered his tracks to her completely. He had left his old gym. David never went back or looked back. With that gone, he knew their paths were unlikely to cross. Except for the gym and each other, their worlds had been entirely separate. To make certain, he also wrote off the other places she enjoyed. Again, this wasn't hard. They were fine establishments on their own, but without her, they were just places. Washington was full of places; so long as they weren't full of Kristin, they were fine too.

David did the same at home. He did not keep a lot of things, and he didn't have a strong attachment to many of the things he did. If it reminded him of her, then it, too, became just another "thing." The one exception was her smashed picture from work. He couldn't bring himself to purge that. Instead, he put it as far away as his two-bedroom condo allowed: in a box, on a shelf, in the back of a closet. He imagined stumbling on it years later, when he was with someone else and happy again. Then, perhaps he would have a fonder memory.

David attempted to do the same at work; this was both easier and harder. It was easier in that only her picture had been there, so there was little to remove. The harder part was removing her from others' memories. Kristin was not someone people forgot—he found it hard even when making an active effort. Most people made an active effort to remember her—especially the men. And most especially one man in particular: Phil.

Of course, David had brought Kristin to work events. Ordinarily, he hated these, but having her there made them fun. Not the events so much, but her reaction to these—the whole hierarchy and intra-office politics were meaningless to her—and, of course, others' reaction to her. The biggest of these had been that summer pool party at Janice's house. As the head of the office, Janice felt obligated to host these, the way Senator Hyde had felt obligated to have his whole staff over on designated occasions. Equally, all invited felt obligated to come. Most of the office dreaded the pool parties. They never had the least intention of getting close enough to the pool to look conspicuous by not being dressed for going into it. Janice had even said as much on her invitation.

Kristin was made for pool parties, and seemingly every swimsuit was made for Kristin. Their attendance, really her attendance, had catapulted David into social legend. People he rarely talked to in the office suddenly talked to him, inevitably steering the conversation toward her and that party. No one more than Phil.

Kristin had definitely hit a nerve with Phil. And Phil had a lot of nerve to hit. David imagined he was closing in on sixty. He was married, but his children were grown and gone. From listening to Frank and Jeff and how their children dominated their lives, David wondered how Phil filled his life with just his wife. Phil had evidently once been physically active, but now his activity was an unsuccessful rearguard action at maintenance. And he was losing ground. David believed Phil lived for work, from which he demanded more and more to compensate for the less and less he got from the rest of life.

At Phil's age, grasping the brass ring of real authority in the company was slipping further from reach. The only thing still within reach was this office. His focus was now here, and not so much on the office's real performance but his and, more precisely, his position. David believed that, like other areas in his life, Phil was consumed with not sliding back here too.

Unlike most people with whom Kristin had struck a nerve, she had struck at least two with Phil. One was obvious, but David believed there was a deeper one also. He had explained it to Jeff once: "I think he sees my dating Kristin as something like a challenge. One he can't match, it irks him into constantly probing for flaws, for ways he can diminish it in his mind and eliminate the threat he perceives. He treats other things in the office that way—why not this?"

Phil had risen through Whitney's hierarchy by dint of seniority. He continually mentioned how long he had been there to anyone who would listen. David could not remember how long that was because he didn't care enough to listen. David's standard was productivity, not longevity. He respected those who could do the job, not those who had the titles. Phil was precisely the opposite. In Corporate-speak, Phil "managed up" extremely well. He paid close attention to who was where, who was moving—or likely to be—in Whitney's leadership game of musical chairs.

Frank had nailed it when he told David early on that "Corporate sees the D.C. office as a satellite orbiting the planet 'Government,' which they don't understand or like."

Janice, who had made her mark in a big way on the Hill, ran the office. Phil had no government experience except what he had picked up from being in the Washington office. Frank summed up the two's relationship: "There's a neat complementary nature to it, but there's no substitutability. The office has to have Janice. Of course, Phil doesn't see it that way. But the office does. And everyone reserving all their most pressing questions for Janice galls Phil all the more, only fueling his insecurity. Why Janice, you, and most everyone else here who came from government are so important escapes him. In any other part of the company, his seniority would trump hands-down his coworkers' lack of it. But not here—and, therefore, not back there either. It drives him nuts."

Phil forever sought ways to reinforce the position he felt due but Washington denied. More cynically, David thought it was to justify his presence and poke holes in the barrier Phil felt between himself and them. This came through in his frequent forwarding of articles with big-picture observations: "Are we following this?" and "Why aren't we doing this?" They were meant to obscure the fact that Phil didn't grasp the smaller details on which issues really rested. It didn't work, but Phil never stopped trying.

David's long-dreaded outcome came in Jeff's text: "Phil knows." The text meant he could expect Phil to find a way to probe it.

David replied: "How?"

"I don't know. He probably just put it together."

"Put what together?"

"You and your behavior over the last however-long-it's-been. He's a jackass, not stupid."

David knew it wouldn't take long. Phil couldn't, wouldn't, resist.

He was working, facing his window overlooking Pennsylvania Avenue with his back to the door, when Phil came in. The scent of Phil's cloying cologne let David know he was there before he saw him. Immediately stopping time, he braced for what would surely be the worst reliving of his breakup.

Looking at Phil's reflection in the window, he restarted time and slowly spun his chair around.

Leaning on the door's frame, Phil said, "Why didn't you mention you were working on the cost issue? I didn't know there was a tax angle there."

David was thrown entirely. "There's a tax issue most everywhere, Phil. That's why Janice asked me to look and see if I could find one here."

"Well, our costs are a big deal for the company right now. The 'glass suites' are really focused on this. We need to be even more laser-focused on it."

Pure Phil: irritated that he had been kept out of a perceived loop.

The big file Stacey had brought from Janice the day David had returned from his Kristin time warp was all about the company's rising developmental costs. They were huge, and the company was looking to pare them back significantly. The "glass suites," Phil's slang for Whitney's top officers, was an entire floor ringed with glass to prevent fratricidal warfare over window frontage. The glass suites solved that but meant they had to find something even pettier to bicker about. The involvement of the top company officers was too enticing to escape Phil's interest. And, of course, "laser focus" was one of Corporate's annoying catchphrases—like "cascading," or "alignment," or David's particular pet peeve, "doing a deep dive," a phrase he had heard so often he was certain it would someday give him the bends. How one could be "more laser-focused" was beside the point.

David, seeking to evade as neatly as he could the fact that he avoided Phil as much as possible, answered, "I figured Janice would've told you…" Then he made his foot fault: "…if she wanted you to know." He didn't mean it the way it sounded, but he recognized instantly how Phil would read it.

And Phil, predictably, read into it an implication of his unimportance. "Of course she told me, but you should've as well so that I could be part of the decision-making on this."

David knew that Phil didn't know the tax code from an area code, and even less about the policy, politics, and players involved. But David knew Phil wanted in on something that would attract the attention of the people whose attention he craved.

Deflecting, David reached for the mammoth tax code. "Okay, so what do you want to discuss?" He knew going into an issue's substance was the surest way to shake Phil. Yet by concentrating so closely on it, he left himself open.

"Say, *cherchez la femme*?"

David didn't know French, but he had picked up enough traveling in Europe to get by, so he knew this one. He also knew Phil loved to use French to elevate his banalities.

"Sorry? What're we talking about?"

Phil stepped into David's office and pointed to where Kristin's picture had been. "Your lovely lady. Where's Catherine's picture?"

Crap. He knows damn well Kristin was "Kristin," not "Catherine." And he knows equally well what's happened.

Recognizing his entrapment, David was livid, mostly at himself. He should have stopped time to think his way out; instead, he leaned in viscerally and said, "Janice told me to take it down. She said too many old married men were using it to jack off, and it was hurting productivity."

He scored more than he had intended. The stony silence, the flush in Phil's face—the veins rising on his forehead and the lock of his jaw spoke louder than words.

Phil said in a guttural growl, "Just keep me informed on this issue from now on. I want to lead closely on it."

Phil spun away, hitting his heel with the door he had tried to slam, then returned to close it loudly.

"Smart," David muttered. "I just raised the stakes."

David knew he was going to have to knuckle down now. When he recounted the Phil episode to Frank and Jeff, they agreed…after they stopped laughing. Both jokingly confessed to the charge David had given for the picture's removal. It took no little time to get the conversation back on a higher plane.

With two weeks to go in November, lowering Whitney's developmental costs now became the primary focus of David's enhanced work. He took the Internal Revenue Code, all thousands of pages and copious pounds, back and forth from the office. Concentrating on its research and experimental provisions, he wanted to know them backward and forward as he searched for precedents to reduce Whitney's costs. In specificity, he might not only find a solution—if one existed—but an escape route when Phil tried to follow. As he surely would.

What a chick magnet reading the Code on the Metro makes me.

Yet David truly liked an intellectual project. This wasn't just another bureaucratic assignment of reading journals, listening to transcripts, and scanning the daily trades. If successful, this would have real value for the company. Already, it was providing real value for him. David felt that time spent actually learning something was time well spent—a complement to his love for reverse engineering, "forward engineering" in this case. On the Hill, and now in corporate lobbying, such opportunity was elusive when everyone was incessantly locked on the present.

Coming out of a Thanksgiving he had spent researching, he finally had something: expand the definition of what qualifies as research and experimental expenditures (R&E). It wasn't sexy, but it would have two beneficial effects for Whitney. More of the company's large developmental spending would qualify for the R&E credit, reducing the company's current tax liability. More importantly, expanding the definition of R&E activity would move developmental spending out of taxable income altogether, reducing the company's overall tax liability. Together, these would effectively cut Whitney's overall developmental costs—without really reducing the spending itself.

It's a two-fer and then some for a company like Whitney ossified in its locked-in processes. And for me, I only need the "one-fer": not Kristin.

CHAPTER TEN

David's impatience with the tedious Monday staff meeting was even greater than usual this week. Naturally, it ran long. Like animals can sense fear, meetings can sense participants' impatience. With only weeks left in the year, this meeting set the remainder of the year's schedule. Janice ran staff meetings while delegating the purely administrative details to Phil.

Phil liked this division of labor; it was more Corporate than the discussion of legislation and regulations affecting everyone's different areas. Unfortunately, Phil's portion always came last, so that by the time of his solo, his audience was itching to leave. *To us, this is the fat lady singing; to him, it's his diva aria.*

Phil slowly and meticulously wound his way through the material, seeming to pad as he went. By the time he hit the topic of the office holiday party, David was only partly paying attention.

"We'll be having our office party the weekend after next. Janice is hosting, and it'll be catered. You're all required to attend." Phil laughed at his joke. "Just kidding. Well, sort of. We're putting a lot into this, and we're looking for good attendance—or an even better excuse if you don't attend. Also, you can invite guests. So, David, we look forward to seeing you with your lovely lady."

Paying only partial attention, David hadn't been making eye contact, but he had heard the change in volume and knew Phil had been looking at him.

He froze time. Even after, he felt himself still blushing. No wonder. Looking around, he could see the stilled faces staring back at him.

He let himself breathe for a bit. He thought about simply leaving the room during the stop. This would have been a neat turn. However, the room was crowded, and he was far from the door, so how he had gotten out without anyone noticing would have been hard to explain.

Phil knows exactly what he did, and he's been waiting for weeks to deliver this. Just take your medicine. But this R&E issue? It's no longer just business.

Calmly, David let the meeting end and the planning for his response begin.

Janice and Phil leaving together prevented David from talking to Janice about his idea. He tried casually strolling by her office later but still had no luck. He finally sent her an email asking to meet that afternoon. He received a response from her assistant saying today just wouldn't work. She offered early the next morning. Feeling his idea would burst before then, he resigned himself to accepting and waiting.

He turned down Frank and Jeff's offer for lunch. They had heard the staff meeting's scattered inhalations when Phil opened fire. They were ready to treat David to a good grouse, but David assured them it wasn't needed. "That chapter's closed, and Phil's ham-fisted attempt won't reopen it."

He didn't bother mentioning that he felt an entirely different chapter was about to begin.

Instead, David opted for a walk to the sidewalk stores that pop up every Christmas beside the National Portrait Gallery. Rather than missing her, David felt Kristin's absence to be now less personalized but no less real. What he really missed, he realized, was having anyone. He had gone from loss to lonely. Despite having sublimated to near-extinction the personal, he still missed having someone, anyone, around.

Her absence forced David to ponder what his loneliness meant to him. Loss is poetic; lonely, merely prosaic. Lonely's even lonely in music. Sure, there was Hank Williams's "I'm So Lonesome I Could Cry," but not much else. "Lonely" was always handled completely fictitiously. Lonely people were always being rescued by their perfect matches in stories.

Real life doesn't do lonely like that, he thought. *Maybe in Hollywood, not in D.C. When you're lonely, you repel what you most want. You wear your worst self like a bad suit. It's not until you've already solved the problem that you find the solution. Like banks only lending to folks who don't need money, love comes to people who already have it.*

Having made it through the mockingly festive stalls, he muttered, "Check that off the list for another year." One Yuletide tradition down, countless to go. Alone.

So excited to talk to Janice, David didn't need to stop time to beat everyone into the office the next day.

Chomping at the bit as they sat down, he let her start. "If you're here about yesterday's staff meeting, let me apologize. I've already told Phil he was out of line with his staff party remark."

Though he hadn't forgotten, David was well past it. He had never considered that Janice wouldn't be. He had to momentarily reset and alter his windup.

"Oh, that's, thanks, that's okay. That's not why I wanted to see you, though." He worried that he had stumbled right out of the gate.

"Well, it's not okay. I've made that clear. But I'm glad it didn't throw you. So, what've you got for me?"

"I've been doing some thinking, a lot of thinking, about the cost issue."

David mentally kicked himself for sounding so Corporate.

Resting her head on her hand, she replied, "Well, what do you think? I'd love to hear something because heaven knows I've heard enough from Corporate about it."

David leaned forward in his chair. "I think we could cut costs *de facto* by getting some qualified as R&E. I think we could keep doing just what we're doing and still save."

She blinked back. "And how do you propose that we get to have our cake and eat it too? I'm dying to see this alchemy."

"We change the definition of qualifying R&E expenses"—he handed her a list—"to include these. It wouldn't lower our actual costs, but by reclassifying some as R&E, we could earn a credit and deduct the spending."

Janice lifted her head and lowered her hand. "You've got my attention. How much?"

"It would reduce them twice. First, by qualifying them for the Section 174 credit and then allowing them to be deductible. We would earn in the mid-single digits on the first—"

"And by the rate of the corporate tax on the second."

"Exactly! And it's that second one that's the real benefit."

Janice's eyes flashed. "Yep. The first's the sizzle, but the second's the steak. So why would anyone consider it on the Hill?"

"The R&E credit's been around for decades. It's changed multiple times and uses various bases for its calculation. R&E's never been more in flux than right now. All of today's various new demands, like environmentalism and AI, argue for rethinking here. A more expansive definition, just as society's expanding the definition."

"Good. But what about others? Is this a rifle shot just for us? I'm not saying I don't like it if it is, but it's a damn sight harder to accomplish." Janice's voice had gone from tired to interested, further heightening David's enthusiasm.

"It would help everyone who fits our profile, so our direct competitors. But it would help us the most unless they also have our high costs. I know this makes it tricky because we all hate each other, but we also all know each other. The education on the proposal should not be hard. We'd just have to be careful on the details—for when someone tries to screw us on them."

David paused to think about the risks. He had not contemplated these much, having been swept away by the reward's potential. He leaned in anyway. "There're always going to be risks in working with partners that know best how to hurt us worst. But really, isn't the risk not that we wouldn't come out ahead, but that we not come out as *far* ahead as a competitor?"

This can't slip away.

Rising, he put his hands on her desk. "Aren't we already behind them on costs? So, the playing field's really more slanted toward us coming out better."

Janice leaned back. "I like how you think. I also think this is worth pursuing. How quickly can you give me a short write-up of your idea?"

He handed her his one-pager. "How about now?" He also had attached a longer, more detailed version behind it.

Janice put on her reading glasses, and David held his breath. Finally, she looked over the top of her glasses. "You've really done some good thinking here. Not that your work isn't always impressive…" Janice paused as she flipped through the attachment's back pages. "But this is..." She trailed off and shook her head slightly. "Let me read this and think about it."

"Thanks. And thanks for taking the time to hear me out." David long before learned a lesson many never do: When you get a compliment, just take it.

As he turned to leave, Janice stopped him. "One last question: Have you discussed this with Phil?"

Suppressing a smile, David replied, "No. I haven't felt that compelled to see him over the past two days."

Janice let her smile through. "I thought you said yesterday hadn't bothered you."

"And you always say, 'There's no education in a mule's second kick.'"

David had gotten Janice with her own Southernism. A generation and gender apart, this bridged both. She was an Arkansas transplant, and he was from Dahlonega, outside Atlanta, which had once been the South before "the influx" had "Yankee-fied" the area so that he sometimes felt a stranger in the place he had been raised—or "reared," as Janice was wont to correct: "You raise chickens, you rear children."

They laughed at their momentary connection.

David left as quickly as he could. He knew well enough that he had just had his perfect meeting…and perhaps found his perfect escape.

It's the first time I've felt good, really good, since Kristin.

CHAPTER ELEVEN

It was two long days before David heard back from Janice. David knew well enough that patience was not just a virtue; at times, it was a necessity. Pushing too hard does not move a project forward, just people away. So, he fought his impulse and waited.

When he did hear from her, it was a simple stop by his office. Leaning in, Janice matter-of-factly said, "Corporate likes your idea. Could you present it to a group here early next week? I'd like to get their take on it too—just to ensure we aren't missing anything."

Talking to Corporate was a level beyond what he had expected, or even hoped for, so soon.

Janice was David's close second in meticulousness. He knew that she liked having everything in order before moving something up in the company. She rarely made mistakes and attributed it to a well-honed process of internal vetting. If there was going to be a mistake, she said that she wanted it made in her territory, where there would be no damage.

If she's confident to be moving so fast, I can be too.

Janice pushed herself out and off the door's frame. Then she immediately leaned back. "Oh, and David…Phil will be there."

Already thinking to the next step, he nodded. "Of course."

Emphasizing with her eyebrows, she leaned fully in on her arms. "Have you told him about the idea yet?"

David countered by leaning back in his chair. "No, I was waiting to hear from you whether there was a point to."

"Well, there is. And you should."

"Good call. I will." Before she could let go of the doorframe, he added, "Oh, and Janice, thanks."

When David told Phil, he got no read from him. He wasn't sure if Phil fully understood it or whether he was distracted by something else. With no sign of particular interest from Phil, David only gave a short description. Holding back the full details left David room to maneuver if needed.

Minutes later, a notice for a meeting next Wednesday appeared in his inbox. It included all the office's lobbyists and would be a tough sounding board. Frank and Jeff appeared on cue minutes later.

"What the hell do we know about tax issues?" Jeff grumbled.

"Yeah, why are you crowding our calendars with your work? You know, we can bore ourselves. We don't need your help," Frank said.

Like an old vaudeville comedy team, each could play either role in their two-man banter. David fought back laughter to play his accustomed role of straight man.

"Y'all are a regular riot," he deadpanned.

"Yeah, we can tell," Jeff retorted.

Frank tossed out, "We're here all week, folks!"

"I was afraid of that," David replied, not breaking character.

"Well, are you going to tell us what this is all about?"

David pretended to turn away. "Why don't you ask Janice?"

Looking around and adopting mock secrecy, Jeff stage-whispered, "I'd rather die."

"Then go ask Phil," David responded, glancing over.

"I would die," said Frank, barely under his breath.

"Look, I've got work to do, so why don't y'all take your little roadshow—"

"We'll let you get back to it—"

"If you agree to go to lunch and tell us," Jeff added.

"Fine. I'll come by at twelve," David chuckled.

They shambled off for effect. "Come on, Jeff, let's go work on our dance number..."

Now David could safely laugh. It would be good to have a few "plants" in Wednesday's audience.

At lunch, David walked them through his idea. Even without tax backgrounds, Frank and Jeff grasped the potential. Saving money by a simple law change was clear. Sure, they could see the possible pitfalls, but as Jeff pointed out, "What plan doesn't have them?" David's confidence rose further—to succeed internally, the idea had to win non-tax types.

Frank and Jeff provided more than just comic relief and moral support. Although they worked on different issues, they knew their stuff—and lobbying in general. They helped refine David's pitch for non-tax types too.

If any idea's going to really move, it's got to be something that can be successfully pursued, not just an interesting tax idea. There are countless good policies that can never be lobbied—because they can't be enacted and implemented. Entire coalitions of the gullible are dedicated to them. Most never go anywhere. They survive by virtue of a handful of true believers and many more naive members who find the price of membership cheap enough to justify pursuing a pipe dream. These are D.C.'s venture capitalists, only they invest in visions rather than start-ups. Such groups, in turn, hire consultants to help pursue their pipe dreams. Depending on the size of the white whale being hunted, these consultants can hire second-tier consultants to whom they farm out even more of the project—media, polling, event staging, an almost infinite list—piling layer on layer. Yet, at the bottom, lies an idea going nowhere.

David had no time and even less patience for that. Frank and Jeff helped him ensure that his idea was both grounded—and could get off the ground. This was what the approaching in-house meeting was for. Janice equally refused to go to headquarters unless she thought David's idea could fly in both D.C. and HQ.

Jeff exhaled for emphasis to signal a change in tone and away from substance. "Now that that's over, we can make this a 'mullet lunch.'"

Frank cut his eyes over without moving his face. "A what?"

Jeff put one hand on his forehead and the other down his neck. "You know, business in the front, party in the back. The haircut! Hockey hair, Frank?" Dropping his hands, he said, "We've talked about work, and now we can enjoy lunch."

David feigned a grimace. "Thanks a lot."

Jeff pretended to yawn. "No, no, it was the most entertaining tax discussion I've ever endured, I mean enjoyed. But shouldn't we break from the levity that is tax and talk about this weekend's Christmas party?"

"You mean '*holiday party*,'" Frank corrected flatly.

"Well, Christmas is *my* holiday," said Jeff. "Frank, you can celebrate winter solstice or whatever you want."

Switching attention to him as though planned, Frank said, "You going, David? You never did say anything about Phil's staff meeting throw-down on Kristin."

Darting his eyes from one to the other, David said, "This is really why y'all came by earlier, isn't it?"

Jeff vamped it up and fluttered his eyelids. "No, we really did want to talk about tax, right, Frank?"

"I haven't decided," was David's honest response. In fact, he had purposely not thought about it because he knew who he wasn't bringing.

"Will you bring anyone?" As always, Jeff homed in on the real issue. "You know Phil really set you up."

"I'm quite aware. If I come alone, then he has the obvious follow-up. If I don't come, it'll look like he scared me off. Anyway, I've just been focusing on work."

"All work and no play makes Jack a dull boy," Frank observed.

"Kristin thought I was a dull boy, even when I played. I'll just stick with work."

"Wouldn't it be great if you showed up with Kristin?" Jeff blurted out.

"Oh, Jeff, I can't take you anywhere," Frank sighed.

"That's over and buried," David muttered.

"Sorry. I just meant to show up that jackass."

Trying to bring life back into what had suddenly gone somber, Jeff said, "You could bring Phil-ette!"

"Oh lord," both David and Frank responded together. "Phil-ette" was really Denise. A young, single woman, she worked in the office. Half Phil's age and the opposite gender, she was Phil in training. Rather than being born to Corporate, as Phil had been, Denise aspired to it. She used all the buzzwords Phil did, plus some new additions. Recently, she had let fly "dimensionalize" without breaking stride. She could also come across like a walking motivational poster from the break room. "Teamwork makes the dream work" had come out of her more than once. You didn't know if she was kidding, but no one cared to find out. Objectively, she wasn't unattractive, but her personality drove everyone crazy; then it drove them away. Topping it off, she had a voice like a Siamese cat. In heat.

David pushed back from the table as though this would also separate him from the suggestion. "I think not. A step down from Kristin is inevitable, but a step off a cliff is something else entirely."

"Actually, I think I'm going to ask Mona," David added.

Both leaped at the news. "Who's Mona?"

"You never mentioned someone new!"

"She's not new. I've been talking to her for years."

"So, who?"

"How?"

Having milked it, David closed. "She's the voice on the conference call dial-in. The one who says, 'I will *now* connect you to your call.' That little inflection on 'now' has always gotten to me. I've had a crush since I first heard her do it. Sometimes I dial into calls that I'm not even invited to just to hear her." Sighing theatrically, he said, "With a voice like that, she's got to be beautiful."

Both roared. When Jeff admitted the same infatuation, David said, "I heard her first. Anyway, Jeff, you're married."

"Just because I'm not eating doesn't mean I can't look at the menu. Or listen to it."

Returning to work, then splitting off into his office, David's mind snapped back in the separation. Now seeing through to the next step, he redoubled his work efforts.

CHAPTER TWELVE

As the meeting approached, David stopped time constantly.

His presentation had to be perfect. In addition to redoing it, he also transformed it into a slide deck. At Whitney, this was how people communicated. They used slides religiously; they were the voice of Revelation. If not said in slides, it had not been said.

Stopping time enabled him to memorize his talk. He never did anything that required him to use more than talking points—the Hill's version of slides—to stay on his topic. This time, he would not need even those. It wasn't easy, but unlimited time made it attainable.

He even stopped time to practice in the room where the meeting would occur—at the same time it would occur. He started with the slide deck, eventually discarding it. His memorization came to include Code citations and law changes. Next, he practiced for likely questions—and for inane ones. Lastly, he honed his delivery—form to supplement substance.

I've earned my Ph.D. in OCD.

Despite the length of his work hours—far longer than any normal person's, and sometimes beyond even the daily two dozen—they rapidly passed. When *the* day came, he was beyond prepared; he was what even he deemed to be perfect.

For everyone else entering the room, nothing was out of the ordinary.

These meetings didn't happen often, but regularly enough that all knew their roles, even if they didn't know the content. Janice ran it. She gave the briefest of introductions to David's idea. Calling it "very interesting" and saying she wanted the group to hear it and provide feedback, she turned the meeting over to him.

And like that, David was on. Ready and raring to go, his preparation readied him for anything.

Except Phil.

Each time he started, Phil sidetracked him with a question or observation. Each aimed to make it appear David had missed the big picture, and, implicitly, that these oversights undermined whatever David was going to say.

To David, the interruptions encroached on eternity—but even more on David's patience. He was not alone. While he could, and did, stop time, doing so twice to maintain composure, others weren't so fortunate. Shifting in seats and audible sighs indicated growing impatience. At one point, even Janice, who in such formal settings was ever the former debutant, gently tried to steer Phil to silence, "and let David go through his idea."

Finally feeling he was clear for takeoff, David said, "Knowing of the company's concern over its high costs associated with work related to its R&E—"

"What's R&E?" said Phil. "Do you mean R&D?"

"If I had meant R&D, I would have said R&D."

"Why not call it R&D? No one calls it R&E. Except you."

"And except the tax code. And it's the Code I am trying to talk about here."

David made another time-stop.

"Auggh!" came the primal scream that had been building the entire meeting. "You son of a bitch!" He was certain he was screaming for others too, and this time-stop went louder and longer.

Then he regrouped with a final quick mental preparation of the presentation that assuredly must begin now.

"I've been looking at the tax code—"

"David, there's no 'I' in team."

It was classic Phil. Just the sort of anodyne aphorism Phil adored.

Without pause, David said, "There's no 'U' in it either, Phil."

The silence mimicked a time-stop. But time was indeed moving. David knew he had hit a bullseye but was not going to acknowledge it and lose the opportunity Phil's stunned silence afforded.

Barreling through, he soon hit his stride. Peppered with questions, he parried them like an expert fencer. He made clear, after the final silencing of Phil, no one was going to poke a hole in this.

The meeting broke. He and everyone else knew it had gone well. But David also knew that he had ensured Phil would be a problem—rooting, if not working, against the proposal.

Frank and Jeff said as much when they met him later. Of all the presentation's points, their big takeaway was, as they howled and said, "There's no 'U' in team either!"

That line would quickly become legendary. David tried to squelch it, but even if he did with Frank and Jeff—and both swore they would drop it—it got out. Too many others had been there, too many who would have loved to deliver it themselves, to not repeat it. David knew that would only make things worse. Unlike their private exchange in his office, this had been public. David knew Phil would relive it over and over.

He will not just want to get even; he will feel he has to.

Before David, Frank, and Jeff could replay much of the meeting, Janice interrupted. "David, as soon as you have a minute, I want to go over...things."

Still soaring, David was already thinking about the next steps for his plan. Figuring out the idea was one thing, doing it another. Of Kipling's "six honest serving men," the most important was the one whose name didn't start with "W": How. He was sure Janice was thinking the same as he entered her office.

"Thanks so much for the opportunity just now," he gushed. "Once it got started, I thought it went okay." He intentionally downplayed his impression of the meeting, hoping Janice would raise it.

"David, please close the door."

David's elation abruptly pulled up short, like a dog hitting the end of its chain at full sprint.

Seating herself, Janice motioned at a chair. Gingerly, David slid in. "Is everything alright?"

Janice blew out her breath. "No. No, it's not."

"What's wrong? Did it go badly?"

"In a way, yes. David, this thing between you and Phil." She inhaled deeply. "It has to stop before it hurts you both—especially you."

"What do you mean? I'd be thrilled if it stopped. You were there. You saw how he acted."

"Yes, I saw. It was a petty performance, to say the least. But you landed a haymaker."

"I'm sorry if I lost my head, but I've worked hard on this. Prepared so much. I couldn't just let it die in the cradle. It was the first thing that came to my head."

Leaning to peer across her desk, she said, "And that's usually the last thing that should come out of your mouth. David, like it or not, he's your boss too."

"You're my boss."

"And if I go?" She shook her head, seemingly more at the thought than at him. "I'm telling you, be careful, for your own good."

"I appreciate your concern. I really do, but what am I supposed to do? He was the instigator! He's twice my age. If he's my boss…to some extent"—David's hands pushed back on the chair's arms and himself with them—"then shouldn't he bear a bigger responsibility for his own behavior?"

Janice sat up. "If you're implying that age equates to maturity, then you're not as smart as I took you for. Look, I'm saying this for your own benefit."

He dragged his right hand through his hair. "My own good would be to have Phil just leave me alone. Period. I'm not looking for anything more."

"Okay, then I'm saying it for your own future advancement. You're going to encounter people like Phil. If you haven't before, consider yourself fortunate. But you must try and win them over, not run them over. It's this that I'm looking for but haven't seen."

"I don't understand."

"David, your work's superlative already. This idea could take you a long way at Whitney. I know what's going on here. He's threatened by you, so he threatens you in return. Look, I'm not going to play psychiatrist. He is who he is. He's an impediment to your advancement, and, if you don't want to advance past him, the surest way to do that is to keep butting heads with him. It's this simple: If I go, he becomes number one and owns you; if you stay, and stay smart, you could be number one."

For the first time, David saw the higher stakes.

"Janice, I appreciate this. Really." Then he simply confessed, "I, I haven't been at my best recently, so I've just been throwing myself into this project. I *need* this. I just want to *work* right now. And I guess I just want something *to* work right now."

Janice relaxed her posture. "I said I wasn't going to play psychiatrist, but here I go. Everyone knows you've had a tough time."

"How? Is it that obvious?"

"Word gets around. And yes."

He dropped his gaze. "Damn. Just damn."

"Look, some free advice here. And it's probably worth no more than you'll have to pay for it. She wasn't for you."

"I thought she was," he replied without looking up.

"She didn't. It went as far as it could go. If you were looking for someone to have fun with, then you had it. If you were looking for something more, you weren't going to get it with her."

Without moving his head, he flicked his eyes up. "I thought it was something more."

"Maybe I'm showing my age, but was it marriage you were thinking about? She certainly had, because that's why she made her decision."

Now his head followed his gaze. "How do you know?"

"Two reasons. Hard as it may be to believe, I was once a girl her age. And a girl that age thinks in those terms about a fellow she's spent some time with because she knows she doesn't have an unlimited amount of it. Marriage is more about roommates than romance. More about getting along than getting it on."

"I've a lot to look forward to," he murmured.

"You do! But it's not what you think, and it's not what you tried to make with…"

"Kristin."

"Yes, Kristin." Her smile stretched. "If every day were wine and roses, then we'd all be alcoholics and florists. I could see what you saw in her. Or at least, on her. Any man would, and every man here did. She had prodigious powers of pulchritude. But how much further did the appeal go than that? You clearly wanted her to like you. But when you were trying so hard to get her to, did you like yourself?"

"I never focused on me."

"You were too busy focusing on her. I know you're an old movie fan. There's a great one called *Shenandoah*. It stars Jimmy Stewart."

Hooked, David let himself be reeled in. "I've never seen it, but I love Jimmy Stewart."

"You never will see it either because it's politically incorrect as hell, which is why it's so great. They were just trying to tell a story when he made movies. There is a great scene where Stewart is talking to his daughter's suitor. He says something to the effect of 'I know you love her, but do you like her?' The point he's making is that a lifetime together is more dependent on daily getting along. Love in the hot, emotional sense comes and goes. And even when it's real, and it's often not, it cools. In the tortoise and hare race of relationships, it's the tortoise of 'like' that beats the hare of 'love.' 'Love' jumps out to the fast and flashy start, but it's 'like' that finishes. So, I would just urge you to ask yourself: Did you *really* like her? And just as important, did you really like *you*? I know I shouldn't have said all this. If you want to tell HR, go ahead. I'm too old, too close to retirement, and too me to care. But I like you and respect your work, and I don't want to lose either or see you diminish both."

"Thanks," was all he could manage. Reaching the door, he turned back. "Janice, if you don't mind me asking, how do you deal with Phil?"

She looked up from her next project and pressed her lips together into a thin line; David watched the thinking behind her eyes. "I shouldn't say it and don't repeat it, but with pity, mostly. He's a fish out of water here…no, in a Corporate fishbowl surrounded by a Government ocean. He can see, he can feel, but he can't attain—can't broaden his bowl or swim in the bigger sea. He's really harmless." She shook her head in apparent resignation; David crossed back, extended his hand, and shook hers. "Thanks…again."

He had a lot to think about, and none of it concerned what he had come in thinking about. At each juncture, his proposal was becoming increasingly less the means to escape from Kristin and increasingly its own end: the perfect opportunity he sought. *If only others would get out of the way.*

Once far enough from Janice's, David stopped time. It was time to go talk to Sailor. There was no better place to think than nowhere with no one else.

The Navy Memorial was right outside David's building. Even had it not been so close, David would have come. It was his place. His gift meant it could always be just his for however long he needed it. So, when he wanted an escape—with or without time moving—this is where he came. Like the ocean itself and the ships that sailed it, the park was just open. Even with a number of visitors, and rarely were there many, it didn't feel crowded.

There was a long circular bench with a bronze *bas-relief* of naval actions running along it. Accompanying it, were masts, from which flew the colorful navy signal flags—Alpha, Bravo, Charlie. His dad had been Navy and had taught him to read them. He had forgotten their letters, but he still spelled words aloud using them—Delta, Alpha, Victor, India, Delta—when called for. Listeners who also knew always assumed he had been in the military. Deep down, he had always envied his dad's service.

For him, the focal point of the park was the Sailor. Sailor was a bronze, slightly larger-than-life-size statue that stood with his feet sea-leg width apart, as though instinctively bracing against the roll of a deck. His hands were stuck solidly into peacoat pockets, and his face was set like flint against a wind only he could feel. He stood there alone, just his duffel beside him, as though he was just ashore or about to ship out.

David felt an affinity with Sailor. The isolation that the statue so clearly conveyed was also David's in a time-stop. Sailor weathered it as did he. Neither could have lived their lives if they could not handle isolation. Like a boxer could never step into a ring if unable to take punches, a sailor could never ship out if he could not take isolation. Sailor and David silently shared that. Both knew they could take it.

CHAPTER THIRTEEN

The meeting behind him, things took shape quickly on the proposal. They would take it to Corporate early in the new year. David ignored those who said he didn't need to do anything more or differently. He did the same things again. He started talking more to the corporate tax team to get a better sense of their interests. He also used the company's consultants to polish its tax-substance side. He knew he would not win a meeting by matching the corporate tax team on details, but he didn't want to lose it there either. Finally, he tried to get a better sense of Janice's expectations. Phil would have been a good source, at least on how Corporate thought, but David let that sleeping dog lie.

The year in Washington ended as it always seemed to when life revolved around the Hill. It refused to. Every year, the desire rose for a respite to enjoy one of the city's two genuinely beautiful times: the cherry blossoms (which never bloomed around the scheduled celebrations) and Christmas (which always came on schedule, just never in sync with the Hill's). Every year it did not happen. There was always some catastrophe; Janice labeled them "crises of legislative proportions."

David commiserated at lunch with Frank and Jeff. "The best you can hope for is that *the* crisis isn't *your* crisis, and you can sidestep others' misery—like avoiding others' wrecks in a NASCAR race."

There was an almost unlimited number of possibilities for celebrating Christmas here. The city looked like Christmas should look—the museums, the hotels, Union Station, the Botanic Gardens, everything wore its Christmas best. Yet, looking was as close as you generally got to doing. If there was one ceasefire in this war of frustration between desire and disappointment, it was the office's Christmas party. This was the one thing that, regardless of the schedule, got its moment.

David's attachment to the party this year was begrudgingly genuine. It filled a void Kristin's absence opened. Her departure had excised most of his social life. The gym was gone. Even people he had seen for a long time, though he'd admittedly not known well, were no more. And the gym in his building was thoroughly utilitarian. Few used it, and among those who did, there was no camaraderie: get in, get done, get out.

Having dropped the places they used to go together, that left him work. He had thrown himself into it—away from thinking about Kristin—and he had largely succeeded. Still, the problem with throwing yourself into your work is that it throws little back besides more work. The social aspect of his job was nearly nil now. Of course, he had friends there. Frank and Jeff for sure, and he was on good terms with almost everyone. But Frank and Jeff went home to their families every night. Even if they hadn't, they weren't David's age.

Its isolation was probably the biggest separation from working downtown and the Hill experience. "Up there" was his milieu—everyone involved in different aspects of the same game. Instinctively knowing what everyone did, its denizens had an innate connection. People forever came, entered, and left your circle; the change kept it different and interesting.

It had not just been possible to, but impossible not to, make your own fun through quickly formed and then abandoned relationships, gossamer connections continuously being created as everyone dreamed the dream that they were changing the world. The freedom and proximity to power made everyone else more attractive too.

Now that he was removed from all of that, the separation of a few blocks and a few years dug a far deeper gulf than seemed possible. *A change of address instantly changed every female congressional staffer into my sister.*

The Christmas party was an opportunity within the office. Plus, David could not pursue professional perfection without at least an appearance. *To move up, I must at least show up.* Despite how far below the proposal he rated this, he knew others did not. As Frank explained it, "Corporate expects the offices to throw one for HR purposes. And this expectation comes with its own budget—a not insignificant one. That's why there's real pressure to go. Everyone knows that if people start not showing, the whole thing will unravel. Then word will get back to HR, we'll be labeled 'an unhappy office,' and facilitators will be sent in, which will lower morale even further. So, there's a love-hate relationship with the office Christmas party; people love to hate it."

Nor was David oblivious to the party's personal aspect. The more he pursued his professional life's perfection, the more glaring his personal life's imperfection appeared.

The Christmas party offered a path of possible transference between professional and personal. *It's getting out without going out.* He could not foresee anything happening there, and he told himself he didn't want anything to. But he wanted something: a chance to be somewhere other than the office. A chance for connection.

As late as the evening of, he considered riding his Harley to the party. It would have been a statement for sure. However, "statement" was not what he was going for tonight; his goal was to reemerge.

The party was at Janice's house, way out in McLean, Virginia. McLean was where former staffers moved once they had married and "arrived." From what he could tell, the swanky houses came with kids. Because no one he had ever heard of lived there without them, he figured they must have come with the property, like the pools—instant families. And people there lived in "properties," not houses, a title that came with the zip code.

He knew most of the people there as they were mainly from the office. Only the men looked like themselves—they just had different ties. The women, on the other hand, were all dressed up in much more than business casual, wearing clothes that made him wonder where else they wore them. As the Georgia expression went, some "cleaned up *real* good." Others, not so much. But all had made a genuine effort. Immediately, he felt underdressed and immensely relieved he had not ridden his Harley.

Fortunately for David, a true son of the South, his mother had made him, *made* him, go through a cotillion as a teenager. He had certainly not thanked her then—*and he wouldn't give her the satisfaction of telling her so now, either*—but it did put him at some ease here.

Other work people from outside the office, consultants, Janice and her husband's friends, some Hill and government people, were also there. It was a good mix and large enough for him to become absorbed in it.

Parties most reward those most adept at small talk. David was terrible at it. *It's the same conversation over and over: what you do, what you used to do, and where you're from.* He chuckled to himself, thinking about how his brother Daniel mockingly summed up such talk at home: "For the women, it's 'Love your hair; how's your mother?' And for the men, it's 'How 'bout them Dawgs!'"

Once David had covered his version of small talk, he looked for a new place to stand. He did so with an eye for keeping Phil at least a room away. While there had been little interaction since "'U' in team," he was taking no chances. Christmas, after all, was the season of peace.

He soon began to feel, if not thoroughly comfortable, at least not uncomfortable. Since he was only a light drinker, this was about as good as it got for David at parties—neither dramatic highs nor dramatic lows. Middle was good, though, and a much better place than he had been for a while. As he mixed and mingled his way through the hours of crowd and food, a natural sifting occurred until he found himself back where he always ended up: with Frank and Jeff. This wasn't hard; if you found one, you found both.

David liked their wives. They complemented their spouses well—Frank's had some of his frump and Jeff's some of his nervous energy. Even had he not known, he could have paired them up. Seeing Frank and Jeff outside of their natural work habitat, David was also amazed to witness how the wives civilized their husbands.

Forgetting where he was, he simply enjoyed himself. Standing at a high table, David realized others from the office had joined at the periphery, expanding their little group. In it now were Stacey and two other women and their husbands.

The conversation broadened. Comments turned to Janice's house. It was beautiful. Beyond aesthetics, it was a treasury of artifacts from her truly illustrious Hill career. Throughout were pictures of Janice with seemingly every important politician of recent decades. *What had become of the insignificant pictures? Surely those had been taken too. But history's vagaries had not blessed them; somewhere, they were now gathering dust in an undoubtedly equally elegant basement.*

Scattered throughout were souvenirs of countless foreign trips, received before ethics concerns had squelched them. Each table had something. On theirs was a simple deck of cards. Seeing no particular meaning to them, Frank called out, "Hey, Janice, when everything here should be in the Smithsonian, what makes these so special?"

"Turn them over. They're from Air Force One. I played pinochle with the president with those."

"Holy cow! It figures everything here has a story." Frank cut the deck nonchalantly, but before he could do anything more, David offhandedly said, "Jack of clubs."

Frank looked at the card and then quizzically at David. "Yeah, how'd you know? How could you see it?"

David said coolly, "I don't have to see it to know the jack of clubs. Everyone knows the jack of clubs."

Lost in the moment and a memory, David had stopped time. He had simply walked around behind Frank, seen the card, returned to his spot, and restarted time. It was one of several tricks that he had used in college to make money doing magic shows for children. He could do the trick in a variety of ways—having them look at the card and put it back in the deck, having him cut the deck and show it to the audience—anything that allowed the card to have its face exposed for an instant worked. His showstopper had been pulling a family pet out of a container. Again, he just had to stop time, go pick up the still pet, put it into the container, and then reveal it. Happening so fast, even the most uncooperative pet was a good subject—usually.

Enrapt, David had lost himself. Unlike his magic shows, where this was expected, this had come out of the blue, with a group of adults who had no idea how David had done this.

Naturally, Frank tried again. He looked at the card, then at David. "What do I have now?"

"Three of hearts."

Frank's wife inhaled audibly; Frank jerked his head. "Damn! How'd you do that?"

"It's a gift. I used to do a magic show in college."

"I didn't know that." Frank's eyes narrowed; Jeff's danced between Frank's and David's; the crowd tightened.

"How about now?"

"Six of diamonds."

"This is incredible!" Frank whipped around and saw Denise standing behind him in the now-growing group. "She's signaling to you! You're both in on this, aren't you?"

Denise raised her hands and shook her head. Still, Frank made her move to the side.

"Queen of spades."

"Son of a bitch!" Frank was thoroughly swept up now, looking everywhere for a solution to the trick. He checked his shirt front, patted his pockets, everything he could think of.

Jeff took the cards and said, "Hey, let someone else try! It's probably where you're standing, Frank."

"Nine of diamonds."

"I'll be damned!" Jeff exclaimed.

The crowd was now pretty big as more partygoers drifted over to see what was happening.

Someone from the office called out, "This is a total con! These guys are always together. They planned this, and they're taking you all in."

"Yeah, they're playing us!" came another. "Give the cards to someone else. Stacey, you take them."

As Stacey stepped to the table, David realized he was now in deeper than intended. What had begun unconsciously had now become something he was acutely conscious of. And he had no idea how he was going to end what he had started.

When he was a college magician, ice cream and cake always ended his shows. *I could've pulled an elephant out of my ass, and kindergarteners weren't going to skip ice cream and cake to stick around to watch. Adults at a run-of-the-mill Christmas party, though; this is something else. They aren't going anywhere.*

Clearly nervous from the unexpected attention, Stacey hesitated as she looked at David and then glanced around the table. "Okay, what do I do?"

"Just pick a card, look at it, and don't show it to me," David replied, thinking he saw his way out.

Peering over shoulders, Janice asked, "Why does she have to look at it?"

"Because I don't read the card; I read the mind."

Stacey blushed. "I didn't bargain for this."

She cut the cards thin. David stopped time. The crowd had swelled and was now packed around the table; moving was difficult. He squirmed to get through. He also really had to lean in. Doing so required him to indelicately go directly over Denise, who had taken advantage of the party to wear an extremely low-cut, NSFW dress.

Coming back, David assumed his former position, restarted time, and looked intently. Stacey held her blush. The group murmured. "What's taking so long?"

"The deeper the mind, the harder the read," David said.

"Hey Frank, he read yours pretty quickly!" Jeff said and laughed.

"And yours, Jeff!" Frank retorted.

"I told you it was a con." Phil had come up to the group.

David smiled. Again, he hadn't picked this encounter, but it offered him limitless possibilities. He now had to fight temptation.

"Queen of hearts."

Stacey went crimson. Putting her face quickly in her left hand, she held up the queen of hearts in her right.

Everyone gasped. The room was David's. There was no way Phil could let this stand. As he came up, he extended his hand; Stacey immediately handed him the deck and moved to the side.

"Janice, are you sure these are your cards?"

David couldn't resist. "You got me, Phil. I brought my own deck of Air Force One cards."

"Yes, Phil, those are my cards." Janice sighed her response.

"Okay, wise guy. Try this." Phil just slid the top card off the deck and left it flat on the table, never picking it up.

Someone said, "Phil, he said he couldn't read them if you didn't read them."

Phil said, "Yeah, right. David reads minds. Go ahead, read it now."

David again stopped time. He had no easy time slipping the card from under Phil's frozen hand. And an even harder one, getting it back. Walking back, he counseled himself, "This is the only juncture where I can easily end this. Don't want to escalate things here; Phil isn't going to let this end if you guess correctly. What he really wants is not just for you to be wrong, but for you to concede. To him. It's not about this card trick. It's what he's wanted all along—for you to concede his superiority in the office, not because he's superior, in fact, he wants it, needs it, all the more, because he's not."

Back in place, he restarted time and then held for a few of the now-moving seconds. Smiling, he tapped the table with his hands. "Uncle. You got me."

Phil clapped his hands. "I *told* you!"

As the crowd returned to the party, Jeff said, "I still don't know how you did it, David."

Janice moved to his elbow. "I don't want to know. I just know I enjoyed it," she said with evident relief. David sensed that she somehow understood what he had done—even if not how. "I'm going to invite you to all my parties from now on, dear boy!"

Just three remained at the table. David, and across from him, Stacey and Denise, sharing in silence their unasked question: "How?" Before they could ask, David whispered, "Four of clubs."

"What?" Stacey was jolted back from wherever her mind had been.

David looked deliberately with his eyes and slightly inclined his head toward the card. It was still where Phil had left it. Denise slowly picked it up.

"Oh my gosh!"

"Shush, don't say anything. This is just our secret," David said softly, just to them.

Almost hyperventilating, Denise said, "Do me, do me!"

David almost believed Denise thought he could read minds. Or perhaps, it was the same way some people have a lark with palm readers, knowing it's fake but still enjoying the personal sensation and attention.

Regardless, Stacey slid away as David obliged.

With each card, Denise became more engaged. Even when they were done, she stayed close. As they were leaving, Denise was still at his elbow as they reached the end of the front walk and a natural point for separation.

"Where did you park, Denise?"

"I got here late and had to park about two blocks away."

David smiled. "A lot of people are having parties around here tonight. I'll walk you to your car."

She returned his smile. "Thanks, always the gentleman."

They walked slowly over the uneven gravel on the road's side. In heels, Denise slipped and grabbed David's right arm for balance. After righting herself, she did not release his arm.

Reaching her car, she turned. "How did you do it with the cards?"

"Never ask a magician to give up his secrets."

She grinned and said, "Can you really read minds?"

David looked away and chuckled.

"Do you know what I'm thinking right now?" Denise leaned in and kissed him.

Startled, David did not deflect the kiss. Nor the second one. Only as he felt her lips parting, did he pull his away and stop time. Looking down to gather himself, he saw fully down the front of her dress.

I don't have to read minds to know where this could go. This isn't smart. It's about as far from perfect as I could get. Jeopardizes everything. What's Jeff always saying? "Don't shit where you eat?"

In the struggle between personal and professional, professional prevailed. Barely. And David knew only his ability to stop time had allowed it. He restarted it only when positive it had.

"I should go."

Her voice huskier, she said, "You don't have to."

"But I should," he said, his breath accelerating again.

"I wish you weren't always such a gentleman," she whispered.

"Me too," David murmured to himself.

CHAPTER FOURTEEN

Monday was an ugly return to reality after the Christmas party. The push to end the year in Washington was always the worst of times. There was a frantic effort to get everything as far along in the legislative process as it could possibly go. Everything was in play, and everything was viewed with an eye to attaching it to something else—a "vehicle" in legislative parlance.

This made Washington's favorite parlor game, the rumor mill, grind even faster. And that meant sorting through countless theories and reports. Unable to review everything, David had to triage the more believable among the unbelievable. Of course, the biggest problem was that Corporate heard rumors too. Usually, the ones they heard were the oldest and worst. Yet they would insist, from having heard something from someone who heard it from someone else, that it needed to be checked.

"It's like having relatives of the patient in the operating room with you," David lamented to Janice. "Undoubtedly, they care and mean well, but they don't know what they're doing. And the more questions and suggestions they make, the more they take me away from what really needs doing."

To accommodate this, he only planned for Christmas with his parents, but without plans for his arrival. Living in Dahlonega allowed him to drive and not have to plan—saving his sanity in the process. It was a holdover from when he had worked on the Hill, and he really did have to work until the last day concluded. He remembered many times having worked on short sleep for days, only to finish on one when he had gotten no sleep, then going back to stop time to sleep before driving home just a day or two ahead of Christmas. Even so, it was preferable to playing airline roulette and praying his chosen date and time came through.

The Hill and home: As distant and distinct as these opposites were, they were somehow connected. When the former ended, David felt drawn to home, like a bird to migrate—instinctual, ingrained—especially now.

So, he and the office hunkered down for the final assault. This was why Washington essentially started the Christmas party season immediately after Thanksgiving. People knew the end was hell, and if you were going to get anyone to come, you better have your party before the craziness came. When it did, Christmas was less a cause for celebration than an escape from the grind's most grueling, cruel part. Christmas became an afterthought in its own season.

Congress members didn't leave as much as the year left them. They worked until the holidays forced them to quit town. Even then, many seemed to leave only because it seemed unseemly to stay, making them appear even more out of touch than normal. Undeniably, a not insignificant number found the holidays an imposition, an interruption in the perpetual politics they lived for. The season simply gave a theme to their fundraisers and an opportunity to send Christmas cards to those who attended these throughout the year.

David approached the end the way he had on the Hill: by being there. He knew there was nothing to be learned from being in the office now.

The ability to stop time had its advantages, certainly. It allowed him to quickly get to someone he saw from a distance. It could also allow him to read whatever someone was carrying. However, it didn't give him the ability to recognize when to not approach someone. It also didn't allow him to understand what a seemingly insignificant piece of paper meant. Being able to read the people *and* the paper were skills David had; all the stopping of time wouldn't compensate for their absence, even as it enhanced their presence.

Stopping time just gave him more opportunities and time to use his skills.

David prided himself on this distinction between his unique ability and his conventional ones. He could not get to perfect if the latter did not measure up. This increasingly mattered to him. With maturity had come sensitivity about the advantage that stopping time gave him. He therefore increasingly differentiated between the two. Of course, it was not a distinction he could share, any more than he could share his secret. In his sensitivity, lay the desire to separate himself from "it" more and more. He wanted to feel accomplishments were "his" and not "its"—a distinction only he could make.

His unique and his conventional skills were on full display now. But while they racked him up his usual untold number of brownie points with his Washington office and Corporate (his email updates were legendary for accuracy, detail, and timeliness), they didn't yield any spectacular results—it just took him away from his proposal. Nothing had gone wrong; the small things he cared about all came out, more or less, the way he wanted. He had gained little but lost time.

The year ground to a halt once it had ground everyone down. Five days before Christmas, it was over. David's Christmas season could finally start. And it started with him sleeping away half of his first day. Even his special ability on the Hill couldn't compensate for showers, real food, and being in his own bed.

The first time he really felt relief was on his drive south. The anxiety that had enveloped him for weeks receded as he moved farther from the city.

The drive also forced on him time to think. He needed this because work had fully occupied his mind since his split with Kristin. David had at first intentionally used work to avoid thinking about Kristin. When the means became the end, work pushed aside reflection on its own. *Just because I reordered my world doesn't mean others understand. Or even know.*

He had never told his parents he was no longer seeing Kristin. Never said a word. Undoubtedly, his brother and parents had spoken about it when he wouldn't. His brother Daniel was five years older and had his own family. The two were not close in any sense—age, temperament, interests, the progression of their lives.

Because Daniel was just a little younger than Jeff, David could understand the younger brother–older brother dynamic he shared with Daniel. But just barely. With ages so far apart, the two brothers had not shared much more than a roof growing up. Even that ended when Daniel went to Georgia Tech. For most of David's teenage years, he effectively had been an only child.

Yet age was not their biggest separation. Their interests were completely reversed. Daniel was "the hard science" son and, true to trajectory, an engineer like their father.

Daniel had tactlessly put it once in a conversation: "David, you're the nonserious son. Hearing about your relationships is like listening to theories. Sometimes, you've got to come up with a proof. Theories are either proven or they're not; you're either married or you aren't. Anything short of the altar is only a theoretical relationship, unproven. How can you expect us to follow them seriously?"

Now that Daniel had twins of his own, his hands were even fuller and his attention even less apt to focus on David's "theories."

Because Daniel lived in Atlanta and now had a family, David's parents were largely centered on him. When they all talked, the conversation quickly went to Daniel and his children. *I understand. They're easy to follow; I'm difficult. I've never even been able to satisfactorily tell them exactly what I do—even on the Hill. My world's thoroughly unknown and unintelligible to them.*

All they knew about David's world was that he was happy in it, and they were happy for him. In contrast, Daniel's world made perfect sense. He had a career, a life, and an address they recognized. David had none of that. It made conversations difficult, like talking to a foreigner; before long, everyone settled on keeping things simple, saying only the necessary and communicating in other ways.

As distant as this sounded when he thought it over, it did not feel that way in action. In many ways, it freed him to a great degree. His brother could be "that son" to his parents. Having one like Daniel, they could afford having one like David. He could then try to sort his life out on his own without feeling he was messing it up for anyone else.

As the miles passed, a long-delayed peace descended over him.

He arrived calmer than he had been in longer than he could remember. Daniel was not there yet. David had his parents to himself for a day.

Oh, they look so much older. I guess I don't see them enough to make it gradual. For years, it had seemed like they never changed. Now, they did so in leaps. He blamed himself for thinking this way. It was natural. Even so, he wished they could stay like he still remembered—like he always would remember them.

Just in their later sixties, he could see age's encroachment. Frailty was not there. Yet. But it seemed to hover just beyond sight. He hoped it was not within theirs or reflected in his. As they hugged, David closed his eyes; behind his eyelids, his parents were as they had always been, despite feeling their age within his grip.

Some things didn't change, though. *They're still wearing the Santa hats they bought when I went off to college! Still trying to soften the blow of the last one having left—holding off the thought that all our returns are now just temporary.*

Daniel was right. It was not whimsy; it was reliving the best time in their lives, when they had their youth and their boys. *Daniel's living that time now; he understands.*

At the same time David was examining his parents, he could see them examining him.

His dad, always better with things than emotions, said, "Let me help you unload."

His mother, always seeing within, said, "You look so tired!"

"I'm fine. Just a long drive."

"You must be hungry. You look like you've lost weight," his mom said.

After pleasantries and some food, they helped take his stuff up to his old room. Upon entering, he felt as though he had never left. They didn't need the space, so they had left it largely as he had. He instantly was back. Even his current place, though he had bought and furnished it, did not feel as much his as this room did. It was a perpetual time-stop with time moving all around it. It was forever the place of someone who would never come back but had also never left. He could not understand its comfort, only feel it—something he could even sense back in Alexandria from knowing it was still there and always would be. The place where his old self still was; regardless of what had transpired to change him, it did not—it could not—penetrate here.

Only his mother's persistently gentle waking roused him. It was darkening outside; evening had stolen up. He thought he had shaken the tiredness, but it had clearly returned today. He felt embarrassed that his visit's first real activity was to drop off so deeply that he had to be awakened. She had woken him up only from fear that he would throw off his whole schedule. More importantly, she reminded him, he wouldn't want to throw off Santa's.

David was dressed up as Santa when he greeted Daniel. Daniel's twins stood behind the glass door so wide-eyed that they looked like crabs with their eyes on stems.

"Ho, ho, ho, who have we here?"

"Santa, you've put on weight," Daniel intoned.

"Look who's talking, Daniel!" David responded with a poke to his brother's midsection. "I think you're on my naughty list this year."

The twins howled but were otherwise utterly stupefied. With eyes agog and jaws agape, they mutely led him on a tour of his brother's house, finishing in their bedroom.

David left them with, "Remember tomorrow night, you need to be here extra early so Santa can get his work done." He winked at Daniel on his way out.

Even though they had not really spoken, David saw the love, despite the demands of the two-year-olds' unyielding schedules. Daniel often seemed completely harried and exhausted, but David saw his satisfaction, a completeness. Even if the part occasionally upset the whole, completeness remained. Unable to understand it, David could only observe it. David had certainly never found Daniel so solicitous of his needs when he had been just a younger brother. He had mentioned it to his parents. They had not tried to explain; they said they couldn't, that it was only to be experienced.

Awakening with the world the next day, David spent the morning in his parents' simple routine. The three assumed the roles they had always played in the same tasks they had always done; he stepped in only when they could not perform theirs, but only "to help." They had the same conversations. Doing so was neither tedious nor tiresome. They all knew these were part of a deeper connection that went beyond the words or even the talking. Of many, though, one conversation struck deeply. The one he had been dreading.

His father started with a statement of fact as they sat in the backyard.

"So, you and Kristin are no more."

It wasn't a question, just a reality, akin to commenting on the weather. "I'm sorry if you're sorry," his father said when David didn't immediately respond.

David didn't try to evade when he did. "I've gotten over it."

"Have you?"

"Yes."

Quickly and equally abruptly, looking squarely at him, his father said, "She wasn't the one anyway."

"How do you know? I wish you'd told me; it would've saved me some grief."

"You never asked. David, you aren't one to be told things. Never were. You've got to experience to learn. Daniel, he was, and is, different. With you, we just have to stand back and watch…and hope it doesn't come out too bad if we see that's where it's going."

David forced a laugh to break his father's gaze. "I don't know whether to be apologetic or apoplectic."

"Don't be either. It's just how you are. You can't change any more than I or your mother or Daniel can. People are who they are. And Kristin's the same. She wasn't what you were looking for."

David now sought his father's eyes. "What am I looking for?"

"In a girl? What Daniel has, I think."

"You and Daniel have always shared a misconception that I want to be Daniel."

This time, his father smiled as he shook his head. "No, I think it's you who has that misconception. I don't think you want to be Daniel. I just think you want to have what he has. A family. A sense of purpose. It's not something to be defensive about. It's called maturity. But you can't rush it, and you can't force it. You were trying to do both with Kristin."

"Well, it's over now. I'm laser-focused on my work." David flinched inside as the Corporate-speak slipped out.

"I don't think it is—I hope it's not. With Kristin? Maybe. You know better than we can about that, so I'll take your word about her. But as for finding someone special? I think that's just beginning—unless you want it to be done. That's something you have to ask, and only you can answer."

David sighed. He had already asked that question. He knew that the lasting pain in breaking up with Kristin was not so much losing her. It was the prospect of starting over after thinking he had done all he could to make everything right—admitting everything he had thought was perfect wasn't close.

"No. But that's the only answer I have. The real crushing sensation is not knowing what else to do. I don't know how to find who I'm looking for."

"I went through the same thing. Your mother's not the first woman I met, you know." His father paused, and David watched him remembering. His father smiled, seemingly more to himself than David. "After many misses with many misses"—they both chuckled—"and finally finding her, I came to believe you don't find it. It finds you. All you can do is to put yourself in places where you'd want to be found."

David knew his father was alluding to his being "unchurched." He also knew his dad was right. It was a twist on Groucho Marx's line that he would never join any club that would have him as a member. It was why David rarely went to bars anymore. It was also a reason he had cut back on stopping time outside work. He had realized he could not get where he wanted alone.

"Don't worry so much. Love isn't work. If it is, it isn't love. You can't simply put your mind to it and finish it like you have most things. You can only put yourself into position to be found and be willing to be found. Look, I'll stop talking. I never thought you'd let me say this much or that you'd listen if I did," his father said.

David was simply struck. He had no witty responses and no interest in finding one to deflect the moment.

As they rose, he said, "Thanks. When'd you get to be so wise?"

"When you quit thinking I, and everyone my age, was so dumb. And don't be so surprised. We never really know ourselves. It's probably self-defense: It allows us to keep living with ourselves. So, our folks likely know us better than we do. After all, they knew us before we knew ourselves."

They paused, each peering into the other, even as their eyes looked away.

"David, you don't have to be perfect. Not for us, not for you. It's always been your cross, maybe because it has always somehow seemed uniquely within your grasp."

"Dad, thanks, I wish I didn't, but you don't know what my job entails."

"That's true. But if you're not working for you, then what're you working for?"

David stuck out his hand; his father shook it. It was the best he could do. He had wanted to hug him but couldn't bring himself to do it.

Christmas was beautiful, even if it felt poignantly empty to him. His dad had been right, all the way down the line. He wanted to hold onto it, but the part he really wanted the most from it couldn't be held alone. He went to a midnight church service, then again with his whole family—his parents, plus Daniel's family—the next day. He said to Daniel, "It's to make up for all the ones I've missed," but really it was to make up for what he was missing. He wanted something more than just him taking care of himself. He wanted Christmas to stay. But, as it always did, it ran through his fingers—the fastest twenty-four hours of the year.

Then he was heading back.

He wasn't going home; he was leaving it. Again. *Home's where you grew up. Where someone cares. A place where there's something more than just yourself.* His talk with his dad had been worth the whole trip. After all the years and all the talks, this seemed like their first adult one.

It was strange how the hours driving alone let him think. *I live in two worlds: one where only I move and another where everything else does. Stopping time to escape's a device, a gimmick—like the party's card trick. It's become more of a place to run from something than a place to run to.*

CHAPTER FIFTEEN

On the one hand, the worst part of Christmas's passing was that it left only winter: long, dark, and bleak. On the other, with little to look forward to and no distractions, it allowed David to throw himself back into work.

The second-to-worst part was New Year's. It was one of "the adult holidays." The ones children enjoy—Christmas, Independence Day, Thanksgiving, Halloween, Easter, and snow days—those were actually fun. The "adult" ones—Valentine's, anniversaries, office birthdays, and generic federal holidays—were completely contrived. None more so than New Year's, the quintessential adult holiday.

In years past, David had traveled to avoid it. When people had asked about his New Year's plans, "going to Paris" was a conversation-ender. They never bothered asking exactly what he intended to do there. The truth was: not much—except not getting drunk and spending too much trying to convince everyone and himself that he was really having fun when he wasn't.

This year, when Kristin had ended "them" and Congress had refused to end itself, he had lost first the interest and then the ability to do something adventurous. He made do instead—simple and single—with friends. He was home, alone, just after midnight.

Winter and work now stretched before him. To avoid the first, he embraced the second even more than before Christmas. His proposal's next test would take place at Corporate. Before the Washington office could devote time and limited political resources to something, Corporate had to sign off. It was not enough that government relations and tax had bought in. The idea had to be blessed before it could be pursued.

"Corporate" was the vaguely accurate term that captured the amorphousness of Whitney's decision process. Who actually agreed to something varied, and David never saw the same process repeat. Somehow, someone would just give the green light, and work would begin.

For David, this meant traveling back to headquarters with Janice and Phil. In January. That meant Chicago—or rather its northern stepsister, Evanston, which was even less appealing than Chicago proper. Being less appealing than Chicago in January took no little effort; Evanston made that Herculean task look easy.

David flew to Corporate as rarely as possible. It wasn't so much that he didn't like it, though he didn't, but his world was Washington. Objectively, he offered the most value to Whitney in Washington; subjectively, it justified him not doing what he didn't want to do anyway. Unsurprisingly, Phil was just the opposite. Oriented toward Corporate and away from Washington, David could tell Phil felt his time in D.C. akin to exile. Phil returned from exile as often as he could, monthly if possible. Janice split their difference, the Goldilocks between David's too cold and Phil's too hot.

Just as their approach to travel differed, so, too, did Phil and David's hotels. Working the system, Phil stayed at Evanston's best. He also always rented a car. Having lived there before his D.C. exile, he knew the area. David begrudgingly acknowledged it made some sense. But only some. *What would I do with a car, even if I knew where to go? I'm there to work and leave.* As soon as the former ended, he did the latter. And each day there, when he was done, he usually went back to his hotel to work out, eat, and sleep.

The hotel David returned to each time was a small three-story building that most derisively dubbed "The Inn." According to Jeff, it was "like staying at your grandmother's." David didn't mind in the least. "I always liked staying at my grandmother's," was his response.

The Inn was almost a hundred years old and completely ensconced in the past. Try as they might, management could only modernize it so much before the last century's limitations intervened. To him, this was The Inn's charm: small, cozy, and unpretentious.

It was one of the few reasons that David tolerated his pilgrimages back to Corporate. That he would never encounter Phil there helped too.

David booked several meetings. He met with the people he felt he must but focused on those he liked. Despite rarely seeing each other, he had friends there. Their different jobs and backgrounds seemed to make the connections truer. Neither fully understood the other, but they connected nonetheless, falling into conversations as though resumed from yesterday, instead of six months earlier.

Back in Virginia, David had recalled his Christmas conversation with his father and imagined that he might use some time to think and walk around Evanston. That thought didn't survive the cab ride from O'Hare. So cold, David swore he could taste it, and it hurt his lungs to breathe deeply. Even inside, just holding his palm near windowpanes was enough to warn him away from outside.

Instead, he emailed a small group offering to meet that night. To his surprise, despite short notice and them not being as untethered as he was, three agreed. All were from the tax team, two men and one woman, all dispersed around his age. They drove into downtown Chicago on an uneasy compromise over the city's best pizza. After three hours and as many slices, David was not about to take issue with the place. It was nondescript, with a sister restaurant right across the street. Even which of these two was better started a debate.

Their group commiserated over Whitney's bureaucracy. Because they were complaining, this did not violate David's sole ground rule: no work talk. Much to David's amazement, they had worse stories to tell about bizarre practices at HQ, especially top officers, from whom David was almost completely separated. As the stories went on, David was shocked that these were the people whose approval Phil so sought.

He also became sheepish over his feelings about the bureaucracy's imposition on his life. His stories didn't compare with his friends' tales. Everything he raised, they easily trumped. He came away with a begrudging gratitude that being in Washington insulated him from Whitney's worst excesses. At least his trash was emptied nightly, and they didn't turn the lights off at 6:30. David instigated a game of Corporate-speak phrases. Going around the table, each person had to offer one. His friends took his best ones, then added many he had never heard of. He managed to get off "level-set," "POV," "dimension" (as a verb), and "align" before tapping out.

As David left them, he was aware of his profusion of thanks. The truth was this had been his most and purest fun in a long time. Clearly too long. That was the biggest jolt: that he had had to fly to have it with people he rarely saw. The experience called to mind Whitman: "I have perceiv'd that to be with those I like is enough, to stop in company with the rest at evening is enough."

As he got out of the car, someone in the group mentioned his proposal. "It's a lot better, clearer than the first word we got on it."

"Thanks, I didn't realize my first description was so garbled."

"Yours was fine; we got it."

"Then which one?"

"Phil's. It came to us from someone upstairs. It was all focused on the credit, and even there it was confused."

Still not believing, he asked, "When did you get it?"

As soon as David went in, he checked his calendar. It had been the same day he first discussed it with Phil.

CHAPTER SIXTEEN

Monday was morning staff meetings followed by one-on-ones in the afternoon. The morning meetings reminded him how fortunate he was to usually attend these virtually; when he could glance at his screen or phone, they seemed a lot shorter. The afternoon ones were more productive, the ones with the tax people particularly so.

His big meeting the next day worried him. He was the central focus. More importantly, this was, had been—and he hoped, would continue to be—*his* central focus. He knew his points; he had the tax team's backing. Still, he worried.

David woke early. He worked out ahead of the big meeting to ensure he would be completely alert. He stopped time on the fringes: getting ready, eating. These were his first stops in several days; he justified them now as building in more cushion.

Just before the meeting began, he stopped time to make a full appraisal of the meeting room. From Corporate's glass-ringed top floor, he could see well into Lake Michigan, its whitecaps running to the horizon. What wasn't glass was wood in the room, most notably a huge table that looked like the room had been built around it. Name cards designated everyone's spot. For a wicked moment, he thought about discarding Phil's. He laughed aloud, caught himself, then, remembering he was alone in the moment, let it out fully as he imagined Phil's reaction. Having enjoyed the release, he restarted time.

Janice and Phil were among the executives who filed briskly into the room. There were none of the pleasantries he remembered; from many, there was not even eye contact. David caught Janice's eye, but she only gave him a quick nod and a roll of her hand, signaling a desire for speed.

Trying not to let the clear preoccupation become his own distraction, David stopped time to tamp down his contact anxiety. In the silence, he gave a pep talk to himself. "Trust your prep. Figure this atmosphere out later. Just play your role."

With the briefest of openings, the CEO gave the meeting over to Janice, who handed it equally quickly to David.

Unlike in D.C., David was unimpeded. Reading the room, he ripped through his proposal. Not needing his PowerPoint slides, he used them only for his audience's benefit.

Closing, he summarized, "It's a really simple proposition—"

"All really good ideas are," interjected the CFO.

"I'm proposing to lower our costs by getting more of our expenses," he said, looking right at Janice, "included as R&E."

The CFO, flipping through her slides, was following closely. "We'd love it, but why will Congress buy it?"

It was the same question he had asked himself and had been asked many times. David leaped into his answer almost before she had finished. "These costs' expanded importance in today's economy argues for inclusion. It's got broader applicability, not just to us."

The group began to murmur. The CEO signaled; silence reigned. "How do you know that?"

Every big meeting has a pivotal moment. David recognized that this meeting's moment had arrived. He swallowed and then deliberately slowed for every word. "I don't. What I do know is it helps us, and it'll help others too. We won't know its prospects unless we try, but there's a need, an argument, and potentially a broader coalition." Then he took his jump toward the unknown. "I think it's worth a shot."

The quiet was so profound that only a glance at the clock's second hand assured David that time was still moving.

Jon, the chief tax counsel, ventured, "The ability to deduct these additional expenses would be huge."

The CFO grasped the two-fer aspect. "We immediately realize a savings equal to our tax rate on that spending; as we cut it over time, we realize even more. But we could never match that short-term savings without the deduction."

In anticipation, eyes locked on the CEO. "We've got to try it."

The reception was strong but extremely brief, and it did not cancel the preoccupation David had sensed throughout the meeting. The executives quickly filed out in the same grimness with which they had entered.

Janice and Phil alone peeled off and pulled David away from the tax team's kudos.

Before they could speak, David did. "Is everything alright?"

"The presentation was fine, more than fine," Janice assured him. "But our balance sheet just took a big hit."

"Enormous hit," Phil interrupted. "And it'll reverberate."

"We just lost a huge airline contract. Massive," Janice continued.

"The red ink's rising. Fast. Without the contract's anticipated revenue stream…" Phil added as they alternated with the stunning news.

"The executive committee is trying to marshal what they can."

"Of the deal?"

"Of everything," Phil responded. "Deal, costs, assets, lines of credit, anything that could be converted to ready cash."

Janice closed with the answer to his next question. "Bankruptcy's staring us in the face, David."

An anxious assistant returned to wave them back. Phil left immediately; Janice turned but locked eyes with David. "Remember how you sometimes say it feels like we're playing for matchsticks?"

Still in shock, David just nodded.

"Well, they're burning now. We'll talk back in D.C. Don't say anything about this."

The tax team regrouped around him, curious to know if David had any insight into the meeting's oddities. He had no choice but to lie to the larger group. Only after he could separate Jon and his deputy did he give them a simple warning. "We've got a huge problem."

On the flight home, David mulled over his trip's divergence—his proposal's ascent and Whitney's descent. He tried not to focus on his idea amid the bigger news—after all, it still was just a proposal; the threat was existential. But he could not avoid seeing the opportunity, beyond anything he could have hoped for or imagined. Pushing the thought aside, he began roughly outlining a lobbying strategy.

Before the final meeting, David had felt ready to cross the Rubicon—from his solely professional focus to at least an accommodation with his personal life. The kiss with Denise, his family in Dahlonega, and then the camaraderie with his Evanston friends, each a different temptation.

David shook his head in thought as he followed the plane's approach up the Potomac.

Before, I wanted work to be perfect to fill my void. Now it has to be.

CHAPTER SEVENTEEN

Exhilarated, David took his motorcycle to work the next morning. January made this a labor of love, but after three days in Evanston, his perception of cold had changed. It still meant layering up, though. Sixty miles per hour in forty-degree temperatures would be cold by any standard. On a motorcycle, it became so quickly and deeply. It wasn't just a question of comfort. Cold could become a huge distraction, and distractions on a motorcycle could kill.

Unwinding the bike on the HOV lane was as exhilarating as it was chilling. Although mostly straightaways, this didn't diminish his thrill. His joy in riding a motorcycle came partly from being in the elements; heightening the elements heightened his thrill.

Even in good riding weather, he didn't bring the bike in often, perhaps once a week to keep the battery charged. Just getting into the garage was a production: It required pulling out an electronic fob from his jacket while keeping the motorcycle from rolling down the garage's ramp—braking with his right foot and holding the bike upright with his left. Then he had to park it with the bicycles—an affront to any motorcycle. Finally, he had to change out of jeans and jacket. Still, riding was fun, and today's nonsensical aspect made it all the better, even as he held his gloved hands to the radiator to regain their feeling.

Janice and Phil had remained in Evanston, so David's was the first report about the meeting. However, everyone in the office had heard "the news," even if just bits. Those not versed in his proposal did not understand its implications for the looming cash crunch. But David did. Seeing the office's foreboding raised its importance beyond David's heightened perception on the plane flight back.

Janice and Phil's absence also gave David the opportunity to informally meet with those covering other areas of Whitney's interests. The more relaxed and candid conversations allowed for a franker assessment. The lost contract was indeed a crisis. It would have a domino effect on revenues and spending. Once word got out, other airlines might cancel their orders too. Undoubtedly, investors would sell the stock. Hard. Short-sellers would inevitably pile on. And Whitney's diminished fortunes would immediately lower its credit rating and raise borrowing costs. Spending would have to go up, not just to cover higher financing costs, but to go into more R&E to address problems that the canceled contract revealed. Bankruptcy had not been hyperbole in Evanston, and if it occurred, Whitney was unlikely to emerge. As Frank said, "After all, who would buy engines that potentially couldn't be serviced later?"

Within hours, he had more to plug into what he had sketched out on yesterday's flight. Because he supplemented liberally with time-stops, he had something to show his small group by the day's end. By tomorrow, he would have a very detailed plan to show Janice when she returned.

Having not felt so energized since leaving the Hill, David used some of it and rejoined his old gym. Not the one downtown he had once shared with Kristin, but his old-old one in Old Town Alexandria from when he was on the Hill.

He was struck by how little it had changed. Every gym has its own vibe, and he had come back for this one's laid-back feel. Starting at the front desk, he knew someone. It was as though he was suddenly restarting time here. This continued throughout his obligatory look around. "Look who's come crawling back" and "They'll let anyone in here these days" rang out. Quickly, he cut his looking short.

Nothing's more awkward than walking through a gym in street clothes. *This is the right decision. Welcome back. This Sunday, I'll start visiting churches.*

That night, he got a text to meet Janice and Phil early the next day. When he did, the angst was only slightly lower than what he had felt in Evanston.

David could tell anything's importance by Janice's split between transmission and reception in communication. Today, it was all transmission. Neither Phil nor he said anything.

"We're going to lay everything out to the office in a meeting this morning, but we wanted you to hear it first. We're looking over the precipice; it's that simple. Your proposal just went up in importance. The D.C. office will focus on everything needed to help Evanston juggle the finances and the fallout when the news goes public. You'll be alone on your proposal. We can't spare anyone else."

The full office meeting was longer, but the message was the same. Leaving it, David felt almost guilty over his energy.

The cards get more interesting as the stakes grow higher. The proposal's always been intellectually stimulating, but it's the wager that really makes the game poker.

This was the game he had missed. The proposal was his ante to get back into it. Now his simple, elegant proposal sported a higher profile. Now it was everything that downtown had not been and everything the Hill had been at its best. Changed feelings made this the best he had felt since the breakup. He did not know which was the cause and which the effect. He didn't care to analyze it—just enjoy it, live it for a bit. It had been so long returning. The important thing was that this was better. That was enough.

Winter dragged on outside; work leaped forward inside. The project now shifted to the retail part of lobbying. Meeting with office after office to pitch the idea. Going to fundraisers to establish contacts with those most likely to help. Reaching out to other companies and associations that might be interested. And drafting language to embody the proposal, a process that always raised more questions than anticipated.

The proposal became a conjunction of David's innate obsessiveness, his unique ability, and rekindled love of the legislative game. As soon as he received assignments, questions, and ideas, he turned off time to turn them back around so quickly and thoroughly that he wore down the handful of people in the office trying to follow his effort.

At lunch, Frank and Jeff raised the white flag. Jeff broached the topic and said, “I don’t know how you’re doing it. You send detailed responses back faster than I can write the simple questions.”

“Thanks, I’m trying to keep the process flowing.”

Jeff straightened up and inhaled deeply. “No, seriously, I don’t understand how. I couldn’t do it.”

“I wouldn’t,” Frank added, “not anymore. I’m too old for that.”

Feeling suddenly defensive, he sought justification. “Different stages of life, I guess. You both have lives, families; I don’t. It’s what I do.”

“Could you do it a little less? Or at least a little slower?” Jeff asked.

Their eyes said this wasn’t just their usual joking.

“Sure, I’ll take it down a notch.”

“Maybe two?”

“Has anyone noticed?”

“Yep.”

I get it. They literally can’t do it. But I can’t help it. Something else to think about.

Yet just the next day, it resurfaced. Going into a meeting with his write-up, he caught a typo he had somehow missed despite multiple reviews. Unable to endure it, he stopped, restarted, stopped, and restarted time to go back to his desk, type, print, and be back in place with a corrected version. Even as he recognized its collateral damage, he couldn’t endure imperfection in his quest.

CHAPTER EIGHTEEN

After days and then weeks failed to change, the seasons did. It was spring, and the cherry blossoms were out for their erratic week of glory. If two things could be counted on during cherry blossom season, one was that they arrived on their own schedule, not an official one. The other was traffic.

Frank and Jeff both reviled the traffic that backed up from the Tidal Basin, where the cherry blossoms were at their most glorious. They loved annually recounting the story when, years before, a beaver had found its way to, and made a surreptitious home in, the Tidal Basin. It had revealed itself by chewing down cherry trees. The local news had given it a mixed press. On the one hand, it had a decidedly comic element: a pedestrian beaver waddling its way into the nation's capital, outsmarting officialdom. On the other, this bucktoothed bucolic was felling Washington's sacred grove. The only thing Washington takes more seriously than politics is its cherry blossoms.

After the beaver was finally trapped and removed, Frank had gotten buttons made up for himself and Jeff that read: "Release the Beaver!" Every year they broke them out. And every year, with fewer who remembered the story, they told it all over again. Each time ending with: "I wish the damn beaver had chewed 'em all down."

A routine Metro rider, David could only sympathize. Yearly, on the peak day of the blossoms' fleeting week, he stopped time. He then walked down, around, and back. It was pure indulgence for beauty's sake. The blossoms deserved their international reputation. He would spend unknown hours there, strolling beneath the trees and through the frozen crowd. It was something he always looked forward to and never skipped. His favorite rite, besides looking, was to, ever so gently, run the back of his hand against them. Their delicacy delivered a sublime sensation, one he believed he would recognize even blindfolded at ninety.

Occasionally, he looked at others equally taken in, witnessing the blossoms' beauty reflected through them. With the especially enrapt, he let time restart just to watch their reaction as they were also transported. Though these people would never know, they and David would share a visual poetry.

He had tried taking women with him to share the experience but had given that up. Their company could not match his ability to control and enjoy every unhurried moment for as long as he wished.

His trip this year was no exception. It was the most peaceful thing he knew. Unlike most in life, it lived up to memory and expectation.

His Metro ride home did not. The chaos he could avoid at the cherry blossoms was unavoidable among the people trying to beat the blossom traffic. These were not seasoned Metro moles like David, used to traveling underground. They didn't have fare cards, or they didn't know how to use fare cards. They didn't know to stand aside as trains unloaded, so they snarled the doors.

Just as David tried to navigate a scrum, he was plowed into. His cell phone went sailing from him; he knew it would shatter on the platform's hard hexagonal tiles. Instinctively, he stopped time. It hung feet away and just a foot off the floor. He slithered his way through the crowd, where frozen faces were all fixed on his phone's impending tragedy.

David lowered himself, wrapped his hand tightly around it, then restarted time. It made for an unbelievable catch. Yet there he was, coming up from the ground with it, so it had to be believed. Even he had some hesitancy owing to the impossibility, but it was overcome by concern for saving modern humanity's life-support system.

The crowd brought back to life, having seen only the beginning and now the end, reacted like an audience at a sporting event—gasping, then roaring.

The woman who had caused the collision went instantly from penitent to jubilant. "You ought to be playing for the Nats!" someone else screamed. Other, more profane compliments followed.

David was gracious to the praise and to the woman. "No harm done, lucky snag."

Seeking to escape unwanted attention and regain anonymity, he slid into the car. Still, he sensed a gaze. He gave the slightest of looks to see whose.

"That was one of the most amazing catches I've ever seen." Said matter-of-factly, it still sounded lyrical. It came from a woman so delicate she resembled a living portrait.

David, knowing he had done a double-take, tried not to stare twice. Conceding defeat, he stopped time to try and collect himself. And to uninhibitedly stare.

She appeared roughly his age. Blonde hair framed her face in rivulets. Like a cameo come to life, she stared intently at him with arresting blue eyes that, even with time stopped, he felt self-conscious under. David alternated between being transfixed and forcing his gaze away. Even with all the time in the world, he was flummoxed. He thought about all the things he could say, but all sounded trite. None more so than what he finally did say when he restarted time. "Right place, right time."

"I'll say. I hope you're nearby when that happens to mine."

"Me too," was all he could cough up.

Think! he yelled inside his head, but nothing was working. Still, she looked intently, as though into him.

He felt the car gently swaying, its wheels beating time beneath, tracking the moments slipping away.

"I guess life just works out sometimes," he finally managed.

"Mine doesn't," she said wistfully while gently shaking her head. "My phone would have crashed every time."

"I'm sorry."

Giving the slightest of smiles that just touched her eyes, she cocked her head so that she was looking partly up at him. "Don't be silly. It didn't. And after all, if it ever does, you'll be there."

"Of course." David smiled back in inarticulate incapacity. "Do you…?" David barely got it out as the Metro pulled in.

"This is my stop. Thanks for the show. And the conversation."

She smiled again as she got up.

David dropped his last bomb. "My pleasure."

Then she was outside the closed doors, and he was pulling away, even as every bit of his insides tried to hold the receding platform. He kept looking and saw her one last time, giving that partial smile and a little wave.

The trip to the next stop was the longest Metro ride of his life. Instinctively, he got out, stopped time, and went to the platform's other side to await the northbound train. Despite knowing he had no chance, he had to try. He rode back to Braddock Road, where she had gotten off. He stopped time and visually swept the platform; then he went to each exit—even going out to look.

Nothing! You just had all the luck in the world, and you let it slip through your fingers.

He cursed himself all the way to King Street. To top off his self-flagellation and embarrassment, at the exit, he could not find his wallet. Panicked, he patted himself down in a frenzy.

Not this too! I had to have it to get on in Washington. How can it be gone?

Only in his third pass over himself did he find it in his right-hand breast pocket.

How? I always keep it in my left. Always! Yet here it is. Well, the fact is the answer.

He walked home with only his mental picture of her smiling up at him as company. It was the first time that he had not thought about work in months. Catching himself, he tried to dispel her from his mind. Yet for what remained of his night, the moment kept resurfacing.

CHAPTER NINETEEN

The next morning, David began the day, not at his desk but at the platform where she had exited last night. When he had reached her stop, he got out and waited. He did, because although he argued this fantasy would become a distraction, he couldn't deny that it really already was. He settled on a truism he hoped would hold true: Proving it's over is its surest purge.

If she left this way, she might come back this way. And she might do so on the same rush hour schedule as mine. Both long shots. She could have been going somewhere she didn't usually go. She could commute some other way, with the Metro a complete aberration—as it was for so many during the blossoms. Or she could go into D.C. during any of the day's other twenty-three hours.

David knew there were only two guarantees: He would get this out of his system, or he would talk to her this time, even if it meant making a still bigger fool of himself. He took strange comfort in thinking the latter would be hard to do. He would casually walk up, pretend he had just happened upon her, and say, "I'm here in case you drop your phone." After countless rehearsals, it was the cleverest thing he could think of.

He repeatedly stopped time to check the boardings of the cars heading into Washington. He spent an hour and a half stopping, searching, and restarting time.

And ninety minutes of not finding.

Uncharacteristically, David was late for work. With her still in his mind, that evening, he left at precisely the same time he had yesterday. David repeated the morning's stop-and-search exercise where he had first encountered her. He also repeated his previous failure. Next, he rode to her stop, only to strike out there too.

Beyond frustrated but still fixated, he was out of options. He had seen her once. She had struck like lightning. And like lightning, vanished in the instant of recognition. David racked his brain to think of all he could remember about her. Not just her physical appearance, but anything that could give him any clue to finding her. Yet, as much as he couldn't forget her, he could not recall anything that helped now.

The next morning, David acknowledged that all his unrealistic expectations and perfectionism had resurfaced. What he had justified as a purge of a distraction was fully distracting in its own right.

Just let it go. It's gone anyway. You've raised her beyond what reality could deliver. She's probably forgotten our meet-cute—even if she had paid any attention then. She's undoubtedly got someone else. If she struck you like this, she has certainly struck other men that way.

It was just seven thirty; David stopped time to ensure he got a seat. He looked out the window at the early morning and ran through his work schedule.

Turning back, he was startled to see his pack had somehow slipped from under his seat and spilled its contents onto the floor in front of him. He had felt no sudden jerk, but this was no time to question when everything would soon be trampled and scattered further. The rest of the car, immersed in their morning commutes, had yet to notice. Once more, he stopped time; over the past two days, he had done it so frequently he didn't hesitate. Collecting everything and himself, he returned it to its place under his seat, bracing it behind his legs.

So focused on his pack and himself, David hadn't noticed someone standing over him.

"You're as adroit with packs as you are with phones," she said sardonically.

The woman he had been neither able to drive from his mind nor find had found him. Stunned, David's planning went where his gaze had just been—out the window. Immediately jumping to his feet, he was fortunate that manners are instinctive. He offered her his seat instead of becoming the mannequin he otherwise would have been. It was not smooth, but it was, at least, a decent recovery.

"Adroit and a gentleman." Signaling the seat with an incline of her head, she declined. "That's very kind, but I don't want to take your seat."

David garbled out, "I can't sit while you stand." Then, recovering, he said, "What if you drop your phone? I couldn't catch it sitting down." *It's the first intelligent thing I've said to her.*

What had been just a curl of her lips broadened into a smile. "Well, we *are* in a quandary. Two polite people and one unforgiving seat."

Their awkward staring was interrupted. "Hey, Galahad and Guinevere, I'll take it," said an overweight older woman without compunction.

David, more grateful than gallant, gladly obliged. Now they rode next to each other, holding onto the pole overhead.

Feeling the pause's pregnancy, he forced through. He opted for honesty over any attempt at being cool. "It's good to see you again."

"Likewise."

"I didn't think I was going to."

Again, David felt his uncomfortable inarticulateness.

She seemed to sense his difficulty. "Well, now we're both fortunate. Which one's your stop?"

"Whichever one's yours," he replied.

"Then *we* get off at L'Enfant Plaza. If you weren't getting off at L'Enfant, where would you typically get off?"

The Metro's swaying caused them to brush lightly against each other.

"Sorry," she offered.

I'm not, he thought but said, "Navy Memorial."

"I am flattered, then. Do you always make spectacular recoveries on Metro trains?"

David paused. "Well, I thought I'd missed this one."

A seat opened up beside them. This time, David insisted; this time, she didn't object. He was trying desperately to read anything he could from even the most inconsequential occurrence.

Sitting down is positive; she let me do something for her.

She grinned back at him as she had two days before. With the same impact. He thought it was the most beautiful, the most delicate smile he had ever seen. *As much as I've played that brief meeting through in my mind, my memory hasn't done her justice.*

David finally conceded to necessity and stopped time.

This moment isn't slipping away without an indelible memory. I've come so close to having the whole experience—opportunity, memory, everything—disappear forever. Not again. At least not without doing all I can to hold it.

Her arms and legs were slim and long, a trait that held true for her neck and hands. As she sat, she seemed taller than she had been when they stood together. David guessed she was about four inches or so shorter than his lanky 6'1" frame. He had remembered her eyes being a striking blue but not their full expressiveness. She could have communicated perfectly through them alone, never needing a word. Her left arm was foreshortened toward him, with her hand languidly dropping back to her blonde hair that fell below her shoulders. She was a sculpture. Of course, frozen in time, everyone could be said to look like a statue. But she, she was something more. He glanced around. The rest were mere mannequins—stiff and lifeless compared to her. Sculpture, she seemed to move even in motionlessness. The slightest of creases at the end of her nose made him laugh. "Well, the Venus de Milo has no arms," he said to the stilled car.

He could not keep himself from comparing her to Kristin. But there really was no comparison. Kristin had been beautiful, but there was a flatness to her beauty, as though it had been captured in a photo. But as an image, this woman was something more—a portrait imbued with depth and refinement that somehow emanated from her. She was more than just extremely pretty. Elegance pervaded everything about her. The way she held herself, the way she had moved and spoken. Even sitting on a hard Metro seat now, she did so with perfect posture, yet still remained completely relaxed. She had an unstudied composure; other women would have looked forced trying to replicate what clearly came naturally for her.

The understated, effortless elegance struck David as more than natural to her, but rather something of nature itself.

It's like watching a cheetah walk; even going slowly, it looks fast. Although only implied, speed permeates everything it does. Despite being stopped in time, so, too, is grace in her.

David restarted time, and they talked casually about nothing. He felt as though everyone on the train was listening and watching. He didn't care, even as he tried to will the train to L'Enfant. Anxiously wanting to ask her name, he didn't want everyone to realize he didn't know it.

Stepping into the crowd rushing to work, David was fully aware of his separation from everyone else. He just wanted to be where he was at this moment. He didn't want it to end, despite not knowing what he was going to do with it.

"May I walk you to wherever you're going?"

"That'd be great," she replied. David followed. "But once there, I've got to go right in—early meeting, got to get ready."

David stammered out his understanding. "I didn't mean to complicate your morning."

"Don't be silly. You didn't. My morning was complicated before you wandered into it," she said as she laughed.

They walked without David realizing where they were going.

"I don't know…I mean, I must know…I'm sorry, what I meant to say is, my name's David."

"Julia. Julia Anne Stewart."

"I'm David Preston. I should've given my full name. Here, I know this is so Washington, but please take my card. I was wondering, perhaps when you had more time—and fewer complications…Could I contact you?"

"So formal," she said, raising her eyebrows for effect. Then smiling again, she said, "I'd like that. Please call. Call, don't just text or email; that's too much like business."

David's heart restarted, even as his voice fought to. "I will. You can count on it. Maybe around lunch? How can I reach you?"

"That'd be great. Here's my card. We're both very Washington now."

David extended his hand. She took it. At first touch, her simple handshake was no less electric. Now, he just wanted to get away before he did anything to ruin this. "Julia. Julia Anne Stewart." He kept repeating it, just as she had said it to him.

David made the long walk across the Mall and through the museums' morning quiet to his office. He didn't stop time for it. He wanted to enjoy the real moments with things in motion around him. As he passed his Metro stop, David went down and bought a paper he did not intend to read from the man who always sold them, and he always ignored. When he finally got back to his office, he sheepishly realized he had not thought about the proposal at all.

CHAPTER TWENTY

David was still first in the office. Only once he was waiting for the elevator did he pull out the card she had given him. David had been saving that moment until after he had fully reveled in her having given it to him at all.

"An architect?" David said out loud, causing someone passing with their morning coffee to jolt around.

He had never known an architect, and he certainly didn't expect to meet one in artless Washington. Everyone here seemed to work in government, live off government, or support those who did. To the countless questions he had already asked on his walk, he added many more.

His first was when to call. He wanted to before he sat down at his desk, but he had just enough willpower and common sense not to. Nothing makes a morning drag like checking the time every fifteen minutes; it moves even slower when checked every five. Mostly, David spent the time in between time checks thinking of what to say and how to say it.

I've got to ask her out. But foremost can't come first. I've got to hold her interest long enough to make her want to see me again. So foremost must come last and the least come first. I've spent my professional life around politicians; I'll follow their golden rule: Always ask others about themselves.

He had seen countless politicians move through entire rooms with "Good to see you, how're you doing?" The targets of recognition were immediately flattered that the politicians knew them (though even when they didn't, the targets never knew); then, with the conversation ball tossed, the targets fumbled it, trying to come up with responses. The whole time the politicians were striding deliberately by and on to the next targets.

The key point was that people want to be heard. To be heard, they have to talk. And the easiest way to get them to talk was to invite them to. David knew little about Julia, but he wanted to know everything.

He made it to noon. Barely. Julia answered on the second ring. Already, David was in heaven, having conjured up every reason that he wouldn't reach her.

"You're prompt, David Preston," came across the line. He swore to himself he could see her saying it.

"Did I catch you at a bad time?"

"No, this is great. I was just going to take a break."

"Did you get your morning uncomplicated?"

"Not uncomplicated but at least less complicated. That's the best I can usually do."

He heard her breath across the phone and smiled broadly in response. "I'd love to hear about it. I can honestly say I've never met an architect before."

"You can't anymore because you have now. In the flesh." He could hear by the change in her inflection that she was smiling back.

"You're right, I suppose. I guess you can't say you'd never met a lobbyist before we met."

"I can honestly say I never *wanted* to meet one before you."

He responded to the playfulness. "Ouch. I see our reputation has preceded me."

"You're good with words, Mr. Preston. Is this the famous 'spin' I've heard so much about?"

"I'm trying not to. We lobbyists are a dime a dozen in this town. I'd guess architects are about one in a million."

"There're a few more than that, but not many. You're unquestionably the dominant species here."

"Regrettably, the lemming species," he said and laughed, now thoroughly relaxing in the back-and-forth.

"Don't be so hard on your kind. You certainly don't come across like what I see on the screen."

"I'm relieved. Otherwise, I'd need to hang up now."

"Don't do that." She drawled out the last word.

"There are so many things I'd like to ask about what you do; I don't know where to start."

"Whatever you think an architect does, I can assure you that you'll find the reality more boring."

"Now, don't you be so hard on your kind," he kidded.

"Touché."

"If we lobbyists are lemmings, what are architects?"

"That's a home-run question, Mr. Preston. I knew I was right to ask that you call and not just type. Let's see," she said and then paused. "We architects are, I would say, ants or beavers. Because we're very organized, but ants and beavers must be engineers. Perhaps, spiders? You really got me on this one," she said while giggling.

Caught up in the wordplay, David threw out, "I think you're a cheetah."

"Well, I don't know where you came up with *that*, but I'd love to hear it."

Fearing he had let himself get carried too far, David sought to cash out while still ahead. "A phone and a few minutes can't do justice to my questions or my answer. Could we meet sometime?"

"That would be nice. How about in a couple of nights? I need some time to research cheetahs." Her laugh sounded light.

"Great. Would supper work? I could meet you at L'Enfant."

"That works. Is six okay? We can just walk to someplace nearby."

"Yes. I look forward to it. One thing, why'd you want a call?"

"So many reasons. The mundane part of my work is written, while what I enjoy doing is sketching, drawing, and designing. I like to keep my worlds separate, I suppose. Also, it's more…more…human. I find too often life being reduced to a series of emojis and memes. I don't want mine to be. I mean, with books, I can hold the writings of the smartest people who ever lived. So, communicating in the here and now should be oral and direct, live human to live human."

"I like that. It's quite an answer."

"You asked."

David's head swirled, like he'd just stepped from a tornado. She spoke as she looked and moved. He found, of all the three, this last had raised his interest the highest—something he would have thought impossible. He couldn't remember a conversation so challenging and enthralling in a long time. If ever. In his few minutes speaking to Julia, he had already had a more stimulating call than any he had ever had with Kristin.

When I meet her in two days, I'd better be ready.

Reveling in the call's aftermath, David went to share it with Sailor. Feeling he'd shared enough of his lows with him, David wanted to treat him to a high. As he came into the circle, an honor flight was coming out. These groups of aging veterans were regular visitors to the Navy Memorial. He stopped to let them pass; most still wore some emblem of their service, and many needed walkers or wheelchairs. As he watched them pass, he noticed one man being wheeled by, his uncovered head tilted sideways in fatigue. Just feet behind lay a cap. David stopped time. The cap read, "World War II Navy Veteran." David walked over and matched it to the man in the wheelchair. Gently, David placed it under the man's hands, returned to his position, restarted time, and watched the man disappear into his bus.

CHAPTER TWENTY-ONE

Time over the next two days seemed to stand still, even though David did not stop it once. He spent it as best and as quickly as he could, diligently working and impatiently waiting. Between the two, he pondered the many blanks he had to fill in. Whatever he did, his thoughts kept circling back to her.

What's she doing now? What would she think about this? Would she be interested in that? How would I describe something from my world, and what would be her comparable experience?

One thing he no longer thought about: whether there was someone else.

With someone like her, there'll always be someone else if she wants there to be. But if there really was, she wouldn't have agreed to meet. She'll let things go as far as her interest holds, which, after all, is what everyone does. Life's constant selection is the best choice available. We all take it. She will too. But I'll do my damnedest to make that choice be me.

David judiciously parceled out his communication. Another call, the next day. A playful text—yes, she did accept them after all. It was thoroughly premeditated and orchestrated. Without conscious planning, his impulse would certainly have scared her off. It was already concerning him that he wanted too badly for this to work, even before he knew what *this* was.

Because their offices were not far apart, and there was no place she particularly liked between them, she suggested they meet at the carousel on the Mall. She also asked if they could move their meeting time up from six to five thirty. David readily agreed: It was closer to now, which is what he had been wanting for the past forty-eight hours.

The late spring afternoon was gorgeous—one of the twenty or so perfect days Washington manages in a year. The supple new leaves wore a light green and moved even more than their older, darker brethren. But the breeze loved them all, caressing each gently as it passed.

Yet, when he caught sight of her, she still surpassed it all. She was sitting on a bench, watching the children ride the carousel's horses. She wore a flattering dress. Accentuating her bearing, it revealed and obscured simultaneously. As the gentle breeze shifted it, he felt himself consciously aware of her beneath it. When she saw him, she rose as he knew she would—grace embodied.

"I'm sorry if I'm late," he said.

"You're not late; I'm early." Glancing at the children on the horse, she said, "I enjoy watching them."

His gaze followed hers. "I don't think they could be having more fun."

"No," Julia said dreamily, "they couldn't."

"Do you think there's anything we could enjoy that much?"

"No, we know too much to get that lost in anything. We know it'll end, then we worry about it ending. They're just abandoned to their enjoyment."

David said, only half-seriously, "Would you like to try it anyway?"

She turned quickly and fixed him with a look, instantly making him regret his question. David scavenged for recovery. About to stop time, instead, he clumsily forced out a few words, "That's probably not a good idea."

"David, it's a wonderful idea," she said with excitement.

Thinking she was trying to extract him from his childish suggestion, he responded, "Now's probably not a great time. We can always come back."

"Now's always the best time. Never forestall joy. We should ride."

Still unbelieving, he said hesitantly, "The way you're looking at me, are you saying that to get me out of this?"

Grabbing his wrists, she leaned into him. "I'm looking at you like this because I'm not going to let you cheat me out of your offer. I was hoping you'd ask. It's why I asked that we meet a half hour early—before it closed."

Still skeptical, he said, "You're not exactly dressed for it."

"I'll ride sidesaddle," she said and exhaled out for emphasis.

They rode. Twice. She rode a horse in front. Looking back at David, she wore the broadest smile he had yet seen from her. The spinning's breeze swept her hair back across her face as her dress flapped beneath her. The Mall's west end was the backdrop; as they came around and around, the sun's approaching setting painted the sky pastel. When Julia hit a certain point in the turn, she turned from person to Impressionism. *I think she might be enjoying the ride more than the children.* She seemed as lost in it as he was lost in her.

She said adults couldn't be captured by a moment the way children could. She was wrong. I am.

David had no other thought in his mind or care in his heart than to watch her enthralled by the carousel.

Afterward, both were exhilarated and laughing, sounding exhausted as though they had just galloped on real horses. Neither thought of food. They decided to follow the Mall toward the sunset. Other than laughter and catching their breath, they did not speak much.

Julia broke the reverie. "I think the first and last hours of daylight are the day's most beautiful. The light's so soft, so golden, the shadows so long. It transforms everything into a different city."

"I enjoy the sunsets as I ride across the river," David heard himself artlessly second. "But I don't have an architect's level of appreciation for them."

"It's not so much how you appreciate them, it's that you do. I come out here for special sunsets and am struck by how often I see people wholly unaware. I'm sure they have places to be, things to do, but I'd hope that they'd pause to just look."

"I confess I fall victim to ignoring." Regretting and thinking, he replied, "If we saw abroad the same sunset we see here, we'd be awestruck. The same sight there'd enhance it; here, the mundane overwhelms it, lowering it to the everyday. Then to unnoticed. Do you sketch or draw when you come out to look, or do you just look? I mean, do architects do that?"

"I do; architects don't. I just do it for myself."

"I'd enjoy seeing one of your drawings someday."

She laughed. "Let me determine how tough a critic you are first."

They walked until the setting sun had shed all its beauty. Then they did the same to the night. Eating was barely an afterthought. But the talking, that David remembered. He ran it over again and again later when he was alone. He had asked everything he had originally prepared to ask. Yet when they finally parted, he had more questions and a greater desire to ask them.

It's like I have always known her—and like she's always known me. Like we're renewing an acquaintance rather than beginning one.

CHAPTER TWENTY-TWO

David had learned the particulars that several hours could reveal. Julia was from Kentucky. She grew up just outside of Lexington, where her parents still lived. She had two sisters: a younger, with whom she was very close, and an older, with whom she had less contact.

When Julia spoke of home, her very soft Southern accent became a little stronger, just as David noticed his did when he spoke of Georgia. Julia's Lexington upbringing had left her with an affection for University of Kentucky basketball. They had determined quickly that this presented absolutely no problem. Since David was from a football state—and the University of Georgia never challenged UK in basketball—and she was from a basketball state—and UK never threatened UGA in football—they could still be friends.

Instead of going to UK, as her family had, Julia had focused on colleges for architecture. Cornell had been her dream; she never considered anywhere else once she had been accepted. She had enjoyed it, but being an architecture major was "like being on a separate campus, if not college entirely." She'd lived in the architecture building, only venturing away for required classes. Her studies had taken her six years—architecture taking five, plus another to study in Europe.

She had come to D.C. straight from Cornell. Washington offered its own architecture and a great opportunity in a small firm. She now lived in Del Ray, after having bounced around D.C. before buying a small house. She lived there with her dog, Brandon, a Jack Russell. Thanks to dog-walkers, she had not worried about their late night. "But I'll get his scolding when I return."

The gracefulness that captivated David had come from years of ballet. Flattered he had noticed, Julia said she'd danced before college and done some local troupes. Now, she just did it for exercise, occasionally helping out at schools in Northern Virginia.

She also enjoyed what she called "real art," not modern art. Because of her dance background, she listened mostly to classical music. She did listen to other types of music, but only when drawn by a song's musicianship. Their musical tastes intersected at the Allman Brothers Band. David had avidly latched onto them given their Macon, Georgia, roots. They were "home," and an early conduit for his love of backward engineering. Hearing them play blues standards, David had avidly tracked these back to the Delta blues.

They also came together on movies. Notably, both viewed them as movies, not films, and certainly not cinema. She liked art turned into movies. Again, they connected on the old ones. She had laughed when he said he only needed three things to hold him: a director, a script, and actors.

Though she was his age, even David's ability to stop time did not allow him to match her range of experiences. With most of them in a world so different from his, David often could not believe their separation.

Finally, from David's perspective, Julia's rarest quality was that she was apolitical. No one he knew was. Politics was so inherent to Washington, the city's only true industry, that he had no more than a passing acquaintance with those undefined by their politics. David explained, "It's like the Capulets and Montagues: You're of one house or the other. Crossings between the two often turn to tragedy or farce." And as she explained back, "When your politicians get as interesting as Shakespeare, then I'll care."

David laughed uncontrollably when she recounted accidentally setting off a scene at Del Ray's dog park by calling out "Let's go, Brandon" to retrieve her dog. Even after David had recovered and painstakingly walked her through the expression, Julia was dumbfounded. "So, I'm the one who's supposed to feel ignorant from our little *tête-à-tête* because I didn't make the connection from a chant at a stock car race to a president to my dog? You've chosen a very peculiar occupation, Mr. Preston."

None of this diminished his interest in the least.

Julia had also learned a lot about David. However, David felt his half of their "big reveal" was the lesser. Coming away, he felt run-of-the-mill at best—just another duck to her swan. He consoled himself, thinking *At least the motorcycle's an ace.*

Because she was not political, he had spent much more time describing what he did than he usually had to. Longer didn't make it sound better. Still, she had seemed absorbed, which was also different. Usually, Washington politicos immediately categorized their counterparts—by party and placement in the system—before introductions ended. Failure to meet the necessary marks usually led to a gaze over your shoulder for someone else. David was very conscious that Julia's eyes rarely left his. He was aware because his rarely left hers.

David had only stopped time once and then not because he'd wanted to. Just the opposite; he had wanted time to keep rolling with her in it. But he had inexplicably misjudged the location of his water glass. Having just begun to launch it, he stopped time to catch it. Julia had complimented him on another great save. "I'm coming to expect these," she had said. *All in all, there are worse things to be remembered for—like drenching your date's lap.*

David was conscious of not stopping time with Julia. Having used it to get and keep Kristin, he desperately desired to appeal to Julia as himself, not his ability's attributes.

They planned to meet again that weekend.

"It'll be a real date," David said.

"Our first night felt pretty *real* to me," she responded.

David didn't disagree.

But the "real date" never got past his planning. Work intruded. Janice offered David her spot on a weekend fundraising trip for someone possibly helpful to David's proposal. *Days ago, I would've leaped at such a chance.* He went, but he didn't leap.

Julia said she understood, but because she wasn't political, David worried. His concern rose further when she canceled their midweek makeup plans so she could finish a project. Of course, they talked, and this was good, but David was aware that "them" was based on few actual hours together. If she could meet him on the Metro, she could meet someone else too.

CHAPTER TWENTY-THREE

They settled on the following Saturday for their "real date."

David picked *Hamlet* at the Shakespeare Theatre Company and then dinner at an Italian restaurant. Both were near his office, where he planned to show Julia around. Then they'd ride back to Alexandria together.

From there? David purposely blocked further thoughts. He just wanted to end the evening well.

It began at Julia's house. It also started with him being very aware of his pickup truck. His heart and money had gone into his motorcycle; he devoted little of either to other transportation. Tonight, it showed, and he saw. When he apologized, Julia reminded him, "I'm from Kentucky; ridden in plenty of 'em."

Her place was a small two-story building that looked to have been built in the 1920s or 1930s. Its front porch roof sat like the bill of a cap pulled low over the house's eyes. Beneath it hung a heavy swing. The front yard was minuscule, the house close to the narrow tree-lined street that was effectively a single lane when cars parked on both sides. A weathered sidewalk ran alongside. Here and there, old trees' large roots buckled it into gently undulating waves. As David paused to ring the bell, he felt transported back in time to Georgia.

Julia answered. As she stood in the doorway, it seemed the house owned her, instead of the other way around. Clearly, she loved it and it, her. She immediately introduced, and admonished, a bouncing Brandon, who clung to her feet like a second pair of shoes. The grand tour took just a couple of minutes until they came to an arresting back room upstairs.

"You take your Halloween seriously," was all David could think to say about a room thoroughly drenched in black and orange.

Julia laughed as loudly as David had heard from her. "I take my Giants seriously!"

His confusion must have been clear because Julia added, "The San Francisco Giants? The baseball team?"

"Oh, of course. I mean, what?" The closer he looked, the more he saw it, but he still didn't get it. "Why?"

She shrugged. "I got attached as a little girl. Daddy took me to a game in Cincinnati, and instead of falling in love with the Reds, as I was supposed to, I fell in love with the team they were playing. The Giants."

"Well, that explains it," David deadpanned. "You're mentally ill."

Julia laughed again, just as before.

"Okay, this room deserves its own tour." She excitedly showed and explained every keepsake, its origin and significance. She concluded with, "And Brandon is named 'Brandon' after the Brandons Crawford and Belt, two Giants players."

"Of course…" David said, drawing it out for full comic effect. "I knew that right off."

Julia smiled broadly and laughed lightly, touching his arm casually as she did. David knew that the laugh was genuine—that she was genuine.

The rest of the night, his planned part, didn't match its impromptu beginning. Only introducing her to Sailor was great. The restaurant was just good; David had never noticed how cramped it was. The tables were so close that it felt like a group meal. And the play: Only by closing his eyes could David tell it was Shakespeare and believed Will himself would have had trouble as well. It was staged to look like the 1940s, with acting more conscious of the staging than the text.

At intermission, he had offered to cut their losses. Julia politely agreed. They left the theater for what David hoped would be the night's recovery.

"Just to wrap that up, he dies at the end."

Julia grinned back. "I wouldn't be so sure in this performance."

David felt his phone ring. His only impulse was to ignore it. Until he saw who it was.

"David, this is Janice. Sorry to bother you on a Saturday night. I won't ask if you're in the middle of something because I know, even if you're not, that going into the office isn't what you want to be doing. But I need you to work on something with an immediate turnaround time."

David tried not to sound as deflated as he was. "Okay."

"I need you to put together some board slides on your proposal; they're to be reviewed tomorrow at noon by the CEO."

Now getting into the conversation, David protested, "But I didn't think this was anywhere near that level yet. The proposal's just that, a proposal; it may never be considered, let alone enacted. It's just an idea we're working on to determine its potential."

"You know that, and I know that," Janice said flatly through a sigh.

"So, how has the corporate process leapfrogged the legislative process?"

"Someone was talking it up to people near Corporate's officers—"

"The tax team wouldn't—"

"The tax team *didn't*."

Now thoroughly engaged in the ramifications, David fought unsuccessfully to keep his voice from rising. "Then who? How? Why?"

"Phil's out there this weekend," Janice said in a way that needed no further explanation.

David pivoted away from Julia, as though his mere turn could keep Julia from hearing. "Oh crap; he doesn't even fully understand the proposal or the process."

"No, but he understands Corporate's desperation. He wants in."

"Alright, there's no point talking. I'll head in shortly."

Janice wrapped it up, saying, "I'm sorry about this. It's just Phil being Phil. I'll send you the contact for the CEO's office. They'll format what you send, and I'll review it. Hopefully, this'll only screw up tonight."

Feeling everything crashing, David dejectedly turned to Julia. "You probably heard. I'm so sorry. Sorry about everything."

Julia's face showed she somehow understood—or wanted to. Not just about now, but the whole night. How much it had meant to him.

"It's alright. I understand. I have a job too, and sometimes it stinks as well."

"Thanks. I really mean it." His shoulders fell, and his hands followed in surrender. "I wanted tonight to be so perfect, but the only thing perfect about it has been you. Can I see you again? Can we make it up tomorrow?"

Julia winced. "I'm doing something tomorrow with my old roommates. I can't."

Feeling everything slipping away, he pushed it. "During the week?"

She moved her hands up, as if about to reach. But she didn't. "Let's talk tomorrow night."

I want to say I love her. But he knew what he really wanted was to rush ahead to them being in love. Instead, he was staring at everything ending before anything had barely started.

"I will. Even if I have to quit," he responded.

Julia laughed. "Let's get you into work now, not fired."

David tried to drive her home, but she refused, saying it would only lengthen a long and miserable night for him. Of course, he knew he could have stopped and restarted time to eliminate that, but he also knew he couldn't tell Julia that. So, he conceded his night's final defeat.

Having seen her off in exactly the opposite way than he had wanted the night to end, David sullenly resigned himself to going upstairs to work on something that he knew was at best premature and at worst an end before the proposal had gotten a real beginning.

Between Phil's assassination of David's Saturday night and Julia's ex-roommates' monopolization of her Sunday, the weekend passed with them apart.

The week was no better, and David became aware of forcing his attempts in desperation. The earliest they could meet was next Friday, for which their plans were simple: not see a play.

After months of purposely excluding people for work, now I can't include someone when I want to. Work is jealous. I've known Julia for more than two weeks and have barely seen her twice.

CHAPTER TWENTY-FOUR

David fully appreciated Julia's assertion that talking was far better than texting and emailing, but it was still a poor substitute for seeing. He was therefore doubly surprised when he got her text just after four on Wednesday afternoon. "Can you see me waving?"

"What?" he said and then texted.

A quick reply came back. "Can you see me waving at you?"

"Of course, I can. I'm gazing into my crystal ball right now," he typed back.

"Look out your window!"

He spun his chair slightly. "Oh my gosh!" sprang from David as he sprang from his chair. "What're you doing here?" Only after hearing himself say it did he remember to type it back.

"Waving at you, Silly."

"Can you stay?"

"Only if you come down. The cabs keep stopping each time I wave."

"Why're all the cabs stopping outside?" David heard from behind. Jerking his eyes from his phone, he saw Frank leaning in, both hands braced on his doorframe. Before David could respond, his friend moved in as though bewitched.

"I wouldn't be looking at my phone if I could be looking at her," Frank mumbled.

"I am, I mean I'm doing both. I mean, I also have to respond, though."

Snapping from his thousand-mile stare and into full attention, Frank said, "You mean you KNOW her?"

"Yes. That's Julia."

"Give me your damn phone," Frank said, grabbing at it. "You mean to say you're sitting here while she's standing there?"

"I was just finishing some things."

Indignant, Frank said, "Nothing good happens in an office after four o'clock. Get the hell outside. Now! Or *I'm* going to go down there."

David needed no further prompting and typed back, "Coming. Don't leave!"

So overjoyed, he didn't care how long the moment lasted and was just grateful it had come—and that she had brought it. He punched the elevator button; when it didn't arrive instantaneously, he took the stairs. His footsteps reverberated like a bass drum in the empty stairwell. Then he pulled up short, his breathing and his heart now the only sounds. In a panic, he stopped time. His last unexpected encounter with a woman filled him and his consciousness. *What if she's here to say she doesn't want to see me again?* Julia wasn't Kristin, and he hoped then wasn't now, but he couldn't shake the feeling of dread.

David's steps dragged the rest of the way and him out onto the sidewalk. He was next to her, staring for any clue before he remembered he had not restarted time. He retraced his steps to the building's front door. Re-exiting, he tried to suppress his apprehension and assume a casual pace.

As he approached her, Julia's eyes redirected David's back up to the windows. "Which one's yours?"

The glare made it impossible to see in, even as he found it impossible to focus. Still, David knew by now both Frank and Jeff were looking out.

He pointed to his best guess. "That one, I think. They're pretty much the same."

Julia laughed. "Never say that to an architect. They're not the same. Windows are the eyes of a building. And besides, one of them is yours, even if you don't know which one."

"Thanks for the architectural lesson, but even more for making my day.

What're you doing here?"

"I was dropping off some drawings for a client not far away; recognizing your neighborhood, I decided to walk back. Anyway, I thought we could both use some cheering up."

David's tension relaxed so completely that he uncontrollably exhaled it out. "You're so right. I guess my frustration's been pretty obvious."

"Let's walk. Then talk," she said, pulling him down the street. Before David could say anything, she asked, "Do you like your job?"

David looked straight ahead as though the answer lay somewhere beyond rather than within. "Do I have to answer that?"

"You just did." The sound of her voice told him she was looking at him.

Turning toward her, he said, "I didn't really mean to. At least not like that. I'm immersed in what I'm working on, but it's irritating that I haven't been able to see you."

"Don't worry about that. Or anything really. You worry too much, at least about me not understanding. I do. But I appreciate you saying you want to get together but can't. That's enough."

He was determined not to release this chance moment after having recently lost so many. "If you're walking back, let me walk with you."

"That'd be wonderful."

As they walked, David felt this was them at their best. But, realistically, he knew that wasn't true. As much as he wanted this to be "them," it wasn't yet. *This is me at my best. Even when I'm not.* Other things were good with her, but by simply being together and talking with Julia, he reached a height he had never known in his other relationships. And he found a peace in himself that he had never known to exist outside of stopping time.

By the time they had reached the Mall, they had decided to turn east away from Julia's office. They walked slowly and talked long. David felt the world stop and somehow spin faster at the same time.

Watching the shadows lengthen ahead of them, Julia mused softly, almost talking to herself as much as to him, "I'm forever amazed that civilizations, separated in time and place and without contact, have a conception of God."

"The concept of nothing is equally amazing," he replied unconsciously.

She stopped abruptly. "What do you mean?"

"Nothing doesn't exist," he said earnestly to what seemed to him self-evident.

"Of course it does," she said, her voice rising slightly as though chasing her disbelief.

Stooping, David picked up one of the Mall's countless pebbles and took her hand. "Nothing only exists relative to something else." He put the pebble into her hand, then took it out. "What's in your hand now?"

"Nothing." Her eyes widened to punctuate her point.

"While there seems to be nothing now, it's only apparently so." Touching the top of her hand, "There's still residue from the pebble here, along with oils and moisture already there." Touching beneath it, "The same applies here." Circling it with his, "And air is all around it." Pressing gently down, "Gravity is pushing down too; your hand would fall if you didn't hold it there." Holding it, "Without your hand to define the space where nothing's supposed to be, we couldn't be having this discussion at all." His look shifted from her hand to her eyes. "Nothing doesn't exist. Man had to conjure up the concept of nothing to make it seem like nothing existed."

Whether Julia thought his idea deep, David didn't know. What he did know was that when he was done, he did not let go of Julia's hand as they walked.

CHAPTER TWENTY-FIVE

Their connection continued for hours. Just as on their first long walk into the sunset, the intervening interruptions seemed to have never been. Their talk became increasingly personal, unguarded. Things David would never have expressed—had never expressed—he now heard himself discussing with hardly more than a stranger. He did so because he felt Julia doing so too.

As their thoughts and conversation grew closer together, so did they in their strolling. By the time they reached their walk's eastern endpoint, they were arm in arm, and by the time they reached where they would part, her head was on his shoulder. Their walk had become a long, slow dance to the music of their conversation.

Walking past the Capitol, Julia had explained the architecture that still put David in awe. He described the interior's process and procedure. Each in turn was teacher; each in turn, pupil. David learned more than he knew there was to know about columns—and more than he ever imagined he would want to. Yet, listening to Julia talk animatedly about them made them fascinating to him for the first time. He heard himself doing the same, taking energy from his audience of one, he heard himself describe in vivid detail what he often took for granted but truly loved.

Their tour had reached its farthest extent at the Jefferson Building of the

Library of Congress. This was Julia's favorite Washington building. She soared, so clearly in love with it that David was envious. As the lights came up on the hedonistic Neptune's fountain at the base of what Julia called "a Beaux-Arts masterpiece," her eyes caught and reflected them back with greater intensity. They circled a building he had passed countless times with barely a notice. He felt his first description of her as a cheetah apt as he watched her stalk it in the twilight.

When they finally finished near her office—where hours earlier they had originally planned to be—David knew he had to kiss her.

The whole evening has called for it; now this moment is screaming its insistence. If I've somehow missed every signal and this isn't something she wants too, better to know it now.

After so many words, now he said nothing. David gently turned her face up to his. What he had planned as just a short, tentative show of affection, a search for affirmation, turned immediately into a prolonged passion. To him, kissing her was better than having sex with most women. And kissing her was unmistakably a sexual experience so strong that when their lips separated, their bodies clung together for support. Finally, they spoke but in such low tones with deep breaths that neither sounded themselves.

"I better go," was all Julia managed.

"Yes, yes, you should. Because if you don't, I won't let you go at all."

One more kiss, a shorter version of prior ecstasy. Then David was left alone to count the hours.

He realized that tonight was the first time he had made no clumsy mistake. Nothing. Only enjoyment, not embarrassment. After his initial fear, he had never needed to stop time—or thought about it. He had simply let it roll on. Now he needed it to rush even faster so he could see her again.

It didn't, and time crept by like Christmas. Whitney's crisis continued, and the demands for—and on—his proposal grew within Corporate. His only respite came when his thoughts ran to Julia. Frank and Jeff insistently pressed him for details—who she was, how they had met, why he hadn't said anything.

David told just enough to get by. Until last night, he had not known the most important one: where he stood. Even with a far better idea, he still had doubts. His biggest was that this was too good; not too good to be true, but too good to be happening to him. In contrast to Kristin, where he had worked so hard, with Julia, things were best when he did the least, when they did nothing.

For tonight, David's only real planning centered on his greeting. Last night's parting left no doubt that they were changed.

How do I approach her now? I can't presume to start where we ended. But I also can't pretend it didn't happen.

The one thing he did know was that he did not want to start awkwardly. When her door swung open, David realized he had already failed. Speechless, he had thought it impossible she could look more beautiful than his memory's picture. Yet, here she did. Framed perfectly in the doorway, every limb exuded the grace he found to be her most mesmerizing feature. Her dress, the simple cotton print that had first captured him, did so all over again.

The setting sunlight exquisitely illuminated Julia, turning her hair from blonde to gold. The spring breeze delicately shifted it and the dress. His silence lengthened; he had to stop time to avoid embarrassing them both.

Brandon hung in midair and mid-yip, just above Julia's knee. Now David could unabashedly stare. And did. He always wanted to remember this. After how long, he did not know, David composed himself and restarted time. Brandon landed, only to immediately vault up again.

"Sorry to stare, one of your pictures really caught me."

Julia looked over her shoulder. "Which one?"

"I'm sorry. That's not true. I wasn't looking at a picture. You're the picture, and I was searching for words to say how beautiful you are."

David moved his eyes from hers, because he saw them change with her blush.

"I didn't mean to embarrass—"

Without a word, Julia reached up and gently kissed him. It became a kiss David sensed could become far more. On this threshold and in her doorway, he sensed them both consciously retreating from beginning at the end.

Another perfect evening with no particular plan, they wandered Del Ray's streets, stopping here for supper, there for dessert. When they ran out of reasons to go into places, they simply strolled. Only Brandon's walk brought them back. It was close to eleven o'clock when they returned with a finally subdued Brandon.

When they did, David felt far different than when he had arrived. Brandon seemed to sense it too. Never docile (David suspected he ran while he slept), he treated David as a "regular" and, to some extent at least, accepted. Julia declared, "It's progress."

When he had arrived, David had just looked; now he observed. Instead of just seeing, he focused on things as windows into her. The house was punctuated with her drawings—everything from finished architectural sketches to actual paintings. What hadn't gotten to the walls had made it to shelves, with sketch pads neatly stacked and catalogued by years. Unable to draw beyond stick figures, he was especially impressed by what she lightly brushed off. Julia compared them to his notes on a work pad.

"I don't frame my notes," David replied.

At her laugh, David slid his arm around hers.

Now the night ended as its beginning had intimated. At one point, she seemed to hesitate, then resumed. David asked, "Are you sure? Really sure?" He knew he was; he wanted her to be. Without reservation, she was, they were.

Both were now clearly "us."

David woke the next morning disoriented, searching for where he was. For months, the furthest he had been from his own bed was falling asleep on his couch in front of the TV. The sun entered from an unusual angle, he was on the wrong side of the bed, and his hand rested on fur.

"Good morning, Sleeping Beauty."

Retrieving his mind from sleep and recognizing first where he wasn't, then where he was, he mumbled, "You can cancel the call to the paramedics."

His head still down, he blinked the sleep out of his eyes and looked up. Julia stood over him, hands on hips, head cocked to the left, a sardonic smile on her face. "Oh, we may still need the paramedics. Who's Philpot?"

David sealed his eyelids tightly and cringed. The last furry thing he had known, that cat had spent eight of its nine lives making his miserable. Now it was reaching a paw out from the relationship grave to pull him back.

His mouth muffled by the pillow, he mumbled, "A cat."

Hearing her voice grow louder, he cut his eyes up to see her kneeling with her face close to his. "Well, that clears that up. Do you have any more details? Is it yours? A childhood pet? A stray you met that introduced itself to you, perchance? If it had a name, it must have had a person to give it one."

"No, someone else's, a person's. Someone I used to know"—he said as he tried to soften it—"a long time ago."

"Well, you're just a babbling brook overflowing with information. It's not like *I* want to know, but Brandon does—after all, you called him Philpot," Julia said, punching the last syllable for emphasis.

"Just my mistake," David said, fearing he had blown the day—and everything else—before even being awake to know he had.

"Come on!" she said, pulling him up. "You owe Brandon a walk. And an explanation."

David, still groggy, was hungry now that he had time to realize it. But he was more than grateful for her humor and a chance to escape his near-death experience.

The walk was short and his answers painful. David could feel Julia's concern when she tried to talk him out of more. But fearing she might think Philpot was in the present and not the past, David welcomed the chance. He wanted her to know she had eclipsed everyone else, that there were no other stars in his sky.

They stayed together all morning. They had not made plans beyond Friday, picked only because it had been their first opportunity to get together.

David broached the unknown first. "So…do you have any plans tonight? I mean, I understand if you do."

Revealing her first hint of shyness, she said, "I'd told some friends I'd come over to their party. It's just something small; I don't suppose you'd have any interest…?"

His heart soared. "I'd love to."

For a moment, David thought Julia was tearing up, but a second later she was bright and buoyant. "I'll tell them I'm bringing 'Him.'"

Suddenly, they were a flurry of excited activity. She stayed to make preparations for an "extra person." He left for the gym, a shower, and to change.

David was not a party person; for him, they needed to have a purpose or a commitment. This one held both. He would get to know Julia better and differently, plus he would get to show her that he wanted to.

Usually, he didn't like large groups. To him, it didn't mean that he didn't like to talk or meet new people. He was just selective. When he met someone he did enjoy, he wanted a longer, real conversation, but that was no more the way to converse at a party than eating the entire hors d'oeuvres tray was the way to dine there.

Regardless of his usual disposition, this was different. He bounced from one person to the next like a pinball on a Bally table. He did not mind the multiple interrogations—he expected them—and used them to learn about Julia indirectly.

He only knew her one-on-one through what she had revealed. What he learned from her friends was that Julia was even more of an enigma. All her friends, even those who had lived with her, had things they could not believe about her. Of course, all said she was creative, even brilliant, and they were as overawed as he had been by her vast experiences and prodigious work ability. They rarely saw her dance; usually, it was just in a production somewhere. And she could seemingly function for extended periods on little food or sleep.

They said she could be emotional, something David had seen occasional hints of. One incident that stuck with him was her loss of a stray dog that she had not had long.

"His name was Willie—"

"Mays or McCovey?"

"How did you know?"

"Just an educated guess; sorry to interrupt."

"Well, she took it super hard. I mean, we all love our pets, but this seemed to resonate within her."

What he saw directly was her clear enjoyment around her friends. So relaxed and happy, her joy reverberated to David.

He was somewhat shocked at how dissimilar her friends were to her. Not that he had expected a room full of ballerina architects, but he had expected some hint of similarity. Instead, there were swaths of connections from across all segments of life—some from dog parks, others from dancing and gyms, a few from work, others just friends of friends—as disparate, David thought, as his were clustered around his life's limited points. They were nice, very nice. But, to his eyes, she so clearly stood apart—a rose among daisies. Had he been there without her, he would have had a good time, had a few pleasant conversations. But with her there, she rose like a full moon in the night sky—obscuring all but the most brilliant stars.

After they left and were out of earshot, she reached up and kissed him on the cheek. "You passed." Their earlier awkwardness returned when he pulled up to her house.

Am I expected to stay? I certainly want to, but I don't want to look like I expect to. Is she thinking the same thing?

Standing on her porch after what Julia called Brandon's "nightly constitutional," David reached for her hands and volunteered, "I understand if you want some space tonight."

His feet shifted as he counted his breaths.

She squeezed his hands. "I want you, if you want to stay. But I get it if you can't or don't want to."

Exhaling more on the inside than the outside, he replied, "You know what I'd really like? I'd like you to describe some of your sketches."

Far from a feint, David's interest had been raised by her friends' awe of them. Her creativity matched her beauty in his eyes. So different from anything he had known, it hung like an aura about her. Her drawings were works of art—buildings so precisely lined they looked as though incised on an etching plate. And Julia also had sketches that were truly art—landscapes and still lifes. The most striking was a figure sketch in charcoal. It was a nude study of a young woman sitting with one knee drawn up high, the other leg extended straight out, and the torso turned back to her left. Unable to leave it, David looked at the slight crease in the tip of the young woman's nose, then at Julia. His eyes and the tilt of his head asked the question.

"I did it years ago. It's a self-portrait," she said casually.

It was the last picture they looked at that evening.

David had determined—as much as he had been able to think or will in the drowsiness of satiated bliss—to rouse himself when he awoke and avoid his first morning's embarrassing, and uncharacteristic, lack of control.

He now watched Julia. Time felt stopped, but he let it move; he was hypnotized by her soft breathing, her slight shifts of position.

Her eyelids' subtle flutter announced her waking. David gave her time. She looked languidly at him, stretching and reaching for him simultaneously.

"How long have you been watching me?"

"Not long enough."

She smiled sleepily but mischievously. The mood that had carried them into sleep had carried over into the morning. As their hands intertwined, a clear prelude to their bodies doing the same, barks came from behind the door. David wasn't the only one who had been awaiting Julia's awakening.

"Can't you ignore him?"

Julia shot him an incredulous look. "This isn't Philpot." Julia huffed with exasperation as she rose.

"How'd you get my shirt?" David asked.

Wearing nothing else, Julia turned. "Stay right there and in that mood, I'll just be a second."

As good as her word, Julia returned so fast that David was surprised she hadn't run into herself coming back.

"How did you get back so quickly? Did you just throw a bone out the back door?"

Putting her hands on the front of David's shoulders, Julia said in a sultry vamp, "Remember the bone. Forget the dog."

David started to laugh out loud at this character's farcical contrast with her every other aspect, but she ended further distractions with a kiss.

David thought he must have fallen back to sleep. One moment, Julia was spent beside him, the next he heard the shower. As he slowly tried to keep pace, he questioned whether he also lagged in giving her insights equal to what she had given him.

Just three days had taken her far beyond a persona and into who she was. Simply being in her house revealed so much. He ruefully considered what his place would tell. Still, against all his nature, David was aware of inexplicably wanting to show some of what he always worked to keep obscured.

At his dilemma's core was that Julia simply had more to reveal. Their difference in experience seemed vast. He couldn't point to an age difference, but David felt Julia had used her time so much more fully—despite David having complete control over his.

He was not envious. Their worlds were thoroughly different, to the point he was amazed she found enough overlap for interest. Nor was he jealous. He was simply humbled by reality: a gulf existed that he could not close, only accept and navigate as best he could.

CHAPTER TWENTY-SIX

Their weekend's intimacy added a playfulness only familiarity brings. As David was about to throw out the cores and pits of his breakfast fruit, Julia stopped him.

"Don't put that in the garbage, put it in here." She pointed to what looked like a tiny stainless-steel garbage can on the counter.

Dutifully opening it, David reeled back from the smell.

"What's that?" he gasped.

"It's where I collect things for my composter."

"It's well on its way," David said, wagging his head for effect.

"It turns waste to nutrients for the soil," she explained in a clipped tone.

"So, it's a dirt-maker?"

Julia silently looked at David with mock wonder that he had somehow missed the obvious.

"Wouldn't it do the same thing at the dump?" he inquired.

"Not for my garden."

"But..." He craned his neck to look into her backyard and said, "you don't have a garden."

She drew out her answer to his willful obtuseness. "When I do, I'll have compost for it." Summarily putting dishes into the sink, she squinted at him.

"Look, as soon as we're done with breakfast, we're going over to your place to critique it."

"I don't think that would be advisable. I wasn't planning on company."

"With your manners, I think not planning on company is very sensible. But we're going, nonetheless. I have come to doubt you even have a Harold Davidson."

"Harley," he corrected, suppressing a smile.

"Harley, Harold, what's the difference? Anyway, we're going," she said, tossing her head in finality.

So, they went. Her one remark, after David gave the quick tour (which was one more than it deserved): "Where does the rest of the frat live?"

"You spent the whole ride thinking that up, didn't you?"

A slow, theatrical wave encompassed the whole condo. "Dahling, no, this was pure inspiration." Snapping back into her regular speech, she said, "Now, let's see that motorcycle."

David had chosen his condo partly because he could afford it, partly because he could walk to the Metro easily with a time-stop, but mostly because it had a covered garage. The bike was his most important single possession. Even when he was not riding it, his Harley was like a parachute to a flyer. Just knowing it was there—even without riding it—was enough. When he had decided to buy, he had gone down into *real* Virginia to find the right store. He had chosen the blue color and added all his specifications. After getting the call that it had finally arrived, he had gone into "the nursery" with the same anticipation he imagined awaited the entrance to a real one.

David saw all this as he removed the cover; he wondered what Julia saw. He waited, looking at her with barely suppressed apprehension.

"David…it's beautiful. Does it have a name?"

"You're the first person to ever ask that. Yes. 'Blue.'"

"That's original." She grinned.

"I used up all my originality picking everything else."

"Do you love it?"

"Probably only slightly less than you do Brandon."

"Are you going to get on?"

"I'd feel strange. I don't ride in street clothes."

"Would you? For me? I want to see you on it."

Her look was so earnest, he could only accede. "Sure."

Even though David was improperly dressed, he slid onto Blue like his hand into an old glove. Almost 80,000 miles together had made them as close to being one as two can get.

"It's you," she pronounced. After a long pause, her eyebrows arched, and her eyes widened. "Well, are you going to ask me to ride?"

"I never ask anyone to ride. I don't want to feel like I pressured someone into something I know is dangerous. Anyway, you're not dressed for it."

"I understand the danger, but I'd still like to go. Will you take me? Now? What do I need?"

"You're serious?"

"Yes, I'm serious," she said, inclining her head in emphasis.

"Have you ever ridden? You know there's some participation required. You're not just a sack of taters back there."

With a mock huff, she drew her hands to her hips as she replied, "Well, David Preston, I'm extremely flattered that you don't see me as a sack of potatoes. No, I've never ridden."

David smiled. "Let's take you upstairs and get you dressed."

Back in an extra helmet and gloves and David's jean jacket, Julia listened to her passenger lesson.

"You have to look over my shoulder to the side we're turning. Control your head; the helmet makes it heavy. It'll move and bump mine if you're not careful."

David pulled down the passenger foot pegs. "Your feet go here."

David looked at her intently. "You sure you want to do this?"

"YES!"

"Okay then, one last thing. If you feel yourself falling off, remember…let go of me." David smiled; Julia laughed.

David eased them out onto a side street. He wasn't normally nervous on a motorcycle. Usually, Blue was where he felt most comfortable. Not now. A passenger, even one as light as Julia, was a large marginal increase in weight on a very light vehicle. The bike handled very differently, stopping slower, turning wider—and that was even with an experienced passenger. Julia wasn't, and this was David's real nervousness. He had never been so concerned about someone's safety on a motorcycle—not even his own. He did a few simple maneuvers—just to get the new feel and to give her a sense for riding.

David asked if she enjoyed it. She nodded. When he asked her if she wanted to keep going, she playfully punched him.

"You worry about what's ahead, not what's behind!" she yelled over the engine.

With Julia all smiles, he headed for the Parkway. He took Blue up to fifty miles per hour. It wasn't fast by any real measure, but for Julia, who had only experienced the road from inside a car's cocoon, he knew it would feel a lot faster. At this speed, neither could hear the other, but David could feel her tighten around him, her arms around his midsection and her legs around his hips.

Heading south on the Parkway to Mount Vernon was a perfect ride for them. It was a straight, divided four-lane road, with the Potomac on their left. At Mount Vernon, he followed the road west to Washington's mill. There, he pulled in to see how she was doing.

Raising her helmet's vizor with both hands, she asked, "Why're you stopping?"

He joked, "I wanted to check the cargo."

"The cargo is fine, but the motorcycle-go is better. Let's do some more!"

As they were about to leave, a woodchuck waddled out of the brush.

"What's that?" Julia exclaimed.

"A woodchuck. You see them all over out here."

"Are you going to say it, or should I?"

"Say what?"

"How much wood would a woodchuck chuck, if a woodchuck would chuck wood?" Julia said, smiling with self-satisfaction.

On cue, David replied, "A woodchuck would chuck wood all day, if a woodchuck would chuck wood. But woodchucks don't, so a woodchuck won't chuck the wood that others would. So, if you'd have your wood chucked, you'd better chuck your woodchuck, if you'd have your wood chucked, like the wood that others would."

Julia stared in stupefied silence, her jaw not hanging open only because the helmet's chin strap held it tight.

David shrugged his shoulders. "You spend a lot of time alone with your thoughts when you ride a motorcycle."

David retraced the route. Now far more comfortable, Julia pointed to things. Spontaneously, David pulled into the lone restaurant between Mount Vernon and Alexandria. The restaurant had a patio that ran its full length and the best view of the river stretching out as far as you could see in either direction.

Close to three o'clock, the brunch crowd that packed the place on weekends was gone. So wrapped up in being together and then riding the motorcycle, David and Julia had let time get away. Here, they let it come back. The place's green lawn rolled down to the Parkway; across it, more grass extended to the river. The water shimmered as the current carried it slowly south. David imagined the view unchanged from that of two hundred years ago.

"That was fantastic! I've never experienced the road like that—the sounds, the wind, even the smells! And I could see so much! How fast were we going?"

"Just around fifty."

"It felt so much faster! How fast could it go?"

"You're not going to find out," he said and chuckled.

"How fast have you gone?"

"You're not going to find that out either."

After eating, they crossed the Parkway on foot to walk on the trail. With arms around each other, they walked slowly, their heads inclined together. Only waning sunlight made them stop. The weekend was ebbing too quickly away; there was a dog that needed walking and a workweek to prepare for.

It was just as well that they couldn't talk as they rode home. There was really nothing left to say but goodbye, and David loathed saying it. He didn't go to his place but took Julia to hers. A neighbor's surprised recognition of Julia on a motorcycle was a bright spot in the twilight.

As they stepped on her porch, David snickered and said, "That'll cause some gossip."

"I could use some. I'm just the boring young woman who lives with her dog."

"You could be many things—anything—but boring will never be one."

"Why didn't we go to your place to drop off all my biker gear? How're you going to get it home?"

Smiling, he laced his arm around her waist and pulled her close. "I was hoping you might have me over again sometime."

David had raised the unspoken topic that had to end the evening. Was it now presumed that their available time was going to be each other's?

"Oh, David…" Again, David thought Julia was about to cry, then instantly she brightened.

"When do you want to come back?"

"As often as you'll have me and work will allow me."

"Done," she said, lightly kissing him.

Both then started to speak. Awkwardly, each deferred. David sensed he and Julia knew what the other thought: a hesitancy about overextending and encroaching.

In place of his hesitancy—and his usual caution—David put honesty. "I don't know if I have ever had a better weekend. Ever. I don't know what else to say, but I know I have to say that."

Immediately, Julia moved into his arms and gave David the most meaningful kiss he had ever received. Their lips barely apart, she whispered so softly that only their closeness allowed him to hear, "I don't want you to say anything else…I don't need you to say anything else."

She moved her head down and, once more, David thought Julia was about to cry. Until this weekend, he had not known how close to the surface her emotions lay. Again, he was surprised at her quick recovery. He wanted to tell her that she didn't have to suppress them, that this was not going to scare him off. Instead, he let her regroup.

He also knew that the emotional had laid open the way to the physical. Any initiative, by either of them, would pull them into the house and then into bed. Even a few months ago, and perhaps with any other woman, David would not have demurred. Now he did. This woman was different; he was striving to be so too. A physical connection could not have elevated the emotional one they had just had. He wanted this weekend, which had meant everything to him, to end as perfectly as it had unfolded. They parted on the porch but without really separating. He sensed she knew, too, that the separation was only distance, its time only temporary.

As David went home, he mused on the proposal. Until recently—until Julia—nothing could force it aside. Now, he had to prod himself back to it. His concern for it was still there, but it was no longer alone.

CHAPTER TWENTY-SEVEN

The happiest weekend of David's life was followed by another frenetic week of work. The only way David could balance his worlds was to stop time for work and reserve his real time for Julia. David effectively lived two lives simultaneously: one as frenzied and demanding as any he had ever had on the Hill, the other as happy and relaxed as any he had ever known.

After meeting Julia's friends, David was conscious of needing to introduce her to his. Not because he was eager for his friends to know her and for Julia to know them, but primarily because he wanted Julia to know he *had* friends—even if far fewer and more casual, more acquaintances than friends, some of whom he only knew by first name. His were mostly from the gym and their gatherings, which were far more informal than the one Julia had taken him to. Usually, plans were made on the fly. The willing and able going to a restaurant. A core group existed, supplemented by others each time—not unlike a Rolling Stones tour.

Bringing Julia, therefore, meant taking her to the gym. An empty aerobics studio was the first place he saw her dance as she went through her routines. Attracted to her grace initially, he had only seen it in routine activities. He was unprepared for its full extent. He had never witnessed someone he knew move so. Spellbound, he tried repeatedly to capture mental images, but each was superseded by another more beautiful.

On little day trips, they took different combinations of Blue, Brandon, her sketch pad, and his books. David's favorite destinations were small places he had found riding the backroads of Virginia and Maryland. Not major attractions, they were just "his." Now he loved making them "theirs." They would drive his truck with Blue in the back. At the day's destination, he would take her for a ride on quiet roads, a world apart from Washington and the proposal. Afterward, she would pick a view perfect for spreading a blanket; she would sketch, and he would read until he fell asleep. Invariably, she would have completed an entire composition by the time they left.

His biggest coup was getting tickets for the Giants' entire weekend series against the Nats. Having splurged for Kristin, he was determined to do better for Julia. She was in heaven. She had planned to go, but not in these seats.

He had arranged for each game's seats to be progressively better. He had not fully appreciated her love for the team. He doubted she missed a pitch and was amazed anyone could so quickly negotiate a bathroom line between innings. She didn't miss a moment of her "*El Gigantes*."

As they approached the turnstile for their last game and best seats, Julia looked at David. "I appreciate this so much, but you didn't have to spend so much on tickets; I would have been just as happy being in the bleachers with you."

David laughed. "I wish you had told me sooner." Then turning deliberately serious, he said, "Do you mean that, really mean that?"

"Of course, it's the company…and the Giants, of course…that matter."

Pointing to a father and daughter in Giants caps just ahead of them in line, he said, "Then let's surprise them."

Once through the turnstile, David, with uncharacteristic impulsiveness, switched seats with the thunderstruck father and daughter. "We Giants fans have to stick together," he explained. "Here's my cell if anyone says anything." At the seventh-inning stretch, he got a text with a selfie from the beaming pair in David's seats. He showed it to Julia; she leaned in and squeezed him. "It reminds me of my first game. Now, I don't mind as much that they're losing."

Other than in small episodes, David realized that he rarely stopped time around Julia. He had when he'd surprised her by putting the Giants tickets under her plate at a restaurant. He occasionally did so at night to prolong his favorite part of their day: the quiet when work was over and the phone off. But other than such diminishing episodes, he enjoyed time moving too much with her.

Despite their changes, their walks on the Mall remained. When Julia asked David to take one at four on a mid-June Friday, it seemed like just another. Their plans on Fridays were usually loose. Meeting at her carousel bench, he instantly sensed her distraction. Julia declared it was the east's turn for their walk. Despite knowing they had walked east last time, David said nothing, waiting to see if she would realize. Instead, hers was only idle conversation—the kind strangers would have had.

Without warning, the summer sky turned ominous. Heavy raindrops fell sporadically, each seemingly triple normal size—a warning of menace. Scrambling for shelter, they ducked into the Hirshhorn Museum as the deluge started.

David asked Julia if she wanted to walk around the museum.

"Yes. From the outside," she grumbled.

"Well, you do, and I do, but the weather doesn't."

Julia said, "Oh, alright. This place is always good for a blood-pressure rush."

Although modern art was lost on him, he thought it would be interesting to see it through Julia's eyes. Perhaps her perspective would expand his appreciation.

As they moved through the building, Julia became increasingly agitated. David finally ventured, "I wonder if it's quit raining."

Julia sullenly responded, "I don't care if it hasn't."

They went out, and David, knowing he needed to lance the wound lest it explode, cautiously offered, "I never cared for modern art."

That was all it took.

"It's not modern art. Modern art is an oxymoron. There's no art here. Instead, it's a collection of individual self-indulgences masquerading as meaning. When you shift all the effort onto your audience—to decipher, to extract, to really infuse some semblance of meaning into something—what've you done? Nothing! Less than nothing, because in the final verdict, you've created a lie.

It's not what you say it is."

Gathering momentum from her own steam, she used her hands to emphasize her point. "You've lied! Perhaps unintentionally, because you're deluded, and others have facilitated your delusion. You really believe that this garbage, that this 'crap,' because that's what it really is—unquestionably something best done in private and then disposed of—is suitable for exhibition, and you leave it up to your viewers to figure out why. It all screams, 'It's art if I say it's art!' Then what should we see in there? Virtually those exact words: 'It's art if I say so.' No, it's not! It's patronizing, it's condescending, it's self-indulgence. It's a participation trophy for wanting to be an artist!"

His eyes following her, David smirked. "So, you didn't like it?"

She reached for David's throat in mock strangulation. Reinforcing each word with a pretended shake, she intoned, "I. Hated. It. Whatever. It. Was!"

Lolling out his tongue and pretending to gasp for air, David responded, "I guess the artists succeeded since they provoked such a reaction."

Julia lowered the fist of one hand onto the anvil of the other. "No, they didn't. There's more to it than reaction. Emotion without content is animal, not humanity. There's supposed to be meaning. And there can't be meaning if, from twenty feet away, you don't know what it is. When you see *David* in Florence, you know it's David. The Florentines weren't asking too much of Michelangelo to do that."

Rapt in her rant, he said, "Okay, I agree, Your Honor; knowing your judgment, how'd you reach your verdict?"

"You ask the best questions; that's why I love you. I believe art should be judged by three criteria: what the artist said, how the artist said it, whether it was worth saying. Clarity, dexterity, and necessity. This place's contents fail on all three."

Although David had heard everything Julia had said, one thing stuck out. Having witnessed her intensity, he now stopped time to look at her intently.

Did she even know? She was so passionately engrossed in soliloquy it might've been unconscious. Even if aware, she might not have meant it literally. The last time I reached this juncture, it didn't go well.

David always tried to follow a rule: Don't "love" anything that can't love you back. The Atlanta Braves taught him that. Relegate the things that can't to "like," and don't set yourself up for the heartbreak of a one-sided relationship. Most people don't follow this rule. Still, this was Julia. She was hardly "most people."

He knew his answer. *I love her.* The question now was whether she had admitted it too, and whether he should.

David restarted time and led them back west. Both were silent, the only sounds the crunch of wet gravel underfoot and the city's motions melding into white noise. For time restarted, it still felt stopped to David.

Nerves prevented him from looking at her as he spoke. "Did you mean it when you said you loved me?"

Only after he spoke could he look over. His heart sank at the sight of Julia looking down, her hands running through her hair as she shook her head.

"David, I was just running on, I got caught up in my thoughts. I get so excited and tend to make a fool of myself..."

"Then let me make one of myself. I love you."

This time, Julia wept. Trying to pull herself back, she dissolved again.

For all her near misses, it was the first time David had seen her cry.

Oh no, not again. David bent down so he could enter her line of sight as she gazed at the gravel. "I didn't mean to upset you. You haven't seemed yourself today. What's wrong?"

Julia gasped, trying unsuccessfully to catch herself. Between sobs and gasps, she said, "You didn't upset me. I...meant it, I just thought I'd messed everything up. I got lost in my diatribe, and it slipped out. I've wanted to talk to you about something for two days but couldn't figure out how; then trying to avoid scaring you away, I lost myself and said exactly what I didn't want to say, and now you aren't scared, and now I'm so happy, and I don't know what to do, and I'm not making any sense."

Thank you, God. He felt relief's chill raise goosebumps over his skin. "Perhaps if you just stopped doing so much at once? Why don't you just come into my arms, cry for a little bit, and then we can talk for a long while."

She did. When they finally resumed their walk, Julie said, "A college friend's getting married in downstate Virginia. I need to go, I want to go, but only if you go."

"Is that all? Of course, I'll go!" David exclaimed.

However, his happiness did not relieve her seriousness as he had hoped.

"College wasn't always the happiest of places, and my memories weren't always the best. I've struggled with reliving, deciding, and asking."

"We all have our ghosts. We can exorcise yours together," he assured her.

Julia did not respond but stared into the distance. David pursued it no further; instead, they focused on their terrible secret—that they loved each other.

CHAPTER TWENTY-EIGHT

Preparing for the wedding and their first trip away was a welcome distraction for six hellish weeks of work for David. As Congress moved toward its inviolate August recess, the pace accelerated to get as much done as possible before all activity ceased for five weeks. To make the external pressure worse, there was the internal one: Phil and Whitney were feeding off each other—ego and exigency in an unbearable and unreasoning urgency. To this, Phil added the idea that David's proposal should be introduced as a bill. As with most naive ideas, this struck Corporate as a great one. The problem, of course, is that getting something introduced as a bill becomes its own project while not getting the proposal any closer to the goal: enactment.

As David had pointed out in vain to all but those who understood the process: "This isn't *Schoolhouse Rock*; the goal is law, not introduction. The more controversial or esoteric the proposal, the less exposure the better. Like a sniper: better unknown until impact. Introduction as a bill not only advertises the intended shot but wastes political capital on a pointless 'ask.'"

Everyone in the Washington office, except Phil, accepted this. Frank had called the idea, "Just a piss short of perfect"; Jeff's was more vulgar still. David described it more sinisterly to Julia. "I worry Phil's just playing dumb. It's his idea, so he gets to preen in front of Corporate. If it undercuts the proposal, that's on me."

David was now squeezed between two projects. The only way he could manage the work to his standards and keep seeing Julia was to stop time more. His days in "David time" became increasingly longer. At first, time-stops merely allowed him to get everything done. Then they became stress releases. Finally, he began using them for simple physical recovery. But still, work's twin pressures pressed tighter.

The days got longer; the nights became fundraisers. The final blow was that this got him booked into a fundraiser on the weekend heading into Independence Day, dashing plans he and Julia had been considering for the long weekend. His frustration over the circumstances had provoked their first fight. It had not lasted past David's abrupt exit onto Julia's front porch, where he acknowledged his fault and then apologized. But again, it required a time-stop to get right.

David could tell Julia was trying to understand what she saw him enduring. During a visit to David's condo, she asked about the government memorabilia—redline bills, signed pictures, campaign trinkets—that were largely its only decorations. These were the remnants of what those on the outside normally spent their time trying to avoid seeing. He explained the process as best he could. But to her question about the difference between different types of lobbyists, David fell back to Jeff's coarse description: "Corporate lobbyists are mistresses, association lobbyists work in a brothel, and consultants walk the streets. They all do the same thing; they just do it for different prices with different people." David had never seen Julia—or Jeff, when he told him the next day—laugh harder. Julia had said, "I'm grateful that at least you're a 'kept man'; the other options are too sordid to contemplate."

To escape thinking about work, David quizzed Julia about the wedding. He immediately got off on the wrong foot, observing that weddings were much bigger for women than for men. Julia took issue with his stereotype; David parried, "I don't see any magazines entitled *Groom* when I check out at Safeway."

Silence. Followed by a grudging "Touché."

"Seriously, why are women asked to so many more weddings than men?"

She replied while pouting, “With your penetrating wedding insights, I’m surprised you’ve been asked to any at all.”

“But shouldn’t it balance out? Who do women bring, or do y’all just go alone, or what?”

“Not surprisingly, they haven’t been asking you, Mr. Romantic. How early in relationships do you usually offer your nuptial observations?”

They agreed that David would ride Blue down, and Julia would drive. This way, they would have both car and bike. The destination was an extremely ritzy place in way-out-of-the-way southern Virginia, where even David, who thought he had hit every “blue line” road in the state, had never been.

The wedding was David’s first real break all year. To no one’s complaint, he uncharacteristically took off Thursday, Friday, and Monday to make a five-day weekend. Leaving on Thursday would give him a day to beat summer traffic from Washington, but because Julia could only leave the next day, it also gave him two days of riding on his own.

CHAPTER TWENTY-NINE

No matter how wonderful it was to climb off his motorcycle and have Julia with him, there was no substitute for riding unencumbered by a passenger—even Julia. Alone, he could stop whenever he wanted, take whatever road beckoned. He also could really open up the bike, not just for speed, but to be able to lean far into a road's exhilarating turns. And he could just get lost, something he often did. The ride, not the destination, was the point.

Julia, not comprehending at all, had offered to find him a hotel somewhere near the resort. She had been less than pleased with his response: "I don't know where I'll stop the first night." That he had once wound up in an emergency room on such an unplanned trip was even less comforting to her. As he explained, he was younger then; he knew his motorcycle, and himself, better now.

It took 400 miles of riding to cover what could have been a 200-mile trip. Julia thought him "addled" when he described ten hours of travel that ended in a trailer at a crossroads where a creek ran through what passed for a town. Still, it had all he needed: a place to eat that wasn't a chain and someplace quiet to walk his legs back to life.

Finally finding it on a map, Julia observed incredulously, "You're still 100 miles from our destination. How could this possibly happen?"

"Good planning," he said through his laughter.

Her exclamation was even louder when he said he would start the next day riding away from their resort. Just as today was finishing its daylight, he had seen a road he had to follow. And it was heading west, his preferred morning direction because it kept the sun from blinding him. He promised he would turn back east around noon. He pacified her with tales of things seen—covered bridges, odd roadside markers, forgotten little towns, family-owned restaurants, small farms—and felt, and smelled, and heard, and tasted. His enthusiasm became infectious. She didn't claim to fully understand, but she accepted and ended with the caution to be careful and that she loved him.

Early the next morning, he stopped time to continue sleeping without wasting daylight. He didn't know how long, but he knew how needed.

As he expected, this day's ride surpassed yesterday's. He wasted no time escaping development's sprawl to get into the country. He was already there.

His highlight was a hollow. Heavily overgrown sides slanted steeply away from the road, and tree limbs closed into a canopy overhead. Though close to noon, it was as dark as dusk. Stopping to check his map to avoid getting too far from his bearings, he cut the engine, removed his helmet, and let his surroundings immerse him. Instantly, he heard a thrum rising and falling in waves. It filled his ears, then lowered but never entirely stopped. Within the trees were countless cicadas, their separate calls joining together into a single giant insect's call. No other traffic or sound diminished its primal nature. Long after he had viewed his map, he stayed, leaned on a boulder, and took in the overwhelming effect—all because of the happenstance to stop at this nameless place at this timeless moment.

Except for this, David was hardly off the bike. Once yesterday's soreness had dissipated, he rode far better than the day before. Yesterday, he wrestled with Blue; today, Blue pivoted beneath him at his slightest touch. Everything was tight, crisp, the bike jumping when he opened the throttle. Only determination to beat Julia to the resort pulled him from the road.

Getting there was not easy. The place was no less remote than the ride's best parts, but unlike those, which serendipity had delivered, he had to find the resort.

When David pulled up to the main gate, he immediately felt himself an intruder in another world. He had done fundraisers at places like this, but then Whitney was paying, and he was not wearing denim and arriving on a Harley. The security guard's reception underscored that most guests did not arrive in such a state. Pulling out his ID, removing his helmet, and explaining he was there for a wedding took longer than either wanted.

Just riding through what looked like a state park took a good ten minutes. The front desk was both easier, and harder, than the main gate. Easier was that the bike remained outside; harder was that his clothes lost their context without the bike.

Waiting at reception, he felt a hundred eyes on him, despite only a handful of people being there. One was the bride's mother. Overhearing David explaining his registration and connection to the wedding, she introduced herself. Then she called over Trish, the bride. In short order, David became as visible as he had sought invisibility. Both followed him to his motorcycle. He fielded the usual questions, but the bulk centered on Julia riding it. From Trish's questions, Julia clearly had not exuded a desire to ride motorcycles at Cornell. He left wondering how many questions he had cued up for her.

Instead of a room, Julia had booked them a cabin along the road David had taken in. Each had its own animal name; their next three nights were going to be spent at The Bear. On top of a rise, it was far more than a conventional cabin. More impressive still was its view east over a large valley. Having stowed his meager baggage, he settled on a lounge chair to gaze into the reason he so loved being away from Washington. Buzzards and hawks slowly circled along invisible currents of air. Effortlessly, they rode thermals. As free as the motorcycle felt, it could not touch what they did on motionless wings. He was still just riding a bike, not soaring, despite what his imagination conjured. He watched until his eyelids could hold no longer.

David had not heard Julia drive up or even her footsteps on the wooden deck. He did not wake until he felt her hand gently shaking his shoulder. Opening his eyes, her face filled his sight; so disoriented, he did not know where he was or even if he was awake at all.

With a doubtful expression, she asked, "Honey, you okay?"

"Yeah," David said sheepishly, grasping for his bearings. "I must've dozed off."

"You were really out. You sure you're okay?"

Back in reality, David smiled and nodded. Julia's brow relaxed; she leaned in to kiss him, only to be jarred back by David's yell, "Bear!"

Julia spun around. "Oh hell, it's got the cooler!"

Lunging to go, David grabbed her waist from behind, spinning her into the chair he had just sprung from. Completing his pivot, David came back around and ran toward the theft.

Julia's bags were still in the gravel driveway, but her cooler was well on its way off. A bear had come from the surrounding woods and was now attempting to tear it away and apart at the same time.

David diverted away from the bear toward his motorcycle. Knowing he would never separate the bear from its quarry—and would be treated even less gently than the cooler if he tried—his hope lay in scaring the bear away. He quickly straddled the bike, started it, and then gunned the throttle. He got the bear's attention away from the cooler, but not the bear itself. There was one option; lowering the throttle, he popped the clutch and spun the rear wheel toward the bear. A shower of gravel arced airborne, like a hundred slingshots firing at once. Bellowing, the bear flipped backward and peeled into the woods. David fought the bike into upright control and shot down the driveway before quickly slowing. He neatly turned it tightly to the left and back around. Pulling up at the deck, he yelled between laughs, "What exactly did you put in that cooler?"

Julia was still frozen in the chair, staring in shock at what had transpired in just seconds. She pulled the hair back from her face. Breathing deeply, she slowly got up and walked over.

Finally, she said in a low voice, "I don't know whether to slap you or kiss you."

He grinned. "Do I get a say in the decision?"

"No."

Julia opted for the kiss. With lips just inches apart, she said, "Let's get these up before my friend comes back. Then let's go inside, and you show me how much you missed me."

Recovering in the bedroom they had barely reached, David said, "I think I know how your cooler felt."

Twisting her mouth, she replied, "Well, we'll have a great story for dinner tonight."

"That's pretty risqué of you to plan to bring this up!"

Having found enough clothes for modesty, she began smoothing the sheets on her side of the bed while ignoring his joke. "I meant the cooler rescue, not our rendezvous."

"Do you mind if I do? That way we'd each have a story to tell."

"I want you to make a good impression when you meet my college friends. Anyway, there'll be children present."

"I've already met your friends, or at least Trish. She liked the motorcycle."

Julia shot upright. "Shut up!"

"Met her at the front desk this afternoon. And her mom," he avidly pronounced with smug satisfaction.

Julia closed her eyes in concentration. "Anything else I should plan on being quizzed on?"

"Your tattoo."

She crossed her arms tightly across her chest. "Shut up! I don't even...You did *not* say that!"

David looked away as though seeing it in his mind, though really avoiding eye contact so as not to laugh. "I said it was very tasteful, but in a private place I didn't feel comfortable mentioning to people I'd just met."

Julia pounced like a great cat. Her hair hung down, just grazing his face. Looking straight into his eyes, she murmured, "I just hope for your sake you're joking."

When Julia emerged from the bedroom a half hour later, David was speechless. She had always excelled at understated elegance. Now she was fully stating it. A sleeveless mesh dress clung to Julia as if spun onto her rather than slipped on. With each move of her bare arms and sandaled feet, the delicately printed flowers on its blue material rippled as though a breeze danced over a field.

She twirled an effortless pirouette; the hem just above her ankles lifted in response, the material momentarily revealing the shapeliness it had accentuated.

“Stop staring, you’re making me blush,” she said, diverting her eyes.

Jarred from unintended rudeness, David said with measured softness, “I didn’t think it possible for you to be more beautiful.”

“It’s just nylon,” she deflected.

“It’s gossamer on you,” he replied.

They drove to yet another venue in the sprawling resort. The dinner itself was formal and stiff, but the party afterward offered a chance to talk casually with Julia’s friends.

What Julia remembered most, and would not let David forget, came from talking with Trish and other women from Julia’s sorority. Trish, of course, brought up her earlier meeting with David and seeing Blue. As they playfully kidded Julia about the motorcycle being out of character, Trish insinuated something more.

Julia shot David an accusatory glance. She then tried to defuse David’s tattoo story from the cabin. David immediately started sidling away as the uproar and laughter told Julia that she had been played. Grabbing his arm, she jerked him back into the maelstrom he had created. It took no little convincing to extinguish it. Even the true story about the bear did not suffice.

What David enjoyed most was getting to talk to Julia’s friends privately. The picture that emerged was of a much quieter and more introspective girl than the woman David knew. One in particular, Kelli, had told him that parts of Julia’s Cornell years had been “somber.” David then understood the kidding about the tattoo was as much relief as joking. For them, a tattoo would have been no more a surprise than her now lightheartedly joking with them. It left David with a much better view of them, but a more complex one of Julia.

Julia’s diatribe about David’s tattoo trap dominated the ride back. He enjoyed it all the more in light of what he had just learned. Despite the late hour, they went into the hot tub. The night was silent; the sky perfectly clear and moonless; the stars hung stark and still, becoming ever more brilliant and deepening the sky's blackness.

Afterward, as he succumbed to sleep, he thought about how much a day can hold. There had been no time or inclination for real conversation when they returned. Now, as Julia slept beside him, he contemplated the allusions to Julia's past. Looking at her now, so peaceful, the words "never forestall joy" kept coming back to him. *How could she ever not have had joy?*

The morning was half gone before David awoke. Julia was gone. She had left a note on her pillow: "Gone to get a tattoo. Back by ten." Having been physically idle for a couple of days, he needed to move but had already overslept an early run. Rather than continuing his sluggishness, he chose to stop time and run now. *There's a risk. If Julia's somehow aware of exactly when I left, she could also figure out that things couldn't add up.* David went ahead anyway, believing he could concoct an excuse if caught.

Even with no hint of where she had gone, it couldn't have been far; her car was here. David looked for her as he ran along a trail across from the cabin. As he finished his run, he restarted time.

David didn't find her until he turned the cabin's corner. Startled, he reflexively stopped time to make sure events added up. She was on the deck with a book and pen in hand. Certain she was sketching, David came around to look. Instead, she was frozen in the act of writing. Before he could turn his eyes away, he caught a fragmentary sight: "happier than at Cornell." He immediately looked away. Great as his curiosity was, he held Julia's privacy sacrosanct. He backed away as cautiously as though in time rather than out of it.

Going back around the corner, he restarted time to come upon her as she still wrote. Instead of putting the book hastily away, as he had expected, she looked up and said brightly, "You're far more energetic than when I left!"

"I thought I should go for a run; I've been missing them. What tattoo did you get?"

"Just as you described: a tasteful butterfly."

"And where?"

Snapping the book shut for emphasis, she replied, "Again, just as you said, in a place that modesty precludes me from mentioning."

"I'm surprised you feel comfortable sitting down then," he said through a smirk.

"I'll let you find it. Come over here and say good morning properly."

Kissing her briefly to spare her his sweat, he asked what she was drawing.

"I'm not. I'm writing in my journal."

"Why writing and not sketching?"

"Some things can't be drawn, like feelings, and I want to remember them. Thinking without writing is nothing. Thoughts are only as much as you make from them."

"I didn't even know you kept a journal."

"There's a lot you don't know about me. We've only been together a few months, after all."

"Anything big?"

"Yes."

"Are you going to tell me sometime?"

Cocking her head to the right, she parried, "Do *you* have any things you haven't told me?"

From the inflection in her voice, David felt suddenly cornered—as if Julia somehow knew. He also saw his own hypocrisy about revealing sizable secrets.

"Yes," he said, the jocularity dropping from his voice.

She set her journal down. "Well, I'll tell you mine when you tell me yours."

His bluff called, he blinked. *There's no way I can tell my big secret.* He had thought about how he would eventually, but before he could, he had to be sure he wouldn't lose her when he did.

"I, I'm building up to it," he said, trying to regain his earlier casualness.

"When you're ready to talk, I'm ready to talk. In the meantime, I'm ready to eat. Let's have that breakfast you so gallantly saved from the bear."

CHAPTER THIRTY

The ceremony took place in a gorgeous setting, but the scenery could not make up for its emptiness. And length. The "minister" was a friend of Trish's, and she did have a tattoo. The couple read their own vows; several times, David shifted uncomfortably. Fortunately, Julia did as well.

A reception, as formal as the ceremony had been loose, followed. This one, Julia had informed him, was family-friendly. Julia dubbed it a "survival-of-the-fittest schedule"—a supper later and then a party—a winnowing away of the youngest and oldest.

With three hours until supper, they returned to the cabin. Because they were not his friends, David was circumspect about the ceremony and reception. Julia was not.

Sliding into a chair, she rocked her head back. With her eyes closed, she sounded like she was seeing the past. "The bridesmaids were all the sorority's officers, each reliving their former roles in taffeta. While people's circumstances may change, their characters don't. Our sorority was Kappa Kappa Gamma, otherwise known as 'Kappa Kappa Glamour.'"

David watched her intently. "I can see why they were drawn to you, but what was the attraction for you?"

"I was a girl from small-town Kentucky. It turned my head, as it did most others at Cornell. I went from being a quiet, nerdy architecture student with a handful of friends to instantly having the social life I never had in high school. Trish was just the opposite. She's still the sorority president—planning the most elaborate party and putting herself at its center."

Feeling emboldened, David ventured, "I missed the service having some religious core; it felt lacking."

Julia's head rocked down and her eyes popped open. "Would you ever want to go to church with me?"

Caught off guard, David said, "I didn't know you were interested in going."

"I've been going—Wednesday nights, Alexandria's First Baptist Church. I just haven't been telling you."

"That's barely a mile from my condo! Why didn't you say something?"

"I didn't know how you'd react," she said with a slight smile.

David grinned back, more in response to what his parents' reaction would be than to Julia.

He thought Julia's funniest insight was about the children at the wedding: "They all have two last names; each one sounds like a little corporation—Madison Sanders, Johnson Thompson. Whatever happened to first names?"

The predicted winnowing occurred as the dinner and the party took them deep into the night. "Trish truly outdid herself—doves released, a wedding cake large enough to have been their first home. All Trish's party planning had been leading up to this. What Godzilla did to Tokyo, Trish did to this wedding," Julia kidded.

David tried to pace himself, drinking just enough to achieve the delusion that he could dance with Julia. He was wrong, of course. *She moves as though not touching the ground, her whole body flowing effortlessly. My movement barely extends beyond my feet; I must look like a statue on stilts!*

She saved him by saying she liked the slow songs better; David knew she was lying and was therefore even more grateful. Here, his cotillion training at least made him competent, and having Julia as his partner made him look almost accomplished.

His evening's favorite moments were watching Julia with her old friends.

Regardless of her earlier jokes, she was genuinely enjoying herself. As he watched her, Kelli approached him. She was showing the effect of drinking more than David, so he tried to distract her with light conversation. Kelli was insistent, as only inebriation makes someone. Oblivious to its obvious cues, she swayed and slurred slightly, neither activity enough to impede her message that they had once been very concerned about Julia.

Seeking balance and earnestness, with her hand on his arm, Kelli clearly strained to make her point. "Has she never told you about her time at Cornell?"

Uncomfortable, David sought his pleasantest smile. "Only that she had studied architecture. That it was beautiful when it was sunny, which it usually wasn't. Just general things."

Kelli's voice lowered. "She didn't tell you about Professor Oglethorpe?"

"No, I've not heard that name."

Kelli's head nodded, and her hand rose and fell on David's arm, as though she were tapping items off a list. "He was her favorite, and she was his. We used to kid her about having a spring-winter relationship. But we stopped..."

David watched Kelli as she paused to fight alcohol's effects and keep herself on track. "He, he...left, David...Julia was devastated. She was never the same. Never seemed truly happy again. She had to fight so hard to stay focused and get her architecture degree. Those degrees aren't easy. She was different from the rest of us. Always so focused, she really had to be then. So somber, so determined. She finished, but I don't think she really cared. This is the first time I've seen her like who she was before...before Oglethorpe. I'm really happy for her."

Feeling awkward as he tried to separate fact from alcohol, he said, "Well, thanks for telling me so much about her..."

She patted his arm and said, "I know I've been drinking too much, now talking too much. Just wanted you to know."

Julia appeared from nowhere; he thought to rescue him, as friends led Kelli away.

After Kelli left, Julia insisted on cross-examining him about his conversation. Knowing he was not at his best and sensing Julia was the same, David defensively stopped time. Looking at Julia motionless, her body language showed her as intent on the conversation as Kelli had been. Gingerly easing into a chair, David fought to regain himself and sort through something clearly bigger than he understood.

Finally steady, he resumed his mark and restarted their conversation. He had no great strategy, just the hope that after his break, he was now quicker in his wits than Julia was in hers.

He did his best to laugh off Kelli as being too drunk for a serious conversation. David thought he had succeeded when Julia suddenly lashed out, "I'm not stupid, David!"

It was one of the few times he had seen her angry, especially at him. Immediately thrown, he tried to calm her. So taken aback and off balance, he nearly stopped time again when Julia paused, visibly trying to gather herself.

Seeing the opening, he smiled hesitantly, put his hands on her shoulders, and said in a voice several levels lower than her outburst, "Let's go back. It's one o'clock. Been a long day, and I'm exhausted."

He held his breath; he couldn't read her. He could feel her heart beating and see her breathing deeply for control.

Shaking her head, she murmured, "You're right. I'm sorry. It'd be great if I could lie down."

"There's nothing to apologize for. We're just tired," he soothed.

He said it and hoped that saying would make it so—that this was all it was. It was as if Julia had avoided an accident. He realized how much he loved her, how he would have done anything to spare her anything—from a scene now, to her pain then. As they hurriedly gave their thanks, David kept his arm around her, determined not to let go.

As they drove back, conversation was more about the unspoken than the spoken. Mostly it was David's monologue: a painful attempt to fill the silence. When they arrived, he was prepared to stop time to get her door and help her out. He didn't need to. Julia was gazing out the window, a million miles away. Her body hung limp, clearly spent and dispirited. David braced her as they walked to the cabin door. Not taking his hand off her, he unlocked the door; then, on impulse, he swung her into his arms and carried her to the bedroom.

He gently knelt to put her on the bed.

"What can I get you?"

Her eyelids shut. "Just keep holding me," she whispered.

David did. He could think of nothing else.

He did not go to sleep until deep into the night, long after Julia was asleep in his arms. He had stopped time to put her into a comfortable position and pull the covers over her. Even then, he remained on watch, truly worried. Not until the sky began to lighten did he feel secure she was alright. Then he stopped time and let himself sleep.

Once awake, he let time resume and himself doze some more to bring Julia, the morning, and himself together. He wanted her to wake on her own and set the tone for what was supposed to be a busy conclusion to the wedding-fest.

To David's relief, Julia was more herself. He had been unsure how much she would even remember. She self-consciously remembered it all. He tried to preempt another apology, but she flashed the faintest hint of last night's adamance.

"David, I'm beyond sorry about last night. I understand if you want to cut today short—or the whole trip—and just go home. Honestly, I'm not sure I don't want that as well. It was probably a mistake to come. I, I…just wanted to. With you. You deserve an explanation, and I promise, I promise I'll give you one. Just not right now, okay? Now tell me what you want to do, and that's what we'll do."

"I want to be with you. I want to listen when you're ready, but mostly I just want to see you happy again. And go on a run."

His last bit provided the first lightness in a long time, allowing both to escape.

They moved deliberately through the last of their obligations as wedding guests. There was a brunch at ten thirty, a time equally inconvenient to all. The group who had left last night's activities at a respectable hour were too hungry; those who had not were too hungover. David and Julia joked they were in both camps.

The final activity had been left up to the guests' choice among the resort's many options. David nixed horseback riding. "Straddling a ride's no novelty for me." Julia rejected skeet shooting. "I've never done it and missing them all doesn't sound like fun."

They settled on ATV off-roading. Neither had done it before, and neither had any idea how muddy it could be. Julia was grateful their final goodbyes had happened at brunch.

By the time they had cleaned up and returned for supper, the other wedding guests and most of the resort's weekend guests were gone. The restaurant looked west onto an empty golf course over which deer were cautiously emerging as the sun set. It was their visit's most peaceful moment.

Lost in enjoyment, David commented as much to himself as to Julia, "To me, a vacation means not having a schedule. It doesn't matter what else it has, as long as it doesn't have that."

David hoped that today had blotted out Julia's last night. He was intrigued, yes, but he was more concerned than curious. He was not going to bring it up again, all too happy to have Julia "back."

Julia apparently felt differently. As soon as the staff moved off the veranda, and they sat alone, she went straight back to last night. David felt she had gotten through today for this.

Her hands on the table as though steeling herself, she exhaled into speech. "David, I've been thinking about it all day and waiting for the best time. Now we're almost out of day, and I don't think there'll ever be a good time…I just want to tell you, so here it is. Professor Oglethorpe was my favorite professor in the architecture department. He was everyone's, I guess. He made architecture come alive. He took me under his wing, always had time for me, always helped me with suggestions on my designs and models. He was more than a mentor, more like an uncle.

"Well, in my third year, he died. I was devastated. No, that's not right. I was virtually incapacitated. My friends, the girls in Kappa, even my family, all thought I was going to have a breakdown. I lost interest in everything and finally withdrew from school for the rest of the spring semester. I didn't come back until the following spring. I lost a year of my life when he lost his. But I also lost what my life had centered on.

"When I did return, it wasn't the same. I wasn't the same. I could function, but that was it. From then on, I basically just pulled myself across the finish line. It was really…hard. It's really hard now, just talking and thinking about it. I wanted to come back this weekend, I wanted to come back with you, to meet these people and write a new ending to the story we all remembered, that I had lived, but that you didn't know. I'm sorry."

She had gone through her soliloquy with barely a pause or break and only fleeting eye contact, as though it came from memory and heart simultaneously.

Wanting to ensure she was done, his pause made up for the ones she had skipped. Having heard, he found himself still listening. Searching for the right words, he could only reach for her hand. "That's a lot. I'm the one who's sorry… sorry for you."

She stared at his hand on hers, then lifted her eyes to his. "David, I feel like I failed. That I didn't rewrite the story's ending at all. I just wrote you into its unhappiness. I was hoping it would go away, but here it is again. And worse, I feel like I used you."

One hand wouldn't do; he rose to put the other on her shoulder. She leaned into his touch. The warmth of her head on his hand brought out his feelings so that he no longer worried about his words. "First, you shouldn't be sorry for hurting over a loss; you should only feel bad if you couldn't feel pain in such a circumstance—even years later. Second, you didn't use me. You asked someone you care about to attend something you care about. Everything you've told me only raises that significance."

Before she could respond, he posed a short, simple question. "Tell me about your year away from Cornell."

For the rest of the night, David prompted her with questions, but only to listen. Maybe if she talked it out, like lancing a wound, the pain would drain away.

He learned a great deal about someone he thought he already knew. She had gone home from Cornell and taken a series of jobs, mostly to keep busy. After several months of doing nothing but work, she took her savings and went to Europe. There she gradually reemerged and began drawing again. Selling many of her sketches kept her going longer than she had expected—just over half a year. When she came home, she had a substantial catalog of work. The architecture faculty had been very impressed, but returning to school triggered the same feelings. The only way she had survived was through detachment, what she called "interludes," when she simply retreated into herself.

Each answer prompted another question. Yet as much as David got Julia to talk, he always sensed something more. Closing the restaurant, they walked the trails leading from it until dark closed so intensely they could only see up—the stars and the thinnest sliver of a new moon.

Lying in bed beside her, he quit trying to sort through it all. Tomorrow's ride home would bring its unique solitude for thought.

CHAPTER THIRTY-ONE

David woke first. With Julia still asleep, he realized he was finally ahead in normal time. Stepping out for a last run on the trails, he saw it had rained overnight. The cooler temperature that brought the rain had also produced a fog that hung across the view from the cabin, giving everything a magically haunting quality as he ran the deserted trails.

Relieved from yesterday's stresses and rested by several days away from work, he felt light, as if springing off the ground. When he reached his stopping point, his closing "kick" was so strong that he kept going on another trail that led him down across a small stream and then back up the other side. He sprinted along this new way, determined to run as fast as he could for as long as he could. He lasted another five minutes. Exhausted and exhilarated, he leaned on a tree to catch his breath. Once his breathing slowed, the sounds of birds and the now-distant stream came back. Determined not to run back, he knew the walk back would take time.

To make up for its loss, he reluctantly stopped time for his return. As always, sound immediately ceased. The fog that had continued to settle now was truly suspended. He walked back, marveling at the remoteness he had reached so quickly. Suddenly, he thought he heard a crack, like a stick snapping. He knew, of course, that this was impossible. Still, by instinct, he stopped dead, straining to hear what he knew he could not. There still were no bird songs, nor the sound of the stream, though he was closer to it. He approached the crest he had earlier crossed. The fog hovered just off the ground, filling the little valley below. As he looked down to start his descent, David thought he peripherally caught a fleeting glimpse of movement descending into the thick mist across from him.

Having thought he had heard the impossible earlier, David incredulously believed he had now seen it too.

I'm hallucinating! What's wrong with me?

Again, he paused to listen. Again, only a time-stop's normal stillness.

The ground was wet from rain, in addition to the valley's dampness under its thick tree cover. Moss grew along both sides of the trail; he carefully steered clear, knowing it would easily give way. He had to be far slower, more cautious, going down than when sprinting up. He heard his own breathing distinctly and was aware of his heartbeat. Reaching the bottom, he looked only down to ensure he didn't lose the trail in the fog and, with it, the footbridge crossing the stream. As he crossed, he remembered the path had sharply angled as it approached from the other side. He proceeded slowly, preparing for the abrupt turn to the left that he knew lay somewhere ahead.

Turning, he almost walked headlong into Julia.

David jumped back at the sight of her still figure posed in the trail before him. "Oh hell, you scared me!" he shouted in instinctive shock, though he knew she couldn't hear or see him. He slowly reached up to her with relieved laughter.

Julia reached back and touched his hand! Now, truly panicking, David leaped back reflexively. It was beyond seeing a ghost.

"What the hell! What the fuck's going on?" he said as he toppled over and then pushed himself away, his feet ripping up trail and moss.

"Such language," Julia said.

"Okay, okay, this, this is a, a…" David searched for coherence amid the inexplicable.

"Dream?" Julia said. "No, it's not a dream. But it is my interlude, and I'd like to know what you're doing in it."

"Wait! What? I stopped time and you…you…I mean, I thought I stopped it…But the stream isn't running! Nothing else is moving! How are you?"

David was completely unmoored. Everything he had known with certainty about his unique ability was being violated as he struggled vainly to make sense of what didn't.

"Calm down," Julia said softly but firmly. "This is real. This is us talking, really talking in real time, not in a dream. I'm asking myself the same question you're asking, and I'm just as surprised—I'm just handling it better. I can only think of one answer: Somehow, we stopped time simultaneously. We're each in the other's interlude. My guess is that if either of us restarts time, then that person will immediately be stopped in the other person's interlude. That's the only thing I can imagine. Does that make sense to you?"

"Nothing makes sense to me right now!" David said.

"Okay, just take your time. I'm not going away; you're not going to wake up. Just take your time to come to grips with this."

David closed his eyes and breathed deeply, as Julia directed. He took a drink from the bottle she offered. Then several. He closed his eyes and opened them repeatedly, met each time with Julia saying playfully, "Still here."

Finally, David was back and said, "Okay, you're real."

"Thanks," Julia said and laughed. "Why don't you get up and kiss me just to be sure?"

David awkwardly rose and, no less so, hesitantly kissed her.

"Not your best effort," Julia said, and she pulled him back to her. "Real enough for you now?" Julia asked with their lips barely parted.

David exhaled. "Yeah. That's pretty real."

Julia's eyes glinted. "Since it's just the two of us…let's make it really real."

Although discombobulated, even in his current confusion, this was clear. "Here? Now? You've got to be joking!"

Julia reached for her T-shirt. "Do I look like I'm joking?"

David tried to deflect. "I wouldn't want you to get dirty on this wet ground."

"I don't intend to," Julia said as she gently, but deliberately, lowered him.

As they recovered from intimacy in ultimate privacy, David finally broke the silence. "You're taking this awfully well."

Julia laughed loudly and said, "You also seem to have recovered nicely from your initial shock."

Leaning on his arm, David looked at her. "Seriously, how have you been so calm through all this?"

"I knew you could freeze time," Julia said.

"What? How could you? No one knows!"

"I suspected the first time I saw you spectacularly grab your phone. Then, as we were around each other, I froze time to create situations where you'd be tempted to freeze it to get out of them. Before long, there'd been so many I knew there was no way you could've successfully avoided them all."

David thought back on his many awkward moments in their early meetings. "So, I wasn't just being clumsy?"

"Nope. You were being tested. Did you ever suspect me?"

"I knew you could stop a clock; I didn't know you could stop time."

She giggled and touched his hair. "That's sweet."

"Were you ever going to tell me?"

"Yes."

"When?"

"As soon as you told me. I figured until you thought it was so important that you had to, I shouldn't."

They lay there talking until hunger forced them to return. Even then, they did not restart the day. Julia said, "As in the *Rubaiyat of Omar Khayyam*, we have struck 'from the calendar unborn tomorrow and dead yesterday.' We hold all there is to hold, all that can be held: now."

This was their chance to experience each other without the escape hatch of extrication. They essentially were meeting all over again—their full selves—for the first time. They talked about their whole histories with their ability: how long they had known, how they had first discovered it, the ways they had used it.

They walked in the middle of the small road as they talked. For David, it was cathartic. Once open, he could not turn it off.

"It's the first time I've ever talked to anyone about it—the first time I've even tried to as an adult. When I discovered that no one else could do it, I mean when I thought no one else could, I just shut that part of me away. But there were times I felt like it owned me—times when I still do. I'm compulsive, a perfectionist—always have been, always will be."

"I know," she said, sighing.

"But many people are. That's not unusual. Unusual is what I thought unique until just now: the ability to bring perfection continually within reach. By stopping time, I can almost infinitely reorder circumstances to fit what I think they should be: perfect. Being internally driven to control and externally able to control...It can be like..."

"Hell?"

David stopped and stared at her revelation. "Yes. Hell. I can feel so alone, then I'll turn to it to actually be alone. I've felt less so ever since...you."

"I wish you could let go, David. I can see what it's doing to you at work."

"I wish I could too, but how do you let go when you can hold on?"

"I hope you don't feel that need around me. I don't want you to have to be perfect. I just want you to be you. That's enough."

David put both hands on her shoulders. "That's what's so strange about being with you. I was actively avoiding relationships before. I didn't want one getting in the way. But we connected on a different plane. It felt like I've always known you. Now I know why."

Julia slid her hands up and over his wrists. "It fits introverts like us, but then it drives us even more into ourselves. That's why finding you was so special; once again, it could bring me out."

As they walked slowly back, he realized that they had reversed roles from the night before. Now, Julia was the interviewer, he the subject. Neither wanted to let the moment go, so they let it go on and on. In gloriously infinite time.

It seemed like they lived a whole day with no one else in it. David felt he could have spent a lifetime here. Even more than its utter uniqueness, what the day impressed on David was this relationship's singularity. With Kristin, with every woman he could recall, David had intentionally stopped time to control the moments and direct them—both moments and relationships—to what he imagined they should be.

In contrast, this shared moment had happened seemingly of its own accord. He had neither caused it nor could he replicate it. Yet it was more than anything he could have created. Or even imagined. And it was simplicity itself. With time stopped, they could only be together where they were in their infinite moment. But as they walked, stopped, talked, there was nothing more that he wanted to do than to be in this moment with her and no other place he wanted to be.

When they finally conceded to end it, David let go first. Of course, he didn't know how long Julia held hers, but their magic seemed to vanish in an eye's blink.

His motorcycle ride flipped the hours he had just spent. Now, he seemed to not move as the scenery did. He now also understood he had an unshared solitude to think about more than he could comprehend. He knew one thing for sure: Getting to know Julia all over again was making him fall in love all over again.

David reached Alexandria too exhausted to see Julia as he had hoped. His new questions from the ride would have to wait.

Still, their shared ability opened the possibility of extending time sequentially—effectively prolonging moments indefinitely. As soon as they had restarted time, they had tried repeatedly to simultaneously stop it again. As Julia had guessed they would, they failed every time. With each attempt, one would be frozen, the other moving. Giving up, they agreed to try to live together in actual time as much as possible. They also agreed to say when either was going to stop time.

Julia called her episodes "interludes in time"—fittingly, far more elegant than his "time-stops." She had started as a teenager. She had tried not to use them unfairly at school, particularly during her architectural studies, where she could have made masterpieces overnight. Like him, Julia used her interludes as opportunities for withdrawal. She had also taught him pranks he had not tried. The best included "disappearing." Julia would stop time and move continually away from where he was turning to look. Doing so almost instantly, she could forever seem to have vanished while still being right there.

Despite all he had learned, David still had gnawing unknowns. *Is her attraction to me or to our shared ability? How had she truly known I could stop time?* As much as he yearned to know, his questions had to wait.

CHAPTER THIRTY-TWO

Work ensured that David had to wait the rest of the week. His days off had put him several days behind. He fought the impulse that comes from a return to a heavy workload: to resent the break instead of the work.

David was less successful in fighting his resentment over the new, inane assignment that awaited: getting his proposal introduced as legislation. Now, in addition to the necessary work—educating others about the proposal, building support for it, refining it, and preparing the material these required—he had this unnecessary diversion that, if anything, threatened the real goal of enacting it.

During one of many calls to bridge their separation, Julia had said, "You do not suffer fools gladly but greatly." David had burst out laughing. *If she can see this, it must be obvious to those at work—especially Phil.*

Julia's own schedule further impeded their time together. They thought about manipulating time at odd hours to manufacture opportunities. But the amount of planning required took away its joy. Frustrated, David had never felt closer to Julia, even as he couldn't get near her.

The weekend's break from work and now their separation brought home more clearly than ever the limitations of stopping time. *It's becoming just a means, not the end it once was.* With work, stopping time meant work could never physically wear him out. Mentally, it was different. Just physically withdrawing from work was not enough. *Eventually, it's no escape at all. It just makes the cage more pleasant but, in doing so, it makes the cage more confining.*

His time with Julia, and now the revelation that she could match his escapes, forced him to examine them harder still. So long as she and he were together, stopping time allowed them to manipulate moments almost limitlessly—even if only separately. And they could have spent a lifetime in that Monday's surprise shared interlude. Like self-exiled castaways, they could have resided on an island uninhabited by time. But to what end? They were just escaping from real lives—a real life he knew with increasing certainty he wanted to spend with her. In real time.

By Friday, when they finally met, David was consumed by work's external pressures and the internal ones fermenting since he had climbed on his motorcycle and left her Monday. When he arrived at her house, he held her as though four years had passed instead of four days.

Still in his embrace, he heard her say, "Are you okay?"

"I'm just stressed about work."

As they walked into Del Ray, David sensed himself becoming even worse company, which only tightened his accelerating spiral. Finally, unable to stand it any longer, he asked to go back.

Feeling squeezed from all directions, David knew he was ruining the evening he had so anticipated.

"Maybe I should just go. I'm miserable company. Honestly, I wouldn't want to be with me right now, but I'm stuck with me, so I've no choice."

"David, honey, I don't expect you to entertain me," she said, holding him at arm's length. "But I'd love it if you'd talk to me. What's the matter? You see, I'm not stuck *with* you, I'm stuck *on* you."

"Are you? Or is it our shared ability? Because I can do 'it' too?"

"David, is that what's bothering you? If so, you're selling us both short. I was attracted by our similarity—how could I not have been? But I'm attached to you—fully, completely. To you. Not to 'it,' to you."

David pulled Julia to him—there in the middle of the sidewalk—as he had when he first saw her that evening. As much as he had longed to be close to her, his doubt had been pushing her away. Now, he dropped any pretext about what tonight meant. He whispered into her ear, "Oh, Julia, I need that to be true. Because I really love you. Really, really love you. I realized when we were apart all week, that's when time really stops for me."

He heard her voice come from behind his left ear. "David, let's go home. We're best when we talk."

As they walked, David already felt better. The air was soft, humid, but not heavy and oppressive like midsummer can be. It was made for strolling slowly. When they reached the porch swing, they talked about their week, meanings and not just details. It took time to recapture last weekend's closeness; as they did, conversation came easier, more open.

"How did you really know…?" David asked.

Julia began rising before he finished speaking. "I think I know what you're about to ask. It's better if we talk inside."

Closing the door, she led them to the couch. As soon as they settled, David began again. "Last weekend, when you said you knew I could stop time, did you mean it? Did you *actually* know?"

Expressionless, she said, "Yes. I meant it; I meant it because I knew it."

"But how? I saw the same clues you did, but even knowing I could stop time, it never occurred to me you could."

Uncharacteristically, Julia looked away. David paused. "Did you know someone else who could?"

"Yes," Julia said hesitantly and in a low voice.

"Who?" David leaned around, trying to see Julia's eyes.

"Someone I was very close to."

"A relative? Does it run in the family?"

"No and no," she said, turning back with a sad, slight smile. "Oglethorpe."

"I'm sorry." David's heart fell. "I didn't mean to take you back there."

"It's alright. I needed to bring it back up. I didn't tell you everything…"

David simultaneously cringed and kicked his selfishness as his mind leaped back to Julia's sorority sisters' jokes about an affair.

Her eyelids batting away tears, she murmured, "He didn't just die. He committed suicide."

David's heart raced; he now desperately wished to stop what curiosity had started. "You don't have to tell me this. It's none of my business."

"It's your business if I am, because other than being able to stop time, it was my life's defining event. Until you. He sensed I could stop time, just like I sensed you could. My work was too good; it seemed too easy for me. He tested me like I tested you. When he was sure, he called me to his office and asked me point blank. I reacted with the same shock you did on the trail. But the age difference, my respect for him, I simply confessed. It made us incredibly close." She shook her head vigorously as though by reflex. "Not like you may be thinking, not sexually. Suddenly, I had someone who understood, not only what I cared most about, architecture, but also about something I didn't understand about me."

"You don't have to—"

"Yes, I do. I've relived it more often than you could know just since last weekend. You should know." She dabbed her eyes, then took two deep breaths. "Now, here goes—and please don't stop me, or I'll never be able to start again.

"One day, a note just appeared on my drawing table in the studio. I saw it appear from nowhere. I knew instantly how it had gotten there. Reading it, I panicked. I stopped time and, though senseless, I ran as fast as I could to the nearest of the gorges that run through Cornell's campus. When I got there, I knew I had not seen him on the way. It took all my strength to look down; I was so sure he'd be at the bottom. When he wasn't, I was relieved that I'd beaten him there. After I caught my breath, I restarted time, hoping I'd see him and stop him. I waited for what seemed like forever, looking both ways on the bridge. Then I heard a scream behind me. A woman was pointing at a body now in the gorge."

Julia began to sob. David gathered her into his arms, hoping somehow to change the outcome.

Julia struggled through her words. "David, he hadn't been at the bottom. I know he hadn't. He must've walked right by me and then…I don't know why. I'll never know. Maybe he was sick physically. I keep hoping that was it. I know that's wrong, but I fear even more that he felt he was a failure. That he owed his career to a gimmick, that he wasn't really great like people thought. But he was wrong, his biggest talent was reaching students..."

She paused to draw a long breath. "I knew that fear. That I was only good at architecture because I could simply use more time and do what others couldn't. He took me beyond just replicating and into creating. He *was* architecture to me. But then I came to feel I couldn't do it without him."

David held her to him, clinging to her in his attempt to fight the futility that there was nothing more he could do. He had led her back here, and now he could not make it better.

"I didn't mean to put you through that again." He pulled back to see her, to let her see how much he meant it.

Breathing as though exhausted, she tried to smile. "You didn't *put* me through it, you helped me finally *get* through it. I've replayed this over in my mind, over and over—not just this week, but countless times since it happened. In all those episodes, I've never been able to tell anyone. I could only give the normal version, but it's the abnormal part—the part only you heard, the part only you understand—that's the hardest, the most haunting.

"Ever since it happened, I've been telling a half-truth—to the campus police, the Ithaca police, the Cornell administration, my parents, other students, my sorority sisters, my family—over and over and over! But I could never tell the hard truth, the part that I walk up to each time I tell the half-truth, then retreat from, only to wake up to at night. I thought all week that this time I wasn't going to run away anymore. Now I'm going to throw this away like I threw away his note. I hope that one last time I've cried away all the tears I've cried since then."

For David, there were no words except two: "I'm sorry," and these he kept repeating.

Julia did not speak again for a long time. When she did, she spoke of everything that had followed, the easy part memorized into soliloquy from constant retelling. How she had completely collapsed. How all she could do was get away, first to Kentucky and then to Europe. How she had withdrawn so deeply into interludes that real time had become the interruption. Everyone believed her recovery had taken months; she admitted now that it had taken far, far longer.

He understood. When Julia pulled out the sketches and drawings from her time "away," their beauty, their intricacy, their sheer number made David fully appreciate how long it must have been, how deeply she had been hurt.

Only Brandon ended their conversation, and only he roused them late the next morning. David realized he had awakened to a fuller relationship. There was no longer any question whether they were just dating, seeing each other, or any other version that all spoke of some lack of full commitment. And of uncertainty. David was certain. Last night had been his confirmation—not just about Julia's feelings for him, but his admission to himself about how he felt about her. This was where he wanted to be, and Julia was the woman. He now eagerly anticipated each step, because, in his heart, he knew where they were going.

He confided that stopping time now held little for him. It could be a necessary respite but being there without her was empty. They tried again to recreate their shared interlude. They never succeeded. It was just as Julia had guessed; without asking, David now understood how she had known.

Revelation's aftershock hung over Saturday, so that doing nothing still felt like something. In her search for something, Julia said with exasperation, "It's the last place I looked!"

"I should hope so."

"That's mean!"

"No, that's common sense. Things will always be in the last place you look; unless you keep looking after you've found it."

"Is this what you do with your interludes?" she asked. "Ponder the minor annoyances of life?"

"I like to contribute to growing humanity's collective knowledge any way I can." He laughed back—more at her look than her question.

Julia then turned serious. "You can plan the rest of the weekend, but I want you to take me to church tomorrow morning. Please."

"Of course." Far from conceding, David had been thinking about this too, but had hesitated to raise it since he didn't have a church. He thought about how happy his father would be. That connection led to another: He had to not only start mentioning Julia to his parents but also begin planning for them to meet her.

A large, airy building, Alexandria's First Baptist Church could have been the First Baptist Church of any Southern town. It was one of Alexandria's few surviving Southern elements in what had become just another suburb of another large city. The service was like many he had attended growing up in Georgia when his family had made the rounds of various churches without formally settling on a denomination.

David was struck by Julia's popularity. He expected this among men his age, for she was the pearl of great price that each would have sold all to possess. But even older people knew her well. Understanding her high profile brought him heightened scrutiny, he played it simply. She was the stone; he was the setting. As they greeted the minister in the receiving line after service, David merely smiled and shook hands beneath Julia's halo.

Julia's happiness was obvious. David felt humbled to have delivered so much by doing so little. Humility brought with it a sense of responsibility: a realization of his outsized impact. He could not remember when making someone else happy had given him so much too. Determined to maintain the momentum, he took them—and Brandon—to Occoquan, a small river town just south of Alexandria. Essentially a single-street town, it had retained its charm along with its buildings. They walked until Brandon docilely settled beneath the table of their outing's last meal.

Impulsive in the glow of the best day of a seismic weekend that had shifted his feelings like an earthquake, David asked, "How would you feel about going to Europe and showing me parts from your past?"

Her face radiated the depth he had struck. She struggled for words until David intervened, "A simple 'yes' is all I'm looking for."

"Yes," she nodded more than said.

Then she was off. Throughout the rest of the fast-disappearing day, they discussed a thousand different things to a dozen different destinations. By the time they returned to Julia's, they had decided on Venice and dates. David realized that over one week his life had changed forever.

CHAPTER THIRTY-THREE

Planning for Venice added excitement to the week's early days. Making arrangements with short notice was hard, but between them, everything was set by Tuesday night. Before putting money down, they would clear it with their offices.

David assured Julia, "The conversation with Janice will be perfunctory. August recess is inviolate with Congress, so everyone plans vacations then."

Not one hour into Wednesday, Julia texted him a thumbs-up emoji and "Ciao!" David had only told Frank and Jeff; showing them Julia's message, they also gave him their thumbs-up. Jeff had been there with a woman he dated before marrying, so he could never talk about it around his wife, while Frank had it high on his bucket list.

"They're enjoying it as much as I am," David mouthed to himself as he headed to get Janice's approval.

Janice called out from down the hall. "Just the person I was looking to see! Can you meet quickly with Phil and me on the proposal?"

David said "Sure" back but "Shit" inside. *This is going to be about the bill sponsor I don't have.*

Phil barely let the door close when he said, "I've found you a fundraiser in Las Vegas with Senator Nelson."

As David's heart sank further, he stopped time. "Damn it!" he screamed into the others' frozen muteness. He jerked his body in disgust. "I can see four without needing to put two and two together. Senator Nelson's a key member on the Senate Finance Committee. If the proposal's introduced as legislation, the bill will be referred there."

Had David supported introduction, he would have agreed this was a good approach—extended time alone with an influential member on the key committee.

Finally calm, he restarted time, only to then listen to Phil give the same explanation he had just given himself. Bigger than the professional blow, however, was the personal one. The fundraiser overlapped with Venice.

With each step back to his office, his dread of calling Julia increased. She picked up with a sing-song "Ciao!" on the first ring. Silence resounded to his news.

He was sure she had stopped time to absorb the disappointment, just as he had when he had received it because her reaction was far too good. "Let's both go to Las Vegas and travel from there. After all, it's not where you are; it's who you're with."

David warned, "It'll be hotter than the hinges to Hell," but was so thrilled she wasn't crushed—and that they would still be together—he'd have agreed to anything.

Janice leaned in as he was hanging up with Julia.

"Everything okay? You didn't seem exactly thrilled at the prospect of Las Vegas in August."

Through sealed lips, David puffed out his breath in frustration. "It's not the heat, it's the stupidity."

Janice barely got the door shut before exploding in cackling gales.

"Sorry," he tried repeatedly to squeeze in during her attempts to catch her breath.

"Oh, don't apologize!" she wheezed out. "That's the funniest thing I've heard all summer."

"Seriously," he said, and he truly meant it. "It's just that the time crushed plans I was about to spring on you."

Janice's residual grin through his explanation didn't make it come out any easier. When he finished, she said, "I'll tell Phil why you seemed less than enthusiastic." As she opened the door to leave, she looked back over her shoulder. "Phil thinks you've got a bad attitude," she said and flicked her eyebrows.

"Tell him I'm sorry, but it's the only one I have; I'll be taking it to Vegas as my carry-on item."

David listened to Janice's laughter float down the hall.

Julia and David threw themselves into the new plan with the vigor they had just trained on Venice. Since Whitney would pay for David's trip, this allowed them to splurge.

At work, David plunged into fully using August. He doggedly accelerated his frenetic meeting pace, now meeting with everyone he still needed to, then swinging back to many he had already. He particularly focused on the staff of Senator Nelson, whose fundraiser he would be attending; David wanted to ensure Nelson had the proposal's details ahead of Las Vegas.

Julia told David she was excited about both parts of the trip—his lobbying and their traveling. Increasingly, she quizzed him about his "official" part: what to pack, what his office expected, who else would attend.

Fielding all of the questions, David warmed to the telling and bringing her closer to his world. Julia commented on the gulf between David's enthusiasm when discussing Hill versus Corporate activity. It came out starkly when she asked him a simple question: "What's the difference between various Hill offices?"

"There are three types of offices: Personal, committee, and leadership. Personal offices are the Army. Their life is a constant slog where victory and defeat look little different; they live in a foxhole either way, under a constant barrage of mail and constituent service. Committee offices are the Navy. Each sails its own ocean, and life's better—the quarters, the food, and there are amenities. Leadership offices, oh, they're the Air Force. They fly to wherever the action is. They see all the combat, but, from their altitude, they have a perspective the Army and the Navy don't. After each sortie, they return to base—no foxholes, no sinking—and if they do get shot down, they usually parachute to safety. Republican or Democrat, House or Senate, they're just different militaries, but they've all got the same three branches. Each staffer can immediately size up another, just by knowing the other person's branch and their rank. It's very straightforward."

Neither of them had ever been to Las Vegas; fortunately for David, Frank had in his mind many times, and Jeff had, in fact, once. While sympathizing over the loss of Venice, both seemed equally keen on Las Vegas—especially Frank. When David asked, Jeff explained, "Venice is like Mark Twain's definition of a classic: a book no one really wants to read but everyone wishes they had. In contrast, Las Vegas is pure beach read."

When David and Julia finally arrived on a Thursday afternoon in late August, they immediately appreciated Jeff's accuracy. Las Vegas was a pure pulp-fiction paradise. Nothing seemed real except unmitigated hedonism's constant search for excess. Had it been any less self-conscious, it would have been sad; instead, David said, "It's a Disney World of debauchery." Julia seconded, "It's so honest in its dishonesty that it's as comical as Shakespeare's Falstaff."

In most places David had traveled, there came a point where he felt he could be anywhere, in an indistinguishable sameness. Not Las Vegas. Because there was neither ignoring nor escaping it, they embraced it.

As both a joke and surprise, David had reservations at the Venetian. It had been meant as an apology, but it worked even better as parody. Then they strolled the Strip, going into the most outrageous hotels and avoiding the touts.

Jet-lagged, they closed an early night watching the Bellagio's fountain show. Without looking over, David said, "I'm sorry the Venetian wasn't Venice."

Gazing at the fountains, Julia responded with a little laugh through her yawn, "The Venetian was much more efficient." Then, turning to look at him, she said, "I would much rather be at the Venetian with you than in Venice without you."

David leaned to kiss her lightly. “Thanks, I just wish you could've had both.”

“Next time.” She sighed. “David, leave perfect for work, and let's just have us. That's enough.”

As tiredness completed its descent, Julia asked, “I've been wondering. You do fundraisers all the time in Washington. Why have one way out here?”

“Money.” He turned his gaze back at the fountains. “This one costs twice the normal amount.” David paused. “I also think that it's a lot like Las Vegas itself. These weekend events add a novelty to the mendacity—like all these hotels. They're trying to create some difference that makes people feel comfortable doing to a greater extent here what they do to a lesser extent at home. Look at all the signs; they're really hawking the commonplace—sex, alcohol, gluttony, greed—all happen wherever these tourists come from. They just give people a reason, cover, for doing them to a greater extent here.”

“You're awfully jaded for someone so young,” Julia said and snickered.

“I'm old and wise beyond my years. And I've seen enough fundraisers to last a lifetime.”

“You know, the hotels remind me of the miniature golf places on the Gulf.”

“The Redneck Riviera?”

“That's the one. We used to go to different beaches—Panama City, Gulf Shores, Destin, Sarasota—but they all had the garish miniature golf courses, with pyramids, castles, dinosaurs. I loved them. Well, here it's like each hole on one of those has become an entire hotel!”

Transported, David also remembered. “We used to go too. I loved those courses, the crazy colored balls, and the last hole where your ball disappeared forever.”

The fountain show ended. The crowd dispersed to pursue their vice of choice; so, too, David and Julia: sloth.

The next morning, jet lag woke them at five. No one was moving, except for some still in the casino. The gym was deserted, and they were done, back up, and back down in just ninety minutes, still way ahead of their tour to the Valley of Fire.

They were the youngest on the tour by a generation. Withstanding

103-degree temperatures, they visited rock carvings and saw a herd of bighorn sheep.

Afterward, thinking the temperature would make a visit to the hotel pool refreshing, they were surprised that it was just four feet deep. They guessed that any deeper and the hotel would be fishing guests out by the hour. The downside to the hotel's reduced insurance premiums was that the winds coming off the desert made it cold to stand up. People-watching was great, though, including seeing some of Las Vegas's finest escort someone away.

Upstairs, sequentially stopping time, with only seconds off the clock, each took an extended nap before the fundraiser's opening cocktail party.

For David, the event was work, but for Julia, it was theater. He could sense her filing away a barrage of questions for later. The cast was the usual assemblage: regulars from Washington's circuit, others in town for a convention, a few locals attracted by the chance to meet a national political figure.

Avoiding the scrum around the senator, David walked toward his staffer. David knew the senator would find him. All politicians make it their business to spend time with everyone who made the effort and paid the money to spend a weekend with them. And anyone willing to go to such lengths was a potential host of their own fundraiser later.

Having been "the staffer" in his Hill life, David also knew staffers were grateful for any break in the tedium from being in tow. He'd done his homework back in Washington, and David had met Nelson's staffer, Shelly, several times; he liked her. Thanks to their meetings, she thoroughly understood David's issue.

When the senator made his way over, the conversation quickly moved from introductions and pleasantries to substance. Shelly had clearly done her work. Nelson knew the issue well; his questions were good. David knew them all because Shelly had asked most of them back in Washington. The only hard part for David was "the ask": Would he consider introducing the proposal as a bill? More artful in making it, David was no more convinced of its value. Regardless, here on Whitney's dime, he had to. Knowing his role as well as David knew his own, the senator was properly noncommittal.

Like that, round one was over. If David did nothing else on the trip, he had done his job. Of course, Julia's questioning lasted much, much longer. Their evening, after the supper for contributors, was a Cirque Du Soleil show featuring The Beatles' music. It was tailor-made for David and Julia, who loved the vintage material with acrobatics as visuals—an extended live music video. They closed the night with a walk through their hotel's casino.

Back upstairs, each shared the same thought, but Julia beat him to it. "So, how could we have stopped time to beat the house?"

With mock horror, David said, "Really, Julia!"

"Don't tell me you haven't thought about such things! I'm just theorizing, not proposing."

Dropping onto the bed, David curled his lips into a sarcastic grin. "Well, I guess we could do a variation on a card trick I used to do. But getting the cards out of the shoe, and then back in, would be harder than it looks," he mused.

"Another would be for us both to play, but one person wagers substantially more. One of us could stop time, then mix the cards into the larger wager's best possible hand."

Leaning back into the pillows, David said, "Really, there are surprisingly few things we can do in general that don't come down to immorality."

Julia sat down beside him on the bed's edge. "I know, it's always the big limiter. Stopping time's greatest advantage would go to the most unscrupulous."

David leaned his head onto her shoulder. "Long ago, I realized I could steal virtually anything I wanted. That's its real advantage: rearranging things to give yourself an unearned edge."

Her head touched his, and David could feel her nodding. "Only when directed inward does it come without strings."

"Well, our humble circumstances testify to our inherent honesty," David said with a chuckle.

The next day was the anchor activity that fundraisers always offered. Julia got the better of this because one option was a spa; David got stuck with golf. In August, golf meant drinking gallons of water, still dehydrating, wearing a cooling towel continuously, while roasting on a spit. Nor had David ever figured out how stopping time could dramatically improve his poor game—or cared enough to do so. Here, it just gave him more time to cool off, but it barely helped. Additionally, his foursome included "that person": the one who truly cared about the score. For David, it was like playing 180 holes in Death Valley; it couldn't end soon enough.

When he dragged through their room's door, their contrast couldn't have been greater. Julia looked like she had been exactly where she had been, while David looked like he had been dragged over the course.

"I'm time-stopping for perhaps a day's worth of hours," he gasped.

Julia barely redirected him with, "Not on the bed!" before he collapsed on the couch.

Julia didn't get another word in before he switched off time.

The night's supper was the fundraiser's central event. David had to follow up on yesterday's initial conversation. It started with cocktails, then transformed into the inane awards presentation that accompanied the day's golf.

"Are you going to win anything?" Julia whispered.

Beneath his hand, David whispered. "Hope not. I don't know which would be worse: winning a gag prize for being bad or winning a real one and implicitly admitting you spend way too much time on a golf course."

Tonight, he and Julia were seated at the senator's table. Julia nudged him when she saw, but David dismissed it: "Never do business in public." Instead, he aimed for a moment alone. For two hours, it didn't come.

"There's always tomorrow at breakfast," Julia said before taking a break.

As David waited, the table emptied. Then the room. Staring into nowhere, David jolted to the realization that the senator and Shelly had returned.

The senator's voice boomed into the room's vacancy. "David, I like your proposal. And I want to help."

"Thank you, senator. That's great," David stammered back.

"But David, I don't like your idea about introducing it as legislation. I don't see what that gets you besides a press release. Personally, I'd rather have it passed. What about you?"

David's mood plunged as fast as it had risen. Of course, he agreed—and even if he hadn't, only a fool disagrees with a senator to his face. He stopped time to think where he could take the conversation, but having done so, he couldn't come up with anything better than, "I agree."

Senator Nelson leaned back and pointed at David simultaneously. "Then why're you asking me to introduce this?" The senator's arm dropped, his voice fell, and he grinned. "It's not your idea, is it?"

Trapped, David couldn't throw his boss under the bus, but he also wasn't going to take Phil's place there either.

Fighting the urge to look away, he kept eye contact. "No, sir."

"Thanks for your honesty. I wanted to make sure you're as smart as I thought you were. You don't have to say more." He reached into his coat, removed a card, and offered it to David in an uninterrupted circuit. "Here. Call my scheduler and set up an appointment with me and your CEO for later in September. Let's see if we can straighten this out then."

They shook hands, and the senator was gone, on to his next stop. Shelly stayed back.

"David, he means it. He really likes the idea." Her face a picture in earnestness, she accentuated each of her words. "I mean, he *really* likes it. He doesn't just say those things."

David's shoulders dropped, and he sighed as though he had just exited a stage. "Thanks, Shelly, for saying that and for all your help getting it in front of him."

She cast a look behind her. Turning to follow her gaze and her boss, she spoke over her shoulder as her feet pulled her away. "I gotta go. We'll talk back in town. And I'll tell our scheduler to expect to hear from you."

He was alone, except for the cleaning crew now cleared to begin. Julia rejoined him moments later.

"I saw you and the senator talking. What did I miss?"

"I'll tell you upstairs. But I'm stuck between the senator and my company."

Returning to their room, they could not avoid the casino. They idly commented on the faces as they slowly passed. One young couple particularly stood out. Looking like their replicas from ten years earlier, the similarity only grew stronger as David and Julia came up behind them. Sitting at the Texas Hold 'em table, they were ingenues circled by sharks. David remembered his father's admonition about gambling: "If you're at a table and can't find the chump, then you're the chump." That, and something about never playing cards with a man named "Doc."

David and Julia could feel the couple's angst descending into despair as their hands grew worse and their chips became fewer. David and Julia stopped, unable to look away.

It took only a few hands of overheard conversation to get the story. Too young to get married at home, they had come to Vegas. Now, they were on the verge of having to call home to confess it—and that they didn't have the money to get back. With each revelation and each fold of their hands, Julia's clutched David's tighter.

"Let's see if we can help," he whispered to Julia.

"I don't even know this game; what can you do?"

"Just watch and don't act alarmed—follow my lead when I fold. And don't stop time."

Returning with chips, David and Julia sat down on either side of the couple. They were now down to playing one hand between them.

From frat games and casino fundraisers, David knew how to play. He also knew there was not much he could do without attracting a lot of attention.

As soon as the hole cards had been dealt to David, the couple, and then Julia, he stopped time. David looked over the six cards and made the best pair he could for the couple: the jack of hearts and the jack of diamonds. David and Julia joined the first bets.

As the flop's three cards were laid down, David tried to suppress any hint of recognition at the jack of clubs among them.

When the young couple looked back at their cards, they were stunned. Their tell was obvious, the mark of amateurs, but they had been so regularly feasted upon that the sharks evidently dismissed it. As the betting came around to David, he folded, unwilling to subsidize the couple more than he already had. Julia did likewise after the couple pushed a sizable fraction of their depleted chips onto the table.

David and Julia sat frozen through the turn's betting. He was more nervous than if it had been his own money. As the river approached, the final card that would complete the seven, David stopped time once more. This time, he went to the dealer's hand and ensured the jack of spades would follow the burn card.

Seeing two jacks on the table, the couple went all-in with all they had left. When the last shark to bet tried to raise the couple out of the game, they blanched; David flashed white-hot inside. Knowing they could not match the raise, the girl began to whimper.

"Have you got a good hand?" David asked the boy.

"Y-y-yessir," the boy said.

"Here, let them see it then." David pushed in the necessary chips.

"Hey, what the fuck?" the shark protested.

David cut him off. "What I do with my money is my business, and it'll spend just the same if you win it."

David was both exhilarated and shaken as they left amid the squeals ringing from the table at a haul so sizable that it had attracted a lot of attention. He didn't feel bad for the people who had lost, especially the prick who had tried to buy the pot, but he also didn't feel as good as he thought he would for the couple either. "Use it wisely," was all he said to them as they pumped his hand in thanks for the loan. And he refused their offer of "interest" on it.

When they were safely back in their room, Julia had wheeled on him. "Tell me, tell me." When David described it, she glowed; he called it a moral "push."

The next morning was a sprint through formalities over a quick breakfast and then everyone rushing to the airport. Many of the Washington lobbyists were heading to another event just like this one for another senator in another fancy location. "I don't know how they do it," he said sideways to Julia as he waved to some. "I know I wouldn't want to." He was grateful that Julia and he finally had their trip to themselves.

Now on their own time, they walked as quickly back to their room as decorum allowed. It was still before ten in the morning, either very early—or very late by Las Vegas standards. Suddenly, Julia pulled up abruptly, jerking David to a halt.

David stumbled back. “What the…What’s the matter, you want to try your luck?”

Julia motioned with her head to one of the tables. It was the same couple in the same position they had found them last night. David’s face fell to match Julia’s expression.

Dejected, David called Janice when he was back in the room to tell her the mixed news: The senator loved the proposal but hated the strategy.

“Send a quick email to me and Phil—but only about the good news. I’ll reply immediately and tell you to go offline for your vacation. I mean it! Oh, and try not to worry about our pickle.”

As he hung up, he was still in a funk when Julia slid her arm around him. “I heard, I couldn’t help it. How do you feel?”

Still feeling the effects of what he had just seen downstairs, he heard his honesty slip mindlessly past his censor. “Like every other day in my job, really.”

She lowered him down beside her. “What do you mean?”

“The personal and the professional don’t sync up for me, I guess,” David said.

“Do you mind me asking, then, why do you do it?”

Stunned, he looked back with the realization that she was asking—and that he was answering—a question he had never allowed himself to broach. “Because Washington is no different than Vegas actually. Like the couple last night, they’re still there this morning. It’s not the outcome that drives us; it’s the action. My job’s the only way I can still have a seat at the table.”

With work done, they picked up a rental car and left Las Vegas as fast and as far in the rearview mirror as they could. Pulling away, Julia started and David finished the *Blues Brothers* line, “106 miles to Chicago,” both closing with, “Hit it!”

Instead of going to the Grand Canyon’s north rim, as most do, they had chosen the parks of Utah. “The road less traveled,” as Julia had said, to which David had responded, “And that will make all the difference.” It did.

Immediately on leaving the confines of Las Vegas, the road opened on the vistas and vastness of the West. Southern newcomers, neither had seen anything like it. Both had "mountains" where they had grown up, but those were mere foothills here.

Miles and miles to drive, hours and hours to talk, and scene after scene to experience; everything was an adventure—both what David saw and the prolonged, uninterrupted contact with Julia. Either alone would have affected him, but the interplay heightened both, making indelible experiences for replaying in his thoughts each night. He need only touch his day's memories to instantly find tranquility and then sleep.

Julia mused on one of the sunsets they watched. "Do you suppose our days are like the day's light? Most beautiful at the beginning and the end?"

Caught off guard, David said, "I guess it depends on the person, just as the sunsets and sunrises depend on themselves and their observers. Not every sunset or sunrise is beautiful; even when one is, a person may miss it."

"I guess we can't know. Our sunrise, even if gorgeous, happens before memory. And our sunset…I suppose is the only one we can hope to consciously control, to pray it's beautiful, and to hope we have the time and the perception to appreciate it."

CHAPTER THIRTY-FOUR

Riding in on the Tuesday after Labor Day, David knew work would resume with pent-up fury. He had been promised no help on his proposal, but with nothing tangible to show for his efforts on it, others' work was now being shifted to him. The pressure from Whitney's dire straits was also becoming excruciating, and the measures to relieve it were becoming increasingly draconian. All purchases now required approval by a corporate officer. Budget cuts were underway, headcount reductions were in the works, and everything but the most essential corporate travel was being halted. At the top of the list of essential trips was the CEO traveling to meet Senator Nelson about the proposal. Janice had scheduled a nine o'clock meeting with Phil and David to organize it.

To Corporate, this was as big as it got. The CEO going anywhere was the equivalent of Zeus descending Olympus and entailed a host of unnecessary work to accommodate the trip. Phil would be beside himself from now through the visit. David could only imagine the effort Janice had made to keep him from ruining David's break. There was nothing she could interpose between David and Phil now.

David was prepared and stopped time for it. Yet as much as he willed his thoughts to work, they drifted to Julia.

The last week, last two weeks, last-however-long-it-had-been, has been the best I can remember. Despite its duration and the continuous contact, it's not gotten old.

David had prolonged their last night so long that only stopping time could catch him up. Still, Julia crowded his consciousness as he watched the Potomac skim by below.

Phil would be in by eight, which is why David arrived at seven. When Phil appeared on cue, David was thoroughly prepared. He didn't let on, knowing Phil would immediately ask for documents and begin urging changes. Better to save it for Janice. That he could make Phil sweat for another hour was admittedly another bonus.

"An hour's a lifetime!" he had cheerily reminded him.

By ten, the three had emerged with a plan for a meeting with the senator in two weeks. Seemingly the entire office had been shuttled in and out of their ninety-minute meeting, each leaving with assignments. Only Janice, Phil, and David stayed through it all. David forewarned them that the senator was skeptical about introducing the proposal as legislation. Janice had heard; Phil had ignored. David had done his job; he left with many more to do.

Everyone had questions about his time away. David could tell their closeness to him by whether they asked about the fundraiser or his vacation. Frank and Jeff were all about the trip—Las Vegas, especially. Denise and Phil asked about the fundraiser.

The general office was consumed with the CEO's upcoming visit. David's centrality to briefing the CEO and handling the meeting preparation—background papers, talking points, compiling the latest intel from other corporate offices, and arranging additional meetings (the CEO didn't fly in for just one meeting, even if Whitney's existence depended on it, so other things had to occur) had to be cobbled together—put him in the vortex of the whirlwind. As he did and redid his work, David watched everyone else's routines being upended. Groups were focused on feeding the CEO, his transportation, his security detail, preparing a private office for his visit. The list spiraled. David could only imagine the production if he were to spend the night, instead of returning that afternoon.

The easiest person David worked with was outside the office: Shelly. He apologetically alluded to his internal frustrations as he called her repeatedly over increasingly trivial things. In contrast, it had taken just one quick call to give her all she needed for the senator. That she took it all in stride with good humor was a reminder of some staffers' consummate proficiency—the ones of good Congress members.

In the dwindling moments David got away from work, Julia held him together. She provided his only sanctuary; she was his interlude. With her, he could stop the world—shutting everyone and everything out—even without stopping time.

For him, the question had become simple: What do I have better to do with my time?

The obvious answer also spurred him to broadcast her within his world. Now sure, he had to make sure others understood too—especially his family. David's personal reticence made this as unnatural for him to say as it was for them to hear. A call from Daniel assured him that his folks were listening. As though he were a third party in their conversations, David heard them asking about her; stranger still, he heard himself talking about her to them.

Clearly, Julia had been doing the same. Within a week, they had begun joint plans. Julia would come with him for Thanksgiving; he would go to Lexington just after Christmas.

David chuckled as he said, "My parents' preparations are rivaling my office's planning for our CEO visit."

The first meeting of their families came unexpectedly sooner. Cindy, Julia's younger sister, came into town as her company's last-minute representative for a conference. Much closer to Cindy than to her older sister Lydia, Julia was thrilled at the chance to introduce her to David.

Normally, David would have been equally excited. Here was the first contact with Julia's family and her closest member in it. From his parents to his friends, all had said a real relationship went deeper than one-on-one. Jeff called it "a group thing, not just a two-thing," while Frank summed it up, "Unless you marry an orphan, you marry a family, and good luck finding an orphan."

For David, the timing could not have been worse. Although Cindy was in town for three nights, he got to see her for only one. Determined to like her regardless, he was relieved to discover that he really did. She shared Julia's directness and sense of humor.

On introduction, Cindy said, "I'm the little sister and the family's advance scout." Julia elbowed her, but David immediately relaxed, not just from the humor, but because it was clear everyone was on the same page.

Julia was relaxed around Cindy, even allowing David to take a picture of them in front of a drawing she had just begun—something Julia usually guarded. David had seen pictures of Cindy many times, but, looking at Julia and Cindy in the same one, he was struck by the resemblance in the eyes and mouth. Other than that, they didn't look related at all. She was not as attractive, and she was shorter and brunette. Nor did she have Julia's disarming grace. Cindy was more extroverted and trendier in her dress and makeup. Separated by only two years, the gap seemed inestimably greater. But their interplay testified to the closeness. David both enjoyed and envied it. They were truly friends, not just siblings—unlike his relationship with Daniel.

Julia started the conversation and then let them go. Cindy was easy to talk to and, once begun, the three barreled on. It was Julia who finally had to bring up the fiction that he needed to get home for some sleep. David also noted Julia's implicit signal about where he was not sleeping: there.

When he saw Julia the next night, just as when he had met her friends for the first time, Julia simply said, "You passed." More detail followed, but David concluded: *We passed.*

As he left, he was stopped in his tracks at the sight of Julia's completed drawing of a beautiful building from four different angles.

"Do you like it?" she asked.

"It's wonderful."

"I mean, really like it?"

Sensing her eagerness, he tried for more. "I can't give you technical reasons, but it's stunning."

Her body relaxed. "Thanks, I finished it today. It's for a big project."

As soon as he walked back to his truck, David reveled in the happiness that he got from hers. *The beam of her smile's everything. It was as big as hers with Cindy.*

Inside his truck, on a whim, he looked at his phone to see it again. Then he looked at the one he had taken of Julia and Cindy. He stared. The drawing behind them: It was unquestionably the one that she had just shown him—the one she had begun last night.

These take a long time. Usually. Well, more than a day.

What had been a gnawing question now became a consuming one: How often and how long were Julia's interludes?

CHAPTER THIRTY-FIVE

David arrived early. Not because this was his first big meeting; on the Hill, he had done a lot of them. He knew from the Hill that this certainly was not a big meeting for the senator. CEO meetings were routine. There was a standard briefing paper to support it and a pre-meeting walk-through with the staffer handling it. Then they had the meeting; there would be several like it most weeks.

David was in the office at six in the morning because, in Whitney's office, only Janice had regularly done big meetings. His biggest unknown was not everyone else's preparation—he knew this was overdone—but the CEO's. The danger in a meeting between a public sector and a private sector eminence is each discounting the other's importance. To an important politician, CEOs are commonplace, their importance doesn't communicate—and whatever does is inherently undercut by the fact that the CEO is usually the one doing the asking.

As David told Julia, "To a CEO, politicians are a dime a dozen. After all, there are 435 representatives and 100 senators—more than the Fortune 500. And those are just the big ones; every local jurisdiction also has its own. My job is to make each participant feel like they're more important, or at least equally important."

What David didn't know was whether his CEO had put in the time and would make the effort to allow this to happen. He knew he had done his part with the senator. The biggest fear was that his office's fawning would inflate the CEO beyond equality.

Just thirty minutes. That's all. And for it, I've spent the better part of a year getting ready.

Leaving nothing to chance, David abandoned his preferred Metro for the day and drove. At this hour, there was no traffic, either on the roads or in the garage. He knew no one would be in before seven at the earliest. First, Rhonda the office manager, for whom this was easily the biggest day of her year, would come. Then, the support staff. Next, Phil. Finally, Janice and the rest of the office. Everyone would then await the CEO's private jet landing and his entourage arriving at eleven.

All unfolded on cue. Rhonda checked everything for the hundredth time. Then Stacey and Melanie, another assistant, did the same. Then Phil came and told everyone to do again what had already been done.

When Janice arrived, she had come straight to David's office and into his question. "Do you want to go over everything?"

David smiled at her reply. "No, I assume everyone knows how to do their jobs."

He knew Janice was there to avoid Phil. As she spoke, they heard him pass outside shouting, "This is how we lose, people, this is *how* we lose!" Not until everyone exhibited an equal degree of agitation would his be assuaged. Janice's respite lasted five minutes before Phil discovered her and pulled her away to discuss the catering for the CEO's lunch.

The rest of his coworkers just seemed to materialize in their offices. All were dressed better than usual, and most found reasons to keep emerging at any commotion that might have heralded the CEO's arrival.

David understood why Frank and Jeff had slipped in the back doors to avoid being seen and pulled into what had become a make-work maelstrom.

David texted Shelly as soon as was decent. Her response came quickly: "Everything on schedule. Will text if anything changes."

David knew Phil would ask. He did. Three times.

The CEO arrived: a satrap, sans the litter. His security detail entered first. Then, the CEO's support staff—Jon, the company's top tax person, and a few others David never identified. Next, the CEO immediately sequestered himself away in a guest office. Finally, the drivers for the group.

"How's it going?" Julia texted.

"Like a period movie when a noble visits his country estate: The entire staff's assembled for inspection, and I'm practicing tugging me forelocks," he typed back.

At twelve, David got the call for the pre-meeting briefing. He stood up, pushed his shoulders back as far as they would go, let them drop, and took a deep breath. *This is it. Now begins the three hours that determine the day, the year—and to hear Phil tell it—Whitney's future. And mine with it.*

He had only met the CEO once in passing. Most Whitney people memorized each meeting and went out of their way to add to them. To David, if there isn't a purpose to a meeting, what's the point? It was like people lunging to get on television at a sporting event. If you weren't the focus, you were a distraction.

Nor had David been particularly impressed when he had watched the CEO in large company settings or investor calls. The CEO did not cut an imposing figure either intellectually or personally. He was a little shorter than David's height but now with a softness that emanated from his waist throughout his frame.

How can someone so clearly out of shape be so enamored with sports metaphors? Do professional athletes use business analogies to aggrandize their occupation?

Following introductions, David faced an immediate divide. If the CEO had read his voluminous briefing book, there would only be questions to field; if he hadn't, David would have a full briefing on his hands. As soon as David began, he knew the CEO had not looked at the material.

Stopping time, he vented loudly as he paced around the still figures. "Why fly all the way here for a meeting of this magnitude and have not prepared? Jon was with you the whole time! And why does his staff insist on so much material? They have a standard format everyone must follow. And the result? A gigantic binder that at first glance dissuades anyone from opening it! Hours and hours of wasted work, but even more, a wasted opportunity to raise this meeting's chances for success. The curtain's rising on an actor who doesn't know his lines! Instead of rehearsing, we're learning the script!"

Once composed, David plunged headlong into it. Playing off the company's tax person and Janice, he emphasized the substantive issues and style points the meeting required. He finished just ahead of deadline. During the break between sessions, Janice came over to congratulate and calm. "Trust your relationship with the senator. He wants this to work. He's a consummate professional; he knows his role."

Regrouped for questions, the answers betrayed the lack of preparation but went well enough. David's confidence rose. On schedule, they headed to the cars. David was tapped to ride with the CEO, Janice, and Jon. It was fortuitous because, as they rode, the CEO threw a curveball. "There's another issue I want to raise as long as I'm here."

David fought the urge to lurch forward and speak. Janice beat him to a response. "This meeting is about securing one big request. Raising another implicitly disparages the favor you're hoping to get. First, let's establish the relationship and just be grateful."

Heading into the Russell Senate Office Building, the stateliest of the three Senate office buildings, David got another curve.

David glanced at Shelly's text—"Senator delayed in Capitol. Has to remain for a vote. Chris, the senator's chief of staff, will take us to Nelson's hideaway instead."

David tried to suppress any concern, but must have betrayed some because Janice made eye contact and then flicked hers toward his phone. Without speaking, he showed it to Janice.

Already self-conscious about the Whitney group's size at six—at least two too many with Phil and the CEO's assistant insisting they be in the meeting—now they would have to march *en masse* through the tunnel system. David had made this subterranean trip hundreds of times and Janice thousands, but the rest: never.

The trip over—or rather under—was akin to a backstage pass to Washington politics. Along it, their group split into three—Janice, the CEO, and Chris; David and Shelly; and Jon, Phil, and the CEO's assistant. Walking, they passed senators; all spoke to Janice.

Reaching the stairs to the Capitol, the crowd compressed, as if approaching the stage. Emerging into the Capitol itself, its features were recognizable to even newcomers. They were now on the stage. Twisting and turning through hallways, they passed the Ohio Clock, turned left with the Senate floor behind them, and headed toward the rotunda before branching off down an innocuous hallway.

An unmarked door swung open into the hideaway. The senator was in conversation with his party's leader, but waved them in nonetheless. The leader left, introductions followed. Senator Nelson seated them in a circle.

"I'm sorry, but I've got to get right to business—a series of stacked votes, I'm afraid."

David saw faces fall across the party—all except Janice's. She began a truncated intro to the topic, concluding with, "Our CEO can explain it best."

Nothing happened. She tried again.

The CEO tried to assume his role but couldn't, stumbling through things they had just discussed barely an hour ago. Whether stage fright from the office, the senator, the Capitol, or some combination, the CEO was frozen.

Eyes, panicked ones from within the Corporate group, shifted around the circle.

It took the senator to step in and direct the conversation back to the one he and David had had in Las Vegas. "You have a good proposal here. Really good. It's insightful, and it's good policy. I know it'll help you, but it also helps the industry, and the country, by giving greater encouragement for doing this research here."

In seconds, Senator Nelson summarized to the CEO the points the CEO was supposed to have made to the senator.

The CEO managed to say, "Thank you."

"But there's a problem," the senator continued. "It's not in your proposal;

it's in your process. David tells me you want this introduced as a bill."

Janice and David were silent, neither willing to claim that mistake. Looking and nodding at the CEO, Phil jumped in. "That's right."

"No, that's wrong," replied the senator flatly. "Introducing this'll tip your hand to no purpose. Everyone in town'll see it, and everyone in town'll want in on it. Like a crowd trying to climb into a lifeboat, they'll sink it. You'll get a press release, but you won't get a law."

There was silence; both the CEO, and now Phil, sat dumbfounded.

The senator added, "I'll be happy to try to get this into a bigger bill as an amendment. Quietly, as my amendment. I think that could work, and I commit to you I'll work it."

Unbearable silence filled the room, broken only by bells now sounding for a vote on the floor. Everyone in the Corporate party—except Janice and David, who knew the bells—jumped. The senator's offer hung in the hideaway's air to no response.

Dying inside, David saw defeat being silently snatched from victory's closing jaws. To his surprise, the senator leaned forward, his incline accentuating his eye contact, and spoke once more, this time slowly and with his pronounced Texas accent.

"Listen, you've got to decide what you want. In horse racing and in this Senate, there are three ways you can make an appearance. You can win, you can place, or you can show. Showing in horse racing means finishing third, and in this Senate, it means just showing up with your press release. Placing in horse racing means finishing second, and in this Senate, it means fighting but losing. I assume I don't have to explain what winning means in horse racing, but in this Senate, it means making laws. I'm a *workhorse*, not a *show horse*. There are more show horses than you can shake a stick at around here. If you want this proposal introduced, you should ask one of them. But if you want to..."

David heard himself say it as though listening to someone else speaking. "Win," David said resolutely, both finishing the senator's sentence and supplying the only answer his company could give but was fumbling away.

Senator Nelson, smiling, pointed at David, then finished his thought. "Win."

"Senator, you have to go vote," Shelly said, standing up.

"We want to win," David replied, standing up with the senator and keeping his eyes level with the senator's. He knew he was taking his job in his hands, but never had an answer been clearer or an opportunity more obvious. *Here's more than we ever could have bargained for, being offered on a silver platter.*

David's eyes darted to Janice, in whose eyes he saw recognition that the moment was now or forever lost. She said, "We leave it in your capable hands, Senator Nelson. Let us know how we can be of assistance."

The rest of Whitney's group rose slowly. The senator's smile broadened. "Great! I'll take you up on that."

Hands were hastily shaken, and the senator quickly exited, already caught up in conversation with Shelly about his upcoming vote. The meeting was over. They had won, even if David and Janice were the only two who realized it.

They walked out of the Capitol—Janice looking down to hide a smile like the cat's that had just eaten the canary, David floating, the rest in shock. Janice whispered to David, "That was impressive."

David tried to demur; Janice cut him off.

"Bullshit!" she uttered in a whisper. "No one's ever impressed by something they can do. So, I'll tell you again: That was impressive."

"We may both get fired," David whispered back.

"It was worth it," Janice said, almost chuckling.

As they walked out of the Capitol, David looked back. Despite countless viewings, it still thrilled him. He had always said to himself, "When you get tired of seeing this, it's time to go." He never had. It was especially sweet now as he rolled his memories of the meeting across this backdrop. He was tempted to stop time just to savor these moments, but he was enjoying them too much. He chose to stay with them and everyone else.

The others instantly changed. Once outside, the CEO's entourage began calls. Another financial issue required them back in Evanston. The company's plane would leave shortly.

Instead of a planned debrief back at the office, they would have to do it on the ride to the airport. Janice and David stayed in the same car with the CEO.

Both braced for the CEO's reaction. David could tell Janice was equally stunned when the CEO said in the privacy of the car, "How'd we do?"

He doesn't know! He doesn't realize how he had folded and how close we had come to losing everything!

Never had David felt more elated in the moment or more deflated in the person.

David recounted it all to Julia that night. "Janice and I explained all we could in the little time we had—how they had secured the commitment of one of the most powerful senators to work to get our proposal into law. We had so far overshot our expectations that we couldn't believe it, only to have our surprise trumped by disbelief that our CEO was thoroughly unaware of what it meant or even that it had occurred. To him, it was just another meeting: box checked, nothing more."

David looked to Julia for grounding. "Were we too close to it to have perspective?"

Laughing, Julia hugged him. "You so clearly love it, and I so love you. That's all I know, and all I care about. It thrills me to see you like this for a change!"

David knew she was right. He had been throwing himself into his work since their return, making him as distant here as they had been close there. Julia had regularly checked in with him, and David had always replied, "I'll tell you when I have something to tell." It had peaked this afternoon before, during, and after the meeting with her texts, emails, and calls. When he had finally gotten his first chance, he had texted, but she demanded to hear in person.

"How did Phil take it?"

"He was beside himself!" David said. "I think he thought Janice and I would both get fired on the ride to the airport. I half expected it myself! I know he wanted us to be. But when we weren't, there was nothing he could do but fume. The CEO was happy, and the CEO's the center of his universe. So, he feigned happiness for us and took as much credit as he could. Now we've just got to watch our backs."

Julia leaned back at the last bit. "That sounds ominous."

As David's mind left the triumph and now seriously considered the future, he became equally serious. "Phil's taking this to another level. It was always personal, but now it's business too—and that's as personal as anything gets to Phil."

After the Capitol meeting, David's mission changed. The goal remained the same, but the means fundamentally shifted. Senator Nelson's patronage meant David was no longer flying solo. The proposal was now the senator's. David became a junior partner in a Senate operation. Despite having been so ardently sought, reduced control was difficult; he knew it would be harder still to adhere to. There would come a point when the senator would make the decision on what the proposal would be. When he did, David, Whitney, and everyone else would simply have to accept it.

"It's not that I don't trust Senator Nelson," he told Julia. "I do. Completely. But the legislative process shapes legislation at least as much as legislators shape the process. Myriads will be involved—Senate and House members, staff, other lobbyists, the administration. Each plays their parts—some major, some minor—each affects the course. Nelson'll have vastly more information than we'll ever know. At most, I can try to guess what's influencing him, but that's all. The proposal's no longer just an idea I can perfectly design; with luck, it's moving toward legislation that will be imperfectly enacted."

The positive in David's ambivalence was some respite. His work became not easy but more focused. Rather than stretched across the whole Senate, it now centered on Senator Nelson and his office. This meant working with Shelly a lot. In regular contact before, they were in constant contact now. Of course, the proposal was not either's only work. But it was the biggest for David. He tried his best not to assume it was hers.

David's notes and insight gained from months of meetings were impressive, even to his perfectionist self. For Shelly, who could not imagine how he had been able to compile them, they were incredible. When they met to go over different offices' opinions on the proposal, she couldn't keep up with his flow of information. And had there been any doubt whether he was just glibly elaborating memories, his voluminous notes showed he was not. Once she had called in Senator Nelson to listen. The senator had dubbed the notes "David's psalms."

Despite anticipating being able to relinquish control, David found it agonizing at times. He begrudgingly tolerated it when working with those he respected, who offered something as Nelson and Shelly did. They were good and made him better too. In his own office, he felt that way only about Janice and a handful of others.

To compensate, as the Hill's accustomed fall cadence unfurled, David wrapped himself in it. There were now regular breaks to pace work slightly below his former sprint. These breaks overlaid Washington's attempt to change seasons—when summer hangs on tenaciously before abruptly conceding.

Over years of motorcycle rides, he had stored countless memories of things to do with "the right woman." Now, finally having her, he returned to them with Julia. He was surprised at how little most had changed from his memories.

The weekend before Halloween, David had saved his best for last: a trip to a "haunted forest" run at a local farm well beyond the suburbs—and the threat of lawsuits. Run only at night, costumed figures appeared in scenes or leaped out as you passed. The most frightening episode had been a solitary figure walking past them. So focused on it, they ignored the trees from which leaped a headless character that provoked hyperventilation from fright and laughter. Both asked how often the other had stopped time to regain composure. Neither believed the other's answer for a second.

When with Julia, time-stops were aberrations for David. Outside of work, where time-stops proved invaluable, he had largely abandoned them.

While David focused on being with Julia, she was focused on a birthday surprise for him. All he knew was that it would take the weekend, and she would be fully in charge—and that she was very excited. Her infectious excitement shifted David from ignoring to anticipating his birthday. It also prompted him to redouble his preparations for their Thanksgiving trip to Georgia.

With each passing confirmation that Julia was "the one," David increasingly prepared his parents. He called more regularly because he finally had something worth sharing. He mentioned her constantly, to the point "they" were one in conversation. Rarely was it "I." Usually it was "we." He even heard himself giving updates just on her.

It had been Daniel who had flatly informed him. "You're in love, Bro."

Tingling coursed through him at Daniel's recognition, and David asked, "Do Mom and Dad know?"

"Absolutely. They're just too afraid of saying anything and spooking you! Brother, everyone knows. We were just wondering if you did!"

"I do," David said, smiling back at the phone.

"Keep those words handy; you're gonna need them."

David knew that too.

CHAPTER THIRTY-SIX

Julia insisted on picking David up at the office on Friday. She had wanted him to leave early. Work prevented it. Their getaway, therefore, was not. Mired in traffic headed to the Bay Bridge, they slunk along to the mystery destination. Hours behind schedule, hunger, the long wait, and short tempers forced them into a random pizza place.

David wanted to joke, "You take me to the nicest places," but seeing Julia's face outside the car warned him away from that precipice. Instead, he tried to make it better. "You're trying too hard…"

"No, caring too much is my problem," she grumbled back.

Eating helped. But only a bit. Hours late, they limped into the town of St. Michaels, a place David had visited during one of his rides. The Eastern Shore was one of his favorite places: flat and far removed from Washington. In early November's deep darkness and drizzle, he barely recognized it.

He was surprised when they pulled into The Refuge, the town's signature destination. Everyone in Washington knew it; going there told everyone everything about whoever you were with. He understood Julia's frustration at their delay. David immediately felt guilty over the expense and sad that the experience had fallen short of undoubted expectation.

The Refuge and the room immediately equaled its reputation. With one exception: The front desk informed them that their room's fireplace was not working. Julia grimaced and hardened around her eyes. They were also stymied when attempting to salvage their night with a walk into town; increasing rain forced them back before they finished The Refuge's long drive. He tried a final rescue with dessert in the dining room—where Julia informed him that she had planned a romantic dinner.

Back in their room, David knew the expectation; nowhere was sex more the implicit subject than here. But the mood was anything but. David could tell Julia had stopped time repeatedly. Stopping time seamlessly required returning exactly to your mark—the place, and the pose, you had when you stopped it—to restart it. Without that, there was a discontinuity, as though a movie's film jumped several frames, the actors jerking through their scene. *She knows, but she's so clearly distracted she's ignoring it.*

They lay in bed, not having the sex so clearly anticipated. David wanted it to be right, more than right now. It needed to have the specialness that had eluded Julia's entire evening. As he tentatively reached for her hand and any hint of a change, his phone rang.

"You should get that. I'm sure it's work," Julia said, jerking her hand back.

"It can wait," he soothed.

"It has to be Shelly," Julia said, emphasizing her last word.

"No, it's alright."

"Get. It." Julia said icily.

David took it into the bathroom. Julia was right. Shelly's news was huge, worthy of a call well into the weekend.

"The senator believes he's close to convincing Senator Davis to join him on the proposal," Shelly gushed.

"That'd make it bipartisan," David responded, trying to bring his voice back to a whisper.

Davis, a woman senator from a swing state, was a political maverick, and she, much to her party leadership's consternation, was never a given on any vote. She went her own way—sometimes this kept her with them, sometimes it took her across the aisle, sometimes it put her on an island.

"I never considered approaching them," he admitted.

"Well, you will now," Shelly said, "because the two of them want you to walk them through the proposal."

David's mind locked on the possibility.

"Does Senator Nelson want Whitney's CEO to come in for the meeting?"

Shelly laughed. "Ah, no. Look, there's nothing to do now, but the news was too good to wait."

"You're right; I can't believe it."

Thanking her profusely, he hung up and put the phone down. *This elevates the proposal to still another level! A bipartisan proposal backed by these two heavyweights, that's headline news. They could immediately draw others with them.*

David desperately wanted to tell someone—everyone. His first instinct was to call Janice, but he knew that could be the last straw for Julia. And as much as he wanted to share it with Julia, he knew that would be even worse.

All he could do was to stop time and celebrate alone. Jumping and pumping his fists, he knocked his phone from the basin into the trash can, where it disappeared beneath a pile of tissues. Pushing them aside, David found two home pregnancy test strips.

Both negative.

When he returned to bed, he found Julia asleep. Or at least feigning it. He lay there in the dark, between frustration and elation.

David did not know how long he slept, if at all. He kept hoping Julia would wake up during the night in a different mood, and everything would be alright. She did not. When the sky finally faintly lightened, he dressed for a run, hoping to expend his energy and tire himself into sleep. The rain had stopped and left behind a washed landscape, now distinctly cooler. Immediately into a strong pace, he came to the end of The Refuge's drive. He turned west onto the main road, away from town. He enjoyed being alone with the world, hearing the satisfying crunch of the gravel beneath his feet and feeling himself cut through the cold. Deer looked up apprehensively, on guard in hunting season.

He did not stop time, hoping Julia would continue moving to a better morning. He also wanted to know how long he could run. Feeling like he could go on forever, he bounded off the ground. Usually on his runs, the ground hit back hard; now it lifted him. Finished, he was amazed at having been gone just over an hour—twice his usual time and surely well over twice his usual distance.

The sun edged above the trees as he walked toward its rising and then up the drive. Save for concern for Julia, he had never felt better.

As he approached the room, David grew cautiously deliberate. He opened the door as slowly and quietly as he could. Julia was no early riser, and he wanted to leave her that way this morning. Today had to be different. He would make it so.

David was relieved to find her still in bed as he crept in. Her back to him, facing his empty spot in the bed, he did not notice immediately. Her side rose and fell too quickly. Springing to the bed's other side, he found Julia sobbing silently. David did not know if she had heard him come in at all. Kneeling, he leaned into her.

"Julia, honey, what's wrong?"

"I am. Everything is!" she choked out, not opening her eyes.

Putting his left hand on her shoulder, his right brushed her hair from her face, he whispered, "No, you're not, and no, it's not."

"It is! This was supposed to be our weekend away together, but we've never been more apart. Last night was horrible, and this morning you're gone and…"

"What can I do? Let me make it better," he pleaded. "We still have the whole weekend. Together."

"Just the three of us! You and Shelly. And me."

Suddenly, it hit him. "Oh no, baby, baby, you don't think…" He couldn't finish the thought, let alone the sentence.

"What else can I think? You talk about her all the time. You rave about her, how you love working with her…"

"Working with her. I enjoy working with her. I like her. I love *you*. You, you, you. No one else and never like this before."

He draped himself over her. For the first time since meeting yesterday, he saw a hint of happiness. Pressing reassurance, he cradled her. As he comforted her, he blamed himself—for working too much, for ignoring her, for being so blind to where these could lead Julia's thoughts.

"David, I'm sorry. I'm just not myself. I don't feel right sometimes. I've never been this moody, and, when it starts, I can't seem to control it," she said as she sniffed, and her hand dabbed her eyes.

"You can't control stopping time?"

"Worse, I can't control me," she responded. She took the tissue he offered. "My moods sometimes. I try and try. I even stop time; I'll think I have them under control, and then they flare up again."

"Tell me. How can I help? Just tell me. I just want you, no one else. Tell me what you need and when you need it; I'll do all I can to give it to you."

"I just need you. I just need us," Julia said, leaning into a kiss. It was their weekend's first real one. Together, touch spoke more eloquently than words could have. Finally, the dam burst into exquisite release. Refusing to relinquish their recovery, they extended it well into the morning.

When they finally left their room, their weekend had been reborn. As much as everything had been foreclosed yesterday, today all things were wide open.

They arrived so late for breakfast that they had to grovel for it. Suppressing laughter at what they knew everyone was thinking, they traded the whispered accusation, "It's your fault."

Recalling what had transpired before, and determined not to lose their day in their room, they chose the more innocent and public option of the town.

A strong sun made everything stand out starkly—as if more finely focused—beneath a sky so blue it seemed on the verge of cracking like ice. Their walk turned into hours of exploring, but more importantly, unconsciously recovering. They then drove west on the road David had run that morning, not stopping until it ended at the water. Their heads touching and hands intertwined, they watched the sun fully set.

Watching its descent brought his mind back to how he had watched its rising this morning. And all that had unfolded between the two, encountering her as he never had. Looking at the sun's slide, he was thinking of hers this morning. "It happens every day, and we know it does, but how often do we actually see it?"

"I don't know that I've watched it, completely watched it disappear, more than a handful of times in my life," she sighed in reply.

"The simple things we take for granted, that they'll always happen as they should."

"It goes so fast when you actually watch it. It's there; then it's gone," she said with a voice whose distance belied their proximity.

David squeezed her hand tightly. Julia lifted both to her lips and kissed his.

Finally having the romantic supper last night had denied, their exuberance led them to Easton for dessert—for no other reason than extending the night.

The next morning was David's birthday. Julia had told him the previous night not to go for a run before she gave him his presents. When he woke, several packages showed she had stopped time to set them out.

The highlight was an expensive sweater that he would never have splurged to buy. As soon as he opened it, she swore, "I don't mind if you return it."

"I wouldn't for the world," he said and grinned. "Even if it makes the rest of my wardrobe look shabby."

"Do you mind if I buy you clothes?"

"Women should always buy clothes for men, and men should never buy clothes for women."

"Why such a one-way street?"

"We can't dress ourselves; how can we presume to dress you?"

Laughing, she insisted he try it on. After she pronounced him "handsome," David thought his gifts were done, but Julia made him sit down.

She brought out a large, flat package. Silently guessing a picture, his first rip of its wrapping confirmed it. However, he halted as he realized what the subject was. Staring out of the shredded wrapping paper was a stunning rendering in pen and ink of Sailor from the Navy Memorial. Julia sat quietly, her hand over her mouth, trying to suppress any expression.

"Did you? Is this yours?" David stammered.

Julia, still silent, nodded in affirmation. David could not take his eyes off it; as he stared, a deeper recognition came.

"The face…it's…is it…me?"

Julia nodded more strenuously. Now tears came to David's eyes. So profoundly touched, he joined Julia in speechlessness.

Julia managed to force out the words in a choked voice, "He *is* you, David. Your face set to the world. Unencumbered, facing it alone, wherever the tides and fate take you."

"No," David said, his voice thick with emotion. "Now I do it with you."

Each closed upon the other.

"It is the second-best gift I've ever received."

Julia pulled back.

"You're the best," he said.

When they finally left The Refuge, they stopped to see Easton in the daylight. For good measure, they took the Oxford ferry on a whim, simply for the experience, despite it adding miles to their return. David did not want to break the spell they had cast on the day. Or on life.

CHAPTER THIRTY-SEVEN

Monday, David could barely wait for Janice's arrival to tell her the news that had nearly ruined his weekend. Janice stifled a yell when she heard. Then she muffled a laugh when David gave her Shelly's reaction to whether their CEO should return for the meeting.

"Did you tell anyone else yet?"

"No, you're the first."

"Then don't; it'll just be our little secret."

He cocked his head. "No one?"

"No one," she hissed through pursed lips.

"Not even Phil?"

"Especially not Phil. We'll tell folks after the fact. If there's one thing I've learned: It's better to ask forgiveness than permission."

Not having to bring anyone up to speed, the meeting preparation took about the same time as the meeting itself a few days later. David handled the proposal, Janice the politics. Senator Davis was a quick study and asked probing questions, to which David apparently gave the right answers. She seemed enthusiastic, which fed Senator Nelson's enthusiasm. And David's.

Davis's support stemmed from the prospect of a company building a major facility to produce electric vehicle batteries. David did not understand that industry or that of the vehicles they would power, but he understood that the tax change would be as favorable to their advanced research and engineering as it would be to Whitney's. His assurance of that, coupled with the fact that the battery and vehicle industries were not asking for this yet, Davis hoped would give her state a leg up on others if she championed the proposal.

David also knew his and Janice's impressions of the meeting meant nothing. Only two opinions mattered. Shelly would relay them. That she did so in less than twenty-four hours was all the evidence David and Janice needed that, although still not public, the proposal was now at a top level. As for how it could cross the finish line, they knew better than to offer suggestions to the experts now shepherding it. Janice summed it up: "It's in God's hands up there and in good hands down here. All we do is what they tell us."

A couple of days later, Janice confided to David that she had told Phil. Through pursed lips, she pushed out a confession. "I felt so damn guilty. I didn't want to tell him; instead, I just let it come out. But I was afraid it somehow might come out, making it even more awkward later." Striking her thigh, "And I don't want him to feel marginalized."

David immediately regretted it as much as Janice had. As she lamented, "No good deed goes unpunished," she adamantly opposed Phil's suggestion to tell Corporate about a Nelson-Davis alliance over the proposal. Janice voiced the Hill's wisdom, "Rumors only hurt, never help. The only real news that follows a rumor is that it was wrong."

They would let it lie quietly and let the senators make the news. That would be both sweeter and safer.

The timbre of November changed entirely. The proposal was way ahead of their initial hopes. Its opportunity could come as early as the big legislative push between Thanksgiving and Christmas, when Congress concluded its year-end business.

The proposal's potentially higher profile made his work significantly harder. As his work and worry load increased, David diverted what little attention he could spare to Thanksgiving. He wanted Julia's visit to his family to be perfect, and he struggled to plan it as meticulously as his pursuit of the proposal.

By sequentially stopping time on the Tuesday night before leaving, they got on the road well before sunrise and past the infamous Fredericksburg bottleneck by dawn. They pushed so hard that they were nearly to the North Carolina line before they ate.

The drive home to Dahlonega—David had spent the drive's first few minutes tutoring her on how to say his town's name—seemed the best he had ever had. It was not the fastest; he had often covered the distance alone with remorseless efficiency. Yet this one felt faster because they talked throughout—about their families, their memories, their homes, and how much they loved the start of Christmas that followed in Thanksgiving's wake. When they stopped for a lunch of comfort food at a Cracker Barrel, they picked out a Christmas CD for the ride back. Both equally determined to "give the bird its due and its day," they would only play it coming back on Saturday.

CHAPTER THIRTY-EIGHT

Pulling into his parents' driveway, David was more anxious than nervous. He knew his parents, but what he had not fully appreciated was how important it was to him that the people he loved like each other. They hadn't even left the driveway before his parents began fussing over her so much that finally, in mock exasperation, he held out his arms and declared, "Look who happened to come with her!"

"Oh hush, we see you all the time!" his mother responded with a mock scold.

Only his reminder that they had driven a long way and were tired got them into the house. Even then, his father had joked, "You go right on up to your room, you know where it is. We'll just keep talking to Julia."

As David and Julia parted for the night, she said, "David, they're lovely. I adore them. How am I doing?"

"Better than I am! I could leave, and I don't think they'd notice unless I took you."

"Shut up!" Grabbing his hands and swinging them chest-high, she leaned on them and toward him. "Really, do they like me?"

"No. They love you. And so do I."

Before everyone woke the next morning, David stopped time for a run. He went through a stillness that would have been there, even had he not ensured it. He was grateful that here, in its deeper eddies, time stood still on its own. Regardless of where else he might live, this would always be home.

David restarted time as he came in. A moment later, he heard a door open. Julia emerged, whispering in code, "Did you?"

"Yes. I thought you were asleep when I looked in."

"I was probably just lying there. It would be hard to tell the difference when I'm in your interlude. I'm sorry I missed your run; I would've gone too."

"What? I didn't know..."

Julia pretended to pout. "David Preston, I can run. It's just not my preference, but I'd like to see your haunts."

"I'll walk you out, show you a route, then you stop time. I'll be right where you left me."

Gone and back in a moment, they walked to cool down. As they did, David went through his memories as though dealing cards off a deck. They came up the drive hand in hand, and David's father greeted them, giving David a look that said everything.

Thanksgiving at his parents' house was the usual chaos. David had warned Julia, "It'll be Grand Central Station with turkey instead of trains." It was. Assorted members of David's extended family began arriving just after noon, capped by Daniel and his family. Even relatives David did not see except at holidays knew about Julia.

Clearly, Mom's been actively handling the advance for Julia's debut.

Julia navigated them all—if not perfectly, at least better than David. She embarrassingly confessed, "I just called Aunt Clara, Aunt Sara."

"They're twins. Daniel and I've done it so often that we now only use their names when they're together, so we can't screw it up."

Julia responded with a jab, hissing, "Thanks for telling me after the fact." Her coup had come in winning over his sister-in-law—something David felt he had never accomplished—by "quickly" sketching David's nephew and niece.

He knew she had captivated his parents, but his biggest surprise was how much it had meant when Daniel had pulled him aside—even if he had closed with, "Don't screw this up."

With their Friday morning unplanned, David's mother offered, "You should take her panning for gold."

"What?" was Julia's all-too-interested response; "You gotta be kidding" was David's.

His mother, talking to Julia as if David were neither there nor had spoken, replied, "Sure, everybody who comes to Dahlonega goes to do it."

Trying to insert himself into their conversation and between Julia and this bad idea, David countered, "It's a tourist trap. Besides, y'all never even took me."

His father, who had been glancing at the paper, joined in. "We didn't take you because we knew every year your elementary school class would take you."

"But—" David tried to protest.

"Did you ever find any gold?" his mother asked.

"No."

"That's why we didn't take you," his mother concluded. "If you'd found gold, your father would have dropped you and Daniel off every day during the summer."

David was ultimately saved by Julia's insistence that they tour his past. Besides his town, they visited Emory, where he had gone to college. He even showed her his old fraternity house—and he was internally relieved it was locked for the break.

That afternoon, his parents met them in Midtown at Margaret Mitchell's house, where she had written *Gone with the Wind*. Of course, Julia knew the book, but she became enthralled by the stories behind it. By evening, David was completely comfortable. His mother and Julia particularly seemed to hit it off, so much so that they chased him back to his father and a football game that neither was really watching.

Attempting to explain his regret at leaving the next morning, his father stopped him. "We understand, understand more than you know. We're just so happy for you and so grateful you shared your happiness with us. Do you remember our conversation last year?"

David felt his blush at the memory. "About me being obsessed with perfection?"

"Yes."

"I've been trying."

"I think you've done better than try this time."

The next morning, David repeated yesterday's start, but this time they ran together in real time. When they returned, David's parents were making breakfast.

All too quickly, it and the visit ended. And all the ways he now could think to extend their stay fell away. A bittersweetness began welling up within him. To counter it, he hid in conversation about his upcoming Christmas visit, focusing on a promised future rather than the quickly impending past. He and his father could barely speak. As David held the door for Julia, his mother ran back into the house.

She returned with a wrapped package for Julia. "I won't see you at Christmas, so I wanted to give you this now. You shouldn't wait to open it, though."

Now Julia's eyes welled up as the four silently shifted, unable to speak despite wanting to, yet without needing to. David finally broke the silence, saying they had better get on the road. After closing Julia's door, he wordlessly kissed both his parents; they could only wave and smile as the car pulled away.

As David drove, Julia leaned over, kissed his cheek, and pressed his hand.

David, only holding himself together by distraction, deflected the moment. "You should open your present." It was a biography of Margaret Mitchell. Julia gushed over it as she flipped through; David was struck by when and how his mother had found time to get it.

The drive back was quieter. Julia, subdued, contemplative, turned several times to her new book. They played the Christmas CD they had saved—listening, commenting, singing to their favorites. They had much to talk about, but more to think about.

Julia, interrupting a prolonged stare through the scenery and into her own thoughts, said, without turning her distant gaze, "Home is more than a place; it's a past. A past so richly woven into you that it stays forever the present. It never leaves you, and you never can leave it. Yours is like one of my interludes. Is that how time-stops seem to you? Is that how they feel?"

"I never linked the two that way." David faintly laughed and said, "I remember using mine to escape home."

She turned to look at him and asked, "Why?"

"It's not what you think," he responded as he stared ahead into his steering. "I love my family, and I loved home. It was just part of the natural breaking away, a breaking away that came so easily for me—partly from 'it,' partly from not following a path they understood like they did Daniel's."

Squeezing his hand hard, Julia leaned toward David. Even with his eyes on the road, he could feel hers intently on him. "Thank you for bringing me."

"Thank you for coming and making this all I had hoped. I pray my visit to Lexington will be half as successful."

CHAPTER THIRTY-NINE

For David, Thanksgiving had not been a time-stop but a time surge. Within twenty-four hours, he shifted from Thanksgiving's hiatus into Christmas's frenetic frenzy. Each day was as precious as they were finite. David threw himself into two things: Placing his proposal and preparing for a proposal. He immovably anchored one foot in his professional world, one in his personal.

In his professional life, he braced for his proposal becoming public and the attention this would attract. Already, Senator Davis had begun showing it to the electric battery companies she hoped to lure to her state. This created still more work for David. He had to lead new people through the proposal, working to ensure their concerns were addressed without Whitney's being harmed.

Senator Nelson confided to Shelly and David, "We're aiming to place this into the year-end tax bill that's needed to extend provisions expiring on 1/1."

In Hill parlance, such "extender legislation" was "must-pass," an ideal means—"a vehicle"—for other legislation. From experience, David knew the drill. Things would change at a moment's notice, defeat and victory would alternate between imminent, then impossible; any outcome would occur in a last-minute whirlwind, requiring absolute focus and patience.

In his personal life, he was equally preparing for what he felt was now destined. Daniel, in a phone call the Sunday after Thanksgiving, had impressed it in his straightforward, laconic fashion, right out of the old *Dragnet* reruns their dad had loved to watch.

"She loves you."

"I know." David stood up and began to pace under the interrogation.

"You clearly love her."

"Yes."

"So, when are you going to propose?"

"I've only begun thinking about it."

"What? You don't believe she's only 'begun thinking about it,' do you?"

"I hadn't thought that far ahead…I still wonder if I'm ready. If we're ready. I mean things are so great right now…"

"Look, it's simple. There's only one real question: Do you ever want to be married?"

David stopped. "Yes."

"Then who do you expect to find better? If you say to yourself that you don't want to marry *her*, then what you're really saying is that you don't want to be married."

David paused for a long time at Daniel's blunt truth.

The question's not about "who." It's really about "if." If not Julia, who? If not now, when?

Put so starkly, it cleared the clutter. He could not imagine going on without her, and he could certainly never imagine breaking up with her.

Once he saw it in Daniel's terms, he understood. And once he understood, he embraced. During the week, he began asking Frank and Jeff for advice; on weekends, he began visiting jewelry stores. Besides preparing to propose, he also resolved that it would not be over Christmas. There was too much work to allow him to give it the attention he wanted, plus he would just have met her parents for the first time on his visit after Christmas. Instead, he aimed for her birthday in April—just a week before he had first met her.

During the week, David was almost never in his office. Whitney's deteriorating finances made it miserable, and there was nothing he could do about it there. He spent as much time as he could on the Hill. Following Janice's advice, he sought to be "around without being omnipresent." This was an art not easily managed. As a lobbyist, he had no office there, no single place to be. He tried mimicking administration lobbyists he had known from his time on the Hill. He had watched them rotate through a series of key places, never haunting one too long. Always moving along his circuit, he looked for opportunities to apparently bump casually into staff and perhaps senators or to just watch and interpret comings and goings.

The problem with the proposal going public was that it brought the public in—into every aspect of its possible passage, but, most importantly, to its heart: the legislative language itself. These interlopers were not only those new to the proposal, like the electric battery companies, but also companies from his own industry. Earlier, they had casually signed off, viewing it as just one of many conceived, but never realized, ideas. Now, not just possible but plausible, predators started to circle.

These were his industry's lobbyists. Probing for ways to gain more than an advantage for their industry, they sought a competitive advantage within it. His most dreaded was also his least liked. Sandi Shearson was his polar opposite and disproved the adage that opposites attract. She worked for his company's closest competitor, Consolidated Aeronautics, and did so in a style diametric to David's. A relationship lobbyist, she relied on knowing people, not policy. Sandi traded on a seemingly infinite number of contacts that she continuously and blatantly networked to augment.

Phil liked her, and they got along well. This made sense on both sides. For Sandi, he was just another link in her network's chains, plus Phil was higher in the office hierarchy. Sandi always zeroed in on the biggest target available—usually House and Senate members—but always the biggest. For Phil, Sandi was a shameless flirt who dressed the part. Her clothes were always too tight, her skirts and heels too high, her breasts overexposed, her makeup heavy, and her fragrance heavier still.

Sandi flatters Phil's ego, but, even more, she's his unacknowledged role model. Phil's never going to master the substantive aspects of Washington, but knowing a lot of people—that's something he can grasp, and the one thing he could aspire to.

Actually, this worked to David's satisfaction. Phil and Sandi getting along spared David from getting phone calls from her. David thought she was a snake. Neither trusting nor liking her, he wanted nothing to do with her—especially now when he suspected she would be working every channel to tilt the language toward her company and away from his.

What little time he could carve from this, David spent with Julia. He did so by stopping it continuously at work and then letting it flow with Julia. No season matched Christmas for him, and he wanted to recreate every wonderful memory with her. Before he could, he had to get through the Christmas parties.

As he explained to Julia, "In Washington, these take place as far from Christmas as possible and have even less to do with it. The first occurs because most in Washington are from somewhere else and leave town for their Christmas; so, if you want them, you have to get them before they go. The second is true because Washington Christmas parties are about repaying social or professional debts; rather than celebratory, they are obligatory." He summed it up, "Guilt is the perfect Christmas gift; it goes with everything and lasts forever."

David only went to the ones he had to, most importantly for work, his office party. Fortunately, it coincided with the one he wanted to do: Julia's office party. Because he had little contact with her office, they went to hers first.

He was pleasantly surprised. Their difference from government people made them far more interesting, while they seemed to find him more entertaining than he thought himself to be. Best of all was their perspective on Julia. As Ross, their managing partner, said, "We love her, we're impressed by her; our only surprise is that we've been able to keep her."

When David asked Julia about this later, she said with a shrug, "The work I get to do is interesting. I work for the work more than the money. I could make more in a bigger firm or in another city, but I wouldn't be doing what I like. They let me, so I stay."

Amazing. In government, people constantly struggle with that choice. Eventually, money always won. But she's got no conflict at all! There's no question, just an answer. And for her, an easy one.

Having started and stayed at hers, they arrived late to his. As always, it was at Janice's, with the full cast—Frank and Jeff and their wives, Phil without his, Denise without a date, Stacey with another new one—plus government people. He had described them all in detail to Julia, who mostly concurred with his assessments. However, she surprised him with two.

She said summarily, "Phil's a letch."

"What? How can you tell?"

"You can't stand him, so you don't even look at him, except in passing. I don't care; so, I watched his eyes. Let's just say they stray, and stay, where they shouldn't be."

Julia's other insight: "Janice really respects you."

Embarrassed, David deflected with a chuckle. "How can you tell that from a party?"

"The way she looks at you. It's the same way your mother does. There's a pride in her gaze, an affection. It's sweet, and it's real."

With their mandatory holiday tasks done, they could focus on what they wanted to do. They shared many of their experiences, despite having done them separately before. First, they bought a tree for Julia's house, because as she observed, "A tree in your condo would die of loneliness."

"The tree is already dead, and dogs don't have a good reputation with trees," David said flatly.

Julia ignored him, and the tree went up at Julia's.

On David's free weekends, they shopped in Occoquan and Old Town. Usually, David hated shopping but grudgingly enjoyed it with Julia, whose insights on gifts were far better than his. Then they split up to shop for each other. This, David truly enjoyed.

When they had time for nothing else, they drove around Alexandria to look at lights—critiquing, but ultimately enjoying, every effort. And they went to Julia's church, an addition David readily welcomed. It felt right, really right, for the first time with her.

David pulled off his most pressing need with help from Frank and Jeff.

"I want my first great New Year's Eve. I used to take someone and hope the evening would somehow transform her. Now, I'm starting with a transformative person. New Year's never worked before. Now it has to. How?"

Frank and Jeff tossed out options until Jeff snapped his fingers at his insight. "Ardmore! It's a resort in western Pennsylvania."

"Hey, that's not bad," Frank seconded.

Jeff tilted his head and copped a fake smile. "I get the occasional good idea—after all, I'm not as long removed from romance as you are."

"Hey, I know that place. I once went to a fundraiser there," David replied. "It's ideal! It's also on the way back from Julia's parents and close to two famous Frank Lloyd Wright houses."

Jeff smirked back at Frank, who muttered, "Even a blind squirrel finds the occasional nut."

David ignored them both.

The end of the year on Capitol Hill whirled down to its usual blur. A centrifugal force seized the participants, hurling out everything that was not work. David expected it and warned Julia, but neither expectation nor warning cushioned it. Festivities ended, and David just worked.

Rarely was he in the office when others were or getting home when Julia was awake. As they approached her departure, they sequentially stopped time in the middle of the final night to get some time together before she drove home. Even so, it was far from them at their best. Her disappointment fueled his, and both approached their breaking points when she left at the outlandish hour of four in the morning.

He walked Julia to the car while she carried Brandon. He watched her somehow buckle him into the passenger's seat. As she closed the door behind her, David put his arm over her shoulder. Each leaned into the other as they walked around the car; David hoped touch could make up for their parting.

After what he thought was their last kiss, Julia pulled him back for a harder one. Remaining in his embrace, she leaned her head back. "David, I'm worried about you." He tried to smile away her concern to no avail. "Seriously. You're taking this too hard. Too far."

Both from reflex and admission, David felt his smile fall. "I intend to finish this. I can't stop; I don't know how."

David stood, seeing his breath hang in the cold morning air as he watched her drive away.

Alone, David plunged into the final push. But though he pushed—himself to the breaking point and every button he could imagine—the process fizzled. No tax bill came together. There were many reasons: Senators were tired and leaving town, this senator asked for too much, that senator would not agree, this bloc opposed that bloc. He knew and related them all to Janice, the last person with whom he was having regular conversations.

Besides Shelly, Janice alone understood. Phil did not. His overpromising had done just what David had sought to avoid: raise expectations at Corporate to unrealistic heights. Phil was now in so deep on the proposal with Corporate that he kept telling David, "Failure is not an option!" David privately scoffed at this absurdity. "Unless you're God, failure's always an option."

Now there was nothing to show for Phil's overpromising and everything to explain. To those who knew, there was nothing unusual. The Senate would simply start again from where it had stopped. But to Corporate, undelivered promises were beyond unusual—especially now—they were existential. Phil had not put just himself, but all of them, in a yawning hole. Now sucking the life out of the proposal David still loved for itself, he was making David's life a misery. And David a wreck.

Phil called or texted for continuous updates on the Senate's lack of progress. Corporate held an increasing number of conference meetings on its cratering finances. Janice was required to conduct brainstorming sessions with the office for some government-based solution—each progressively more far-fetched. David heard from the tax team that the same was happening throughout Whitney. But the result remained unchanged and became ever clearer, ever closer: There was David's proposal or bankruptcy or bailout.

David arrived home on the last flight out on December 23; it was the only reservation he had felt safe making, but there was small solace in having been right. He feigned physical exhaustion; with his schedule, everyone expected it, and he could never explain how he had avoided it.

His real exhaustion was mental. Christmas was more stay of execution than reprieve. Nothing was over; everything still hung over him and was far beyond his pay grade to solve. All he could do was worry. Despite attempting to project calmness to Janice, Phil, and Julia, he endured the stress internally with only momentary respites. He did his best to attribute any manifestation—a nervous tic, weight loss, and growing circles under his eyes—to anxiousness over meeting Julia's family. Only Daniel sensed there was more.

David felt semi-honest in his diversionary explanation because there was no little anxiety there too. He returned to his old escape. He needed it just to sleep some nights, and some nights, despite his induced infinity, it still took forever. Normally, he slept best when sensation ceased—none of his five senses registering. But pressure added a sixth that even stopping time had limited effect in evading. Still, he time-stopped to separate from whatever had renewed his cycle of worries: sometimes just physically moving—often a walk, even if just to another room. Occasionally, he would sit with the silent tableau around him to simply breathe.

When he spoke to Julia, she was particularly relieved he was using his ability and urged him to do it more often. Their conversations helped more than anything. Even though she did not understand his work, she understood him. She got him through the four days at home so that by the end, he was somewhat better than when he had arrived.

David knew his parents silently wondered whether he was going to propose when they dropped him off at the airport. Of course, they had said nothing, fearing, in Daniel's words, that "they would spook him out of it."

If they're thinking it, I can only imagine what Julia and her family might be thinking.

CHAPTER FORTY

As he flew, he rehearsed what he would say when he saw her. Having undergone their longest separation, he wanted a worthy reunion. The small plane descended into a very different landscape from Georgia's. Unlike Dahlonega's Blue Ridge foothills, Lexington's landscape rolled. If the grass was indeed blue, he couldn't tell beneath its dusting of snow. Watching, he polished the soliloquy he planned to use to sweep her off her feet.

All was forgotten at his first sight of her. While he had been concerned about finding her, she had laughed and said, "This isn't Atlanta, honey!" Indeed, it wasn't. The whole airport was no larger than a few gates at Hartsfield. When he got past the small security barrier, only a handful of people scanned the arriving trickle. He saw her instantly; he instinctively stopped time.

Frozen in first recognition, her arm rising in a wave, her feet extending to tiptoe, her face flashing joy. In that moment, David knew he would have found her among a million people, just as she had found him on a crowded subway.

Forgetting his practiced eloquence, forgetting himself, forgetting everything but seeing her there, there for him, he ran. Only at the last moment did her unmoving countenance remind him to restart time. Their distance had closed in a flash, startling her; he did so again by lifting her off the ground and into his arms.

"Have I told you I love you?"

"Never," she said with a faux nonchalance.

"I love you."

"Do you really?"

David kissed her to make up for all the ones they had missed. And in it, time neither moved nor stopped, if it existed at all.

"I believe you."

Looking at herself in his arms, she said, "I believe I was supposed to pick *you* up!"

"You did. More than you know."

The drive to her parents' house felt like the resumption of a conversation that had been but momentarily interrupted. David had always noticed that the closer people are, the quicker their relationship resumes; with Julia, he felt theirs started again, right as it had been, as if he had stopped and restarted time.

When they arrived, he was caught up on everything but could have continued their talk and the drive all the way to Virginia. Set far back from the road, down a long, tree-lined gravel drive that circled across its front, was an elegant two-story brick house that looked more than a century old. A small fountain sprayed water serenely in the middle of the drive. David could imagine a Model T or a horse carriage having once pulled up there. That Julia lived in a place she would have enjoyed sketching did not surprise him.

As they stepped out, Julia's father greeted them. He carried himself with an easy casualness that immediately resonated with David. Waiting at the door, Julia's mother exuded formality. David mentally labeled her mother Julia's exterior, her father Julia's interior.

Although David and Julia had agreed to exchange presents once they left, Julia's parents had made no such agreement. David dutifully exchanged small gifts with them and was grateful his mother had insisted on him bringing her fudge. The first question out of any Southern parents' mouth was whether you were hungry. Neither David's nor Julia's parents were exceptions to that rule. But though he was, David was not about to start their impression of him being behind a plate alone. Not until her father broke the ice to say he was hungry did David admit to it too.

Julia's parents were about a decade older than his. He had not considered the effect this would have on him. There was no way he could call them "Bob and Delia"; they would be "Mr. and Mrs." unless he could artfully avoid addressing them by name. Her father was only slightly taller than her mother, both of medium height and build; gray generously appeared through their hair. Even though her mother had Julia's blue eyes, her father's eyes were the closer match, laughing and lighting up just like Julia's.

Delia clearly had been a beauty. But now, she tried too hard to retain its remnants when age's natural weathering would have been more flattering. He was reminded of Jeff's line, "The older the house, the more the paint." Again, it was her father who seemed Julia's closer match through his relaxed acceptance of time's forward march. David deliberately worked to evenly balance his attention between the two despite his inclination.

As they toured the house, he was struck by its ordered precision and stylish correctness—even down to the Christmas decorations. David deliberately complimented Julia's mother on it, but later whispered to Julia, "Does anyone live here?"

"You should see Lydia's place," she replied with a smirk.

He was drawn to the many beautiful, framed photographs throughout the house. They looked professional, and he was surprised to learn Julia's father had taken them. He deflected David's compliment. "I can only shoot what Julia can draw." This genuine pride emerged in his office, where he had hung drawings, sketches, and paintings that David immediately recognized as Julia's.

By the time they finished, the winter sky was bluing into dusk. He and Julia only had time for a stroll before all its color dispersed into black. When they returned, the Christmas lights had come on; he laughed internally. *They're all white.*

He stopped and turned to Julia, struck his most serious tone, and said, "I don't think this is going to work."

Taken aback, Julia asked, "What do you mean?"

Closing his eyes and tightening his lips, he sighed his confession. "I come from a colored-lights family."

In mock horror, Julia recoiled. "You don't!"

"Yep. Got inflatables too. Everything but the trailer."

Julia feigned a swoon into David's arms and gasped, "Don't tell Mother."

When her parents offered him a choice for supper, a steakhouse or the Red State BBQ, he looked quickly to Julia for guidance. Receiving none, he chose the BBQ, figuring they should know what lay in store for their daughter's future.

Her father clapped his hands. "Hot damn! Just saved me a hundred dollars!"

Her mother responded, "Oh, Bob!" in such a way that David, for the first time, saw the fun in both.

He went to sleep that night, imagining he was in a B&B and thinking how good it was to have Julia just across the hall. Throughout the day, he had answered and asked questions to which they and he already knew the answers. None of it was about information or even conversation; it was about intention. Everyone was obviously striving to make this time they had together great, most of all David.

The next morning, Julia showed him Lexington. Horses figured prominently. After visiting one estate, David overrode Julia's protests and got her to show him her past, not Lexington's.

Overcoming initial reluctance, she warmed to her tour of her former self. As her inhibitions fell, she volunteered more. He saw her schools, the family's church, places where she had just hung out. David's favorite was a small park Julia had often gone to for interludes after Cornell. She hadn't needed to tell him; he had seen it in her eyes and heard it in her voice's wistful tone.

The day's central focus took place back at the house. David knew meeting him was its purpose. He looked forward to seeing Cindy again, who was bringing her boyfriend, Ronnie—someone much discussed in Alexandria by the two sisters. Based on those conversations, he was a little apprehensive about meeting Lydia. They had left no doubt that Lydia was, as David's mother described, "the queen bee," and the queen was bringing her entire court—husband Robert and three children, Elizabeth, Carolyn, and Robert Jr.

Lydia and family arrived first, or as Lydia pronounced, "Cynthia is late…

again." The children were perfectly dressed, looking like they had tumbled forth straight from a catalog. An engineer, Robert was slim, nice-looking, and about ten years older than David. He welcomed David with a thin, reassuring smile. David had expected to have topics of conversation—after all, Daniel and his father were engineers, and David worked with engineers frequently at Whitney—but Robert was one of the quietest people he had ever met.

Lydia was formality personified. She closely resembled Julia physically, unlike Cindy, and was instantly recognizable as her sister. Yet despite being very attractive, she seemed unapproachable, exuding a meticulousness that approached severity. And while her eyes and Julia's were identical, Lydia's smile never reached them; Julia's always began there.

Twenty minutes later, Cindy and Ronnie came blowing in. Cindy was as effervescent as Lydia was restrained. David marveled at the sisters' differences; had he not been the object of inspection and needing to be on, he would have lost himself in watching them. Cindy, in her rush, kept her coat on and her hands in it; David became aware that only her left hand remained inside its pocket. Finally, Lydia said pointedly, "Are you planning to stay?"

Cindy distractedly asked her what she meant, and David realized Cindy had been subtly toying with Lydia, who responded exasperatedly, "If you are, you should take off your coat."

"Oh, silly me." As Cindy took off her coat, her left hand emerged with an enormous engagement ring. Julia squealed, then everyone converged on Cindy.

Although everyone outwardly focused on Cindy and Ronnie, David felt for sure that they were all inwardly focused on him. Lydia's immediate turn and comment, "No pressure," verified that feeling.

His night's best conversation was its most unexpected. Momentarily alone in the crowd, he felt a tug at the knee of his pants. Looking down in surprise, he saw four-year-old Robert Jr. looking up quizzically.

"Hello, there. What can I do for you?"

The boy's eyes widened. "Do you really ride motorcycles?"

"Well..." Disarmed by directness, David confessed to the four-year-old what he had never told his parents, "Yes, yes, I do."

"Is it *scary*?"

"Sometimes, but mostly it's just fun."

"How fast do you go?"

"The speed limit."

"What's the fastest you've gone?"

Under cross-examination, David smiled. "We won't talk about that."

"Have you ever crashed?"

"Yep."

"Did it *hurt*?"

Remembering, David nodded back. "Yep."

"Bad?"

"Yep."

"Did you *cry*?"

"Nope, but it hurt enough to," David confessed.

Their eyes locked across their one-foot separation, with Robert Jr.'s questions apparently exhausted. David knelt to the boy's height and offered, "Would you like to see a picture of my motorcycle?"

With a hearty "Yessir!" all formality vanished.

David's heart was squeezed by hearing the same answer his daddy had taught him. They sat on a couch, and David pulled out his phone and scrolled through pictures. His new friend told David he could call him "Bobby."

David was unaware of how long they had talked or what had made him look up, but when he did, he saw Robert smiling in the doorway with Julia beside him, her face with the same faraway look David had seen at the park that afternoon.

"It looks like you've made a friend," Julia said.

"I asked if I could ride with him!" Bobby interjected.

David assured Robert, "I made no commitments; I said he'd have to ask you first."

As Robert led a thoroughly animated Bobby away, David called out, "What do we always wear when we ride?"

"A helmet!"

“And why?”

“Because we want to keep our brains in our heads and off the road!”

“That’s right!” David laughed as Julia eased her arm around him and kissed his cheek. “You were wonderful just now.”

“I’d love to hear how the conversation on the ride home goes,” he said with a chuckle.

“Oh, you will,” Julia said, patting his hand for emphasis.

When David woke the next morning, another light snow had fallen; infrequent but usually a nuisance in Virginia, it was beautiful here. He slipped quietly out the front door, and out of time, for a run in it. He could return at the same time he had left and still have time for a walk with Julia.

Julia’s itinerary was Louisville for the day. Cindy worked and lived there, so they had quietly made plans for lunch. Their first stop was at the Louisville Slugger bat company because, as Julia explained, “Everyone needs to see how a bat’s made.” David, having never felt the necessity, didn’t argue.

He could not resist buying her one decked out with the Giants’ logo and colors as a Christmas present. Cindy immediately seized on this at lunch. “How romantic! I was hoping for something closer to a diamond—”

“Cindy, shut up!” Julia reprimanded.

Cindy laughed innocently. “Baseball diamond, Julia, baseball diamond!”

Then the two sisters were off. David jumped into their conversation where he could but had to be agile. And ready. When he asked why they had not asked Lydia, Cindy instantly replied, “Oh no, she might have accepted!”

Julia laughingly explained, “There’s a forty-eight-hour rule—”

“Seventy-two-hour,” Cindy immediately corrected.

“Seventy-two-hour rule,” Julia continued, “between visits with Lydia.”

The two went on for more than an hour, back and forth. To his surprise, both had already thought a great deal about many of the details for an event, the reality of which was less than a day old. Even without Cindy’s wedding to talk about, the two could have rambled indefinitely. They synced on a level David had never experienced, one he found himself now envying.

Only when Julia excused herself did David become more participant than audience.

"Sorry, we've gone on and on. I just love her so much. I know my engagement is a further signal that what we have is stretching further apart. There'll be another relationship between us."

"Another?"

"Of course," Cindy replied as though obvious. "There've been several. Her leaving for school. Me leaving for school. All degrees of separation. They keep adding up, taking us further from when we were always together. Now we grab it when we can; while I have it, I don't want to let go."

"I understand, even if I haven't experienced it. Except once, I guess."

"With your brother?"

"No," David scoffed, "with her."

"I know. You're another of my degrees of separation. I'm glad. Really. She loves you, David. Julia doesn't love easily, and she doesn't love lightly. No pressure…"

David felt a tingle. "You're the second sister to tell me that."

"But this one means it. Lydia was Mommy's girl; Julia was Daddy's. I got to be the tiebreaker; I chose Julia. But she always seemed able to slip away, off into herself. I just had to wait for her to come back from wherever it was. Since she met you, she's…different. No, that's not right. She's like she used to be at home."

David tried not to let his curiosity betray him. "Did she used to slip away…a lot?"

"Not before college. But the year she came back—"

Just then, Julia returned, and Cindy had to leave. As much as David loved his time with Julia, he was sadder that his with Cindy had to end. He sensed there were so many things only she could and would tell him.

They wandered away the rest of the day around Frankfort Avenue. They visited a historic house; its name David immediately forgot, but he loved listening to her describe the building. They went into places on whims or when the cold became too much. Soon, they were late and hurrying back to Lexington for a fancy last supper with her folks.

By the evening's end, David had absorbed so much that on his next morning's run, he was still going over yesterday's events. He had arrived ready to leave; now he found himself regretting having to. He had seen so much into Julia that could only be viewed from here.

His goodbyes were easier than Dahlonega's had been: a solid handshake with her father, a semi-embrace and an air-kiss from her mother. She drove the first leg, but after crossing into West Virginia, David took the wheel to take them to his New Year's surprise. When he pulled them into the swanky resort in Pennsylvania's mountains, both were dazzled. Wreaths hung on the entrance columns and carved wooden doors. In the fading afternoon, the resort's snow-covered grounds sparkled under the reflected twinkling of strands of Christmas lights that seemed to stretch into infinity.

"White ones," Julia pointed out.

She gushed over the resort at supper as they planned their stay. In addition to its winter activities, nearby were Frank Lloyd Wright's Fallingwater and Kentuck Knob, and closer still, Ohiopyle. But first, they had Christmas gifts to exchange.

She gave him a leather jacket. Not like the stiff, heavy one he wore on rides for safety but an extremely elegant one to be seen in. She also gave him a pair of cowboy boots. On one of their Christmas shopping excursions, he had seen a window full of them. They had talked, but he dismissed them as impractical. "The top of the left toe always wears through under the motorcycle's gear shift." This, of course, made them her preferred gift—something desired but unobtained.

Julia fidgeted excitedly as David opened his gift. "Just because your horse is steel, doesn't make you any less of a cowboy. Do you like them? You can always exchange them if you don't."

"I love them. You know my rule: Women should always give clothes to men."

"Yes, 'because men can't dress themselves.' What should men give women?"

"This." David held out a small package, but heeding Daniel's advice, not so small as to be mistaken for a ring. In it was a gold pendant on a golden chain. A figure of a woman drawing graced the front of the pendant. He had also found his present during their Christmas shopping together, and he had hustled Julia out of the store before she saw it. When he returned alone, he had them set small sapphires around the woman's head; his hope had been that these would catch Julia's eyes. They did.

She was speechless for several seconds, then looked up misty-eyed. David fastened the necklace around her slim neck. She let her hair fall back around her shoulders, and David looked from the pendant's sapphires into her blue eyes, unable to distinguish between them. He pulled her close, and their two bodies soon dissolved into one. Only the necklace remained between them as they slept.

The next morning, David gave the last of his gifts, Ayn Rand's *The Fountainhead.* Forgotten in the prior night's passion, it was better saved for today; David had managed to reserve them a tour of Fallingwater that morning. From having stopped time to scour her collection, David knew Julia did not own the book; it was the only one about architects he knew. He hoped its novelty would offset Julia having visited Fallingwater several times.

As much of an impact as Wright's masterpiece had made during his only trip years ago, he hoped it was still a pilgrimage for her. Its power remained undiminished by time or repetition for both of them. Each stopped time repeatedly, signaling their returns and that the other could depart.

In the afternoon, they returned for cross-country skiing. Neither was terribly good, but the setting, and doing it together, masked that. Finally, they donned their new finery for their New Year's Eve supper in the resort's best restaurant. After, they strolled through the property, cutting it short when Julia said she was tired. She offered to stop time to recover so they could share the beginning of the new year, but David refused. "There's nothing in a clock striking twelve." Unlike past years, he was neither lonely nor apprehensive; he was eager, knowing what he intended it to hold. For them.

Awakening early, shared soreness lowered their ambitions. They chose a quiet day hiking at Ohiopyle, just below Fallingwater. Recounting his first visit, he pointed north on the town's only road. "Long ago, I ended a ride on that crest there, staring at this road winding down into what looked like a model train set. I couldn't bring myself to leave."

"What did you do?"

"I went to this store, over there. In the window was a sign that read simply 'Rooms.' I went in, and there was an orange cat on the counter. Felt like I was meant to stay. So, I did."

Julia pulled his arm. "Then we've got to eat there now."

As they left, she asked him, "How's it compare to the memory?"

He stopped and looked at her. His heart, more than his lips, answered, "You complete it." As they kissed, David let his admission ripple through him. The old year had ended better than any David had known; now the new one had begun the same way.

As they physically separated, he knew he could not truly separate from her. Ever. Feeling the almost unbearable weight of honesty, he grinned. "Oh, and the cat's different."

Before they left for home the next day, they toured Kentuck Knob. It wasn't Fallingwater. Nothing could be. But that heightened its charm for him. Its reduced pressure for greatness seemed to accentuate it all the more. Again, they stopped time by turns, but David knew instinctively his were the shorter and fewer.

Only a stop at a small local restaurant—another of David's ride-finds—in Hancock, Maryland, broke their return. Julia slept for the final couple of hours. David could tell she had stopped time during their drive and had to wake her at the house. Only Brandon's greeting cheered their return to reality.

CHAPTER FORTY-ONE

Though they had returned, Congress had not. Not until later in January would senators and representatives return for the president's State of the Union address, which signaled the start of the Hill's new year. David had three weeks for the transition to separation from Julia that would come with Congress.

The work would then be full-out until the deal that had eluded Congress in December was reached. Failure had bruised egos and more tangibly left businesses in the lurch, as needed vital tax provisions had just expired. What exhaustion had not delivered a month earlier, pressure would now—along with its effects, which had only recently disappeared.

David knew this as much as he dreaded the inevitable hell that would transpire until his proposal was either passed or discarded. As the hell reheated, he spent all available time with Julia. With winter fully set in, and their budgets depleted, they kept things simple: cooking together, watching movies, having friends over. It was more real than memorable, but its realness made it special. It was particularly so for David, who remembered all too well last year's misery.

On one of their quiet nights, Julia had put *The Fountainhead* down and, looking at David, said, "Life is a novel. We write it, or if we don't, time writes it for us. We're either the author or the audience. We hold the pen and turn the page, or time does both. I know this isn't deep, it's just reality."

David responded, “Where does God fit in?”

She paused at his question. “He edits. He lengthens it or shortens it; he accepts it or rejects it. We only get to keep a part of it. We recall only episodes, not entireties. These glimpses comprise our story.”

“I’m not sure I understand.”

“Recall something. You really only remember a few of its moments and the feelings it left. Time is so ephemeral. You and I have been given the gift of holding its moments longer, but, in the end, we still come away with only moments.”

Days later, watching the president’s address, David remembered Julia’s words. The last moments of their extended time together were slipping away. They had never spent more time with each other, yet it was not the amount he felt, but the goodness. That was the feeling these simple three weeks had left with him. He had to successfully close this work chapter, one that once was everything, and begin writing the next one with her—one where all their time would be like this.

Washington wore winter like a shroud. David could see it in no other way as he drove at six thirty in the morning through its cold darkness. It was Wednesday, the day after the State of the Union. Because it started a new session and Congress had unfinished business, David braced for the onslaught. He was forsaking the Metro because he would be leaving after it stopped on many of the upcoming nights. Until there was a verdict on his proposal, he was stripping his life down to the barest essentials. As Phil continued stoking Evanston’s expectations, Janice tried to lower David’s. “Proposals rarely arise and get adopted in the course of a single year. Just because we need it, doesn’t mean we get it.”

David was already looking past these extremes. Regardless of Whitney, regardless of realistic expectations, he wanted this perfection for himself and to pair it with the one he had with Julia.

It was just before seven. As soon as he had printed out everything he needed to read—and these days he read everything—he stopped time to review it. He did so without concern for its duration; now it was always the same, however long he needed. Nor did he care how often he stopped it. Whenever he thought it would help, he used his ability.

Finished, he restarted time and worked out downstairs. *Then, get out before others get in. Don't need their questions or added pressure.*

The little time he saw his coworkers contrasted with his Hill contact. First, there were staffers and occasionally senators. He had essentially farmed himself out to Senator Nelson and Senator Davis's offices. But while doing everything needed to advance the proposal, he worked as hard at not being omnipresent as he did at being available.

His attention did not stop at the top of the food chain. He spoke to the Capitol Hill police, cafeteria and coffee shop workers, the shoeshine men, people in the barbershop. David gleaned from all. And he spoke to his own people—lobbyists, who traded in information the way bankers exchanged currencies. He did not care if he heard the same thing repeatedly. *Repetition also tells me something: Nothing new has pushed the old aside.*

He dutifully answered Julia's question about his "rounds."

"I move from one spot to the next in a revolving circuit. As the day wanes, the circuit shrinks—cafeterias close, the barbershop closes, the credit union, the post office, the offices themselves, and finally the coffee shops. Eventually, I'm left with just paths of transit—the tunnels connecting the office buildings and the Capitol—and vending machines. But so long as I feel any pulse, I stay."

Of all these, the only one with any obvious connotation of work to the uninitiated—and the only one he regularly told Julia about—was reading proposed revisions to legislative language. By this stage, David had effectively memorized the proposal; more importantly, he had memorized all the changes that had occurred since its inception—why and for whom they had been made.

This was vital because as the process moved, and the proposal with it, people's interest in it grew. Suddenly, a "small clarification" or a "technical fix" was needed. Some were innocent, as David understood from dealing with Whitney's bureaucracy: An issue wound its way through every conceivable office, everyone seeking to make an impression and show their value. Others weren't and were intended to fundamentally change the proposal; of course, in this category, David watched his company's competitors most closely. Sandi, closest of all. These changes could never be trusted—any more than they would go away until the bill was finally passed.

David's unique familiarity with every aspect of the proposal effectively made him its gatekeeper. It was a role he implicitly recognized but never explicitly acknowledged. He knew his place—just a lobbyist, the help, not even a staffer—and remembered well the dislike of lobbyists who didn't.

Even on slower days, as Wednesday turned out to be, he stuck to his pattern so long as it offered a hint of help. He saw it like a runner building endurance for a marathon. When he did return to the office that evening, the last there were leaving. He talked to Janice in passing to give a recount of twelve hours on the Hill.

Tomorrow, I'll do it all over again.

He knew he would not physically burn out. When he was fatigued, he stopped time to recuperate. At times, things became so slow that time-stops and real time became indistinguishable.

Mentally, it was different. To keep sight of life outside work and a semblance of sanity, he texted Julia throughout the day. At night, he called. Before this push had started, she had insisted, "I want to help any way I can."

"Just being there when I have chances to talk, those are enough—they keep me grounded," he had replied. And meant it.

To make "them" work, regardless of the hour, both were stopping time. She would wake up and they would talk about their work; David gave only the barest descriptions of what was boring, even to him. Then each would stop time to catch the sleep they had missed. Far from all they wanted, it was just sufficient to get them through.

If weekends existed, he turned them completely to her. This was both a small recompense for her and a huge release for him—to not think about anything. Winter lent itself well to these weekends' small respites. The long dark of the days drew both into sleep. Even with his time-stops at work, David was exhausted; Julia readily adopted this slower pace. Occasionally, sleep would just overcome her before she could stop time to hide it. David used it to do small things for her around her place, fixing something broken, walking Brandon.

For two more weeks—five days alone, then two with Julia—David kept this routine. Curled against him on a couch on a Sunday night, Julia shifted to look at him and asked, "When is this going to end?"

David shifted his gaze from her stare to his mind's eye. "The Senate's slowly putting its pieces together. Like a jigsaw puzzle, the final image is beginning to emerge. The deadlock's real; pieces are tried, then rejected when they fail to fit. The final deal looks to be coming toward Nelson and Davis to close it."

As he finished, he felt a tic flick his eye.

Julia touched it, whispering, "Until it does, please stop time more."

CHAPTER FORTY-TWO

The last push looked to begin the second week of February. On Monday, staff finished their final preparations as senators returned to town. The feeling was entirely different now, an atmospheric change only discerned by those who had lived it: determination leavened with desperation.

Shelly called. "The bigger tax bill's going to get done; it has to. Even though the senators are only just arriving, staff are setting up the deal, and senators are agreeing on phone calls. Our proposal, your proposal, will be included in the final grand amendment that the committee chairman managing the bill on the floor will offer. In return, Nelson and Davis will bring their supporters with them; together, they'll oppose any attempts to amend and change the bill. It'll then pass—*if* everything holds."

David told only Janice.

Tuesday, the bill went to the floor, and David went to the Hill. As he had been for weeks, he would stay throughout all, and any, action; this time, though, the action could run into the next morning. It did. Tuesday cemented the deal, but the language in the Chairman's amendment risked alteration until offered at the very end. While activity on the floor took center stage, it was just that: theater. Statements would be made, amendments would be offered, but all—regardless of eloquence or success—would be wiped away when the Chairman's amendment was offered at the end.

Tuesday's proceedings, which ran until two in the morning, was no more than the process speeding to conclusion. Centripetal force shrank his circuit, reducing the places David visited. He watched, he waited. When it was over, he left. But he only returned home because he could stop time to lengthen his stay there. Without this, he would have slept at the office to start over again at seven on Wednesday.

The next day started with the rumor that today they would finish. He dutifully reported it but was dubious. Janice reminded him, "The Senate votes when it has the votes and generally does not get them without a deadline—Thursdays, with their flights home."

Regardless of rumors, David remained focused on attempted changes to the proposal. These came more slowly now with the process so far along, but the most dangerous always came late when patience was thinnest and mistakes most likely. Sandi was up there almost as much as he was but had been noticeably distant yesterday. Today, she seemed equally so but more animated, more actively engaged than simply watching to ensure nothing undid the deal.

What particularly caught David's eye was her binder.

She's not substantive but transactional. She has no need for paper; a phone and purse usually suffice.

The more David saw, the more he focused. With two staffers, he watched her open the binder, take out a piece of paper, and show it. With the third, he was consumed by concern and curiosity.

Approaching her, ostensibly to trade information and compare rumors, yielded nothing. She moved away, but not far from where the Senate subway dropped everyone going to and from the Capitol.

David waited. As another staffer approached, and she began pulling the paper out, David stopped time. He weaved his way through living statues. Her hand was just extending the paper. David was careful not to take it from her; instead, he twisted to read it without touching her or the staffer frozen in her approach.

He recognized his proposal instantly. Now contorting, he read it closely.

Not relying on memory, he pulled his copy and cross-checked hers. Right at the beginning, he noticed a change in definition. It seemed innocuous, but still, he wrote it down on his clean original. Not until he reached line seventeen did he notice another discrepancy; a comma had been removed. Other than this, there were no changes. He felt sick.

Having walked back to his earlier spot, he restarted time. She went through the same procedure of showing the paper.

She's clearly shopping a language change.

David's stomach knotted tighter.

Immediately, he stopped time again to walk to where he could make private calls. Restarting time, his first was to Whitney's chief tax counsel. David had been right; the first change was inconsequential. His instincts were also right on the second change.

Jon blurted out on the other end, "It's huge! That comma substantively alters the language to our extreme disadvantage!"

David's second call was to Shelly.

"I think Sandi's shopping a last-minute change," he said as calmly as he could.

"You're friggin' joking!" Shelly replied, almost as upset as Jon.

"I wish. Have you seen it?"

"No, and I better not," she hissed.

"If I'm right, you will. If you do, will you call me? I'm worried."

"Of course, sure. I'm worried too. It's too late, and we've worked too hard and too long on this."

David could feel his pulse in his temples as he made his last call to Janice.

"We've got a problem. Consolidated is trying to change the language and screw us."

Silence. Then Janice, in typical understatement, replied, "That *is* a problem. How do you know?"

David paused then, realizing the issue, he stopped time again.

Leave it to her to ask the tough questions. Can't admit actually knowing; can't explain how I actually saw it. As far as I know, she hasn't given it to anyone.

He had been purposely careful not to take it from Sandi, but claiming exact knowledge could make it look like he had.

He restarted time. "I know; not exactly, but circumstantially. She's playing dumb and avoiding me like the plague, but she's approaching staffers with something on paper. And she never carries paper."

"She also wears too much makeup and too few clothes, but that doesn't make her a prostitute."

"You forgot to mention enough perfume to make a bloodhound bite off its nose," he growled.

Janice cackled. David continued, "It all makes her a cocktail waitress, but that doesn't mean she doesn't have new language. We just have to be careful."

"Always, dear boy. Always."

"Doubly so now."

David hung up. Janice was right. There was nothing he could do until Sandi played her hand.

He waited the rest of the day, through the night, and until today became yesterday and finally died at two in the morning tomorrow. Again. Just as he had expected, today hadn't been the day. Surprisingly, he had never heard anything about her language, and Sandi had left well before he had.

All the clutter had been cleared. Tomorrow must be it. He texted Julia; as usual, she responded quickly. He regaled her with accounts of, in her words, "nothing happening."

Feeling Thursday had to be the day, David took no chances. He got to the Hill two hours before the Senate would start. Before he could assume his post, Shelly called.

"You were right; she's got language. Senator Davis's staffer just called me and said he heard from Senator Wilkerson's office that they want a technical fix. The chairman's office is fed up and said we all have to sign off on it."

"If it's what I think it is, you shouldn't."

"Apparently, she says your company already *has*. Can you meet me? I want to walk over to the Capitol and figure out what's going on."

David's mind was reeling as he hung up. His first thought was that Sandi was lying.

I wouldn't put it past her, but such a bald-faced lie would be too quickly exposed to make its attempt worthwhile.

He met Shelly; on their way, they were joined by Allen, Davis's staffer. He knew no more than Shelly did, just that a change was in the works. Accompanied by staffers, David could go past the subway exit where unescorted lobbyists had to stop. Up the small escalator, then the elevator, through a labyrinth of turns he knew by heart, and then onto the antique tiles just outside the Senate chamber.

Sandi was with Wilkerson's staffer just before the landmark Ohio Clock. There were no pleasantries; everyone was too tired for that. Wilkerson's staffer looked uneasy, knowing his action risked throwing a wrench into everything. David said nothing; he had no role here unless a staffer invited him into their conversation.

It was immediately clear Sandi was pushing this hard. At the first opportunity from Wilkerson's staffer, she leaped in with the new language.

"It's just a technical fix," she said, holding out the paper.

David watched intently. He stopped time to check the tableau, person by person. Seeing nothing out of the ordinary with anyone else, he focused exclusively on Sandi.

She's aggressively thrust forward, clearly insistent. But that's her. It's unnatural to see her holding paper, but that's expected under these circumstances. The paper looks the same.

He cross-checked it again, word by word. The same.

Still...wait! Look at how she's holding it—her grip!

It was the same wording in the same place, but the key was the comma on line seventeen. He couldn't see it. She held the paper so that her finger covered the crucial spot where the comma should have been at the paper's edge.

David restarted time, dying to be brought into the discussion. After what seemed like forever as Shelly and Davis's staffer read the proffered paper, Shelly asked David what he thought. Before he could say anything, Sandi interjected, "They've signed off on it."

"I've never seen it," David replied.

"I didn't say you had," she shot back.

"Then how did we sign off?"

"Phil signed off on it," she replied smugly.

Party meetings were just convening before floor action resumed; the hallways were growing hectic as senators, staff, and reporters converged into nearby rooms. But all David could focus on was the feeling like he had just been kicked in the balls.

"Who? When?"

"Phil. Your *boss*. Last night," she said, clipping each word, as though laying down trump cards on a table.

He knew, without taking his eyes off hers, that everyone was staring at him. The room had just grown thirty degrees hotter.

He did not stop time. His mind simply raced in the never-ending moment. At that moment, Senator Nelson joined the group.

David didn't break mental stride. And he didn't stop time, he wanted this to be him, not "it." "This language change at the top is all you want?"

"Yes, and Phil's already signed off."

Searching for calm, David said, "You've made that clear. Is this all you want?"

"Yes."

"May I see the language then?"

Without changing her grip, she turned the paper toward David.

"May I hold it?" David asked slowly.

"Look, Phil's already signed off," she said in a strained voice.

"Then it won't hurt for me to see the paper, will it?"

"But here it is…"

"May I have it?" Senator Nelson demanded, more than asked, in a slow, low tone.

"Of course," Sandi said, still grudgingly.

The senator took it. Then handed it straight to David.

"What do you think?"

Just as he had suspected, beneath where Sandi's thumb had been, there was no comma.

"There's a typo," David replied in self-restrained understatement.

"That's impossible! What? Where?" Sandi retorted.

"Line seventeen, at the end. There should be a final serial comma before the 'and.' Otherwise, the last two items must be combined to count, rather than applying separately."

"But Phil signed off on this!"

"And *you* said all you wanted was the language change at the beginning. That's fine; it's just a technical fix, like you said. But the comma, as *you* said, was not what you wanted. It's not in the original, so there must've been a typo during drafting."

She was trapped and knew it.

Everyone there knew it. Senator Davis and Senator Wilkerson had now joined the growing knot.

David, a picture of magnanimity, concluded, "Your technical fix, with this nasty typo fixed, is fine."

"Are we good then?" Senator Nelson asked, looking directly at Senator Wilkerson. The conversation was now well above staff and lobbyists. Everyone else stood silently; mere mortals' speaking roles were done.

"I'm fine with it the way David said," Senator Davis seconded.

"We're good," Senator Wilkerson concluded and squinted at Sandi as he looked to exit the quagmire into which he'd been led.

The senators left, the staffers went to hastily redraft, and David and Sandi were alone. David couldn't restrain himself, so he didn't try. He stopped time instead. There, in a silent, still crowd, he exulted, letting loose every vulgarity, every classless gesture he could think to use on his vanquished foe.

Finally done and recomposed, he restarted time and stuck with simple. "It's good we caught that typo."

"Yeah," was all she could manage, while her eyes screamed, "Fuck you."

As soon as David could get outside, he called Janice. Although she wanted all the details—particularly when she heard Phil had supposedly agreed to the change that nearly sunk them—David begged off, saying he had to go back inside to ensure the bill passed without any more problems. Before he left, he called Julia. "I can see you early tonight."

David had to hold the phone away from his ear at Julia's piercing squeal. "Tell me, tell me!"

"I can't right now," he said as he laughed, staring and smiling goofily at his shoes. "Got to get back and finish. I love you."

The Senate's vote came shortly thereafter. For the unaware, it was high drama, the chairman's amendment passing narrowly as the deal had preordained. With David's proposal now in, the deal that had cemented the amendment would hold; the dealmakers now locked arms to protect it. Still, it took hours. Vain efforts to further amend the bill had to be beaten back, then interminable speeches praising the now inevitable had to be made, finally, the whole bill had to be passed. But it all happened. David was now more than halfway home.

CHAPTER FORTY-THREE

Even with Valentine's Day only hours away and his preparations nonexistent, he went straight to Julia. Beating her home and overdosed on exhilaration, he went from pacing her porch to sitting on her swing until he heard Brandon's warning, then greeting, through the door. Acting on a desire to do something—anything and everything—for her, he took Brandon on a walk that was almost a run.

They were just coming back as Julia was going in. Her broad smile lit his world. After a long kiss, the first thing out of her mouth was a request that they celebrate privately tomorrow night. David knew that, although she hadn't wanted an elaborate night out, she was thinking of him. With his weeks-long work schedule, there had been no time to plan anything. Tomorrow he would; tonight, he did not want to think about anything but being with her.

Despite their ability to stop time to see each other and recuperate, the weeks had taken their toll. Tonight was the first time that either had not been bleary from the grind of stopping and starting their lives to scratch some stolen moments together in the early mornings. Now and through the weekend, David assured her it would just be them. What he meant was that it was just going to be her. He knew that she had also been working on a big project, but her reticence rebuffed all his attempts to learn about it. She had been propping him up throughout his ordeal, and now he wanted to be her support. He also did not want to think about what would come next for his proposal in the House.

So excited to be together when the rest of the world was also awake, they went straight to Monroe Street and into the first place that could take them. It had been so long between meetings that tonight felt more like a first date than a reunion. They acted the part too. Each awkwardly interrupted, immediately yielded, then laughed at their conversational clumsiness. They made it through pizza but dragged into dessert. Conceding exhaustion, the last weeks' toll had to be paid. As much as the moment beckoned, as much as both desired, it was all they could do to make it to bed before falling asleep in a light embrace.

David woke up before Julia. Not wishing to wake her, he stopped time to slip out. Leaving, he realized he had just ended his abbreviated run of not stopping time—his longest hiatus in weeks. He had been doing it at a continuous pace, longer and more frequently than he had ever recalled. He laughed at the irony of vowing to cut down on stopping time while stopping it. Today, everything seemed worth a smile.

He went straight to the market to pull together Valentine's Day. He got everything before the essentials were picked over by other desperate men overtaken by the last minute. Naturally, he used his advantage.

Nothing speeds shopping like going through the store effectively alone.

After dropping everything at home, he swore off time-stops for the rest of a day that he wanted to speed by until the evening. He also knew no one expected him at the office today. The only reason he went was to find a real Valentine's present.

Regardless of his real reason for coming in, David was drawn into impromptu celebrations of the proposal's progress. At each, he had to recount how things had happened. Each group had its own focus. Janice wanted to hear everything; Frank wanted to know about Sandi's reaction when David caught her "typo"; and Jeff wanted to know what she was wearing. Phil wanted to exonerate himself. Much to his own surprise, David let him—and graciously—something he could never have done had Sandi succeeded. With hours to reflect and a night of real sleep, David told Janice, "I can't be sure Sandi hadn't removed the comma after showing Phil the text. In a contest between her duplicity and Phil's naivete, I can never be sure which prevailed."

"It was enough you and, because of you, that Whitney did."

This consumed the whole morning and through a lunch that Frank and Jeff insisted on. Not until he lied about missing so many workouts and needing to get to the gym did he finally break away. As soon as he got there, he left his gear and raced to look for Julia's gift. Mindful of his own rule that men should buy women jewelry, he first went in that direction. Regardless, once there, nothing struck him, and he found pricing engagement rings had depleted his mental budget for jewelry. Walking back equally empty-handed and empty-headed about what to get, he passed the lingerie store that he still subconsciously blamed for his breakup with Kristin.

Disregarding his other gift-giving rule that men should never buy women clothing, he was determined to redeem the store and himself. That he felt more confident with Julia than he ever had with Kristin helped. He made a purchase as close to tasteful as he could find amid the lascivious, did so quickly and without making a fool of himself—at least in his own mind.

As he returned, David beat back his already mounting doubts with the argument that no woman would ever be insulted that her man found her sexy. He hoped. And he had never known a woman as appealing as Julia.

I'm going to say all this to her at the first hint of trouble, then stop time, whisk it away, and swear she had imagined the whole thing.

So engaged in his thoughts, he lost track of himself as he swung his hand, the hand with the bag from the lingerie store, to block the elevator's closing doors.

"You must keep that place in business!"

All his self-confidence from the morning's triumphant return vanished in the sarcasm. It was Stacey.

Feigned bravado could not overcome the real blushing he felt lighting him up. He tried to stammer out a response, but he could have stopped time for a year and still been unable to come up with one.

Stacey mercifully let him escape and did not follow up on her score.

"You have a right to celebrate. As little as I understand all its details, I still can appreciate its magnitude. Evanston is ecstatic."

Still recovering, he managed to say, "Thanks."

Her voice changed to earnest. "I'd enjoy hearing about it sometime."

Flattered and surprised that anyone would want to hear more than the outcome, he said, "Sure. I'd be glad to, but I warn you, it's dry."

"All the more reason to hear it. I'd like to start working on something with more substance and a chance to move beyond just taking notes and filing reports."

Fortunately, the elevator ride was short and the locker rooms nearby, so David was quickly free of everything but his embarrassment.

As soon as he finished his work, he followed Janice's advice and left early. It was his first Valentine's Day with Julia, and the first one he could remember looking forward to since elementary school classroom parties.

Excited and anxious, only Julia's strict order to arrive no earlier than seven o'clock kept him away. As a compromise, he waited in his truck for ten minutes outside her house before faking a nonchalant arrival. He felt deep contentment—the house aglow in winter, his love inside, success's satisfaction still fresh. It was a completeness from all being as right as he could make it.

Julia opened the door. At her most basic, Julia was beautiful; tonight, she was not basic. Her dress hugged her above the waist before flaring out to her knees, and she seemed to float above her heels. A minimalist in her makeup, tonight she wore a touch more to highlight her sapphire eyes and a light fragrance, both to devastating effect. David froze as though she had stopped time on him. If Julia had been in hibernation the past few weeks, she was wide awake and out now.

Cocking her head to interrupt his stare, she sweetly teased, "Hello. Happy Valentine's Day to you too."

"I'm sorry, my eyes overrode the rest of me. Happy Valentine's Day."

"Aren't you going to say anything about the finery?" She pirouetted, finishing perfectly at eye contact.

"I thought my boggle-eyed staring said it all."

"Not mine, thank you, his," Julia said as she pointed to her feet, where Brandon was sporting a bow tie with red hearts.

"I was talking about Brandon," David deadpanned.

"You..." Julia jokingly raised her hand. David caught it and pulled her through a kiss and into his arms. Suddenly serious, he said, "I didn't think you could look more beautiful than I've always seen you; I was wrong."

He handed her this morning's flowers.

"Oh! It looks like I just won the Derby!"

Julia put the flowers into a vase, which she placed on a beautifully set table. Her small dining room was transformed by candlelight—the only light that lit them as they ate. Music played softly. When they were done, he tried to give Julia her presents, but she deferred them with a request to dance.

David knew he was way beyond his depth with her, but the tilt of her head and the graceful stroke of her left hand drawing back her hair was irresistible. He brought her to his body; she brought them closer still. Closing his eyes only heightened the contact's sensuousness. His breathing slowed and deepened as he lost himself in her.

Julia whispered just below his ear, "Make love to me."

He sighed. "I thought you'd never ask."

"I'm not asking."

As he lay recovering, David was amazed at the eloquence of their passion.

Julia lay beside him with her eyes closed, lost in the moment's release. David, marveling at her beauty and his happiness, said in genuine admiration, "No one does nude better than you do."

She smiled back. "Well, you know what they say, 'Nude goes with nothing.'"

David saw his chance. He gave Julia the package, partly explaining, partly apologizing as she unwrapped it.

"I suppose it's a little anticlimactic now," he offered.

"More post-climax, I think."

"It seemed a good idea at the time: Now I'm afraid I've attempted to paint the lily. I just wanted you to know how I see you—in every way, including physically." He found it as hard to say as to admit. "You're everything to me."

Julia listened, expressionless. David did not know how his gift, or confession, had been received. The pause was so long and pregnant that had he not been so uncomfortable, he would have believed he had stopped time.

She leaned back into a pillow, then exhaled deeply. "Thank you. I was a little hesitant about approaching you so directly tonight too. I like being the prey, your prey, but I wanted to be the predator tonight to show you the same thing."

David felt a tentative smile. Julia returned it. "Now, let me slip into something less comfortable."

When she went into the bathroom to try on her gift, David told himself that there was only one thing appropriate to the approaching moment. If he had to stop time to make it happen, he intended to. He didn't. Framed in the doorway and backlit by indirect lighting, her long body posed in unconscious elegance. The blue of the material caught her eyes, while her hair fell in graceful curls over the straps. The spell was complete; he did not need or want to stop time.

The rest of the weekend was hers. Their limited time together recently had unintentionally afforded the perfect opportunity to affirm his feelings about her beyond any doubt. He wanted to pass his happiness to her, to ensure she knew his certainty.

With her, the mundane wasn't. Having fallen into bed early last night, they awoke equally early and walked to the farmers market in Del Ray. On his suggestion, they went into D.C. to the National Gallery, "the real art museum," Julia called it. He listened as she led. Julia pronounced, "Here, there is no doubt—not in the artist, the work, or the audience—simply truth." David understood—not just the art but the truth—as he never had before.

Sunday, they went to church, now a regular habit. More than ritual, being there with her felt spiritual. He did not know if it came from God or from Julia. He did not care to explore the source, only accept it. Simply feeling was enough to know.

That night, he stayed with her. It was something he rarely did heading into a work week, but he wanted to do it now. Only her questioning about what lay in store for his proposal's bill brought him back to the work he had shunted aside for the past three days.

David heard the anxiousness in her voice. "Will the grind start right back tomorrow?"

He sought to reassure her. And himself. "As much as I wish it wouldn't, it'll resume. But it won't be the same."

"How do you know? I mean, even with an architect's knowledge of American government, I know the bill's just halfway home—no pun intended—the House still has to pass it."

"Technically halfway, but the next steps are much less fluid. Before, we weren't sure the Senate would pass the proposal. Now that they have, the House is really in a take-it-or-leave-it position. In Hill parlance, they're getting jammed."

"Couldn't they reject your proposal?"

"Not without upsetting the Senate coalition needed to pass it again if the House changes it. The Senate has them over a barrel. It's usually this way. While they play on the same board, the House plays checkers, and the Senate plays chess. Individual senators have far more freedom of action than House members. Senator Nelson and Senator Davis will vote against the bill without the proposal; they'd also take others with them. Any defections will bring the supporters below the magic number of sixty needed to prevent a filibuster—a filibuster Nelson and Davis would likely lead to protect their reputations, both now and for their Senate futures.

"For his part, the chairman only built his coalition to reach sixty. Doing so allowed him to quit making deals with other senators and save himself aggravation, but it also gave him all the leverage with his House counterpart. When they meet, he'll flatly tell him that he can't pass anything that diverges from what he sent over."

She nodded. "Ingeniously devious."

"Checkers and chess."

"And the president will sign it?"

"Yep. No way he's giving up a 'win,' and there's no time to put Humpty-Dumpty back together again if he pushes him over."

"So, I get to keep you?"

"As long as you'll have me."

"Be careful what you say, Mr. Preston."

David wanted to say, "I will, Mrs. Preston," but held himself for a better time—a real one he would soon make perfect. Instead, he opted for, "As long as it's with you; I like living dangerously."

As they parted Monday, only his body left.

Trips' artificiality can't be replicated indefinitely. Life must be lived somewhere; trips' constant change makes anyone seem more exciting, special. But this weekend could be repeated. Forever.

The only shadow on their homey Valentine interlude had been their divergence in stopping time. David was trying to avoid it and had, for the most part, succeeded. Julia appeared to be stopping it regularly. He had not raised it as an issue. The weekend had been too good, and he had not wanted to break the spell over something so minor. Yet just as she had originally detected it in him, he saw increasing signs now in her.

CHAPTER FORTY-FOUR

David began the week in the House, and in the realization that he had undersold the difficulty. Having never worked there, this was comparatively foreign territory, making it uncomfortable in every way. Amazingly, Sandi was not letting go. But just as persistent, so, too, was David.

His advantage was that here he played defense—his proposal was already in; he just had to keep it there. For three days, he bird-dogged Sandi constantly. Her connections here were better than his. What he did was to learn who she had talked to, then report that back to Shelly and Allen. They then applied pressure to the Finance Committee chairman's staff. In frustration, Sandi became increasingly hostile.

Just inside the Longworth House Office Building's main entrance, David had taken up a vantage post inside one of the old telephone booths. From here, he could see those entering, as well as the offices of the House tax committee staff. Sandi rapped hard on the door's glass. When he opened it, she hissed, "I don't like being stalked," a tad too loud.

Looking past her to the eyes now looking on, he replied, "And I don't want any more typos." David would not be baited. Nor would he be shaken.

When the vote finally came, her connections were not enough to undo the dynamics that David had described to Julia.

On Thursday, the House passed the bill with David's proposal intact. The next week, it went to the president, and, by that week's end, it was law. With that signature, David had pulled off the lobbying feat of a lifetime. He had run a novel and obscure idea through the legislative gauntlet.

Over two weeks, he enjoyed his fifteen minutes of fame, parceled into bits. He gave a rundown of the drama in a staff meeting. He gave more in a meeting with Janice and Phil. More still, to Frank and Jeff. And he gave the real details to Janice in several private conversations.

The Hill's accolades were better because they fully understood David's accomplishment. He had lunch with Shelly and Allen; both had feathered their bonnets from the ordeal.

The accolade that left David unmoved came when he flew back to meet Whitney's CEO for his personal congratulations. Janice and Phil both came, the latter embodying an iron rule of a project's completion: reward of the non-participants. Janice had graciously turned her praise to David, but Phil ensured he basked in what he could garner.

When David met the CEO, it was his most uncomfortable moment of the proposal's entire process. He felt like a fish out of water—not unlike the CEO's reaction on the Hill. He had gotten another picture and a handshake. Both were admittedly nice, but the CEO, while knowing its impact on Whitney, had no real idea of the legislative feat itself.

"It was like throwing a perfect game and having the club's GM saying, 'nice win,'" he shared with Julia.

When the handshake and photo were over, he was whisked out of the wood-paneled, glass-surrounded penthouse and the next meeting ushered in. One of his fifteen minutes of fame gone and forgotten.

The encounter in Evanston that touched him came with the tax team. They spelled out in detail what it meant to Whitney. Although it would not be booked until the next tax return, already the company was releasing lines of costly—and now unnecessary—credit. Of all Corporate's people, only among them did he feel a part.

CHAPTER FORTY-FIVE

Other than going to Evanston, David's schedule seemed like a vacation by just being normal. His anxiety and its myriad symptoms had begun to ease. He regularly spent nights with Julia. A cold continued to sap her, but she brushed it off. "Every year, I sublet my body to one. It stays for the season and leaves with the cherry blossoms."

Several nights, she fell asleep as they watched a movie. Knowing she was stopping time, he was surprised when she dropped off; she had used interludes to nap before but apparently was unable to do so here.

Their first weekend after the House's passage, they had planned to celebrate and go to a party some of David's friends were throwing. Instead, Julia had headaches so bad that she called them migraines. David welcomed reciprocating for her weeks of being there for him at all hours.

On Saturday, when she just needed to lie quietly, he narrowed his search for the right engagement ring. In addition to the ring, he wanted the right place. Of all the ones he had visited, he settled on a small shop in Old Town's north end run by Peter and Mary, brother and sister twins right out of the Haight-Ashbury sixties.

After a couple of visits, David had kidded, "Where's Paul?" He wondered if they would get the joke. They rolled right into "Leaving on a Jet Plane," punching "wedding ring."

Mary had owned up immediately. "It's exactly where our names came from! If there'd been another boy, he undoubtedly would've been Paul."

For David, the place had the right vibe.

He had already decided on the time and place. After talking with Frank, Jeff, and Daniel, he would propose on the weekend nearest her birthday in April. They would go back to Easton, Maryland. There was an old theater there that booked eclectic acts; the weekend of her birthday, there were two he thought Julia would like. Right across the street was a picturesque old hotel where he booked a suite. He had begun rehearsing the scene and his proposal with attention to detail equaling his preparation on his legislative proposal.

On Sunday, when Julia's headaches persisted, he wanted to take her to an urgent care clinic, but she insisted her migraines always passed given time. When Monday came, and he had to return to Evanston, she pushed him out the door, saying "Go!" as loudly as her head permitted. Though he checked back constantly, he knew distance could obscure anything.

Returning Wednesday, he went to her house from the airport. She was little changed. If anything, she was worse. She had no appetite; then, when she tried to eat, she became nauseated. David knew she had stopped time because he detected the smell of a quick cleaning.

Late that night, when she tried to eat just some crackers and applesauce that David had brought, it was even more obvious. In an instant, she had gone from one blouse to a different one. That night, he pleaded, "Please be honest about how you're feeling. I think not stopping time would be best, so you can get through the night as quickly as possible."

David stayed up most of the night, intently watching. As soon as the urgent care facility opened on King Street, David bundled Julia into her coat, then into his truck. More than concerned, he was now worried. When she finally went back to the doctor, he called work to tell Janice he would be late. She heard David's anxiety, though he tried to assure her—and himself—everything was okay.

He watched the door like Brandon sometimes did, eyes unmovable for more than a heartbeat, then returning immediately. When she finally emerged, he sprang up, putting his arm around her, as much to steady himself as her. He held back a torrent of questions.

She said in a weak voice, "They took some blood, but the results won't be back for a day. I also got prescriptions for antibiotics."

David ushered her back to the truck, then went next door for the prescriptions. Time seemed to be going backward as he scoured the drugstore for anything she might need.

Climbing in, he feigned brightness as he closed the truck's door—and hoped pretending could make it so. She tried to reciprocate, smiling back wanly. "The doctor said the antibiotics should knock out what my body's been unable to fight off."

"And the blood tests?"

"Just a precaution to confirm the diagnosis."

Having gotten her back to bed, he took Brandon for a real walk. He had wanted to make Julia lunch, but she had dropped off too quickly. Trying to do something, anything, he cleaned the house, doing every odd chore he could think of. What he could not do was leave. Whether Brandon sensed David's concern or merely his own, David didn't know, but both shared it.

Julia woke feeling and looking better. Now with some appetite, he insisted she eat. Then he waited to be sure she could hold it down. Only after his hovering had elicited Julia's complaint, "Honey, quit worrying, you're going to make us both crazy," did he finally go. He sat perfunctorily in his office a few hours—enough to allow him to honestly say he had been there. Unable to concentrate, he returned as soon as he could.

Further improved, Julia was better than David had seen her in days. To his chagrin, she had made them supper. David was far more grateful for the sign than the meal. They started *His Girl Friday*, but as soon as David saw her second yawn, he shooed her off to bed. He took to the daybed in her Giants room, so he could be close without disturbing her. During the night, he checked on her several times; each time, she was asleep.

Stopping time at five thirty, David topped off into his own ragged sleep; he then stayed up to ensure he was awake whenever Julia was. Her first stirrings were not until eight in the morning. He held his breath; she had rallied more. His confidence did as well. Mutually relieved, they exchanged demands: He insisted that he make whatever she wanted for breakfast; she insisted that he go to work. Each complied.

At work, David regularly checked back until Julia playfully snapped at him to give her a moment's peace. David went to lunch with Frank and Jeff, who observed that David's lovesickness was more serious than anything Julia likely had. Friday allowed him to leave early. He stopped to get flowers and everything he needed to make "breakfast for supper," which he explained was his family's ritual for patients. He had returned to her being better than he had left her and better still after he had made her breakfast of choice—pancakes.

They had just finished a movie, and David was putting their dishes into the sink when she said, "I went back to the doctor this afternoon."

David wheeled around. "What?"

She laced her arms around his waist and leaned back. "It was nothing. They just wanted some more tests—to be sure they got it right. They'll have the results sometime Monday."

Putting his hands on her arms, he pulled her to him. "I wish you'd told me."

"I'm telling you. Now." She chuckled, biting her lower lip and arching her eyebrows mockingly.

"I meant sooner, Smarty. I worry, you know."

"Don't I know!" she laughed until she coughed. "That's exactly why I *didn't* tell you sooner."

He rocked her gently side to side. "But I like worrying about you."

"And I like you caring, but I don't want you worrying. You worry too much."

"I can't help it. You should get to bed."

"*We* should," Julia said as she raised her eyebrows comically.

"Let's get you fully back to health first. As much as I want you, I want you well more."

Julia embraced him tightly, really tightly, then kissed him as softly as her hug had been hard. Their night ended; each going to their separate corners, like boxers coming out of a clinch.

Julia's recovery caused David to drop his guard; on Saturday morning, he did not stop time to ensure he woke up before her. He was surprised by her coming into the Giants room when he sleepily asked, "How're you feeling?"

"Good enough to have made us breakfast."

The rest of the day was so normal that David did not dispute Julia's decision to go to a work "command performance" that night. He even went to the gym. The only thing he flatly refused was her request for a motorcycle ride. He said it was not only too cold for her, it was too cold for him. The latter was a lie, but a white one at worst.

Her night event was an even bigger surprise. As they entered, his eyes immediately fell on several beautiful architectural models, precisely cut from cardboard and meticulously assembled. David had been mesmerized by some of the items in Julia's portfolio, their detail reminding him of the beautiful symmetry and converging lines of nautilus shells. Instantly drawn, his eyes had moved to a series of sketches and drawings, each progressively more finished. He recognized her hand, despite having never seen these. Neophyte that he was, the connection was obvious.

David was utterly stunned to learn all were for a competition Julia had won for the firm to design a museum. He was also utterly humbled, not only by his own lack of such creativity, but because he had been completely unaware of her efforts. As he told her fawning colleagues, "She never gave anything beyond vague hints." All he could think of was how wrapped up in his legislative chase he had been, how supportive she had been—night after night—while saying so little about what her colleagues repeatedly lauded as a major career landmark.

CHAPTER FORTY-SIX

David had loved the whole evening, but driving back, he was lost in reflection. Only her question roused him from unconscious silence.

"Now it's my turn to ask. Are you alright?"

"I'm embarrassed. No, perhaps 'ashamed' is more apt."

"What? Why?"

"Of myself. I've been—and you've been—so focused on my work. I wish I'd pressed you harder. Why didn't you tell me when I asked? I hope you didn't think I would've thought it distracting."

"You were fine. It was me; I didn't say anything because I didn't want to."

"Why not? I care about your life too."

"I know." She reached over and caressed his arm. "I wouldn't be with you otherwise."

"So why didn't you tell me you were working on something so big?"

"Fear. I was afraid I'd fail. Again."

"You? After what I saw tonight, that doesn't seem possible."

"For every success, there've been countless washouts. You get used to it—it's like hitting in baseball, only your odds of success are lower in architecture. I don't know how my Giants do it. I'm used to it, but I wasn't prepared for someone I love to see it."

David started to reply, but Julia continued, and he could hear the emotion. "If you didn't know I was doing it, you wouldn't have to know if I failed. Silence was a defense mechanism. This is so damned personal! They can say rejection's only professional, but who're they kidding? It's completely personal—they're not rejecting someone else's work; they're rejecting yours. And if you put yourself into it, then damned right, they're rejecting you. I didn't want you to see me that way."

"I'd never see you that way."

"But *I* would. That's my point, and that's the reason I didn't say more. I knew there'd be tonight if I won. It really helps the firm, at a time when we really needed it. So, I knew they'd make a big deal out of it—maybe not *that* big a deal, but I knew I'd be able to let you see it then."

David glanced from the road to her. "It must feel great to have worked so hard and have it come through."

"You should know that feeling too. But you know the best part? It was *you* getting to see it. I'm so happy you enjoyed it. I so wanted you to see me that way."

"I always see you that way. I *will* always see you that way."

They were quiet again as they parked. As they walked in, David asked, "When did you do it all?"

"I stopped time. A lot."

By Sunday morning, although David was still observant, Julia pronounced herself well. They followed their now-predictable pattern of church, returning with lunch, then walking Brandon. Today, they took Brandon to Jones Point Park on Alexandria's southern edge. Reaching their turnaround point and looking down the Parkway toward Mount Vernon, Julia held David's left arm with both hands and said, "Take me on the motorcycle."

"You were just sick; I'm not sure it's a good idea..."

"David, I'm a person, not porcelain. Please."

Looking into her imploring eyes, he could deny her nothing. David agreed, telling himself that it was a dry day, cool, not cold, and an easy, straight ride. Julia hustled them back before David could change his mind.

David did insist that Julia bundle up far more than she thought necessary.

He knew from experience that riding into the motorcycle's induced wind affected someone far more than the inexperienced knew and far faster than they expected—even if a shielded passenger.

"Do you want to ride, or do you want to argue?"

Julia conceded.

To David, the ride was nothing special: a straight shot to Mount Vernon and back—though Julia did pad it with a dogleg down to the mill. Yet in just its hour, he felt the creeping deep cold. When he got them back to her house, he saw Julia's body shiver reflexively and knew she was feeling the same. He got them both in, quickly removed the riding layers, pulled them both into her bed and tightly wrapped his body around hers. Lying there and restoring their bodies' heat, he recounted, "I once rode all the way down Indian Head Highway in Maryland, only to realize at the farthest point I was cold. The ride drove my temperature so low that I went straight to the gym afterward. Shaking and with teeth chattering, I dropped my clothes on the locker room floor and went directly into the sauna." A tremor ran through him at the memory.

She hugged him tightly. "I like this way of warming up much better," Julia said.

"So do I. I don't have to worry about my clothes getting stolen here."

Julia punched him playfully. Then they lay silently and enjoyed the return of feeling to their extremities.

"David, let's make love."

Despite all of their past experiences, each was always different. This time, their lovemaking had never felt gentler. Externally subdued; internally, a mutual transference of passion.

As Julia basked in the low light of the setting sun, David permitted himself the now rare indulgence of stopping time. Although Julia had earlier declared herself a person and not porcelain, Sunday's fading light argued against her. Her long frame draped across the bed was too graceful, too elegant for mere flesh and blood. Julia lay unconsciously as gorgeous as a sculpture she would have sketched.

David stared at her in solitary, silent wonder, unable to believe her outward beauty, but even more the inward beauty she held for him and through this contentment, this peace, she gave him. Just days before, he had gotten the barest hint of what it would be like without her. He knew he had never known a deeper, more profound happiness than he knew now—and that he would never know it with anyone else. With Julia, he now had the completeness, professionally and personally, he had so long sought.

Having been at Julia's for days, David returned to his condo just to catch up on things he had let slide. He planned to make a stop at the jewelry store before work. Since Friday, when David's hope had become belief that Julia was not seriously ill, he had waited for something else. For two days, he had expected Julia to tell him she was pregnant. For two days, she had said nothing, and for two days, he had not asked. He wanted to give her the latitude to tell him in the way and at the time she felt right. What he had done was send every signal that he welcomed the announcement and that he was ready. In his mind, it did not change his plans at all; it only accelerated them.

CHAPTER FORTY-SEVEN

David was at the jewelry store before it opened Monday morning. Having thought everything through repeatedly, he was convinced Julia was pregnant.

When she tells me, I want the engagement ring with me. I don't want to produce it after she tells me and leave any question that I'm proposing because she's pregnant. The proof will be in my hand—and on hers—that I'm proposing because I want her.

During a late morning staff meeting, her text came. "Can you meet me at Sibley Hospital at 2?" That was all. David shot straight up in his chair. Flustered, he stopped time; he didn't know what else to do. As prepared as he thought he had been, he wasn't now. He ran through scenarios and tried to calm himself out of his descending cold sweat.

He restarted time to respond. "Of course! Do you need me to take you?"

Her reply came back instantly. "No. I'm already here."

Stunned, he had not known she was going at all—let alone into D.C. Anxiously, he answered, "Do you want me to come now?"

"No."

Then moments later: "Yes, if it's not a problem. Otherwise, I can wait."

His fingers flew in response. "Leaving now. Do you need anything?"

"Just you."

David abruptly left, with only the briefest glance at Janice to acknowledge his departure. One last time, he checked for the ring.

It was the longest wait for the longest Uber ride of his life. He leaned forward in the Ford's backseat, like a jockey on his mount, as though somehow this would hasten it. His trembling hands made texting difficult, but he did at each passing landmark—as much to assure himself of the progress as for the comfort it might give Julia.

Once there, he stopped time so that Julia would have no more time alone. She was by herself in a waiting room. Its functional plastic furniture, fake plants, and old magazines made her seem even lonelier than he knew she must be. He had practiced how he was going to act when she told him about the baby.

I'll be surprised, but immediately supportive. Then, I'll drop to one knee, draw out the ring, and tell her I'd planned the proposal differently, but with this wonderful news, I didn't want to wait. He would be perfect; everything would be perfect. Everything was perfect.

David moved just out of sight, restarted time, and approached like an actor on cue to his mark. With nowhere to put her gaze, Julia saw him instantly and as quickly started toward him. As she did, her composure began to crumble; by the time they met, a large tear was tracing toward her quivering lip. David caught her shoulders in his hands.

"What's wrong, darling?"

"I don't know how to tell you. I didn't know."

"I'm here. We're in this together. Tell me what it is."

"David, I have cancer."

David reeled inside. Time stopped without either's effort. They hung suspended in it, each holding the other to keep from falling. He didn't know what to say, or do, or even how to talk. His lips moved, but words did not emerge, and the tears in Julia's eyes now moved to his.

"I just found out an hour ago. The doctor's office called first thing this morning. They told me to come here immediately for tests. I didn't think; there was no time to call, but, honestly, I didn't want to until I knew something. As soon as I did, I texted. I'm so, so sorry. I'm so, so scared." Julia started sobbing softly.

David still could not comprehend what he had just heard. Unable to think, he fought for words. “I'm here, it'll be okay, we'll get you well.”

It was the very opposite of what he had expected when he arrived; it was the very opposite of what he now felt and feared.

They were not long together before Julia was taken for more tests. With each, there were never results, just more tests. David shadowed her throughout.

The worst was an MRI; David could see she endured it only through force of will. David sat in helpless agony. He could do nothing but be there.

I would switch places instantly; seeing her suffer is worse than suffering myself.

He finally went to bring her something to eat, even though worry and pain from the probing and prodding had eroded her appetite. The last blow was the doctors' desire that she stay overnight. When told, she had grabbed his arm with her left hand as her head sank into her right. Her features projected terror and defeat; she was unable to even look at him.

Having not foreseen this possibility, she had nothing with her at a time when she needed the familiar for emotional, even more than physical, comfort. David went to Del Ray to bring everything he could retrieve in short order. Brandon followed in confusion.

He did not return with his truck until after eight. While he was gone, Julia had begun making calls. Cindy had immediately called him in panic. He tried to feign calm optimism, but he knew he had neither convinced her nor himself.

David had also brought a bag for himself so he could stay, but Julia refused. He limped home emotionally exhausted, completely lost.

As unproductive as he knew it to be, David had stopped time more than he could remember. He knew Julia had too. It was the only way he, and he believed she, could cope with their world collapsing. He did so again as soon as he got to her house. She had wanted him there with Brandon. As hard as it was to feel her absence all around him, he had come to soothe at least one of her worries. In his freeze of time and the paralysis of his own fear, he prayed.

CHAPTER FORTY-EIGHT

Tuesday morning finally came. David did not know how much sleep he had gotten. He knew it had been fitful during an agonizing night. Torn between resting so he could be of use tomorrow and allowing time to move so he could get back to her, he followed a jagged cadence of stopping time, trying to sleep, and then letting time creep until he felt he could sleep again.

Wanting to be there when Julia's doctor made rounds, David made sure he was there before 8:00 a.m. visiting hours. He wanted to learn all he could about her cancer, but even more, he wanted to be there when she heard.

After just a single day, David knew his way to her room. He was completely jolted when he arrived to find it empty. After initial panic, he discovered she had been moved. Even when he found her new room, he did not find her. She had already been taken for more tests. Frantically feeling he was letting her down, David could only wait.

He was unprepared to see her being wheeled back. Tubes and wires now ran from her. David knew he had failed his eye test, his shock clearly registering, because Julia tried to make light of her return. He was up instantly, only to find himself clumsily attempting to avoid her attendants as they positioned her and the attached equipment. The role he had planned reversed: She comforted him and explained what had already transpired.

They did not get beyond facts before the attending doctor arrived. He was a nondescript lab coat in David's mind, younger than either of them. After the briefest of forced pleasantries, David listened in stunned disbelief as the doctor told Julia she had pancreatic cancer. Stage Three. Another physician would come by that morning to talk about treatment options. Just like that, it was done. The diagnosis given, the lab coat left, a jury of one who had just issued his verdict and now hurried to his next case—no heart, only a schedule. Now they had to wait for another doctor who would act as judge and pronounce sentence.

Julia took it better than David. He was mortified at his inability to not tear up, to be what he wanted to be for her. He was lost in his shock over the diagnosis. Julia finally had to remind him about the things he had brought this morning. Fumbling through them, he apologized. "I'm sorry how gracelessly I'm handling everything."

"Don't feel bad, I've had longer to process it. I took an interlude to read my chart last night; then I saw they were going to hook me all up."

They waited hours for the next doctor. David was ready to pounce when he finally walked in, but this one was thoroughly different: a human being. Dr. Stimson was grandfatherly, almost bald, rather short, and his face wrinkled into a ready smile that instantly calmed. It made what he had to say that much harder to hear.

"You heard your diagnosis?"

Julia calmly nodded, almost inaudibly answering, "Yes."

"How much do you know about it?"

"Not much, but Stage Three of anything can't be good, can it?"

"No, I'm afraid not. Sadly, it's not uncommon for pancreatic cancer. It's very hard to detect, and its symptoms aren't ones that people necessarily associate with cancer. As a result, when it's detected, it's often late."

"Too late?"

His Adam's apple bobbed as he swallowed. "Often, yes."

"In this case?"

"Not necessarily."

Without a role in this most personal of dialogues, David could only listen as the two discussed Julia's options. None were good. If Julia did nothing, the cancer would kill her quickly. Even with aggressive treatment, Julia's odds weren't great. Finally, they would continue testing.

"You left me with a lot to think about and apparently very little time to do so. I need to talk with David," she said, gesturing toward him. "And my family's coming."

After so much had been said, there was now nothing more to say. An awkward silence smothered the room, and the doctor turned to leave. Seeing his only opening, David said, "Excuse me, and I apologize if I'm out of line to ask, but if you have a diagnosis, why continue with tests? Is there a chance the diagnosis is wrong?"

"It's a good question. I know they're unpleasant." The doctor cleared his throat. "That's doctor-talk; I know they're miserable. I'd like to find that the diagnosis was wrong. I *really* would in this case. We continue doing them to determine if the cancer has spread beyond the pancreas and how fast it's progressing there."

The doctor's parting words, uttered more to himself than to Julia and David, stuck like a dagger.

"We usually see this in someone considerably older."

For what seemed a long time, David and Julia stared in silence at each other. Then awkwardly away. David searched for something positive in the horrors he had heard. He wondered if Julia had stopped time; then, unable to resist any longer, he did. In the past, he had fully vented over minor frustrations. Now facing a cataclysmic one, he was adrift.

There's no rage large enough for this agony. Everything I can think to say seems wrong for this moment's demands.

Unconsciously seeking an impossible physical escape, he jammed his hands into the pockets of yesterday's coat—he hit the ring he had forgotten since seeing Julia.

Restarting time, he thought no more and simply reacted to what had prompted him to buy it, and the despair that now drove him to try to bring her some happiness.

"If this is wrong, please tell me. I wanted to wait for your birthday, but I don't want to wait any longer."

David dropped to his knees. "I love you like I've never loved anyone and like I know I'll never love anyone else. Would you please marry me?"

Nodding her head vigorously, Julia smiled, even as she wept. "Oh, David, never forestall joy. It's the perfect time; it's everything I wanted and do want. And yes, I'd love to be your wife."

For one brief moment, both were able to cry from happiness.

Julia's parents arrived that night only to confront the same shock David had received. Leaving the three alone with their grief, he called his parents, Janice, and Daniel. He did not feel like saying much and certainly less than he knew. His parents offered to come; although grateful, he talked them out of it. This was a time for Julia's family, and they did not need more to think about now. Janice told him to stay away from work and to just let her know what she could do. Daniel seemed the most shaken by his news; his voice cracked repeatedly as he babbled, something his usual fixed assuredness never permitted. In sympathy, David found it an equal struggle to listen to.

As he hung up, he realized. *He knows. Knows better than I do because he has fully the family I am only approaching.*

Privately, David talked with Julia's parents and convinced them to go to her house. Their emotional and physical exhaustion was glaring, but despite it, the only way he could convince them was by arguing that this would help Julia. He would stay with her in the hospital tonight, while they would be taking care of the house and Brandon. They followed him back. He picked up his things and returned while he could still get into the hospital.

David found Julia asleep when he stopped time to go in and make up the institutional chair that unfolded into an uncomfortable flat surface. In case she awoke during the night, he left her a short note, with his love and to wake him if she needed him for any reason. He restarted time and, with it, all the sounds of the hospital that never let him forget where they were.

As soon as he began waking the next day, he heard Julia begin speaking. "I know it won't be long before the day's march of visitors starts. Thanks for just being here. Throughout the night, it was so comforting to look over and see you there."

He tried to pull himself out of his grogginess and into the moment. "I'll always be where you need me to be. You look great. How do you feel?"

"I know you won't approve, but I took some interludes. I don't remember how many; I just know they help. A lot. The nurses' visits would destroy a normal person's rest. Still, it's pretty uncomfortable being so hooked up."

Walking wobbly to her, David confessed, "I took two myself. The best part is the quiet. I'm sorry about the discomfort."

"It's not as bad as yesterday's unknown."

"Is there anything I can do?"

"You could bring me more things from home."

"Of course, and anything else you want. I thought I'd leave when your parents arrive."

"That's fine. Oh, Cindy will also be here late this afternoon."

In a voice straining for cheerfulness. David squeezed her hand and suggested, "Since we're both taking interludes, I thought we could arrange ours at night like we did when I was working nonstop. It would give us our own time."

"That would be great! It's a date. Also, I know you have work, so don't worry about staying here. It's a regular parade during the day. Just always come back."

No sooner said then the parade began. Technicians wheeled her out for more tests. David waited for Julia's parents to arrive, then filled them in on last night and today. They looked better, but their anxiety never left. They congratulated him on the engagement, everyone intentionally leaping away from the present into that more hopeful future.

David returned late that afternoon with a box of things Julia had requested, plus some he thought would make her happy—books, more clothes, her Giants cap, sketch pads, and drawing pencils. He had seen Janice while picking up work at the office. He had led with his engagement but been bluntly honest about Julia's condition. He could not say any more, confiding only to prevent more questions.

He ran into Cindy in the waiting area. He welcomed having someone to speak with without really talking. She knew, he knew. Love for Julia bound them together; everything filtered through it, clearing away the unnecessary. Whatever helped Julia was important; outside that, nothing was.

Giving her parents time with Julia, they went downstairs. Neither was hungry, but both knew they should be. The cafeteria featured equally institutional furniture and food.

I remember the end for Grandmother and visiting the small-town Georgia version with Daddy then. Time, distance, and size change nothing. It's still purely utilitarian, serving tasteless food to people who would not taste it anyway.

David watched her fidget, stirring and restirring coffee that she never drank.

"Congratulations on your engagement. You've made Julia incredibly happy—the rest of us too."

"I'd planned for next month, but when she called from the hospital..." David paused and demurred. "I didn't know it was about...this. I just wanted to make her happy."

"I understand. It's beyond a shock. These things don't happen to people you know, to people you love. They happen to friends of friends. They send a chill, you're sorry, then you go on with your life."

"I've only known her for just under a year, but I know Julia's tough."

"She is, she really is." In thought, Cindy seemed to look through him. "But tough can cut two ways. It can lead you to fight trouble, but it can lead you to run into its teeth too."

"How do you mean?"

"Like you and the motorcycle. It's not the safest way to travel. You do it; she loved it too. I'm just saying there's more than one way to challenge trouble."

That night, David and Julia returned to stopping time in almost simultaneous sequences. Just seconds apart in real time, they seemed instantaneous. Thus, they could sleep out of time; extending their night, they created their only real time together. Although David basically just slept during his, Julia would sometimes draw, write in her journal, or get up as best she could. She could unclip the electronics when time was stopped, then reattach them without missing a second of real time. As for the IV, she walked with the pole. When she said, "It makes me feel like a ghost," David reflexively stiffened. Seeing his reaction, she reached for him. It was the first emotional acknowledgment of her condition that David had seen from her all day.

As though speaking about someone else, Julia said, "The plan's to begin aggressive cancer treatment Monday. Since I'm young and healthy, the doctors feel this gives me the best odds. Lydia arrives Friday, everyone will stay through the weekend, then my folks will do shifts in Virginia during the treatment." Only when she spoke about the proposal did she lighten. "Everyone's excited about the engagement; you'll get dragged into earlier wedding preparations."

Even the most miserable of circumstances routinized into a pattern. David stayed to see the doctors, then, when Julia's family came, he went to his condo, showered, changed his clothes, and worked from there. He did not go into the office; he couldn't bear reliving any of this through questioning. David spoke of Julia only to his parents and Daniel. He then returned in the late afternoon to spend the rest of the night with her.

CHAPTER FORTY-NINE

Both David and Julia had barely awakened when Dr. Stimson made his visit earlier than usual. He came alone and closed the door behind him. His pause drew their attention; once it was clear he had it, he said slowly, "The cancer's spread. It's moving extremely fast. It appears to be in your blood. I honestly have never seen anything like its speed. It's like it's progressed a week in a day."

Julia's head fell into her hands. David knew instantly that she had stopped time because it looked like she had been crying for quite a while when she finally looked up.

Barely managing to speak, she asked, "What are the chances with treatment now?"

"It's very tough, I'm afraid. They were challenging before…but now…Even if we got the cancer in your pancreas…It's just moving so far, so fast."

Now it was David who stopped time. His mouth was so dry; only with the greatest effort did he avoid vomiting as the air left his lungs in heaves. He could not cry, despite desperately wanting its release. It felt like forever before he regained a semblance of composure.

Julia began again as soon as he restarted time. "I've nothing to lose, a wedding to plan, and family coming this weekend. You aren't advising against it, are you?"

He tapped his fingers on the back of her chart. "No, of course not. I…I admire your courage, young lady."

Staring through the doctor more than looking at him, Julia said without emotion, "I will see you Monday then."

"I'll see you Monday," he responded, forcing a bare smile.

Unspoken was the fact that there was no longer a reason for him to return until Monday. David rose instinctively but couldn't move, trapped between staying with Julia to offer what comfort he could and rushing after the doctor in hopes of getting some encouragement. He knew there wasn't a choice, despite the fact that the only support he could give was simply being with her.

David recognized that Julia had just taken another interlude. In addition to clues that she no longer tried to hide from David, since being in the hospital, she always came back with a resolve, moving methodically through thoughts he realized she had just collected. David let her speak while her composure still held.

"David, not a word about this conversation with the doctor to my family. Let's get through this weekend like this never happened."

"Of course, if that's what you want."

"Them knowing won't change anything; it'll just make it harder on all of us."

David couldn't imagine it being harder than now already was. But he intended to match Julia's determination.

Julia's parents and Cindy came in shortly afterward, and David left with Julia's secret, having hardly had a chance to talk with her about what he could now not discuss with anyone else. He went home feeling utterly alone and helpless.

Lydia arrived that evening and joined the rest of the family at the hospital for a few hours. Only after all had left for Del Ray, did David finally have time alone with Julia. As the visitor count increased, their time became even more precious. David wished their night could last forever. He was amazed how so small a realm could become their world when spent together. They would end their night with each taking a final interlude, then both were ready to start another day.

Saturday and Sunday were busier than any days before. Having fully arrived, her family stayed for long stretches. David would offer each breaks in the form of walks outside. His favorite companions were Cindy and Julia's father, but he grew closer to Julia's mother too. Lydia's formal exterior he never penetrated, though he tried to a point he was sure seemed forced.

Word having gotten out, her condition's shock reverberated through her universe. Painfully, David and Julia repeatedly relived these first reactions. Julia held up remarkably. Only once had he seen the evidence of a break in her composure, as a visibly rattled Lydia left the room.

Cindy recounted the story on a walk later, saying with satisfaction, "Lydia had her bitch on, and Julia would have none of it. Lydia cattily implied you only proposed because you thought you wouldn't have to go through with it. At that, Julia tore into her like I've never seen her do. And it rocked Lydia like nothing I've ever known. Her comeuppance has been overdue for years; I'm just glad her 'uppance' finally came."

By Sunday evening, the crowds dispersed. Cindy and Lydia flew back with their mother to Lexington, while their father left early for Del Ray, ahead of many planned shifts. Julia's friends retired to their homes in preparation for returning to their normal weeks. Only David and Julia remained.

They did not speak about much, and nothing about the ordeal that lay ahead. There was nothing to say and less desire to think about it. In place of words, there was touch. David sat on the right side of her bed, where Julia's unencumbered arm could hold his more comfortably. Each clung to the other. For the first time in days, both accepted regular sleep, foregoing staying up as they had been, because neither wanted to prolong what awaited.

CHAPTER FIFTY

Julia spoke first, early Monday morning.

"How was your night?"

"It was okay. Not great, but alright."

"Are you fully awake?"

"Yeah, I'm fine. Just a little groggy. I woke up a little early. I wanted to be with you."

"David, I want to talk."

"Sure, of course."

"I'm not going to go through with it."

His grogginess instantly vanished. "What? You're not going to go through with what?"

"The treatment. I'm going to tell the doctor as soon as he comes. Then I'm going to tell my father. I don't care what they think because I know they can't understand; but I care what you think, because I know you can."

"Why? I mean, I know it's easy for me to argue, I'm not the one who must endure it, but there's still a chance."

"No, David, there's not. We both know. Everyone knows it, but we know it better than anyone. And I know better than you do. I've probably lived half my adult life inside myself—in interludes. When the doctor said this usually happens in people much older, he was talking about *me*, he just didn't know it. While time has been stopping, my body hasn't been."

"How do you know that? You're just assuming…"

"No, honey, I'm not. A woman knows. It's not female intuition or anything like that. I had missed my period before we went to St. Michaels. I stopped and restarted time to take a pregnancy test. Hell, I took so many. They were all negative. Then I made the connection to the other things I was feeling; I was in menopause—'premature' they call it. Having it coupled with my time stops accelerated it even more. It's why I was so emotional. I knew I couldn't have children, and I wanted them—I want them—so. I wanted them with you."

"That doesn't change anything between us. There are other ways."

"I know, I know, baby. And I've told myself this a thousand times since St. Michaels. But the point is my body's racing ahead of me—ahead of us. If by some miracle I beat this now, then I'll just face something else—more cancer, some other condition that makes doctors scratch their heads and wonder why it's happening to someone so young. These things do happen to people: It's not fair, it's not pleasant, it's just life. Or in this case, death. By taking interludes so often, I brought forward what was coming for me. I didn't know!"

Julia hit her right hand on the bed. "We didn't know. But now I do. And I need you to understand because it's so damn hard. I'm not being a coward, or a hero, or anything; I'm just being realistic. If I get past this, it'll just be to go into something else—something that could be worse and will feel worse if I have to endure it after having gone through this. That's not how I want to die, that's not how I want to live. Honey, something's got to kill you sometime. This is mine, and my sometime's now."

David tried to argue, but Julia was calmly adamant. She faced down her father, then she faced down the doctors—especially the young one David had come to despise. She had finally dispatched him and his protests over the schedule, saying, "Then you have the treatment."

Dr. Stimson was the last to come.

"I heard there's been a change of plans."

"More a change of mind: mine," Julia responded.

“I’ve heard it’s a woman’s prerogative to change her mind.”

“Apparently, your younger colleague missed that class in med school.”

The older doctor chuckled, then gave vent to a full laugh that drew in Julia, then David. He made a *pro forma* counterargument, but his heart was clearly not in it when he saw Julia’s was.

“Then let’s get you unhooked from all this,” he said as he waved toward the machines and IV. Regaining his medical demeanor, he said, “You could try to go home for a while if you’d like, but you’ll need to go to a hospice—probably pretty soon. Still, it’ll be a lot better than here.”

Julia’s voice rose as she did onto her elbows. “Can I go home today?”

It was the first eagerness David could remember hearing from her in a long time.

“Absolutely. I’ll get the discharge underway.”

“Thank you. Thank you for everything.”

Stimson turned to leave, then stopped.

“I don’t mean to be presumptuous, but for what it’s worth, I would’ve made the same decision.”

“Thank you. Again.” Julia smiled and settled back.

“No, ma’am, thank you. You confirmed my determination for when my time comes.”

“What were my chances?”

“You might have survived the chemotherapy, but at what cost? And likely it would only have bought you a little more time.”

“Thanks for the honesty.”

Turning to David, Stimson said, “Here’s how you can reach me if you need, or want to, at any point.”

David mumbled thanks. They shook hands firmly, their eyes saying all that they couldn’t.

CHAPTER FIFTY-ONE

The next weeks of Julia's life were the hardest of David's. Julia wanted to go home to Brandon and Del Ray. She had left in such a hurry for the hospital; now she felt compelled to go back to put things right. They found a hospice, but David was determined to keep her at home for as long as she wanted to stay. Her father agreed. Perhaps out of deference to Julia and David, perhaps in defense of himself, he moved into David's condo, and Julia's mother joined him. David again took up the daybed in the Giants room.

Excruciating as David found this, watching her father suffer seemed somehow worse. In addition to the evidence before him, David could feel its depth when he spoke to his parents each night. He also remembered his father's stay with his grandfather at the end. His father only obliquely spoke of that, but now he gave David the best advice he had received: "Do all you can. You'll relive it longer than you lived it, so make sure you do it right."

Julia and David returned to where they had started: their walks. She still loved them, but they grew shorter, and she leaned increasingly on David to manage. Determined to give her everything he could, he took her to places she would never have agreed to had they not been able to stop time.

The first was to Washington's "real art museum." He insisted, "Take as long as you want, then come back and tell me what you see." As they looked at the

Leonardo, she still seemed more in the painting than in the room with him. "I see infinity," she said as she described its background. He got in a visit to Great Falls too, but even with him stopping time and pushing her in a wheelchair, it taxed her more than he had anticipated. Her last outing was to the Jefferson Building of the Library of Congress. When they arrived, he could feel that the long line had dispirited her; David stopped time and avoided it altogether.

In the end, it was not the desire to stay that left Julia but her ability. Her strength ebbed quickly; her pain increased. She simply could not execute the plans she had made when she left the hospital. Despite her determination, she was unable to stay more than a few days.

The hospice she had picked was far to the west, well beyond the sprawl, where she "could see mountains and hear birds instead of traffic." Of course, Brandon came. David would push Julia in a wheelchair as she held Brandon's leash. She observed, "Now you're walking us both."

Their walks remained good. If anything, they savored these even more. She was no longer self-conscious—not for herself, but for those who had encountered her in Del Ray. It had been obvious something was very wrong. More painful than her condition was having to discuss it. "Explaining dying is harder than doing it," she had concluded.

Here at the hospice, dying was meant to be easy. Even so, it was still damn difficult. Her parents found a motel nearby, her sisters returned, and friends trooped out. But the purpose was entirely different. It was to say goodbye. Here, there was no pretense of recovery, as there had been at the hospital. So debilitating was it, most visitors could only manage short stays before awkwardly exiting.

Only David and Brandon stayed. Of the two, only David accepted. Brandon dutifully assumed his post every day on the side of the bed Julia got out on. His paws crossed under his chin, he waited on her. At her slightest movement, his hope seemed fully replenished that she would get up, and all would be as it had been. Regardless of how often circumstances should have proved it wasn't, for him, they never did. After every false alarm, he would resume his post.

Besides their walks, David and Julia held onto their movies. He always insisted she pick. He knew that with each choice, he would never watch the movie again. Julia wanted to see all of Audrey Hepburn's, but threw in *Cool Hand Luke* out of the blue one night. These also measured her rapid decline: They started them earlier and earlier and watched them for shorter and shorter periods. David watched her as much as the movie so he could stop them when she nodded off. He would also read her poems from an anthology she had brought from her bedside. And from her Bible.

The one thing that cancer's ravages did not erode was their intimacy. This evolved and, in its fullest sense, increased. It was no longer expressed the way it had been. It was no longer reliant on the limitations of the physical but became unencumbered in the infinite of the emotional. Their physical expressions shrank to kisses, to touches, to looks. Their emotional ones expanded to topics they had never discussed, and that David would never have broached even days earlier. They were more direct, more honest, the present being liberated by the future's absence.

Alone one day, Julia began discussing the disposition of her things. As much as David understood, he made it through this darkening forest they had entered by seeing only each tree before him. Things like this conversation made such focus—or rather, focused blindness—impossible.

"David, when you go back to the house, I want you to burn my journals. You can read my last one because it's all about you, but then burn it too, with all the rest."

He choked. "You told me that thinking without writing is nothing."

"It is, and nothing would be better in this case."

"Why?"

"There's too much that can't be explained. I never told my parents, and now I won't be around to. They'd think I'd been crazy; it would only add to their hurt."

"I could explain," David murmured.

"Could you? Who've you ever told about your gift?"

"No one."

"Why not?"

He sighed and said, "Because they'd think I was mad if they didn't believe, and a freak if they did."

"Exactly. If you want to explain yours, explain that. As for mine: Promise you'll burn my journals."

David watched the stream of visitors slow to a trickle.

I get it. It's hard. Without love or a strong sense of duty, it's tough to face.

The deterioration in Julia's condition shocked those who had not become inured by daily exposure. He easily recognized those who, having visited once, would never return. They were the ones stupefied by the obvious but equally insistent on ignoring it: Julia was dying. He did not condemn, only commended. In this, he followed Julia's lead: "They did the best they could. It's impossible to accept someone's death without acknowledging the inevitability of your own."

Besides David and her family, the people who remained constant were the members of her church. Back home, David had looked askance at the practice; now it was welcomed as one of the few things that gave comfort. Both were particularly touched that her minister regularly made the journey. Realizing his next one would be possibly his last, David asked Julia, "Would you marry me now?"

David recognized that Julia was now the practical side of their relationship, he, the emotional side. Even so, her adamance against it surprised him.

"These are the last decisions I'm going to make. I intend to make good ones, not just now but forever, and not just for me but for everyone—especially you."

Her objections were all sound and mature. "It would raise a host of legal issues, immediately and later. People might misread the motivation. You'd be a widower. Most importantly, I already feel fully bonded to you by our betrothal."

She held his hand and added, "I considered it too."

When the minister arrived, though, David raised another possibility.

"Could you read the ceremony, let us say our vows, but not file the paperwork?"

"I don't know..."

"You need witnesses for it to be legal, don't you?"

"Yes."

"Then just do it alone with us. God will be our witness."

With the minister's assent, David asked, "Julia, will you marry me?"

She could only nod tearfully but vigorously. Without a wedding ring, Julia handed him back her engagement ring. Her weight loss made it slide back on achingly easily.

"I now pronounce you man and wife. You may kiss the bride."

With that, it was done; David and Julia had done all they could together.

Despite the signs and Julia's acceptance, David was unprepared for the end. It had crept so close that his eyes had grown accustomed to the shadow it cast.

"David, please read to me from St. Paul's first letter to the Corinthians, chapter thirteen, verses four through seven."

David knew it, even though he didn't recognize its citation. He tried to steel himself, stopping time before beginning haltingly.

"'*Love is patient, love is kind...*'" He had to stop time again.

"'*...Love is not jealous, it is not pompous, it is not inflated, it is not rude, it does not seek its own interests, it is not quick-tempered, it does not brood over injury...*'"

Again, he faltered as his voice cracked. Once more, he stopped time.

"'*...Love does not rejoice over wrongdoing, but rejoices with the truth. It bears all things, believes all things, hopes all things, endures all things.*'"

Finished, he wiped his eyes, exhaling as though having just completed a sprint.

Julia reached over and squeezed his forearm. Also struggling to speak, she finally managed to say, "That's how I've always felt about you."

They sat silently for some time, their eyes fixed on each other, their hands entwined. She was clearly struggling with her pain but holding on for this moment.

"Heraclitus said, 'The waking have one world in common, sleepers have each a private world of his own.' That's us, David, we've had our private worlds. I had too much of mine; it cost me one in common with you."

She laid back to recover.

"Please call the nurse. I need another shot. Then I'm going to take a nap."

When the nurse came, Julia also asked for something to help her sleep. As soon as the nurse left, Julia began to speak deliberately, slowly, clearly using all her concentration against the pain and the sedative.

"I love you with all my heart. I looked for you all my life, but I looked too long alone. I will always love you."

He could hold back no longer. He held her as tightly and as tenderly as her condition allowed.

"Let me go."

David relaxed his embrace; Julia stopped him.

"Not with your hands…I want those."

David understood. The thought had raced across his mind, only to be followed immediately by selfish shame. No one could want to cling to this. There was nothing left to cling to. There was only letting go now, and both had to. Julia was willing; David had to fight every emotion he felt—and all of who he had always been—to steel himself to the same. Rather than stop time, he wanted to race through it. To make it go faster than it ever had, to reverse places with his tableau, where he could stand still, and everyone would go on without them.

She quietly said, "Don't stop me, please. Just let me go."

David released his grip. He knew what she was doing as she stared intently at him. She was going to take her last interlude and in it drop off to sleep. She would never wake up here again. When she died, time would restart, and her passing would seem to him to have happened in less than the blink of an eye.

"Kiss me," she whispered. "Now smile. For me."

David tried with all his effort but was sure he failed. He felt his lips trembling and could barely see her.

Then she was gone. He reached for her. As he did, a piece of paper slipped from his hand. In what seemed the same moment, she was already gone from time to timeless. Julia had passed as he had known she would. How she could go so far beyond his reach so fast, David could not comprehend. He could only experience being left and being more alone than he had ever been. As he gazed at her, Julia's interlude had reversed; she had stopped her own time, and now the world moved around her.

As David pulled back to inform her family, his eye caught the paper. Picking it up, he saw it was a page from her journal. It read simply, "I will love you always. PS: Never forestall joy. Yours forever, Julia."

David felt numb. It was not the emptiness his numbness mimicked, but a surfeit of pain. A sensation that came from hurting so deeply and feeling nothing else that he had lost awareness of what anything else felt like. It was intensely emotional: the ache of seeing Julia suffering and now gone. It was physical too; despite his ability to stop time extending his endurance, the trial had still been prolonged. Lastly, it was mental, one coming from pain, beginning to feel somehow normal and the guilt arising from wanting to feel something else.

He could absorb no more; he could only endure as everything crashed over in waves. He could not evade it. Rather, like the tide, it pulled him through the multitude of forms and formalities that death inflicts on those it leaves behind. Until now, he had only known these from the periphery—his grandparents' passings—never at loss's core, where they are felt more than known. Before, he had only to be there; now, it was in him.

Just as physical lack of sensation causes clumsy awkwardness, so, too, David found that his emotional numbness left him stumbling on after Julia's death. Among the first was his return to her house for the journals.

Because her parents had flown in and knowing they had enough to worry about with the funeral, David had volunteered to drive Brandon to Lexington. The trauma of Julia's absence befuddled Brandon to no end. He constantly snapped to attention at every approach and noise, perhaps thinking that finally she was returning. Knowing he could not leave Brandon, David took him to Del Ray. As they drove in the neighborhood, Brandon was beside himself in anticipation of a long-awaited reunion.

Both found going into the house gut-wrenching. Brandon immediately shot in, searching every room, becoming increasingly agitated that she was nowhere to be found. For David, the effect was just the opposite—Julia was everywhere. Every view, every object—from sketches her hand had left unfinished to pillows her head had creased—did not just remind him of her; everything *was* her. He could not leave fast enough, vowing to never return. Brandon would not leave without David's insistence—and the ball that Julia had always thrown for him.

When they arrived at the park, they were alone. David removed the leash and the ball Brandon dutifully carried. David threw it repeatedly, oblivious to all around him. So lost in their game, Brandon in chase and David in nothingness, he did not realize when the woman arrived. He only became aware when she began to berate him for Brandon being unleashed.

Man and dog looked quizzically at a face contorted in indignation beneath graying hair and behind bifocal glasses. Under normal circumstances, David would have chosen between two extremes—responding in kind or laughing; instead, he replied flatly and without hesitation, "You must be Karen, I've heard so much about you." This at least elicited her first non-profanity.

"I've never been so insulted—"

Before she could continue, David did: "Then you need to get out more."

Having said it, he stopped time, scooped up Brandon, walked back to his truck, making sure he was in before restarting time. He laughed to himself the whole way back about what the woman's reaction would be to their disappearance.

Before Julia, that exchange would have sent him over the edge—as when he had hurled the asshole's keys down Washington Street—or worse. Now, even without her, Julia's peace still hovered over him.

CHAPTER FIFTY-TWO

As much as he wanted to get through the funeral, David was still struck by its brevity. The visitation the night before, the funeral service in her family's church, and the final service at the gravesite—together, only about six hours to remember Julia's life. A small gathering followed with a meal everyone picked over more than ate. Then there was nothing more.

He was grateful his parents had insisted on coming. They had relented before, accepting that they would be a distraction, and they only made brief visits to the hospice. But once she was gone, there was no equivocation.

David was shocked by how hard they took it until his father gave it perspective. "We know it because it's every parent's greatest fear. So, every parent intimately feels another's grief. Worse, we had been mentally preparing to meet Julia's folks to celebrate a wedding. And I understand your loss because it foreshadows mine of your mother or hers of me."

David and his father shared few words, but these assured David that they truly shared what was important. If ever David intended to reveal his ability, it would be to his father. And if ever the time was right, this was it. He did not and knew now he never would. He could not endure talking about Julia or bare any more of himself than he felt had been flayed open already.

Throughout it all, he repeated to himself, "Endure." That was his sole aspiration. To hold himself together at all costs, by whatever means, and to run grief's gauntlet as quickly as possible. He refused to stop time.

His hardest conversation was his last one with Julia's parents as he prepared to leave.

They were not coming to the memorial service in Alexandria; Julia's father confessed, "We can't take any more suffering. I honestly think it would kill her mother."

He still spoke of Julia as if she were alive. They had gone from the hospital to hospice to home to bury their daughter. That was enough.

Despite several days of being continually together, they had never been alone to really speak. Now there was no one else; David knew when he left, they would be finally alone. He awkwardly shifted in the spring's late afternoon, wondering how to say goodbye.

He extended his hand only to have her father step into a tight embrace that David knew was his substitute for words he could not form.

Julia's mother followed; by avoiding eye contact, she retained her ability to speak. "Please stay in touch, David. I guess, as the middle child, she was destined to be the glue that held her sisters together, but she was really what held our family together. Even so, there was always a part she held to herself. A place where she went into her thoughts to be alone. I sense she showed that to you. You saw something in her, inside her, that no one else ever did. That made you so special to her; it'll always make you special to us."

Only his promise to Julia held her secret back. "She showed me more than I could ever have dreamed or described."

Her father, having regained some composure, finally spoke haltingly, "There's something I'd like you to see. It'll only take a second."

Her father went inside and returned with a large page from a sketch pad. David recognized Julia's hand in the drawing, even though he could not distinguish the subject.

"There wasn't time to have it made before the service, but this'll be over her."

Julia's mother stood beside him, her arms wrapped tightly around herself and her face pinched in a supreme effort to restrain tears. David stared in stunned silence at a headstone's rendering.

Julia Anne Stewart

Loving daughter of Robert and Delia

Loving sister to Lydia and Cynthia

Betrothed to David

"She drew it herself near the end and gave it to us. She made us promise we wouldn't change anything."

"I, I…I had no idea. She never said anything."

"She didn't want you to know; she was afraid you'd object to your name being included."

It took everything he had to hold back tears that he knew would convulse them all. With slow deliberateness, David managed to say, "I loved her so." Only after pulling away did he submit to his grief.

CHAPTER FIFTY-THREE

He returned to his condo in the early dawn of the next morning. Alone, David could have been quicker, but Brandon slowed him. He hadn't minded; he appreciated the company. He had talked to him, as he would have Julia, until Brandon had curled quietly on the seat beside him. He had not planned to bring Brandon back, but when David went to his truck, Brandon had hopped in as well. Julia's parents had encouraged it, saying they would take him if he proved too much trouble. For his part, David could bear no more pain, even a dog's, so he had taken him without protest.

After walking Brandon, he unloaded the truck and entered a place now foreign. He had not been here in longer than he could remember, and even his most recent visits had for so long just been pit stops from Julia's. He had planned to go straight to his emails and begin unburying from the thousands that had pelted down throughout the ordeal. Instead, he opted for his texts; these were more personal than work. There were more than enough to consume the time until tomorrow's memorial service. Then he would have finished the trial. Until then, he did not want to see or talk to anyone. Brandon was company enough; he understood the loss and didn't try to talk about it.

He opened his phone and lay back on his couch. Instantly he was pulled to sleep, so quickly he had not even attempted to stop time. He slept for hours.

He woke only at Brandon's insistence and from a dream where Julia and he were in her house. So real, so welcome, and Brandon so perfectly placed, that as he woke, he was asking Julia to walk her dog. When fully awake, he was thoroughly unsettled—not just by his location but by trying to determine whether his dream was the reality or his reality the dream. As his clouded head cleared, the realization left excruciating sadness and loneliness sweeping in like drafts through a winter window. There was only Brandon and him. No one else. It was midafternoon. There was no Julia, and he remembered there never would be again.

He was rueful; even sleep had betrayed him. He threw himself into messages and into time as it was. Only Brandon interrupted his determined push. When Brandon was hungry, they ate; when Brandon needed exercise, they exercised. To the texts needing replies, he acknowledged with laconic efficiency. To the first expressing concern, he typed out, "Thank you for your thoughts." Then, copying it, he pasted it into replies to the news having gotten out. He deviated only once from his mechanical resolution to delete himself into the present. Janice had written, "I know what you're going through, but, once you're able, text or call me on my personal number." He vacillated over it far longer than it warranted, almost calling then, before replying with a brevity that belied his debate, "Thanks for understanding. I will."

Only Cindy came to carry the family's flag. She looked haggard, as ready to be done with this as he was. Staying at Julia's, she invited him over, but David flatly refused. Even when he drove to meet her in Del Ray a few blocks away, he altered his route to avoid seeing the house again.

Of all the people from his past with Julia, Cindy was the only one he imagined keeping in touch with. But when she mentioned coming to her wedding, he could not even contemplate it.

"Julia told me about your wedding at the end."

David flinched.

At his reaction, she said, "I won't betray Julia's confidence—ever. I just wanted to tell you. Julia loved to describe you as 'gallant.' I agree. There's no finer description of how you treated her, especially…It meant the world to her. I just wanted you to know—in case the grief ever grinds you so far down that you start doubting yourself. Don't. She never did."

When he returned to his condo, it was over. There were no more duties. He had endured.

CHAPTER FIFTY-FOUR

David awoke in the gray light of what he thought was barely dawn. He was surprised to find it past eight o'clock with a steady rain. He had just been with Julia again in his dreams. Such was sleep's torture now. Her quoting of Heraclitus resurfaced to him. As much as he now loathed stopping time for its cost to her, he desperately sought his own private world of one. To live a dream of his creation had never felt more necessary. Gone from work so long, he knew he must return; yet he knew with still greater certainty he could not bear it. The expressions of sympathy would be well-intentioned, but, as the saying goes, so is the road to hell. And it would be that for him—the questions, any reminders, would just thrust him back into what he was flailing, and failing, to escape.

So, he did what he now abhorred, only because he hated the thought of reality more. He stopped time. Brandon lay still, having just stirred and put his head down. David read; he wrote out his emotions, tore them up, then wrote them again. He worked out as well as he could.

When he exhausted his meager food supply, he walked to the store. It was a good mile away and through rain that hung in his freeze of time. Rather than falling on him, he caught it across his front; he carved a tunnel as he walked, his back staying dry. He restarted time just long enough to pay, hear the cashier's comments about the rain's pattern on him, then stop it again and walk back.

He had no interest in knowing how long he kept time stopped. Little changed, and the only thing that measured its passage were discarded cans of food. At one point, he took a run through the tunnel he had cut through the rain from the store. When that food he had carried home was gone, he drove back, not thinking that in his prolonged time-stop, time had hardly moved for everyone else. It occurred to him only when he walked through the same cashier's line and heard, "You were just here!" Jolted into recall, he mumbled an excuse that he had forgotten something, then stopped time as soon as he returned home.

As he dragged himself from the world, his time dragged on and on. Ordinarily, he restarted time to sleep and minimize separation. Not now. The separation from sensation, the sound of stopped time's silence was what he craved. He wanted nothing more than nothingness.

Leaving only her picture, he methodically cleared away everything else that rekindled the pain of Julia's absence—her gifts, the note her parents had left to thank him for use of his place. The first had been the picture of him as Sailor that she had drawn. It all went into the spare bedroom's closet. Pushing the smaller items into the recesses of its shelf, his hand felt the coolness of metal and the jaggedness of broken glass. Instinctively drawing it out, he stared up at Kristin's picture smiling down at him.

At the sight—at the contrast—between the losses, at who he had been and who the man Julia had forever changed, his body reflexively shuddered. He fell back until his body found the closet's wall; then, it slid down until he reached the floor, where he slumped over himself. There, in the gray morning of his frozen time, he leaned his head back and gulped for air.

On his third trip to the store, David recalled that Sunday had barely moved. Only necessity had forced him to release time for the briefest moments. Other than these, there had only been vain attempts to distract his mood; with each failure, he retreated again into time-stops.

Still morning, still raining, and he still was as utterly withdrawn as he could make himself. Remembering his last encounter, he chose a different store and forgot time altogether. Unfamiliar with this one's layout, he diverted from his normally quick, purposeful approach to wandering. So accustomed to being alone, he was oblivious to others, nearly walking into a woman standing in the aisle. When she jumped at his near approach, he saw first surprise, then the deeper shock of recognition. It was Rhonda, his office's manager.

"David? Is…that you?"

"Um, I…" he replied, then froze time.

Wasn't thinking, need to now.

He searched his unresponsive mind for any explanation as to why he was not the person she clearly knew. Unable to conjure any, he simply left, leaving her with the inexplicable experience of having seen him and then having seen him completely disappear.

Before restarting time to drive, his eyes caught the truck's mirror. "You look like hell itself." His face's reflection showed what looked to be uncountable days' worth of beard and hair disheveled from prolonged neglect.

"I'm a portrait of Dorian Gray."

This physical manifestation and its reminder of what had happened with Julia jolted him as nothing had throughout his self-exile. Once home, while he could—and did—clean up his exterior, his interior was no more reconstituted. His only distraction came from the mundane before him, and he now tried to think as hard as he had been trying to actively forget. He was no more successful in reaching a solution. He simply kept coming back to one thing.

Rhonda will tell. Hell, she's probably already told several from our office. Regardless of my vanishing, regardless of implausibility, she'll repeat it.

David could live in this Sunday forever, but whenever he let Monday finally come, he had to be back at work to dispel the rumors and stop a search party.

His isolation violated, David went to the office to clear away the invariable clutter—memos, mail, packages—that must have accumulated during his long absence. More importantly, he could leave clear evidence that he had been in, not homeless, as Rhonda's description would imply.

To avoid everyone, he allowed time to move to midafternoon before he left. Further minimizing a chance encounter, he entered through the kitchen. Time had to be moving for him to open the electronic lock. Once in, he let it run. The day was so dark, anyone else would have turned on a light; David welcomed the darkness and scooped everything into his backpack. The work he would read at home; the sympathy cards he left.

Leaving as quickly as he had come, he retraced his steps to the back door. Opening it, he nearly ran headlong into Janice standing there with a cardboard box in her arms.

"Oh lord! You scared the hell out of me, David!"

"Sorry! I didn't expect to see anyone here! What're you doing?"

"Finishing cleaning out my office."

"You're what?"

"I take it you haven't been by it."

"No, I came in this way and went straight to mine. What's going on?"

"I'm leaving, David."

"You're joking! I mean, you must be, you can't have decided to retire so suddenly…" David's voice trailed off as he read her eyes.

"I didn't. Corporate did."

"Oh. Oh, I'm so sorry."

"Me too. I didn't envision leaving like this," she said as she held up the box. "But here I am."

Both stared, wordless; Janice wistfully, David sympathetically.

Janice filled the vacuum with condolences. Then, unprompted, she answered the obvious. "Phil's taking over."

David, incredulous, started to respond; Janice cut him off. "I don't want to talk about this anymore. I don't want to say anything I'll regret."

"Is this why you texted me to call?"

"Heavens no," she said and chuckled. "I knew you'd find out soon enough. I wanted to see if you needed anything. Your loss was serious; mine, just an insult."

"Thanks for thinking about me. I'm not really sure I'm ready to be back, but I'm pretty sure that I need to be somewhere other than alone."

"Call me anytime." Twisting a smile, she said, "I've lots of it now." She moved to go in, but then she stopped. "Oh, I also wanted to pass along that Senator Nelson wants you to call his scheduler for an appointment to see him when you're back."

"Is everything okay?"

"Yes," she said with the first genuine happiness David had seen in her. "He likes you. More importantly, he respects you. Call him. But don't wait too long. Senators don't like to be kept waiting."

CHAPTER FIFTY-FIVE

David helped Janice with the last of her things, but they didn't talk much more. He felt strange having intruded on her private exit, and he couldn't bring himself to talk about his past weeks. When they parted, David knew Janice was never returning, while he had to return sooner than he had planned.

Having failed at actively trying to forget, David now resolved to try being active to not think. At least this was his reasoning Sunday night. It would also be his explanation when he went in the next morning. He had to coach himself through reentry to normality after his longest time-stop.

In preparation, he renounced stopping time. He had turned on it.

What has it really accomplished? It makes life easier at moments. But ease came at an unfathomable cost: a life with Julia.

He broke his vow only once. Exiting the Metro, he bought a paper from the usual paperman; however, when he told him to keep the change from a five-dollar bill, the man refused. "That's charity, not a gratuity. I'm a working man." He accepted a dollar extra. David stopped time for a moment and put the rest into the man's breast pocket.

As usual, David arrived at the office before anyone else; the unusual part was that he had done so the same way everyone normally did. He thought arriving first would minimize the focus on him.

Although back, he was not ready for real contact and braced himself.

You've just gone through the worst; you'll get through this.

Just as he knew others would be wary of how they approached him, so too, was he hesitant about approaching them. This included even Frank and Jeff. To avoid awkwardness, he preemptively asked them to lunch—tomorrow.

His day finally ended with him thoroughly drained. Partly, it was from being unused to a normal day. The greater part was due to the whipsaw effect of concentrating only to have someone bring him back to what he had come there to avoid.

I understand their intentions, but, still, it saps me. I never get more than a few minutes respite from remembering Julia's death.

Through his revolving door of sympathy, only Phil's visit surprised him. Their first and only contact of the day, he spoke very formally after closing the door to David's office.

"I am sorry about Julia."

"Thanks. I appreciate the time the office gave me throughout..." David trailed off, not wanting to name it, let alone talk to Phil about it.

"I'm sure it was a difficult time."

"My hardest ever."

"A lot of changes here," Phil said as he offered a tentative smile.

David didn't return it, as any goodwill from Phil's attempted gesture had immediately evaporated. David assumed Phil's opening formality. "So I hear."

Phil retreated when David did not reciprocate his overture. "We'll catch you up on what they mean for you Friday."

"I will see you then."

Phil began to leave, but as his hand pressed down the door handle, he turned back.

"Denise told me you came on to her at the party two Christmases ago."

"Excuse me? Not that this is either appropriate or accurate, but you've got it backward."

"I'm not getting into a he-said, she-said. Just don't let it happen again." Swinging the door open even as he finished, he left before David could respond.

David sat in shock, not entirely sure he had heard correctly. His first impulse was pursuit. But that would have meant talking to Phil further. He had disputed it. That was enough for what Phil's condolences had obviously been: a mere cover.

Tuesday was better simply because it was no longer his first day back. He and the office fell into tentative normality. Most had expressed their sympathy; he kept an emotional distance—just business. David recognized he was defensively avoiding small talk, largely because he did not really have anything to talk small about, but mostly because he did not want to be drawn into conversations when all seemed to take him where he didn't want to go.

He actually looked forward to lunch with Frank and Jeff. Their sympathy was genuine, more accessible—made more so among just the three of them. There are things more easily expressed—both said and received—away from one-on-one. What he found disconcerting, though, was that even after their discussion about Julia, his friends' tones did not lighten.

"So, what happened?" David asked at last.

"Phil happened," Jeff explained in a monotone.

"What do you mean?"

"He means," Frank said slowly, "that while Janice had our backs with Corporate, she forgot to watch her own. Phil spoke their language to them—get rid of Janice, give him her title, but don't promote him within the company structure. He gets the position he's always craved—"

"But never deserved," Frank interjected.

"And they get her salary back, and they get this place back—they get to bring it under their control."

Jeff finished the assassination's summary. "They never understood the magic Janice made out here in her fiefdom, so they left her alone. They understand all too well the mundane Phil brings—he manages up—that, they get."

"We're going Corporate, David, right down to logging hours and contacts."

"David, this new regime under Phil..." Jeff said, shaking his head in exasperation.

David's anger wouldn't allow the conversation to move away so quickly.

"I always thought he was just a hack; parked out here to keep him away from them, while letting him ride on to retirement."

Frank said, "He's all that. But all the time he was making his regular trips back to Evanston, and Janice was running things here, he was undermining her out there. Rhonda told me what she heard from her friends in Evanston. She knows he's not getting a penny more, and she knows what the CEO's suite heard."

Jeff, jumping in as the avalanche gathered momentum, added, "You haven't heard the juicy part…Phil's doing Denise."

David shot back in his chair. Then it dawned on him.

"Oh, come on, you guys had me going!"

"We're not joking, David. All the HR sexual harassment training sessions he's made us take?" Frank chortled and said, "Well, he's making his own now."

David, reeling from revelation, tried to make sense of it all.

"But I haven't noticed any change."

"David, you've been gone, and, even when you were here, you were on the Hill. It fell into place incrementally. Like a chain of dominoes, none of us knew where it was going. Not even Janice."

"But you'll soon see changes," Jeff added, as he shifted to leave.

"We're all being assigned to new teams. Phil calls them 'tiger teams.'" Jeff snorted. "They cover every possible area and issue. I can't even count how many I'm on, but I do know they're a shitload of work. Every time I turn around, there's another one with more work. I've gotta get to one now."

Down to just David and Frank, David looked at his friend, still not comprehending.

"Why haven't I heard about any of this? I don't know that I've been assigned to any…"

"Have you checked your emails? I guarantee there's one—probably more—from Denise."

"Denise? I delete hers usually."

Frank leaned across the table and widened his eyes. "That luxury's gone, pal. She's organizing the tiger teams. The reason you haven't heard is because they decided to hold your meeting until you had a chance to get caught up."

Frank digressed into editorial. "I know you're still dealing with a lot. We all understand you keeping to yourself; I did as well when my folks died a few years back. It's natural. So, you haven't had time to see that everyone's hunkered down on all the assignments these damn things are creating."

Sighing heavily, he said, "It really sucks, David. I'm not one for casual profanity, but it really *fucking* sucks. We're going Corporate as fast as Phil can take us there. I've done my tour in Evanston. I know. That's why I liked it here. I feel sorry for you and Jeff. Especially Jeff."

"Well, you're in it too. Misery loves company," David said, realizing his role had now reversed as he tried cheering up Frank.

"I've already told my wife I could be gone any day. I'm within retirement age already. I'm still doing it because I used to like doing it, and, when I didn't, I liked doing it with people like you and Jeff. But I don't like it like this, so I'm staying only as long as I can stand it. I feel sorriest for Jeff. He has a baby; he just wants this part of his life to be settled so he can focus on family. He *has* to take it."

They left physically together, but apart mentally. Frank seemed to have suddenly aged ten years and was already gone. David's mind was racing to pull everything together. First, his personal life had collapsed; now, the professional part in which he had sought refuge was crumbling.

As soon as he got back to his office, he closed his door and searched his calendar and emails. There were Denise's, just as his friends had predicted.

My meeting's scheduled for Friday, just in time to ruin a weekend.

After his shock passed, it was clear what was happening.

Unqualified for the job, Phil was changing the office to suit his abilities. Unable to do policy or politics, he could manage process. Process was something Corporate understood. They had always fought Janice over her independence. If Phil could point to his process, he gave Corporate exactly what it understood and rewarded. The "tiger teams" would give Phil reports on everything, so he would appear knowledgeable of—and claim credit for—work he could not produce.

He's competent at one thing: cunning.

CHAPTER FIFTY-SIX

David was just leaning in to kiss Julia when he woke up. She had been at her best and wearing the blue dress from the wedding that had floored him. They were at the carousel on the Mall; he had felt his hands on her shoulders and could smell her fragrance. Then she was gone; a few moments later, he realized where he was. Just another dream, a prelude to another day without her.

He reached for his phone to reenter the real world. Scrolling through messages, he saw one from her father. Without thinking, in a couple of quick clicks, David was staring at Julia's headstone. It was now in place. Perhaps in a sense of closure, he had sent a photo to David. David looked at it, remembering the drawing from her parents' driveway. Now, it seemed so final. He gazed so intently that he looked through it and into his memories. Only when the kaleidoscope threw up images from the end did his shudder bring him back.

On his Metro ride to work, he stared vacantly out the window. Certain he saw Julia on the platform, he forgot his promise and stopped time instinctively, impervious to the impossibility. It was just a woman who, seen from his seat on the moving train, must have looked like her. He let time go. He would catch the next Metro. He had no interest when, or if, he got in now. Wednesday was already ruined.

Slinking in through the back door, he ran into Stacey. It was their first contact since she had brought him a card on Monday. David tried to avoid eye contact.

"How're you feeling?" she asked tentatively.

With flat honesty, he said, "I wish I were dead. But barred from that, I wish I were alone."

"Oh, sorry. I'll get out of your way."

She paused, but, as he passed, she offered, "Carl Jung said 'the foundation of all mental problems is the unwillingness to experience legitimate suffering.'"

David wheeled around before she could finish. Stacey drew back as he let fly with invectives. Her eyes watered as each buried in.

Recoiling, she stammered, "I was just trying to say that…"

"Don't say anything, *anything*, else."

He fumbled for his phone, pulling up the picture that had started his day, and he thrust it at her.

"That's how I feel! Is that legitimate enough for Carl?"

He stormed away, past his office, and back out the front door. He stopped time as soon as he hit the street and flopped down at Sailor's feet to let pain, and now guilt, soak in. Barely begun, his today was over.

The next day, he purposely sought out Stacey.

"I'm sorry about yesterday; I've agonized over it ever since."

Throughout his soliloquy, she listened, nodded her understanding, and accepted his apology. But she did so in stiff formality that let David know her discomfort in talking with him about this.

Or even talking to me at all.

David resigned himself to another burned bridge. A day removed from alienating Stacey and a day before meeting with Phil and Denise, he searched for something positive. He decided to call Senator Nelson's office. Even this offered no respite; the earliest he could get in was next Tuesday—nearly a week away. Whatever that meeting's purpose, it was not going to release him from his tightening personal and professional vise.

David approached his Friday meeting with Phil and Denise like a death sentence. Unlike traditional dawn executions, his was after lunch. Had he not already felt the dread, his coworkers put it into him.

Instead of the usual ball-busting from Frank and Jeff, they belatedly tried to downplay it. When he had seen Jeff's clenched jaw that morning, he had comically offered, "Hello-o-o."

"Nope. Today's more 'oh Hell,' than hello," Jeff said and went right past.

When he finally went in, David still hoped to find out that this had all been an elaborate con job—a hoax of masterful proportion. He would then burst in on Frank and Jeff with mock indignation, and they would all laugh.

It wasn't. It was everything negative he had heard. Phil clearly relished it. There was no pretext of Monday's minimal sympathy. Each of the countless tiger teams and their endless work assignments rolled on in steady succession. David purposely quit counting early on; too depressing to think about, he simply didn't.

As David sat in the meeting, the completeness of Denise's betrayal became clear.

Phil doesn't care whether Denise's story is true or not. His overwhelming desire—his need—for it to be true is enough to keep him from examining its implausibility. By believing it, Phil feels he's taking something I wanted but couldn't get. It takes all Phil's frustrations and resolves them by having Denise. In his mind, he's finally won.

For Denise, it's even better. It avenges my rejection. She also knows it's the ultimate aphrodisiac for Phil; it makes her the bearer of what Phil wanted more than anything: my failure. Plus, it gives her the role she's always sought.

David understood that, woven so tightly and tying up their desires so completely, that the story's falsity was irrelevant. It gave them what they wanted: him in this chair, at this moment, at their mercy.

CHAPTER FIFTY-SEVEN

It was not the sheer volume—committing to paper everything he was working on or could work on—but its sheer uselessness. It was a meeting in writing: a large group who didn't know what they were doing, slowing down the core who did—at best, work's interruption; at worst, its impediment. He recalled the scene in *Cool Hand Luke,* where Paul Newman must repeatedly dig and refill holes. The topper was that before any future meetings with Phil, David would have to write a memo about the topic.

David was jerked from his mental resignation to digging and refilling holes by the piercing sound of a fire alarm. Drill or real, he didn't know. He was simply grateful. It saved him from the outburst Phil seemed intent on provoking.

For once, instead of slogging down the stairs, he flew. He noticed several people calling it a day, taking the alarm as a divine omen that the week was done. But now with so much piled upon him, he waited among the building's milling throng for the signal to return. He was in no hurry. When it finally came, he turned, only to have his way blocked by the security guard.

"The alarm sounded, so we can go back, right?"

"Not until I get the all-clear from my supervisor," the guard mumbled.

"Then why have the return signal sound?"

"Just doing my job."

Muttering to what he thought was himself, "Calling it your job don't make it right, boss."

From behind, he heard the equally soft reply, "What we got here, is a failure…to communicate."

Not quite the words, but the cadence was dead-on. David spun to see Stacey there with a slight, hesitant smile.

"You know *Cool Hand Luke*?"

"Can you eat fifty eggs?" Her smile grew.

David picked up the line.

"Nobody can eat fifty eggs!"

David started to laugh, unable to recall the last time he had. It built uncontrollably until he was conscious his face was wet with streaming tears.

Stacey guided him away. He would have stopped time to avoid precisely this happening. Now he could not gather himself to stop.

David lost track of where he was or how long he had been there. He was thoroughly inside his sorrow. When he felt a hand gently squeeze his, he responded on emotion and instinct. "Oh, Julia, I miss you so, so much."

He had tried to stop time the instant before but had clearly failed; he could see it in Stacey's surprised expression; he felt it in her grip's relaxation. Yet he let himself continue feeling the moment. As though rubbing a bruise, despite its pain, it soothed and seemed to release a deeper one.

When he finally readied to regain himself, he did so gradually. He was in no rush to leave emotions he had choked off over and over. Before, it "hadn't been the time." Now it was. He wept his ordeal's hardest tears. Only after he felt himself poured out did they stop; absent being emptied, he didn't know he ever could have.

Completely drained by catharsis, he managed to say, "I'm sorry, I don't know what happened just now."

"Normal happened, David. Be grateful you're a human being. Some people here have wondered. I can't imagine what you've been through. I just hope some of it's gotten out."

"Thanks. I realize what you were—"

"No need. I think I'll go home. It's late; work'll keep."

Stacey was right. As she left, David wished he could join her. He also rolled over her "human" comment. Before, he would have responded, disputed; now he acknowledged his own doubts.

He spent the weekend trying to force himself back into who he used to be. But far from stopping time, he hastened it along—as though living in real time would somehow change its most important part.

Saturday, he went to the gym, not because he wanted to, but because he wanted to get this over too.

The longer I wait, the harder returns are.

Still, it was hard. He appreciated people inviting him out, but he only stayed for supper. He went to a movie alone, not really recalling what he had just seen.

On Sunday, he returned to Julia's church. Similar to the gym, people approached gingerly; he responded in kind. Everyone spoke around the unspoken. They would talk about how beautiful the memorial service was or how much they had cared for her. They spoke of Julia often in the third person, avoiding her name—as if this would keep it from David's mind.

The minister eased him aside as he left. "How are you?"

"I've heard stories of people who've lost an arm or a leg but still feel it—that it itches but can't be scratched. I know she's not here; I can see she's not here; still, I feel."

Like a missing limb, the absence threw him out of kilter; what was left didn't function the same. He felt clumsy, uncoordinated, as though what remained sought to compensate for what was gone.

He sought solace in Blue but found none. He simply rode up and down the Parkway, stopping here and there at places he hoped would distract him. That evening, he called his family and talked, listening to himself say nothing as though someone else spoke.

David returned Monday no better. The weekend had only closed more avenues of escape. Having pushed from his mind the new regime, he could avoid it no longer. On top of the normal meetings that gutted Mondays, he had all the new work.

He felt antsy—unable to log his hours, then get to the reports of all the tax bills in the committees, including the purely partisan ones that were going nowhere—and then finally onto the real work. He had never known this inability to function before.

At best, he had been able to appreciate this from observing it in others: wrenching panic that came from having no control over a situation and no way to gain it, while being swept along in its wake.

I saw it plenty in college. The terror that there's now nothing that can be done because all time was gone; the deadline's arrived with no product with which to meet it. Even now, I know people have "those dreams," the ones where they discover being unknowingly enrolled in a class and learning its final was tomorrow.

David never had those dreams. He didn't because he had never felt the sensation underlying them. Now, he did.

He could have stopped time and done the reports at seemingly amazing speed to alleviate some of the stress. He refused. He was not about to sacrifice himself for this. He also knew stopping time meant obscuring how long the work took. This was the new regime; more than wanting them to know, he wanted himself to know *exactly* how much it cost. Excruciating slowness compounded its futility. Never had he been more conscious of wasting time. Monday ended with just two reports done and more work piling up behind them.

For Tuesday, David had circled his meeting with Senator Nelson. He had blocked out two hours. He knew it would be far shorter—not presuming even the usual fifteen minutes. He also intended to be early. Having heard Nelson use the cliché "if you can't be on time, be early" more than once, he took the hint to heart. After that, he planned to catch up with Shelly.

Denise tried to squeeze an unscheduled meeting into his two-hour blackout. She insisted he had nothing on his calendar then. David neither budged nor divulged. He feared that she or Phil would try to tag along. Neither having their own Hill connections, both frequently looked to hitchhike onto those of others; David valued too much his relationship with Senator Nelson and his office to have either compromised.

Instantly on entering the Russell Building, David felt it. He could not put his finger on exactly where the peace came from, but it was real, made doubly so by being his first in so long. At a glance, he recognized scenes—the nervous young page clearly lost, the news crew testing backdrops for a quick stand-up, lobbyists practicing talking points en route to a meeting. As he bypassed the ornamental elevators for the steps, he found that even the building's worn marble felt familiar.

Despite not knowing the meeting's purpose, he was certain about its trappings.

I'll enter the sparsely furnished, utilitarian office and approach either of two low desks manned by young staffers. They'll earnestly ask who I'm here to see and then invariably offer me water. I'll take a seat on Naugahyde furniture. Then my eyes will wander over the Texas souvenirs, while cable news plays in the background. I'll be called in, the meeting will happen, and its end will be signaled by a staffer entering to hand the senator a folded piece of paper that they will pretend is a message of some importance. Then I'll be politely escorted out as the next "fifteen-minuter" is escorted in.

When he went into the senator's personal office, only Senator Nelson and Chris, his chief of staff, were there. David had gotten to know Chris well while working on the proposal. With the senator from the beginning, Chris was in his fifties and considered one of the Hill's best. As soon as the door closed, the senator offered his sympathy over the news Shelly had passed along. David thanked him; although genuinely appreciating it, he redirected the conversation. They spoke in generalities for several minutes of transition.

"I wanted to tell you again what an impressive job you did on that amendment."

"Thank you, but it was you—"

"No, David," the senator said, holding up his hand to stop him.

They rose, shook hands, and the door swung open. Fifteen minutes exactly. Only this time, instead of going out, Shelly and a photographer came in. The pictures were a nice touch—it never got old for him. He knew where it should hang among his memorabilia.

Shelly and the senator went to another meeting, so Chris walked David out.

As they stood outside, Chris asked, “Do you ever miss it?”

“Sorry?”

“The Hill?”

“Every now and then.”

CHAPTER FIFTY-EIGHT

David walked back from the Russell Building to think undisturbed. He was surprised when he found himself passing Sailor. So lost in thought, he had neither stopped time nor thought of it. He had also forgotten a meeting.

Coming in the back way, he ran into Stacey, who informed him that he had not just missed the meeting but had been missed too.

"Denise is looking for you."

"Is she pissed?"

"She took pissed and ran with it."

"She's all over these tiger teams."

Smirking about the office's open joke, she said, "She's all over a lot of things these days."

"Well, you know what they say: A fool and her legs are soon parted," he said.

Stacey choked on her water.

"That's Thurber, not me," David confessed.

Wiping her chin, she said, "No, David, that's all you. I'll distract her while you find someplace to hide."

David slipped into his office and shut the door. He knew Denise was looking for another memo. Before starting, he texted Janice. "I saw Senator Nelson. Could you meet me sometime tomorrow to talk?"

"Name the time and place that works for you," came quickly back.

David settled into his unnecessary work. It stretched into the night; guilt over his missed meeting pushed out more write-ups. He had been interrupted by Phil and Denise stopping by to upbraid him on lagging production. David came as close to lashing out at Phil as he ever had. Only stopping time had stopped him, but, even after, he came perilously close. The shreds of professional perfectionism held him back. That and his eagerness to talk to Janice tomorrow before doing anything stupid.

Wednesday, David kept to himself. Putting on mental blinders, he churned out more of the endless tiger team assignments. His regular outward focus had become inverted.

Usually, I know everything going on and can anticipate what's going to happen. Now I'm all inside and looking backward—explaining everything that's already occurred. I've gone from being Radar to being Archive.

Now work's only satisfaction came with completion.

He met Janice that night in Old Town. It had been her choice not to go anywhere near the office, or even into D.C. The first half of the conversation was David's. He recounted the new regime and the reactions to it. These went from the absurd—the new tiger teams and their spiraling work requirements—to the serious: cratering morale.

After half an hour, he finally asked, "What should I do?"

"I can't tell you what to do, David. What I can say is what I know about you. You'll always be a foreigner at Whitney. You are of the Hill, not Corporate. To Evanston, you'll always speak with a foreign accent. You will because you make no effort to lose it. The Hill is what's important to you. For Corporate, it's just the opposite—a means to their end, and even then, just one of many. To you, the Hill *is* the end. For you, Corporate's the means, your means for staying part of the Hill."

"Did you want to stay in our office?"

She held a blink and her breath, clearly in thought. When her eyes opened, she released a prolonged exhale. "It was time to go, just not the way I wanted to. But it did remind me of something I'd lost sight of: You're only irreplaceable to the ones who love you. Hold onto what you love as long as you can. You know that better than anyone."

Now, David paused. "Any regrets?"

"Being victimized by irony." She chuckled. "I had dismissed Phil as a pathetic figure, only to find myself dismissed by him in the end. Of all the great personages I've known in Washington, I was undone by the least."

As they walked out, David rephrased his initial question, "What would you do?"

"There are five P's in the Senate: politics, policy, press, process, and people. All are vital, and someone can make a career out of mastering any one of them. In Corporate Government Relations, there is only one P: people. Because they don't know the other four, they often make a mess of people. It's why the lobbying world is populated by folks forever telling you who they used to be. It's not a place for those who still could be. I'd follow my heart and my talent as long as I could."

That night, David couldn't sleep. His thoughts jumped in wild disarray. He actively tried to think away work. After Kristin, and before Julia, he had sought it. Now, after Julia, he had wanted the same: obscurity in continuity. This, too, had been stolen away from him.

David knew alone was not working. As much of a necessity as it was for him—and it was a need as real as any physical one—its limitations were stark. It could be only a retreat, not a way of life. He had recognized its failure as permanency right after Julia's memorial.

Julia, he could not think about. But, still, he felt her presence. Seemingly as close and real as she had been when alive and just a call, a text, a touch away. So often right after she passed, she had come to him in his dreams; it had so upset him that he damned sleep for it. Tonight, he wanted her return so much and longed for sleep to bring even her illusion. But neither came.

Not until dawn did David finally drop off. As he felt the descent, he stopped time for some unknown amount of sleep. As he drifted off, he thought about how "this" was what stopping time had become. A gimmick of convenience. Despite its promises, this was its reality. He had been wrong; he could not stop time. Julia had correctly identified what these "time-stops" were: interludes—interruptions, no more.

I can hide in a moment, but I can't change time's outcome. Outcomes depend on too much too far beyond my impulse to control.

Thursday was a brilliant spring day and still in its dawn when he restarted time. His Metro ride in showcased the monuments, gleaming white stone against azure. As much as he dreaded today, he could not deny the day's beauty.

David's dread came from yet another HR meeting, this one notable for its cruelty, an all-day off-site designed to thoroughly steep everyone in Corporate's culture that Janice had before held at bay. As Phil reminded all who would listen—including those, like David, who were now forced to—"Washington is no longer different." Indeed, it was not.

The off-site was no more off site than his office building's basement. Yet that was far enough. All any HR off-site seemed to require was a windowless room. Frank's explanation was plausible. "With windows, they know you'd be staring out five minutes into it." Jeff's was closer to David's mood. "Or throw yourself out of them."

They had all dutifully marched down. Even before the first break, David was aware of the sensation of more work piling up—"snowplowing" in Evanston's slang. He could almost physically feel the pressure building to finish this meeting, then get back to more inane tiger team paperwork, then finally to the real work now undone for days.

The first scheduled break arrived after two interminable hours. Never had he needed one more, though he did not really know why. He had ceased paying attention to the material—how to write tiger team memos—about five minutes in and had since been mulling his situation.

Got to beat back this urge to screw Phil. I want to on general principle. People like him should get what's coming to them. And I want to for Janice. And I want to for me. It's personal—it's always been personal with Phil, never more so than now.

With each motivation, he relished letting scenes play through his mind. Quitting would be his ultimate "screw you."

While Corporate loved and understood process, it demanded results.

Janice's tenure proved Corporate would sacrifice the former for the latter. If Phil couldn't deliver the latter, Corporate would sacrifice Phil. For Phil to deliver, he had to retain what Janice assembled.

Phil could never hire good replacements. He doesn't have Janice's connections to approach them; if he happened on them by chance, he won't know who'd be best. And if, by sheer dumb luck, he did, that person won't long want to work for Phil.

David also knew that, without Janice, he was the piece of the office that Phil could least afford to lose. This was not simply self-flattery. David had raised his profile with Corporate by securing his proposal's passage. The CEO had not been joking when he had asked what David intended for an encore. David's departure would raise a red flag in Evanston.

So, pure vindictiveness offered huge enticement to quitting. But David knew a decision could not be about Phil. It could not even be about Julia. It had to be his choice. He wished it could be elevated beyond him, but the most it could be about was him coming to grips once and for all with his obsession. Understanding that all a person could do was make the best choice in the moment offered. Not the perfect one, just the best; not for all time, just for this one. Then to let it be what it was.

There's no permanent perfection. Even when it exists, it can't be retained. My shared time-stop with Julia proved it. We could've lived our lives forever in that moment. But in it, we found it temporary—even in its permanence. We both agreed we had to leave it. Like that day, perfection can only be held for its moment, not held forever.

David finally understood what his relationship with Julia had truly meant. It had been one of acceptance—acceptance for as long as it lasted; now, acceptance of its departure. To enjoy the gift that it had been, but that it was no more than that: a gift, not a promise.

Lastly, he saw the irony of what Julia's life and his time with her had been. Their relationship had been perfect to him. What had ended it was Julia's control of time. It had been her extended interludes that had rushed her through her life and ultimately their time together. Despite Julia's admonition to never forestall joy, she had cut theirs short. As much as he had wanted her then, as much as he would always want her, all that remained was this lesson.

I'm left with the barest remnant of the perfection I sought: the money. Numbers on a piece of paper; I watch them go up, then I put the paper in a drawer until the next one arrives. Years ago, I had to let go of what I loved. Why am I still clinging to what I don't? Is it just because it's all that's left? No.

The chase was over. It had to be.

They all emerged blinking like moles unearthed into relentless sunlight that taunted them with what they were missing. He milled around with Frank and Jeff before finding himself momentarily alone with Stacey.

She voiced everyone's thoughts, except those of Phil, Denise, and the traveling executioner brought in from Evanston for the day.

She looked at the sky's deep blueness and inhaled as though to draw it into her. Looking back at him, she breathed out. "Brutal, huh?"

He started to respond with standard commiseration when he heard himself quietly say, "I want to quit."

He had not planned it; the words had just emerged. He was no less surprised than she was.

"Uh, that's…how we all feel, I guess."

"I don't know what to do."

"What would Julia say?"

That was the answer. The one he had been looking for but afraid to admit. It was the corollary to Julia's "never forestall joy." Never prolong agony. As vain as it was trying to hold onto perfect, so, too, was trying to improve the irredeemable. They were two sides of the same acceptance. Of letting go. The first he had learned from Julia; the second he now saw for himself. Even if he did not know what he was going to do, that it *could* be better—*had* to be better—was enough.

The HR rep signaled for their return.

Stacey sighed in resignation. "I guess we've got to get back."

"I'm not going back," David flatly replied. "I don't want to be in the supporting cast of a shit show."

Stacey's laugh sounded fake. "What? But the off-site. This party's just getting started."

"Tempting as hours of an HR presentation in a windowless room sounds, I'm going to be strong and pass."

As David's decision had dawned on him, suddenly it seemed to have on her. "But what should I tell them when they ask where you are?"

"The truth. Just say I vanished, and you don't know where I went. Because that's how it's going to happen. When you turn around, I'm going to be gone."

As Stacey started to turn, David stopped time. It was the first time-stop he could remember really enjoying in a long time. The stilled moment was complete liberation—not just in this frozen moment, but in all the ones he was claiming for himself by leaving a job he realized he was only enduring. He had tolerated it because of Janice, whom he adored and learned from. Then, because of the proposal that allowed him to pretend to himself that he was back on the Hill. Then, because of Julia, whom he had loved and who had loved him in his quest. And finally, he had sought to return to it because he thought it offered an escape from loss. But at its core, stripped of all the things that had masked its reality for him, it was joyless. It would never be anything more than a check.

David intended to walk so far toward the Senate that no one could stop him. As he started, he pulled up short and turned hard to port.

"Goodbye, Sailor."

The figure stood solitary—as David was in reality—in bronze and as motionless as everyone cast in flesh and blood around them. His pant legs forever moved by a breeze that didn't blow, his seabag beside him, his hands thrust resolutely into his pea coat, the slightest smile on his face. Sailor had always known. But he had never told, despite all David's monologues to him.

"I guess you figured I had to discover it for myself. Well, I'm shipping out too. I'll miss you."

Before he left the square, he went into the Metro and put a twenty-dollar bill into his paperman's pocket.

David was blocks up Pennsylvania Avenue and out of sight when he restarted time. He texted Shelly.

"Could you give me just sixty seconds? I'll wait for any time that works."

Her answer came moments later. "Of course. What's up?"

David's reply was equally succinct: "I just quit." But it had said everything that needed to be said. Especially to himself.

It was not the perfect shot—he did not know what he would find. Or where, or when, or even if. And it certainly was not David. But that was the point. This was simply the time and this his best choice—his only real choice—in it.

Hanging up, his pace quickened, and David smiled to himself—and for one who was not there.

THE END

ABOUT THE AUTHOR

This is James Young's first foray into fiction. He has spent over three decades in and around D.C. politics immersed in economic and policy legislation. Alongside degrees from the University of Chicago (B.A.) and Cornell University (M.A., Ph.D.), Young's writing has appeared in the *Wall Street Journal*, *Washington Times*, *Washington Examiner*, *The Hill*, *American Spectator*, *The Federalist*, *Washington Post*, *New York Post*, *Barron's*, *Forbes*, *Chicago Tribune*, *Townhall*, *Blaze Media*, *San Francisco Chronicle*, *Cleveland Plain Dealer*, and elsewhere.

In his early days, James was Kipling's "cat who walked by himself," working in a steel mill, sailing on the Great Lakes' iron ore boats, tending bar, riding motorcycles, scuba diving, traveling extensively worldwide, and "doing all manner of things that would have consumed fully eight of the Kipling cat's nine lives." He is spending his remaining life more sedately, though still traveling with his family to America's national parks—with only the occasional exotic foray here and there.

ACKNOWLEDGMENTS

There are more people deserving of thanks than I could possibly name here. However, there are some who I must acknowledge.

Ross Browne gave me early and continued encouragement in this endeavor. Peter Gelfan gave the novel its first critiques and provided direction for its improvement. To both, I hope what appears in its pages captures your insights.

I want to thank John Robert Marlowe. You have been a guiding voice from afar and someone who has continually believed in this work.

To Lauren, I want to thank you for your constant attention to details (most of which I didn't know existed because of your indefatigable work). I also want to thank you for always being there.

To Merlina McGovern, please accept my gratitude for your superb editing; it always made this novel better. To Jackie Peveto, thanks for catching so much—even after I was sure everything had been caught!

Shannon, please accept my gratitude for the cover design which I love so much and which captures the book.

My thanks to Kristin Perry and the team at Amplify for everything they have done and do.

A big thank you to my friends: You gave invaluable support, even when you didn't know you were giving it.

To my wife, Jennifer. I simply could not have done this without you—and wouldn't have wanted to, even if I could have. To my children, Eliza, Jimmy, and Jeremy: Thanks for your love, which is your greatest gift to me, and for your support.

Finally, although I tried to catch all the errors, I know that is impossible. Know that those which remain are all mine.